LIB
BOUND

NATHANIEL
M. WREY

To ~~⬛~~

A fellow traveller

Best Wishes

~~(signature)~~

Published in 2020 by Waterman Books

Copyright © Nathaniel M. Wrey 2020

Nathaniel M. Wrey has asserted his right to be identified as
the author of this Work in accordance with the
Copyright, Designs and Patents Act 1988

ISBN Paperback: 978-1-9163705-0-0
Ebook: 978-1-9163705-1-7

A CIP catalogue copy of this book can be found in the British Library.

Published with the help of Indie Authors World
www.indieauthorsworld.com

IndieAuthors
World

To my grandparents and their generation, for their sacrifices and the freedom I have enjoyed.

ACKNOWLEDGEMENTS

My sincere thanks to my family, Mary Whinder, Sarah North, Melissa McMahon, Rebekah Morris, Leon Chambers, Delphine Gatehouse (Daniel Goldsmith Associates Ltd), Lee Dickinson and Kim Macleod and all at Indie Authors World.

CHAPTER 1

O n a cloudless, still night made alive by a Ferral moon, an inhuman shriek broke the silence, echoing down the valley, causing a shiver for all those in earshot. The cry belonged to the beast from which the celestial sphere acquired its eponym: a Ferral.

A troop of young guards from the town of Athenia stood listening to the fading, dissonant torment, the moonlight exposing their wide-eyed fear. Although few in number, they enjoyed the protection of a fortified wall and superiority through their weapons. Each man clutched his gun, aware of their responsibility as protectors of a precious commodity: civilisation. To the people of Athenia, their community was the last bastion of civilisation in a wasteland of barbarity and hardship. Few understood how it had come to be thus. Like all before, they took for granted the world they were born in. But all understood their inheritance. Some 10,000 years ago, the world gave birth to civilisation amid a fertile crescent. Cities, kingdoms and empires rose and fell, but the flame of civilisation remained alight, passing from custodian to custodian: sometimes fading to a faint glow, sometimes lighting up the entire world. Now an isolated ember hung on, prized by a society of little more than ten thousand, but its light still served as a beacon of hope and purpose.

In the uneasy stillness, as the guards dismissed their shivers of fear to the chilly air of night, a rifle shot sent roosting birds to flight, their panicked calls merging with the report of the gunfire.

"Who fired? No one fire! Who fired?" A bellow joined the broken silence.

"I hit them!" came a reply. "I got them!"

"You don't fire unless you see them clearly!" The voice of authority quivered with anger. "You can't see them clearly unless they're in the perimeter."

"But I got them! I saw them in the moonlight."

"Finbarl! Is that Finbarl-apcula?" demanded the voice. "You know the rules: you know the reason for the rules. A wasted bullet is no good to anybody."

"But I got it," Finbarl mumbled to himself. "Yes, sir. It's Finbarl-apcula." He spoke with the respectful tone due his superior officer.

"Well hold your bloody fire until they get closer!" growled Officer Vassel. "We may regret not having that bullet if they get through the defences."

"But I bloody got it!" mouthed Finbarl to himself again, crouching on the narrow walkway running along the back of the twelve-foot-high stone wall. No guard dared stand, exposing their head above the defences, an easy target for a Ferral stone.

Beneath Finbarl, beyond the wall, lay a dry moat, its depths filled with thorny scrub and stakes. The defences continued further outwards. Wicker barrels, filled with sand and stone, made three rows of shallow barriers, their tops covered with sharp flint to dissuade and slow down attacking Ferral. Yet, they kept trying.

The Ferrals used the cover of the shadows. Every now and again the moonlight caught a darting movement, reflecting off naked skin, but with incredible agility these beasts shot between one spot of darkness to another, getting closer and closer.

They came forward in twos or threes, with more poised in the darkness, ready to exploit the fearless vanguard's successes. Tension saturated the air around the defenders. Inside, they fought the demons trying to undermine what common sense told them: they were the ones armed with guns, safe behind the lines of defence. The savages possessed nothing but stones, but what if one got through? What fate awaited them then? For all their bestial ways, and the sub-human contempt the citizens of Athenia held them in, the Ferrals were human. Physically they possessed all the traits of Homo sapiens but displayed none of the trappings of civilisation. Somewhere within, they were different – they had lost what it was, in the opinion of the Athenians, to be human: they had no souls. Where was their intellect, compassion or creativity? They wore no clothes, lived under the open sky, avoided washing, preferring instead to daub their bodies in mud. They couldn't even talk or make fire. What they did possess were the worst traits of humanity: the guile, cunning and cruelty. In the harsh and brutal world, with food and water sparse, they thrived, their numbers growing all the time, while the population of Athenia stagnated. However, for the Athenians, what set the Ferrals firmly amongst the beasts, and within their own nightmares, was their taste for human flesh. It was the source of many a tale told to the young of Athenia to ensure they behaved: for a hungry Ferral would surely take a naughty child in the night, stealing their soul!

Yet for all the stories of horror, no one knew what drove the Ferrals to regularly attack the walls of Athenia. It usually brought only death to the raiders, never a meal. A priest declared barbarity and civilisation fought an eternal battle: civilisation's duty to bring light into every corner, the barbarians to bring darkness. Like most people in Athenia, Finbarl paid little heed to the words of a priest and gave little thought to why the Ferrals attacked. As vermin, they deserved a vermin's fate, a belief drummed into him since his days as a cadet. He would have loved to fire his rifle all night, slaughtering every one of the abominations. He was only prevented by the shortage of bullets, rationed as precious commodities in a world where natural resources were rare and the knowledge and skills to do anything with them still rarer. Unless you hit with every shot, you left yourself exposed to a potentially gruesome death. Finbarl understood why Officer Vassel chided him for shooting so early, even if he knew he had hit his mark.

Another screech. Finbarl peered over the rampart, his eye looking down the sight of his rifle. A stone rapped against the wall to his left, making him start. They were in throwing distance! Finbarl made out a limp Ferral body, prostrate upon a wicker barrel in the second row of defences. How have they got past the first line without me seeing? thought Finbarl in alarm. Then, to his horror, he saw the motion of two other Ferrals leaping over the second line, using the dead body as protection against the sharp flint.

"They're in perimeter three!" he yelled. "Two at least. Maybe more."

"I see them!" Vassel shouted back. "Ready lads. Permission to fire if you're sure of a hit." No sooner had the words left his mouth than two rifle shots exploded along the wall, the puffs of smoke glowing in the moonlight.

Amidst the commotion Finbarl heard Vassel continuing to bark out orders. "Cannon readied?"

"Yes, sir!" came the nervous reply from the crew manning the crude, bulbous-shaped mortar. Their rarely used weapon loaded with stone, primed to spray a barrage of indiscriminate death.

As the drama heightened, Finbarl felt his heartbeat quicken, his palms sweat. How many are there? he asked himself, peering into the charcoal distance. So far, he counted three. One probably dead upon the wicker barrel, but the other two vanished since the first shots, back within the safety of the shadows. Were more following from behind? Dead or injured Ferral were easier to see than a live one. Finbarl's eyes felt strained staring into the darkness, and he blinked, screwing them up to relieve the discomfort. As his sight readjusted to the nightscape, a movement caught his attention. A figure crossed over the last line of barrels, weaving through a sentry line of thorny branches, looking pitiful in their defensive role, the moat now within reach. Finbarl aimed his gun and pulled the trigger, sending a bullet towards the shadowed outline.

"Cronax!" he cursed, as the Ferral's left arm whipped back. The bullet hit its target, but only the upper limb. The creature's forward momentum continued, now only ten yards from the moat. Surely it can't get across? Other guards assumed the challenge, firing with a rare abandon. Ghost-like, the Ferral evaded all attempts to stop it. Five yards closer.

At this range, Finbarl clearly made out its appearance. Male, with a wild mane of hair swept back at the front by the mud layering its face. A thick, matted beard framed the bottom half of the face, with ferocious eyes staring out above a wide-open mouth.

"Aaallkkkaaarrr!"

As Finbarl flinched at the scream, he noticed two stripes of blue painted upon the Ferral's cheeks, while other colours appeared dappled upon the chest. As his senses heightened amid the danger, the world slowed down, intricate details coming into clear focus. Blood from the bullet wound streamed down the Ferral's left arm, droplets hanging in the air as the fiend ran onwards. Those childhood stories of monsters and magic flashed through Finbarl's mind as he wondered what creature could ignore such an injury. Did they feel pain like normal humans? Would the Ferral have the power to leap the eight-yard-wide moat and make the top of the wall?

With a graceful motion, the Ferral sank to a squat position on the rim of the moat and pushed off, soaring through the air. Finbarl scrambled to reload, watching in horror, while his brain calculated whether the Ferral's trajectory would carry it across.

"Cannon, fire!" Officer Vassel cried.

As the boom announced the command fulfilled, the Ferral's body came to a mid-air halt, stones ripping through its body. Finbarl looked away in disgust as the tangled remains slumped to the bottom of the moat.

"No reason to stop, you Ferral-whack sons of whores!" screamed Vassel. "There's at least one more out there!"

Finbarl recovered from his sickened stupor and finished loading his rifle. Below, the cannon crew rushed to cool down the turret with a bucket of water, bringing up replacement stones to re-arm their weapon.

Another rifle shot sounded. "I got it!" came a cry from down the wall. Several heads peered over the barricade. Far to the left, protruding out of a bush, a limp, lifeless arm confirmed the claim.

"Good shot, guard!" yelled Vassel. "We stay alert until we're sure there are no more!" His tone conveyed some relief, suggesting he believed the attack at an end.

*

"Stand down, guard!" ordered Officer Vassel to Finbarl. "You've had a long day and your Jumblar levels are low. I don't want any more bullets wasted to the night. You can return to barracks. We'll talk in the morning!"

Finbarl opened his mouth to protest but thought better of it. "Yes, sir," he snapped, turning under the gaze of the other guards. A couple smirked in appreciation of a colleague's shaming, while others offered sympathy. Under the glare of Officer Vassel, all quickly returned their attention to the perimeter stone wall and the barbed wire divide separating them from the wild country beyond.

Finbarl endured a lonely trek back. The wall lay at the far end of Eden Valley, stretching a couple of miles to the north-west, with dominating hills guarding either side. At the valley's other end lay the town of Athenia, a carbuncle adjoining the verdant, cultivated land.

Moonlit plants swayed in a gentle breeze, while the serenity of night distracted Finbarl from his anger and frustration. He never tired of this beauty. He only needed to travel beyond the hills to see the contrasting barren world of scrubland and sand. The imposing mountains to the east kept the rain away, but also provided the precious glacial meltwater that found its way into Eden Valley. Finbarl skirted right to avoid the irrigation ditches, finding the path running down the side of the Jumblar crop. Brushing his hand through the wispy heads, he considered how long since his last dose of Jumblar. Officer Vassel was right on that. Perhaps twenty hours; maybe more. He felt the strange effects of it leaving his system: an odd bedfellow of tiredness and nervous energy, known to everyone as Jumblar's vengeance. He rubbed his arms in a futile effort to satisfy a compulsion to do something with them. Sleep usually provided the bridge to the morning's Jumblar ritual, but the Ferral moon meant an extra shift. The discomfort of a guard missing his Jumblar fix was as nothing to the risk of a breach in the walls by the Ferrals. Those walls meant everything to Athenia.

A fog shrouded much of history. Only an awareness of a huge loss and gratitude for what remained survived. From the apogee of civilisation, some 5,000 years ago, the pressures of population growth and climate change triggered wars for resources, while societies succumbed to an uncontrollable rise in crime. National governments collapsed, trade declined, and local communities sought sanctuary from the anarchy behind impregnable walls. The more fundamental needs of local particularism soon replaced national loyalties, shrinking and shrinking until the focal point of life became the fortified town. How Athenia came to be the only community to survive, no one knew. Legends talked of others beyond the desert and mountains, but who took such things seriously when legends also talked about man travelling to the moon? This version of history explained everything for the Athenians. They understood their blessed position, chosen to guard civilisation until it could grow again; they accepted the hardships they faced, the walls keeping them in but keeping them safe, and they understood the Ferrals. What else could these savage beasts be other than the natural result of breeding by those criminal, anarchic elements responsible for the death of the old world, generations of corrupt genes mutating and evolving into something sub-human? Protecting society from them was vital to save civilisation.

Running along the top of the valley's hills, Finbarl looked upon the regularly spaced watchtowers with their burning beacons, the flames occasionally glinting off the barbed wire. Defences ran the full length of the ridges. The watchtowers were, in turn, dominated by the occasional windmill, whose sails provided the power to pump water across the farmland, into the town and to grind the grain for bread. A magnificent human achievement, considered Finbarl. In their vantage point atop the hills, they sent an unmistakeable message to anything beyond the hills and walls of Athenia's superiority.

Down in the valley, the imposing walls of Athenia sliced across the valley floor, green turning to the harsher tones of stone and wood. A stream, dancing in the moonlight, guided Finbarl to the single-entry point, a pair of heavy wooden doors. The water vanished down a small brick tunnel, carrying it under the town, its departure accompanied by a familiar gurgle. A shallow ditch, filled with stakes rather than water, ran parallel to the walls, and Finbarl crossed the simple bridge leading to the doors.

"Finbarl-apcula reporting back!" shouted Finbarl, thumping his rifle butt against the wood.

"You're back early," came a muffled reply, accompanied by the movement of rusty bolts. "Is the Ferral threat over?" As the door slowly opened, Finbarl found Strathbol-apcula peering at him, holding a lighted torch. He was one of the youngest guards, barely sixteen, and his smooth skin glowed in the light.

"Something like that," replied Finbarl. "A dead Ferral ain't much threat!"

"Cronax!" cursed Strathbol, wide-eyed. "They got that close?"

"Close enough for me!"

Strathbol tilted his head, pondering Finbarl's response before nodding an understanding. Whether the reaction was in recognition of seeing through the bravado or not, Finbarl couldn't tell.

"I heard gunshots at the east side too," commented Strathbol. "That's a true Ferral moon out there tonight. Reminds me of the time … ". Before he finished his sentence, Finbarl brushed past and beyond earshot.

Finbarl liked Strathbol but was in no mood to stop and chat. Finding solace under his bedsheets in the barracks dominated Finbarl's thoughts. How much sleep he would get while his body craved Jumblar, he didn't know, but at least he would be alone with his thoughts.

CHAPTER 2

The background noises of the barracks and town tormented Finbarl as he lay wide awake in bed. The snoring and heavy breathing of guards in adjacent beds, a distant shout from the street or a grating sound from a passing cart, pierced his thoughts with an uncomfortable intensity. A gruelling day of work usually brought a deep, restful sleep, but his lack of Jumblar, coupled with the evening's drama bouncing around his head, prevented the welcome escape into slumber. The humiliation meted out by Vassel grew to a level where it overwhelmed and fuelled his every thought.

Having reconciled himself to a night without sleep, Finbarl's conscious thoughts slipped into the subconscious world of dreams. He stood on parade, surrounded by his peers, all to attention, rifles resting upon shoulders. A voice addressed them. The words were incomprehensible, but belonged to the Governor of Athenia, their leader. Finbarl towered over those around him, the Governor's eyes and words directed at him. He felt proud. Then the pitch changed, becoming more strained. A click of heels indicated a section of the aligned guards turning left and marching away. Finbarl felt confused, looking around. Those leaving were the Familos; those who remained the Orphos. His parents were by his side, dressed in the guards' uniform: why was he left with the orphaned guards, those they informally called Orphos, when it was clear for all to see he had parents? Surely that made him a Familo! Then another command from the Governor, a click of heels and everyone around him marched away, leaving Finbarl alone. He called after his parents, but no sound emerged from his mouth. They turned but with featureless faces. Finbarl looked to the Governor for help but the great man now stood far in the distance, addressing a different parade, full of Familos and Orphos. Despite willing his legs to move, Finbarl remained stuck. All eyes of the parade turned to look upon him. Panic welled up, turning to terror as he realised Ferrals surrounded him. The beasts circled, moving closer, fanciful fangs and claws dripping with blood. Finbarl tried to grab his gun but found he had no arms. Now the Ferrals towered over him, getting closer and closer. Finbarl opened his mouth to scream.

"You all right there?"

Finbarl opened his eyes, conscious of his blood pumping fast, the noise of the barracks and a face above him. It was Strathbol. "I'm fine," said Finbarl, relieved the nightmare was over. A film of sweat coated his body, while a lingering shadow haunted his memory. It was not the encroaching Ferral, but his long dead parents. They regularly appeared in his dreams, but only ever as precursors to something darker. His young companion remained standing over him, and Finbarl lay still, waiting for him to move on.

"You were making all sorts of strange noises," commented Strathbol, as he adjusted his uniform.

"I was dreaming."

"Really? What about?"

"Killing Ferrals," answered Finbarl.

"You sounded a bit like a Ferral," quipped Strathbol, walking away chuckling to himself.

Finbarl sat up, ruffling his hair, aware of the dawn chorus mingling with the sounds of the awakening town. Thoughts of the dream lingered, clashing with the reality absorbed through his eyes, as he watched Strathbol's back disappear into the washroom. The young lad was a Familo, sponsored by his family to be a guard, but he was all right. As an Orpho, Finbarl got on with lots of Familos. When a young cadet, the social divide dominated the barracks. He remembered the bullying and fights; the insults thrown the way of the disadvantaged Orphos. But, now grown-up, the discipline, strength and bravado were all that mattered in the guards' petty hierarchy, as far as Finbarl was concerned.

Despite some sleep, Finbarl's body felt exhausted. Torn between a desire to stay in bed and rest or rise for his usual scheduled activities, the ringing of the duty bell settled Finbarl's dilemma. He swung himself off his bed, as those around him did the same. Memories of the nightmare faded, as the duties of the day beckoned.

Standing with bare feet upon the chilled, stone floor of the washroom was a familiar hardship. Icy water stung Finbarl's face as he splashed from the communal bowl. He let the water drip back to the washbowl, blowing out his lips as though trying to expel the demons. His body still cried out for Jumblar. He splashed more water over his face, hoping it would numb the sensation. It didn't.

Having dressed in his ragged, light green thawb, the loose, airy uniform of the guards, Finbarl followed his companions out of the barracks, they with idle chatter, he in sour silence.

A hotchpotch of muddled buildings, crammed into limited space, made up Athenia. Narrow streets, shaded by overhanging structures, twisted their way across the town. They followed no regimented pattern, going this way and that to accommodate the need to squeeze in another house, stable or workshed. Had Athenia the knowledge, technology and materials to build upwards, they surely would have, but two stories were all the largely wooden edifices supported. Most accommodated some fragment of scrap, scavenged from the past and found in the wilderness. Only the windmills, looking down upon the town, and the central cooling tower, funnelling fresh air down to the town square, built with precious stone, dared reach to a grand height.

Finbarl breathed in the chilled morning air, rubbing his hands for warmth, vaguely noticing the familiar and unpleasant stink of the streets. A trickle of green-brown sludge wormed its way along a worn channel in the middle of the walkway. Before the heat of the day permeated these claustrophobic alleys, the residents of the neighbourhood brushed the waste towards the few drain holes and into the cesspits; water too valuable to spare for such a task. A permanent stain coloured the channel, dappling the flat surface. In the cesspits, the mix of human waste, camel dung, bones and other rubbish festered in the heat, until transported to the fields as fertiliser. Hollowed tree trunks covered the drains, helping carry the overpowering smell upwards but, unless the wind blew in the right direction, the foul air found its way back to the street.

A clucking chicken scurried past Finbarl, escaped from its pen, a desperate keeper somewhere no doubt seeking their escapee. Finbarl contemplated ringing its neck, smuggling it back to the barracks and feasting on its delicious, tender meat, but his need for Jumblar superseded the temptation. He expected someone to follow his initial instinct; some fool willing to risk a life sentence in the Prison for theft. Instead,

Finbarl kicked a pile of camel dung past the fowl and into the waste channel, making the bird leap and squawk in indignation. Increasing his pace, Finbarl caught up with a loose column of guards heading in the direction of the town square. Their green uniforms soon diluted in the dull beige and white clothes worn by the ordinary townsfolk, emerging from their shacks to join the procession.

The town square was the largest open space within Athenia. A few Chitalpa trees populated its outer edges, providing a little shade. The sun, still absent in the sheltered streets, warmed the exposed, hard, sandy surface and air. A faint wind, generated by the cooling tower looming to the right and by the variable temperatures of the side lanes, felt nice upon Finbarl's face. It also brought to his hearing the undulating chants of the priests. Their voices rose and fell in beautiful harmony as they delivered their traditional call to prayer, standing in an ordered line in their blue robes. Ever since a young child, Finbarl recalled listening to the enticing sound of their song. Then, the priests appeared fascinating, magical and important, but now in adulthood, beyond their role handing out Jumblar, Finbarl saw no purpose for them other than their singing. He considered them parasites, kept around by tradition and fear of change. No one knew what to believe in any more, not even the priests. Who could believe in a benevolent, all-powerful being when mankind had suffered and lost so much? What faith did an unreliable deity deserve? Yet at the same time, the Athenians needed hope more than ever. As such, few possessed bravery enough to discard the ritual of religion and hope in God, but neither would they invest their lives in it. Jumblar, that gift from God, provided the one certainty.

The square filled as men, women and children trickled in from all directions. The irony of a world with so few people, cohabiting in such crowded circumstances, remained lost on a people obsessed with their preservation. The dangers beyond the walls defined them all.

By the time the priests' mantra reached an impressive crescendo, the scrum of people had formed into orderly queues. The familiarity of the weekly ritual, known as the Jumblar uchaist, allowed for this controlled spectacle. Everyone waited patiently in their designated lines, symbolising the strict strata of society. Across the town, smaller, similar events took place in several districts. At the main square, only one priest continued his incantation, his brothers preparing for the distribution of the Jumblar. The rumble of the waiting masses drowned out his voice, as they passed the time catching up on the week's gossip; even the other priests chatted amongst themselves, insensible to any spiritual solemnity. The formal meaning of the ritualised exchange of Jumblar for obedience and devotion, was trivialised and irrelevant to most now. They needed their Jumblar, to surrender to its calming embrace and uplifting intoxication, helping them overcome the fears and mire of their lives.

Finbarl joined his queue, designated for guards alone. The green line looked incredibly long to a man twenty-four hours without Jumblar. He shuffled testily, conscious his peers no doubt talked about him and his impending fate with Officer Vassel. A mumbled curse escaped his lips as the queue appeared unmoving. The man in front gave him a momentary glance, turning away on recognising his neighbour. Finbarl ignored him, looking towards the other queues. To his left, a line of the common citizens, the Gulas, edged their skinny frames forward; to his right a line of Moralistas, the civic equivalent of the guards, its numbers largely made up of women, with the occasional ex-guard no longer fit for active duties. The women of the Moralistas, nearly always orphaned, were supported and moulded from a tender age to manage and deliver the will of the Wardyns and uphold the values of civilisation. Finbarl felt envy at the shortness of their queue. He couldn't even bring himself to look over at the Alci line, where the professionals and higher social strata of Athenia waited. Their queue always moved with speed. Bloody typical! This time Finbarl managed to keep his profanities to himself. *What idiot's handing out our Jumblar?*

At the front of each line, a table, manned by a priest provided the objective for everyone and the target for Finbarl's stare. With a blessing, a vow and an exchange of Jumblar for a token, the ritual was complete: what was there in that to hold them up? As a sudden urge to yell out his frustrations built in Finbarl, the man in front took a step forward. The urge subsided and Finbarl quickly followed with his own stride, aware his tormented nerves could not take much more. *Discipline, Finbarl,* instructed himself. *You're a guard, so behave like one!*

He turned his attention back to the adjacent queue of Gulas. Assessing and belittling the plebs offered one way to occupy himself. His training as a guard made him feel apart, suspicious of those threatening Athenia's stability, nurturing disdain and snobbery. On another day, he would focus his condescension towards the Moralistas: a collection of unwanted women and weak and damaged guards. Good families didn't place their daughters in the Moralistas. A suitable social marriage was their fate, and no guard desired to end their days amongst them.

Finbarl's admiration and loyalty pointed one way, towards his superiors in the guard and the Wardyns, the ruling class. The latter didn't frequent the common uchaist, which was fine by Finbarl. He had no desire to be under their gaze. No such concerns afflicted him in the presence of farmers, shopkeepers, dung-shovellers and other workers. Even the Alci held no real power over the guards. Without him and his kind, those helpless saps would be long dead. The arrogance allowed for no appreciation of how much his life depended on them: for the food, the building, the cleaning. Guards possessed guns and the authority; the Wardyns owned the guards and the power. Each cowed head in the Gulas' queue reinforced Finbarl's opinion: they had their place but not his respect.

A small gap opened in the Gula line, leaving one man with room to stretch his arms and yawn. That's right, opined Finbarl to himself, pretend you're tired and not a dung-shoveller who no one wants to stand near! He laughed out loud, earning another uneasy look from the man in front. "Dung-shoveller," said Finbarl to the fellow guard, nodding to the source of his mirth. The guard remained straight-faced, turning away with a whisper to the man in front of him. "Dung-shoveller," said Finbarl again, this time to the back of the oblivious guard's head.

As his own line took a few more steps forward, a short, pretty woman, with long, jet-black hair, caught Finbarl's attention. She stood about ten feet in front, in the adjacent Gula queue, her hands gently resting upon the shoulders of a young boy of about five. Finbarl smiled as the young boy waved a whittled, wooden animal in his hand. For a change he didn't feel the need to condescend or judge. The boy stirred thoughts of his own childhood, a vague notion of uninhibited playing and innocence. Did his own parents hold him like that before their death, leaving him alone in the world? The woman looked over, catching Finbarl's eye. He smiled: she quickly turned away.

"Keep moving!" said an anonymous voice from behind. With the distraction, the queue moved forward and Finbarl advanced to close the gap, turning again to look at the woman and child in gratitude. Did she have a small smile? wondered Finbarl, as their own turn to receive Jumblar came up. It wouldn't be long until Finbarl reached the front of his queue. He noticed the priest distributing to the guards displayed a bored expression, blessing with more haste and less sincerity. All the better, thought Finbarl.

A tiny yelp caught Finbarl's attention. Heads all around turned to the source. A guard stood towering over the boy and mother. Finbarl recognised him. It was Audlech, a sickly-looking man who compensated for his light frame by bullying anyone weaker. He gripped the wooden animal in his hand, teasing the boy, who tried to retrieve it. The mother showed no signs of fear, standing up to the guard.

"Give it back!" she snapped.

"Or what?" replied Audlech.

"Or what nothing!" shouted the woman. "You don't take a toy from a child!"

A few of the younger watching guards laughed at the confrontation, the mature ones looking less amused, but all did nothing. Something in Finbarl, perhaps the lack of Jumblar, stirred him to intervene. He stepped forward, pushing Audlech forcibly away from the woman. "Nothing better to do than steal a kid's toy?"

"Mind your own business, Orpho!" growled back Audlech, trying to regain his composure.

"It's my business to deal with thieves." Finbarl squared up to the other guard. "That's what we have the Prison for."

Audlech laughed nervously. "This ain't feft. Just some Ferral-whack fun."

"Well, I get my fun from beating guys like you to pulp!" Finbarl now smiled as his superior height and build became apparent.

"Finbarl-apcula!" A new voice sounded from behind.

Finbarl turned to see Officer Vassel not ten places back in the queue, his face red with anger. Why did it have to be him?

"Get back in line, guard! We don't fight our own."

Finbarl skulked back to his line, leaving his eyes to linger upon Audlech in a last vestige of a threat.

"And as for you, Audlech-apcula," continued Vassel, "Grow up! Give the boy his toy back and go and take your bloody Jumblar. I want all my guards fit for duty today."

Audlech paused for a second, shocked at his public humiliation, unsure how to react. Left with no choice, he thrust the wooden toy back into the boy's hands and stormed away. The child smiled in glee, his tears gone in a flash, and showed his retrieved treasure to his mother. She ruffled his hair before guiding him forward as their turn came to collect their Jumblar. Finbarl looked on with a sense of satisfaction.

The boy went over to Finbarl, waving what turned out to be a misshaped wooden dog. "Thank you," said the boy.

Finbarl smiled broadly. "Some things are worth fighting for," he replied, bending down to examine the toy. The mother caught up with her son, carrying their Jumblar doses. She looked at Finbarl without emotion.

"I'm Finbarl-apcula."

She continued to assess Finbarl more with suspicion than gratitude, before saying, "Aminatra-gula," and then gently pushed the boy on his way.

"Next!"

Finbarl turned to see a priest beckoning him to the table, rummaging in his pocket, pulling out the small, blue stone token, etched with the town's symbol of a windmill.

The priest took the token and mumbled, "Bless thy soul for through God we seek sanctuary." His mundane task complete, the priest waited for Finbarl to complete his side of the ritual.

"I thank the Lord for what I am about to receive and promise to honour his name."

With the vow completed, the priest passed across a bundle of folded Jumblar leaves, enough to last Finbarl the week. A bucket of green balls stood on the table and Finbarl reached in, took one, showed it to the priest and hurried on his way, desperate to start chewing on the fibrous leaf of the Jumblar plant.

CHAPTER 3

"I can't make you out, guard," said Officer Vassel, as Finbarl stood to attention before him. "You either have something about you, or you're lucky."

"Sir?" Finbarl hadn't expected the dressing down to go this way when playing it over in his mind.

"We found a dead Ferral this morning, 200 yards from the barricade. Had your bullet in it! That was either a fine shot or an unlucky beast."

"As I said, sir, I could see what I was shooting at."

"It was still a mighty risk to shoot at that distance. Should have waited, as trained to do. A kill is just as good at 100 yards."

An hour earlier, Finbarl would have struggled to contain his anger, but the Jumblar worked immediately. Its bitter taste left the tongue tingling but also brought an instant internal peace. Finbarl compartmentalised Vassel's provocative attitude behind a mild feeling of contentment and well-being. The muscles, previously crying out for release, relaxed, sated through the intoxicating infusion, Finbarl remaining calmly to attention as the words washed through him.

"I don't mind luck," continued Vassel. "Just like talent, it shows you're blessed, but the difference is, you can't rely on luck every time. I don't want to be the one exposed because your luck runs out. But that dead Ferral's bought you a reprieve. All I'm going to say is you make sure any future shots hit with certainty, not with the hope of success. Am I clear?"

"Yes, sir!" snapped Finbarl. A warm, elated sensation washed through him. With his fix of Jumblar, the world started to feel in balance.

Vassel's brow furrowed with frustration, indicating the dressing down was not over. "Killing Ferrals is one thing," said the officer, "bringing the guards into disrepute in front of the town is another matter. I do hope it wasn't an Orpho-Familo thing. I don't care the provocation; you do not challenge another guard like you did this morning! Understand?"

"Yes, sir! Sorry, sir! It was Jumblar's vengeance making me irritable. Won't happen again."

"I've had my Jumblar and you're still making me irritable, guard." Despite his words, Vassel's tone changed to a more paternal nature. Poised to speak again, something over Finbarl's shoulder caught his attention. His facial muscles tensed.

"Don't let me stop you," said a voice, instantly making Vassel straighten.

Finbarl turned his head to see the source of the interruption. Despite the Jumblar, sight of the owner of the voice caused him a shock.

Wardyn Torbald-eltar, son of the Governor, stood casually against the doorframe, a broad smile across his chubby face. "I've heard about the little drama in the main square. Sounds to me like you should have knocked his block off, Finbarl-apcula."

Finbarl looked to Vassel's eyes for a reaction. They remained calm, appearing to examine Finbarl with the same purpose.

"Of course," continued Torbald, "that would have got you sent to the Prison, but at least you'd have caused some entertainment."

Should he reply or keep silent? Finbarl remained undecided, confused by the presence of this powerful individual. Wardyns rarely made such informal interventions in the lives of others.

Vassel broke the silence. "Is there anything I can help you with, Eltar?"

An uncomfortable pause followed and Finbarl felt the eyes of the Wardyn on his back.

"No, I just wanted to meet the guard willing to risk his freedom for the sake of a child's toy."

Vassel's face relaxed, indicating the departure of their guest. He shuffled in his seat, resetting his thoughts. "Now, we've two prisoners to transport to the Prison today," began Vassel. "I want you and Gauret to undertake the task and lead on Jumblar distribution at Bruuk's Point. You'll have F Section to support you with security. Understood?"

"Yes, Vassel-apculex. Thank you, sir."

"Dismissed!"

Finbarl turned to leave, paused, thought about asking Vassel what had just happened, before thinking better of it.

CHAPTER 4

Finbarl found Gauret-apcula at the stable outhouse. The prematurely balding guard, another Orpho and not much older than Finbarl, nibbled the last scraps off an apple core. Finbarl looked enviously at the narrow remains of the fruit, teased by distant memories of the last apple he ate as part of his rations. A stable boy led out two camels, who sniffed the air with noble distain. Gauret grabbed the rein of the paler beast and presented the apple core on the palm of his hand. The camel's lips curled round the fruit and gratefully ate the scant remains. As Finbarl took the reins of his camel, he wondered if those big, moist eyes judged him, accusing him of neglect at his lack of a gift. The last thing he wanted was a temperamental beast, personally affronted by his master. Finbarl offered a compensatory scratch under the camel's chin. The creature emitted a distinct groan that Finbarl elected to interpret as contentment, though in truth they groaned for every emotion.

"Where are the prisoners?" asked Finbarl.

Gauret nodded to his left. "Boujet is bringing them. Seems one's having second thoughts!" Gauret laughed at his own joke.

"Should have thought about that before breaking the law," huffed Finbarl. He found it all so pitiful.

A sobbing announced the arrival of the two prisoners, both with hands bound. Finbarl recognised the eldest as a senior farm manager named Gorwell. He maintained a dignity, staring forward in defiance. The other man's cheeks were red from tears; he stood, stooped in abjection. The face looked familiar but in no meaningful sense. Finbarl didn't care. What was there to care about with justice served and troublemakers removed from the civilised confines of Athenia's walls? Each guard learnt this mantra as the unquestionable truth from an early age.

The camels stood, weighed down with bags of Jumblar, ready to distribute to the existing prisoners. It was payment for scavenged goods, representing the final remnants of trade. The oasis of Eden Valley provided so much, but not enough. Salt, flint, guano, certain plants and, most prized of all, scrap metal left by previous societies, lay in the land beyond. A dangerous land feared by the Athenians. The prisoners provided a cheap and safe means to harvest from Ferral country. They followed simple rules: no item to trade, no Jumblar; no Jumblar, then death through madness. The control and supply of Jumblar remained solely in the hands of Athenia. The cruellest form of control. For any crime committed in Athenia, the punishment was banishment to the Prison. The Prison, nothing more than the wide-open wasteland beyond Athenia's walls, with no proper protection from the Ferrals, no access to the bounty of Eden Valley and no escape until death. Death came quickly, but Athenia found replacement prisoners with equal haste.

A long rope tethered the two prisoners to the camels' saddles. Finbarl sat atop his beast as it rested upon the ground, adjusting his rifle strap so not to rub on the ride. "Where's that bloody priest?" he growled at no one in particular. The party would be going nowhere until the man who blessed the

Jumblar turned up. To Finbarl, undertaking the ritual for prisoners made even less sense than for the law-abiding townsfolk.

A braying echoed from an adjacent alleyway and, moments later, a priest emerged, riding awkwardly upon a donkey. Finbarl signalled to the small troop of guards to move on their way. He wasn't waiting for the priest to reach them. When had those sanctimonious hypocrites ever condescended to be polite to anyone? The priest would have to trot if he wanted to keep up. If Finbarl avoided talking to him it would be a bonus – he didn't even know his name, and had no intention of asking it.

Finbarl's camel roared as he tugged the reins sharply, making it rise to its feet. In front, Gauret's camel took its first steps down the alley. Behind, waiting patiently, were the other accompanying guards. Finbarl fidgeted to a comfortable position, rubbed his camel's neck and urged it forward. He jerked backwards, bracing his legs to compensate, and turned to ensure the prisoners were safely in tow. The priest showed no signs of hurrying to catch up.

When they turned from the alley into the main square of the town, a large crowd awaited. It was a customary send-off for convicted prisoners. The Wardyns instigated the tradition, providing the mob with a target for its frustrations. An empty column divided two groups of about 300 baying people. At the front, a row of youngsters stood armed with dried camel dung, thrown with practised accuracy as the prisoners passed. The camels peered nervously but kept a disciplined, indoctrinated pace.

"Traitors! Thieves! Murderers!" The crowd yelled a range of unsubstantiated accusations with a passionate and sincere vitriol. Guards and the Moralista stood amongst the crowd, ready with clubs or a rebuke for anyone stepping out of line. The prisoners tried burying their heads into their chests, shielding their faces from the barrage, but as the rope tugged them forward, they had no choice but to stand tall.

"But I'm innocent!" cried Pryfol. A fruitless gesture. The volume of the mob increased, dashing hope of mercy or forgiveness. They now had a focal point for their dung.

"Your fate's sealed," bewailed the other prisoner, Gorwell. "You'd do well to accept it."

Pryfol acknowledged the advice, slumping his head down.

The huge gates of Athenia inched open, while a drawbridge eased down over the dry outer moat. In the hollowed defensive channel running from the southern hillock of Bymore to the northern ridge, called Cragor, row upon row of stakes and thorny shrub bushes shouted an aggressive warning. The only way into the west side of Athenia was through these doors.

A deep thump echoed through the ground as the draw-bridge dropped into place. The leading camels strolled onto the wooden surface, grateful to escape the noise, sniffing at the air around. A faint odour of death lingered. Finbarl looked down to see the rotting corpse of a Ferral in the moat, its body pierced in several places by stakes. Finbarl felt nothing. For the prisoners, everything had changed. They were no longer protected by the walls or guns of Athenia: the Ferrals were their new neighbours. If a Ferral attacked, they would have to defend themselves with whatever nature provided. Their home was now the Prison, the wilderness before them, where death came sooner rather than later, inevitably involving pain and fear; Athenia's way of main-taining its façade of civilised law yet punishing its criminals in the most horrible way. Another thud signalled the doors closing behind them, and Finbarl ordered the procession forward into the wasteland.

They made their way towards Bruuk's Point, a small outcrop of rock in the barren scrubland a few miles from Athenia, used as the control point for the Prison. Ferrals rarely roamed as far west due to the proximity to the desert. Their natural habitat lay in the cooler foothills to the east. For the rest of the week, the prisoners travelled widely, collecting tradable goods and food and water for their own survival. Their dependency on Jumblar brought them all back to Bruuk's Point. When the sun reached its zenith on the seventh day, they returned like migratory birds.

Finbarl's party slowly marched down a near dry river channel, the longer strides of the camels making the priest, much to Finbarl's amusement, force his donkey into a fast trot every time he dropped back. Athenia used most of the glacial water flowing from the mountains in the east to quench its thirst and irrigate the fertile Eden Valley and the small farming colony of Buchaunia, further to the south. What remained, as the river flowed westwards, formed a gentle trickle, gradually disappearing into the parched, sandy earth. The camels, sated from the troughs of Athenia before their departure, trooped happily along the valuable life source without distraction. Every now and again, as they turned a corner in the channel, their arrival startled a visiting animal grabbing a precious drink, causing a panicked escape as they sprinted off or flew for refuge.

Bruuk's Point broke the flat landscape like a pimple, coming into view at a distance. It provided a perfect vantage point across a large area. Only to the west lay any cover, where a small wooded area clung to the bottom of the hills holding back the desert. A kettle of vultures circled in a vortex on the thermals to the north, waiting for the first carrion feast of the day to invite them down.

"We'll stop for a drink!" declared Gauret. The sun, now high in the sky, beat down relentlessly. He removed his keffiyeh from his head, wiping his forehead with his sleeve. "Hadyn! Willym! Establish a lookout on the banks!"

Finbarl tugged at a rope attached to his camel's left ankle and commanded it to koosh. As always, the camel emitted a protest but eventually succumbed to more forceful persuasion. Behind, the prisoners collapsed to their knees, Pryfol whimpering loudly. Finbarl slid off the saddle, rubbing his backside to relieve the sore muscles. He reached into a small bag, withdrawing a clasp of green leaves to feed to the camel. The beast eyed him with little gratitude, but chewed contentedly.

The priest also dismounted, leading his beast to the water. He spoke not a word to anyone, and no one spared him a moment's thought.

"Can we have water?" Finbarl turned to see Gorwell gesturing hopefully towards him. He curtly directed the prisoner to the stream. "But that's too brackish!" Gorwell complained. "The sand! It adds salt."

"Get used to it!" snapped Finbarl. "It'll soon taste like elixir when you've lived out here a while. Anyway, if it's good enough for an ass, it's good enough for a prisoner."

Gorwell glanced at Pryfol, who shook his head pathetically in response. They crawled to the water; Finbarl unplugged his goat bladder and poured a refreshing mouthful of pure glacial meltwater down his throat. Gorwell glared with pure loathing as he spooned the first handful of stream water. It had a salty edge but not as bad as feared, and he lent forward to splash as much as possible over his face and into his mouth.

Gauret wandered over to stand by Finbarl. "Nice and quiet," he observed.

"A particularly hot one," replied Finbarl, eyeing the blue sky. "I imagine most prisoners are sheltering in the shade of the wood."

"Or toasting on a Ferral spit," offered Gauret.

"Not even I'd wish that on a prisoner," said Finbarl. "You never know if one of your friends will end up here one day."

"Or even yourself!" laughed Gauret.

Finbarl joined in, acknowledging the ridiculous notion.

"I saw you at uchaist this morning," said Gauret, suddenly serious. "Audlech's not someone you should cross. He's an idiot, but a vindictive one."

"He's a disgrace to the uniform. Picking on a small boy!"

"And his attractive mother." Gauret smiled slyly.

"And his mother," replied Finbarl, ignoring Gauret's attempt to tease him.

"She ain't worth standing up for. You know that?"

Finbarl looked at Gauret. "What do you mean?"

"The child! He don't have a father. Or should I say, the mother don't have a husband!"

"A bastard?" A distasteful expression fell upon Finbarl's face.

"No doubt," confirmed Gauret. "She was a prize catch a few years ago. You remember, she hung out with the Governor's boy and his gang?"

Finbarl stretched his memory back to his adolescent years. "Vaguely," he replied, "but I focused on my training in those days." He looked over towards the prisoners, hoping his lie went unnoticed. But, of course, he'd notice her, and all the other potential wives, as his teenage hormones raced. It was unprofessional to talk of such things, argued his conscious thoughts, while his subconscious ones understood his inexperience with women made it awkward for him.

"Really!" said Gauret, less concerned with his professional standing while out in the wilderness. "She was hard to miss. Anyway, she got with child and that was her future done for. She'll be lucky if a dung-shoveller will marry her now!"

"So, who's the father?" asked Finbarl, his curiosity pricked.

"I don't know," said Gauret, shrugging his shoulders. "She's never said anything, from what I've heard. Rumours, however, have reached my ears!" He smiled.

Finbarl's mind was filling in the blanks. "The Governor's son, Hradbar!"

Gauret raised an eyebrow in acknowledgement. "That's what they say. No wonder she doesn't say anything! If she did, she'd soon end up out here."

"Eh? No way!" protested Finbarl. "That's not a crime."

"Finbarl! Are you that naïve?" Gauret laughed aloud. "You embarrass the Governor and his family – you become a 'criminal'."

"Rubbish!" retorted Finbarl. "You can't talk about the Governor like that! He's the custodian of law. Wouldn't send someone to the Prison because of a comment."

Gauret recognised the dangerous territory entered, criticising the Governor to a fellow and zealous guard, and added, through a shrewd smile, "You're right, of course."

"Of course, he wouldn't," reiterated Finbarl, feeling victorious in the battle for truth. "Now let's get moving before we feel Jumblar's vengeance!" He tugged on the ropes of the prisoners who soothed their sore feet in the stream. They looked up forlornly, their suffering to start again.

A bird screeched in panic and annoyance as it plummeted down to the stream only to find the motley group of guards, prisoners and camels climbing to their feet and setting off. The guards all laughed. They were the lords of this realm.

"We'll be gone shortly, my friend!" cried Willym at the rear. "Then this godforsaken spot is yours!" This caused more laughter, and Finbarl smiled in contentment. It was good to be alive, and he could think of no better life than as a guard.

*

An hour later they arrived at Bruuk's Point. A ring of sandstone boulders lay at the base of the mound and several geckos, bathing in the sun, flashed into the shaded gaps as the boots of Gauret climbed up. Upon the summit, a solitary Manketti tree stood as a sentry, its bark marked with a dozen carvings left by guards and prisoners over the years. Gauret scanned the panorama, squinting against the sun, before retrieving a rudimentary telescope which he aimed westwards towards the woods.

"I was right," he called down to the others. "There's movement in the woods but no other activity. I'll raise the flag. Finbarl, see to Gorwell and Pryfol, and you, Kiteli, help the priest set up the Jumblar and bonus handouts. Everyone else set up a perimeter watch!"

Gauret pulled a threadbare green flag from his satchel, and unrolled it, attached it to a rope dangling from the tree and hoisted it up. It was the signal to prisoners of the guards' presence and Jumblar's availability. A light wind caught the fragile material, making it flutter.

Finbarl beckoned to Gorwell and Pryfol to step over. "I'm going to release you," he instructed them. "No funny business when you're free!"

"Free?" retorted Gorwell. "Free to die!"

"Should have thought about that before you stole from the Wardyns!"

"I did no such thing!" protested Gorwell. "I've never stolen a thing in my life. I was framed for questioning the food distribution."

"Wow! Not heard that one before," replied Finbarl. "Why are you prisoners always 'innocent'? One more pathetic excuse and I'll beat the truth into you! Now give me your hands."

Gorwell, fully aware it was no empty threat, offered his tied hands, and Finbarl cut the binding.

"Your turn, Pryfol. Anything to say about your innocence?" Pryfol offered his hands, too drained to offer resistance. "Good, now up you go. You can be first to collect your Jumblar. Your luck's changing!" Finbarl laughed to himself before adding. "This is the last time you get it for nothing. Next time you bring salt!"

"The salt plains are miles to the north!" a horrified Pryfol complained.

"Excellent," replied Finbarl, "you know where you're going."

"Three to the south!" cried Willym, halting Finbarl's fun.

Finbarl leapt up on a rock and jogged to the top of Bruuk's Point. The shimmering scrubland exposed three silhouettes heading their way. They walked with purpose, indicating prisoners rather than Ferrals. Finbarl turned westwards, towards the wood. A large group emerged from its cover, converging on their location. Over 200 prisoners would soon surround them. By the end of the summer, numbers would be down by about a quarter. Nature extracting its price.

The large group from the woods arrived first: a variety of shapes and sizes, all displaying the rigours of the Prison. Their emaciated bodies moved slowly under the burdensome sun. Scars from their brutal lives stood out in sharp contrast against dried, sun-hardened skin. Within their eyes, the call of Jumblar was present; a desperate, needy absence.

The ratio of prisoners to guards favoured the former. Overpowering their keepers would not present a problem. Finbarl considered the scenario. A few prisoners killed before they overwhelmed the guards, cutting their throats with a ragged piece of flint. Jumblar held them in check. Athenia controlled the supply and hence the guards controlled the prisoners. For some, death was a welcome release and so attacks happened, but most, while getting pleasure from the sight, refrained from joining the assault.

Finbarl recognised nearly all the prisoners. Some he knew by name; some he remembered escorting to the Prison. Only a small number survived beyond a few years, from before Finbarl's time as a guard. One, an old woman, never spoke to guards, though Finbarl often noticed her watching them. She stood out both for her longevity within the Prison and for her habit of providing unusual items to trade for her Jumblar, usually medicinal plants. Despite initial suspicion, her claims proved true. He wondered how one managed to survive so long, and how old she was. Living in the Prison added years to your appearance, while taking years off your life.

"I've got some metal," said Haal, a diminutive prisoner with a hideous wart on his cheek. "Found it near Bluebecker." He placed a handful of screws and a bent piece of rusting metal plating on the floor.

Finbarl examined it. "Looks okay. Kiteli, five pieces of dried goat with Haal's Jumblar!"

Haal beamed with delight. Metal always earned extra. The dry air of the local climate allowed many remnants of past civilisations to survive the years and, while the sand and wind buried most, the latter also exposed the odd valuable piece. With easy-to-access ores hard to find, Athenia prized nothing more precious than second-hand scrap metal. Finding the lost resources of old civilisation gave prisoners the opportunity for reward. Metal made guns and bullets, while glass and plastics became telescopes or jewellery. Occasionally, they found something with the capacity to work as originally intended, or at least demonstrate an industrial concept long lost.

"Where's Euphima?" shouted Gauret to no one in particular, conscious one of the more notable prisoners was missing.

"Dead-ed!" replied Johansson, a prisoner whose peculiar syntax and other oddities amused Finbarl.

Finbarl's eyes flicked back to Haal, examining the grinning prisoner as he chewed a piece of goat meat. The prisoner's eyes stared back innocently, but Finbarl knew what had happened. Euphima found the metal, but let his guard down, providing an opportunity for Haal to murder him and steal the hoard. Once a criminal, always a criminal, thought Finbarl to himself. It didn't bother him. It was the nature of the Prison. If the scrap got handed in, he was happy. Finbarl shook his head in disdain. "Come on!" he cried across to his colleagues. "Let's collect the goods and get this Jumblar dispensed so we can get back to Athenia!"

CHAPTER 5

A minatra stood patiently in yet another queue, her five-year-old son, Karlmon, as always by her side. The sweet smell of fresh bread wafted from the shop door, stimulating the senses of the long-suffering individuals waiting outside for their rationed loaves. Within the procession stood those Athenians considered too old or incapable of heavy labour, some youngsters helping hard-pressed parents and, the vast majority, young mothers who, having fulfilled their duty of providing civilisation's next generation, remained obliged to undertake this soul-sapping routine while caring for their children.

Queuing was an essential way of life for the Athenian. They queued for Jumblar, then for food or other precious and essential commodities. State shops, scattered through the districts, dispensed the precious resources, controlling all food and other essentials, like soap and salt. Each member of the community received food and Jumblar tokens for allocated work, from labour in the fields to more specialist roles, such as the blacksmith, carpenter or baker. It was an economic model promising no innovation, only stagnation.

With no husband or wider family to support her, the work was a heavy burden on Aminatra. Once she ensured Karlmon and herself had collected enough to survive the week, Aminatra, like many of the mothers, made her way to the fields or laundry rooms to spend the afternoon in back-breaking work. She heard that during the Golden Age, women enjoyed choices, even equality with men. It seemed hard to believe, in the harsh reality of the present, that the Golden Age was anything more than a fireside tale, but Aminatra liked to think it no coincidence civilisation reached its apogee when women possessed the freedom to make a real difference. Now there was no choice: married off at an early age, risking their lives to regularly produce babies and forgoing opportunities while raising a family. Surely, thought Aminatra, society owed her more than the ration vouchers in her hand. Karlmon was everything to Aminatra, but she knew she was more than a mother. This hard, relentless life offered little reward or appreciation.

The settlement held a population of about 9,000, covering the far west end of Eden Valley, clinging to the slopes of the surrounding hills. A thousand or so lived in the smaller, more vulnerable farm settlements of Buchaunia, over hills a short way to the south, and Hope Spring, lying far to the south-west, before the desert cut across the landscape. It was a fragile existence. Despite a small population, Athenia creaked from its overcrowded environment bearing all the dangers close proximity and poor hygiene brought. Rats, those great survivors, persisted in the alleys and drains, spreading disease. Their natural predators, cats and dogs, almost extinct as man's best friends, became meals during the times of famine. High birth rates only reflected the tragedy of high child mortality. Life expectancy in general was low, but with such limited resources, a constant population level became a chief objective of the ruling classes. If the dice of fate fell unkindly, Athenia would vanish, following the fate of all the other cities, towns and settlements over the last millennium. The only difference was no one else would be around to notice or care.

"I'm hungry," moaned Karlmon.

"I know, sweetheart," replied Aminatra. "Can you taste the bread through your nose?"

Karlmon looked at his mother. "Don't be silly. You smell through your nose."

"Close your eyes," instructed Aminatra. "Smell that bread; imagine its taste."

Karlmon closed his eyes and giggled.

"That's what my mother used to tell me to do when I said I was hungry."

"But I'm still hungry," said Karlmon.

"And that's when she'd clip me round the ear for being cheeky," quipped Aminatra, but ruffled her son's hair. He laughed and hugged her leg.

A woman in front turned to look disdainfully at Aminatra, her eyes condemning such tender behaviour. Aminatra ignored her. She had no time or respect for the notion you desensitised your feelings to cope with the constant spectre of death, or brutalise your children to ready them for a brutal world. A short life deserved to be a full, happy life.

As the queue edged forward, a tall, well-dressed woman approached down the street, passing the orderly line and heading directly into the bakers. The waiting women shifted uncomfortably in silence. They recognised the woman as a Moralista and clerk to the Governor. What right did she have to push to the front of the queue? But no one challenged her. A moment later, she emerged carrying a load clearly more than the normal rations allowed: again, silence prevailed. Only when out of sight did someone speak.

"It is, of course, so important to have a strong husband to help you in the house," a short, mousy-haired woman opined loudly.

"You can't raise a proper family without their guidance and discipline," offered her companion. "And without discipline, you get criminals!"

Aminatra realised the direction of the barbs. Unable to direct their frustration at the Wardyn's clerk, the women aimed at her. "What do you want with your bread?" she asked Karlmon. "How about some Ferral meat?"

Karlmon once again looked at his mother, perplexed. "Urgh," he said, with a mix of disgust and glee.

Aminatra smiled at him, welcoming the look of scorn on the faces of the opinionated women. She played on their prejudices, allowing a seed of fear to grow in their minds.

Twenty minutes passed before Aminatra and Karlmon arrived at the front of the queue. A trough housed a mass of unleavened loafs, while a more refined selection of pastries lay neatly on three shelves at the front. Karlmon put his nose to the edge of the cake rack, admiring the sweet treats.

"Not this week, Karl," sympathised Aminatra. "Two loaves please," she asked of the surly looking man behind the counter, handing him her ration token. He eyed it with a certain degree of suspicion, before dropping it in a bowl and picking up two loaves from atop the pile. Without a word from the shopkeeper the transaction was complete, his attention already on the next person in line.

"Come along, Karlmon!" The boy remained glued to the cake counter, only reluctantly turning to follow his mother. Outside, Aminatra looked along the long queue and sighed. "Right, just milk and butter to collect. Then you can have an hour's nap before we go fruit picking."

When Karlmon refused to hold her hand, Aminatra noticed his sheepish look. "What's the matter, Karl?" she asked.

He looked at her with innocent eyes.

"You not feeling well?"

Karlmon shook his head slowly.

"Then what?" Aminatra began to lose her patience.

Tentatively, his small hand went into his pocket and he pulled out a pastry. Aminatra's hand shot to her mouth in shock. "Karlmon! What have you done?"

The boy burst into tears, as Aminatra checked to see if anyone observed them. No eyes looked in their direction. Could they return the cake with no one the wiser?

"What made you take it? You know stealing's wrong!"

"There were so many," blabbed Karlmon. "And they looked so good!"

Surely they wouldn't blame a five-year-old, not yet schooled in all the world's rights and wrongs? He knew it was wrong but didn't understand why it was wrong. Such a small crime, yet one where Prison awaited. But who ever heard of a child interned in the Prison? Aminatra's mind raced with consequences, options and excuses. The two women in the bread queue surfaced in her memory, their bigoted words and her foolish response. Why had she played their game, feeding their fears? They believed destiny condemned a fatherless boy to becoming a criminal, and now this simple mistake reinforced that nonsense. She couldn't go back and return the pastry now.

"Come with me!" Aminatra grabbed the still tearful lad, leading him towards a narrow side alley. "Put that cake back in your pocket!"

Karlmon did as told, running behind his mother as she cast nervous glances around.

"Now, listen!" she instructed. "You promise me you'll never take anything again! Promise!"

The boy nodded his head, his tear-filled eyes looking up at his mother.

"Say it!"

"I promise." And the tears flowed again.

"Good. Now eat your pastry!"

Karlmon stopped crying, looking with confusion at his mother.

She smiled softly. "Go on, enjoy this moment. Eat your cake. Savour the sweet flavour. But do it quickly!"

He didn't need telling again, and whipped the pastry out, stuffing it in his mouth.

"Not that quickly," laughed Aminatra. "You'll make yourself sick!"

He nodded again, his mouth full, his moist eyes now sparkling with life.

"This is our secret," whispered Aminatra, brushing her son's dark, curly hair from his brow. "We'll never tell anyone, and we'll never do it again!" With no parents, no husband, no friends, he was all she had in the world. On becoming a single mother, Athenia abandoned her. To lose Karlmon would be to lose everything.

Karlmon swallowed the last bite and found himself engulfed in a tight hug by his mother.

"Oh, my baby! My darling baby! I love you so much. You've so much to learn."

CHAPTER 6

Finbarl plunged his head into the camel trough, whipped it out and exhaled a satisfying breath, glad to be back behind the walls of Athenia. Sand, grime and sweat clung to every inch of his body, and there it would have to remain until another day, when the opportunity arose to bathe in the river.

"Anything of interest happen?" Officer Vassel appeared to greet the troop.

"Euphima's dead," offered Gauret.

Vassel pondered and then replied, "Good!"

"Got some metal," said Finbarl. "Not a lot, but it will keep Saul happy."

"Nothing makes Saul happy!" joked Gauret. "He even grimaces when he gets a fresh peach."

"You wouldn't smile if your family had been slaughtered by Ferrals," chastised Vassel.

"They were probably glad to be rid of Saul," whispered Gauret to Finbarl.

"I can hear you!" said Vassel, but merely clipped Gauret's head playfully, fully aware black humour had its place amongst the guards. "For that, Gauret, you can have the privilege of delivering the goods to Saul! He'll be 'delighted' to see you."

Gauret hung his head back in melodramatic disbelief, but there were worse things to do, and a broad smile adorned his face as he brought his head back down.

"Got something special for you too, Finbarl-apcula!" announced Vassel. Finbarl's smile was more hesitant. "You've an invitation to a Wardyn council meeting," continued Vassel. "They're going to want you smarter than that."

Finbarl turned, gaping at Gauret, who returned the expression. "Bloody hell, sir! Why?"

"Because a Ferral looks smarter," replied Vassel.

"No, why have I been invited?" asked Finbarl, too shocked to appreciate Vassel's attempt at humour.

"You still here, Finbarl-apcula? You're not going to get presentable asking me questions. You've half an hour to scrape off that dirt. See me back here then!"

"Yes, sir," snapped Finbarl, realising he wasn't going to get much more from his commanding officer.

*

Vassel knocked gently on the door and, after a moment, it opened. A young man's face appeared, a finger to his lips. Finbarl recognised him as the Governor's grandson, Hradkarl, a stocky, overweight sixteen-year-old with intense eyes. He motioned Vassel and Finbarl inside and pointed to the wall. Vassel instinctively understood, motioning for Finbarl to follow. The veteran guard stood to attention, his eyes straight ahead, his back upright to the wall. Finbarl followed his lead, but with eyes flickering curiously to the faces seated around the long table in the centre of the room.

A deep discussion absorbed those around the table. They paid no attention to the two new arrivals. At the head sat Elbar-enis, Governor of Athenia, his bulky body slouched in his chair as he listened to the discussion. A bunch of grapes dangled from his fingers. Every now and again he plucked one, dropping it into his mouth, before squeezing the juice between his tongue and palate in noisy satisfaction. Finbarl felt a flush of anxiety colour his cheeks. To be in the company of this symbolic father figure, a guide for his childhood and adulthood, was an honour. He had seen him on numerous occasions, heard him address the town so many times, even been spoken to directly a few times, and yet this was the first time he felt in the Governor's presence; somewhere his own company was at the behest of the great man.

To the Governor's right sat his eldest son, Hradbar-eltar, father of the doorkeeper, Hradkarl. He was a well-built and muscular man, whose only resemblance to the rest of the family was his hair, which was curly and light like his father's. Finbarl admired him but retained a sense of unease whenever in his company. His reputation was coloured by rumour, of womanising and brutality; tales of Ferral hunts and prisoners forced to fight to the death with Ferrals at Hope Spring stockade. Finbarl believed the first part but dismissed the gladiatorial stories as malicious gossip, probably spread by Hradbar's younger brother, Torbald. He sat to the Governor's left, the image of his father. He was overweight but with a sparkle in his eye and a personality charming one moment, but striking fear the next. Finbarl's mind went back to the strange encounter a few days back. Was this summons in some way connected? Whereas Hradbar was a man of action, Torbald's reputation rested more on his mind and capacity for manipulation. As designated head of his guard division, Finbarl respected him, but viewed his intellect as a suspicious trait in this world of simple necessities. He also talked a lot.

".... it's good land we need for crops. We cannot allow more building on Cragor. If we let every new generation set up new homes in the valley, we'll soon have no space for Jumblar and maize. The answer is a new colony, perhaps to the south." Torbald looked around the table for agreement. Rhyd-eltar, son-in-law to the Governor, nodded. Utrep-eltari, wife of the Governor's nephew, looked to Hradbar.

The tall Wardyn responded to the look, put his intertwined hands behind his head and leaned back. "To start a new colony," he began, "we need a population that can defend itself. We'd lose valuable manpower for the harvest and the colony would be massacred within the month, just like at Newlon."

Torbald smiled at his brother, their rivalry and dislike of each other an open secret. "Hrad, you aren't seeing the bigger picture ... as usual." Torbald shared his father's condescending manner. "As with a rose, you have to cut back to allow new and healthy growth," continued the younger brother. "Athenia needs pruning to allow it to grow stronger. Newlon happened because we left a fool in charge. We won't make that mistake again. Well, not unless you want the role?"

Hradbar jumped to his feet, his face red with rage. They said he could win any argument, but only with his fists.

Finbarl's eyes tried to gauge Vassel's reaction to the spectacle. The senior guard remained impassive.

"Sit down!" The Governor, yet to show the slightest interest in the disagreement, stamped his authority.

Hradbar obeyed instantly, his face retaining its flushed anger. Torbald smiled at his apparent victory.

"Torbald's right," continued the Governor, his tone firm and controlled, "but it's not something we should rush." The heads around the table nodded in agreement, even Hradbar's. "We find the right location, the right families, the right time. Newlon would have happened with or without Gordwin's incompetence."

Hradbar smiled, acknowledging the minor put-down of his brother.

"We panicked because of the food shortage," declared the Governor. "The foothills provide too much protection for the Ferrals. They spent all day watching Newlon and the night undermining the defences. If we attacked, they just retreated into the mountains."

"You should let me take a troop to the foothills," urged Hradbar. "I'd soon clear them out!"

"Don't be a fool!" snapped the Governor. "It will get you killed one day!"

To Finbarl's eyes, Hradbar seemed to shrink by about a foot.

"Never underestimate the Ferrals!" continued the Governor. "They may behave like savages, but there's cunning in them. I've seen them set traps and diversions. Many a good guard has ended up dead, thinking they're too stupid to outwit a civilised and armed man."

"I only meant ... ". A dismissive and curt gesture by his father cut Hradbar short.

"Utrep, you'll work with Torbald to plan a colony. We'll look to establish in two harvests' time. I'll discuss with the pair of you after this meeting, but enough for now."

Torbald shifted uncomfortably, understanding something deeper in the decision.

"We have guests!" declared the Governor, looking across to Finbarl, who stiffened to a new level of attention. "Finbarl-apcula, welcome! Here, come and sit with us."

Finbarl couldn't quite believe what was happening: him, a humble Orpho, asked to sit at the table of the Wardyns. He turned to Vassel, whose eyes commanded Finbarl to sit down as quickly as possible.

The padded chair, a new experience for Finbarl, felt uncomfortable in the company of the Wardyns, their eyes all upon him.

"Excellent," declared the Governor. "I hear the traitor Gorwell's safely deposited in the Prison?" The other prisoner, Pryfol, was an unmentioned, insignificant detail.

"Yes, Ensi," replied a dry-mouthed Finbarl, careful to address the Governor officially.

"Excellent," said the Governor again. "An evil and dangerous man! Who knows what other crimes he's committed over the years and how much food he's sold on the black market?" The Governor seemed genuinely upset and shook his head. "All those people who died as a consequence!"

Finbarl had not thought about the consequences before but, as always, the Governor was right: food stolen from the state condemned others to starve.

"I knew your parents," commented the Governor, nodding his head. "Good people. Good, honest people."

To think the Governor knew his mother and father, long dead some eighteen years.

"Their deaths were a great loss to Athenia. Your father had a great future. I even think he could have become a Wardyn one day. And your mother … ". The Governor paused. "Well, let's just say you should have had many more brothers and sisters. You've her eyes, you know?"

Finbarl's head swam. His father a potential Wardyn! What an honour and recognition, albeit posthumous. He never appreciated that he came from such a distinguished family before.

"It was a cruel plague that took them from us," continued the Governor. "What were you when they died? Two? Three?"

"Yes, Ensi," spluttered Finbarl before correcting himself. "I mean, three, Ensi!"

"Excellent," said the Governor, using his stock adjective. "And we've looked after you well?"

"Yes, Ensi, and I'm very grateful."

Governor Elbar waved away the gratuity and smiled. "It's what we're here for. You're all our children. It's our burden but also our privilege. Do you understand?"

Finbarl had no idea what was going on. "Yes, Ensi."

"Excellent! Now to the reason we've asked you here. Torbald, I'll leave it to you."

Finbarl fidgeted in his seat, looking across to the grinning Torbald.

"Finbarl-apcula, I've been watching you since you graduated from the cadets." To Finbarl's horror, the Wardyn and son of the Governor got to his feet and walked towards him. Torbald halted behind Finbarl and gently put his hands on the guard's shoulders. "I like what I see!"

The muscles, knotted with anxiety on Finbarl's shoulders, relaxed a little.

"Yes, gentlemen," continued Torbald, now addressing his peers around the table. "Finbarl's a credit to his parents and to Athenia. Unswerving loyalty, a hard worker, a good man in a fight and, oh, yes, did you know he shot a Ferral last night at 250 yards!"

Finbarl frowned at the extra fifty yards, but glowed with pleasure seeing those around the table acknowledge his achievement with an exchange of nods.

"In short, I think Finbarl-apcula has a promising future!" declared Torbald. "What do you think of that, my boy?"

Finbarl felt Torbald's chubby fingers squeeze his shoulders. "Thank you, Torbald-eltar," was all he could think to say in reply.

"I think," said Torbald, and then corrected himself. "We think you're officer material. Finbarl-apculex has a nice sound to it. Don't you agree Vassel-apculex?"

The officer stepped forward. "With the right guidance, he could make a fine officer, sir."

"Oh, absolutely, the right guidance," repeated Torbald. "An officer's a critical position, eh, Vassel-apculex?" He asked without awaiting a response. "They're the glue keeping the guards together: the cool head in a hot moment. We don't want officers who lose their rag at the slightest thing. They're the Wardyns' ears and eyes. They must be above reproach."

"Get on with it!" snapped Hradbar. "I've got a woman waiting in a bed for me somewhere."

Torbald smiled at his brother. "Too old to get out, no doubt!"

"Boys!" The Governor laughed gently. "Not in front of Officer Vassel and this impressionable young man."

"Quite," said Torbald, regaining his line of thought. "Would you like to be an officer, Finbarl?"

A broad smile broke out on Finbarl's face. "Yes, Eltar. Very much!"

"Excellent," said Torbald, now sounding like his father too. "What we can't be having, however, is guard attacking guard. That little confrontation in the town square this morning was regrettable."

Finbarl felt a shiver run down his neck, and was sure Torbald sensed it through the fingers still resting upon his shoulders.

"What I mean to say is," continued Torbald, "Audlech-apcula was wrong, but we can't have the commoners seeing such weakness in the ranks. Fighting between the guards! They trust and believe in the guards to protect them. Imagine what those who saw this morning's shenanigans are feeling now. Fear is what they're feeling. If guards fight each other, how can they protect us from the prisoners or, God help us, the Ferrals?"

Finbarl nodded his head in understanding.

"A guard is never wrong in front of a commoner. You undermine that code again and not only will you not make officer, but you'll find yourself on more excursions to the foothills than is healthy for a guard. Now, do we understand each other?"

Finbarl gulped uncomfortably. "Absolutely, Wardyn. Sorry, Eltar. Won't happen again."

"Excellent!" The Governor rubbed his hands together. "A slight mishap because of Jumblar's vengeance. Can happen to any guard ... once!" A smile remained on the Governor's face as he continued. "The first step towards proving your credentials is to make an arrest. Have you made one before?"

"No, Ensi," replied Finbarl, both nervous and excited by the prospect of fulfilling a task usually designated solely to officers.

"Hradbar, make yourself useful and instruct Finbarl-apcula on his assignment."

Hradbar grimaced at his father's tone, then looked at Finbarl with amused satisfaction. "We have a serious accusation made of theft," he announced. "A food thief. There are several witnesses and you shouldn't have any trouble making an arrest. Are you up for this, Finbarl-apcula?"

"Definitely, Wardyn!" declared Finbarl.

"Good," said Hradbar, the one word demonstrating another difference between himself and his father. "The accused's name is Aminatra-gula. I believe you met her this morning?"

Finbarl's heart and mouth dropped as one, as all those around the table grinned at their fait accompli.

"Excellent!" said Governor Elbar.

CHAPTER 7

A warm breeze tickled the leaves in the orange grove, carrying the delicate aroma of the ripe fruits down the valley. Situated on the gentle lower slope of Bymore Hill, on the southern edge of Eden Valley, the grove covered half an acre, providing a burst of colour in an otherwise green environment. It was Aminatra's favourite place, a perfect picture of nature, and she hummed a tune to herself while reaching to pick a fruit. Few places existed to escape other people within Athenia, so to enjoy some alone time with her boy felt so precious. A light straw hat provided some shade from the still hot, late afternoon sun, but no protection from the relentless flies, which Aminatra patiently waved away. She placed each picked orange gently into a loose sash, hung diagonally across her front. The weight pulled her forward, reminding Aminatra of her pregnancy with Karlmon. She looked down to see him sleeping in the shade of a tree and smiled.

With her sash full, Aminatra waddled across to a large wicker basket, balanced her artificial stomach upon the side and allowed the oranges to tumble in. She took a moment to catch her breath, stretch her tired back and wipe the sweat from her brow. A bird landed in an adjacent tree, releasing a burst of song. Aminatra thought about waking Karlmon to share the moment, but his restful features persuaded her otherwise. Instead she turned to look down the valley and wondered at this oasis of plenty in a barren world. So much life packed into such a relatively small space. It was a wonder.

The production of food and Jumblar dominated every inch of the Eden Valley. Everywhere people toiled in the sun, tending the delicate symbols of survival. Olives, grape vines and almond trees clung to the steeper slopes of Cragor and Bymore hills, orange, peach and berry bushes to the lower gradients, while along the valley bottom a diverse range of crops grew in chequered blocks. Goats grazed the upper reaches of the hills, the only livestock allowed in the valley.

The oasis stood in stark contrast to the surrounding barren landscape. Date trees appeared in small clusters, but the dominant Agore mountain range to the east starved the land of rainfall, its snow-capped peaks shimmering in the hazy distance. The source of Athenia's survival rested there in the form of a glacier. So many miles separated them, yet, as though delivered by divine purpose, the meltwater found its way into their valley, into the irrigation ditches and pumps, turning the land green. It never occurred to anybody life followed the water rather than the other way around. Aminatra once heard all the land, as far as the eye could see, was fertile, with people scattered everywhere. What a wonderful world, she thought.

A working song, sung by a fruit-picker down the valley, carried to Aminatra's ear, disrupting the rhythm of her own humming. Not a problem; she simply changed her tune to match and continued harvesting the oranges. The art to picking the fruit was to grip between finger and thumb and pull and twist at the same time. As she grasped the next orange, Aminatra felt her thumb sink in. It came off the tree with ease and she examined the soft side. An insect had at some time burrowed in, no doubt to lay its eggs. Aminatra placed it within her sash with all the other oranges and put her thumb in her mouth to suck off the juice. Nothing went to waste in Athenia.

The constant threat of crop failure haunted the community's history. Too young to recall the last famine, Aminatra knew the stories: hundreds, maybe thousands, died from starvation and disease. Survival meant leaving the fortified protection of Eden Valley, venturing into the mountains, foothills and arid lowlands, scavenging for naturally growing fruits and nuts, hunting for rabbits, birds and anything moving; exposing themselves to the ferocity of the Ferrals. Prisoners, left to fend for themselves, died like flies. Twenty years passed before the population of Athenia recovered to its current state; the Prison re-populated at a much faster rate. As Athenia regained its strength and dignity, it sought to understand and apportion blame for the catastrophe. As the chosen people, guardians of civilisation, to whom water flowed, only an invisible criminality, insidiously poisoning society, explained the famine. The forces of barbarity had found their way within the walls, attempting to destroy them with their evil ways: the 'culprits', found amongst themselves, restocked the Prison.

*

News of Finbarl's exalted summons spread through the barracks and Strathbol awaited his return, eager to hear all. "Don't tell me," said the young guard, "they wanted you to become high priest?"

Finbarl acknowledged the joke. "They've earmarked me as an officer," he blurted at speed. "The Governor himself said so!"

"You haven't taken a year's worth of Jumblar have you?" said Strathbol. "You, an officer!"

Finbarl frowned, annoyed at the youth's cheek. "Yes, an officer! What, don't you think I'm officer material? You think the Governor's wrong?"

"Whoa! Steady there! Don't want you going all Ferral on me." Strathbol's smile defused the situation.

"Sorry," said Finbarl. "I know it's unbelievable. That was one surreal experience. One minute Prison-bound, then starbound, and now I don't know where they're sending me." He paused for a moment's contemplation. "They want me to arrest Aminatra."

"Who?"

"The incident in the Square with Audlech this morning." said Finbarl, sure Strathbol would have heard the news too.

"Oh, your pretty friend."

"She's not my friend!" muttered Finbarl. "I simply returned her son's toy."

"Well, what's she done?"

"Stolen from the bakery."

"So, what's the problem?" pressed Strathbol. "Arrest her!"

"Yeah, of course. I will! It's just, well, you know, what about her son?" Finbarl sat down, contemplating the issue. He recalled having the same unambiguous view of the world when Strathbol's age, but now he saw things differently.

A serious expression fell on Strathbol's face. "But she's a reputation. If she stole the bread, or whatever, there'll be witnesses. Best thing for the boy. She'd only lead him astray."

Finbarl looked up at Strathbol, considering his words. "Yes, I suppose you're right. I'm just mixed up following the meeting with the Wardyns."

"Well, congratulations are in order," exclaimed Strathbol. "Don't worry, she'll be out of your mind in a week. We'll celebrate tonight!"

Finbarl smiled feebly, then shook himself from the fog. "Yes, you're right. The Kywaczek's on me!"

*

Karlmon groaned as he shuffled in his sleep, breaking Aminatra's daydream. She glanced up at the watchtower high on the summit of Bymore Hill where the guards watched over the workers. No eyes observed her slackness. She made to begin on the next tree. As Aminatra straightened her sash to allow the oranges to slip to the bottom, she noticed a small party of men walking at pace down the middle of the valley bottom. Their green clothes gave them away as guards and Aminatra sneered before turning to stretch for the next orange.

"Aminatra-gula?"

Aminatra swung around to find the four guards striding up the slope towards her. Hearing your formal name used by guards promised nothing good. "Yes," she verified. "What's the matter?"

The guards didn't respond, focusing all their attention on climbing the final ten yards to their destination.

Aminatra raised her eyebrows on recognising the young guard from yesterday at the head of the group. She struggled to remember his name. "Finbarl-apcula?"

Finbarl's eyes gave no reaction, just a grim, set determination. "Aminatra-gula!" he stated. "A serious accusation's been made against you. You're hereby charged with theft. You're under arrest!"

Aminatra turned ghostly pale. "But ... but ... ".

"Mummy!"

She looked down to see Karlmon at her side, his eyes still heavy with sleep.

"What do the men want?" he asked.

"I ... I don't know," she replied, her voice shaking. She pulled the boy to her side and looked Finbarl in the eye. "What do you mean? Why?"

Finbarl glanced at the harvested crop of oranges to avoid Aminatra's stare. "You've been accused of stealing food." He plucked an orange from her sash, inspecting it closely.

"I've not taken a single orange!" protested Aminatra.

"The word of a thief doesn't carry much weight," commented Finbarl, before tossing the fruit back in the sash. "You're not accused of stealing from the farm, but the bakery."

A wave of nausea surged through Aminatra. Her head became light. Had someone seen Karlmon take the pastry? "I … I did no such thing. I collected the rationed bread as was due me. I think there must be a mistake."

"Don't care what you think. Hougat-apcula! Take the boy to the orphanage!" commanded Finbarl to the man on his right. "Laitoni-apcula! Dix-apcula! Escort the prisoner to the cells! As is your right under the laws of Athenia," he continued to Aminatra, "you'll stand trial in front of the Keepers of Justice in a week's time. Until then, you'll be kept in solitary confinement for your own protection and to prepare your defence."

"No, you can't!" shouted Aminatra, her protestations turning to a scream as they led Karlmon away. "Karlmon! Karlmon!"

"Mummy!" The boy, tears streaming down his face, struggled to break free from Hougat's firm grip.

Finbarl looked to the sky, trying to ignore the drama. The orders and attitude came easy to him. His training prepared him for it. Only the child's involvement niggled. Thankfully, the cries of Karlmon soon faded as he vanished down the valley, away from his struggling mother.

"You Ferral-whacks!" screamed Aminatra. "You've no right! He's done nothing wrong. He needs his mother!"

"He needs a worthy mother," goaded Finbarl, as he swished away some annoying flies, before motioning Laitoni and Dix to lead the prisoner away.

Aminatra collapsed to her knees as the guards tried to pull her forward. It was all she could do to be obstructive and delay the inevitable. Her energy drained from her body. She feared never seeing her boy again. It was like no loss she had ever felt. She needed all her strength to fight for Karlmon, but had nothing to muster.

Finbarl began walking back to Athenia. He turned his head to monitor the situation, nodding contentedly as Laitoni and Dix followed behind, the prisoner slumped between them, her feet dragging in the dirt. Aminatra's discarded sash lay in their wake, a few escaped oranges sitting serenely upon the ground. Above in the trees, the bird returned to its perch, its joyous song filling the air. The grove was again a perfect picture of nature.

CHAPTER 8

A long, busy week for Finbarl followed. He accompanied a working party to the foothills to collect timber, undertook sentry duty for the livestock at Buchaunia farmstead, and travelled to Hope Spring in the distant south-west, to escort quarried Raffia clay to Athenia. His duties kept him occupied but his mind raced with the image of Aminatra screaming as her boy cried. Of all the horrific acts witnessed by Finbarl as a guard, why was this incident causing his thoughts such conflict? He slept poorly, as though Jumblar's vengeance tormented him. When sleep overtook him, he dreamt of a small, faceless boy, falling endlessly while the face of Aminatra, surrounded by two silhouetted figures, watched from above. What did it all mean?

The day of Aminatra's trial started like most others: a cloudless sky resting over a chilled land. As soon as the sun began its ascent, the temperature rose swiftly, the accumulated water vapour evaporating in a dancing haze.

Finbarl manned the watchtower high on Cragor Hill for the early shift. It surveyed a wide area over Athenia and the valley and beyond, across miles and miles of scrubland. A short-lived mist obscured the view. As it evaporated under the early sun, a few pockets lingered, exposing the few permanent sources of water in the landscape.

Finbarl leant on the side of his box, staring out in the direction of Bluebecker Woods but seeing nothing. He mulled over the day ahead and his obligation, as arresting officer, to attend and give evidence at Aminatra's trial. The Ferrals could have climbed Cragor Hill without him noticing. What made her do such a stupid thing? Why risk her son's future for a cake? Finbarl's confusion turned to anger. He knew what it was like to lose a mother.

*

When Finbarl arrived at the multi-purpose building, now used as a courtroom, he found Torbald awaiting him, standing with an arrogant gait, chewing on salted camel meat.

"Ah, Finbarl-apcula," greeted Torbald. "I trust the Ferrals are not attacking from the north this morning?"

Finbarl smiled nervously at the jibe. "No, sir," he replied. "A quiet morning."

"Good, because they do so disrupt things! Eh?" Torbald laughed at his own bravado before his face became serious. "Now, I want to have a word with you ahead of this trial."

Finbarl's unease worsened.

"I'm worried," continued the Wardyn. "Worried because there's a real chance a known criminal may escape justice because of technicalities and fear. You see, we know a lot more about this Aminatra-gula than can be proved in a court of law. She's in league with an underground criminal gang and our sources inform us she helps run a black market in stolen food and goods. We even hear, through an unknown corrupt guard, she's in contact with a number of prisoners and may be planning an attack on Athenia!"

Rumours of a black market and secret criminal organisation always persisted, but Finbarl dismissed them as myths. What Torbald said shocked him yet explained so much: the food shortages when the harvest seemed so good and the reports of missing tools from the smithy's workshop. It also gave flesh to Aminatra's character, explaining how she could be so heartless in respect to her son's future. Through coincidence, or empathy, Torbald read Finbarl's thoughts.

"I fear terribly for that boy of hers," the Wardyn confessed. "In a few years, he'll be working for the gang, stealing and lying. After all, who'd suspect a small boy, supposedly brought up on the values of Athenia, of being involved in anything like that?" Torbald let the question hang in the air. "I need your help, Finbarl. Athenia needs your help."

"Of course, Wardyn. I'll do whatever's needed."

"Excellent! There, I knew you were officer material. Now, here's what I want you to say during your testimony." Torbald placed his arm around Finbarl's shoulder, slowly guiding him down the corridor, conveying instructions.

*

Aminatra stood in a makeshift dock, her face and hair lacking the lustre of a week earlier. Her eyes, red from tears shed over the week, retained a flash of defiance. They burnt with hatred when the three Wardyns took their seats as Keepers of Justice and the Moralista clerk read out Aminatra's name. In the centre sat Torbald, smiling, as was his way. To his right sat Hradbar, his eyes examining the prisoner dispassionately. Utrep occupied the final judges' seat, focusing on cleaning her glasses. At the side of the room, a small group of townspeople huddled in the enclosed jury box. An anachronistic definition, for they observed and nothing more. The sole custodians of law – the judge, jury and executioners – were the Wardyns.

Guards stood scattered around the room, keeping the populace in order and the accused in fearful anticipation. As the court clerk stood to address the proceedings, the guard behind Aminatra pushed her roughly forward to the front of the dock.

"Aminatra-gula," stated the authoritative voice of the clerk, "you're here today charged with the offence of theft against the state. How do you plead?"

"Not guilty!" responded Aminatra.

"So be it recorded," announced the clerk, her high-pitched voice grating as she strained to project across the room. Lifting a sheet of paper, she read it aloud. "The evidence against you is as follows: on Tuesday, 14th July, at morning's quarter you were witnessed, while in the company of your son, Karlmon-gula, appropriating two loaves of bread and four cakes."

Aminatra's brow furrowed at this obvious fabrication.

"Salfort-gula, loyal and dedicated baker of District Three," continued the clerk, "was witness to this heinous crime and will testify two families were, consequently, deprived of rations from his premises that day. It is also attested, due to this theft and absence of said ration, Alkreg-gula did die, not two days later, wanting of nutrition."

Aminatra spluttered in disbelief. She knew Alkreg, an elderly man, weak of heart and near death's door for the last few years. Surely his death was natural and no consequence of the single cake Karlmon took. She wanted to shout out the truth, but knew to do so would expose her boy.

On the clerk went. "Also witness to this wretched crime were Pettrina-gula and Wynoda-gula, honest and experienced mothers, now fearful. Were justice not to be delivered today, their lives and those of their children would be at risk."

Aminatra could hold back no longer. "But ... but that's just not true! I'm no thief and no murderer! They weren't even in the shop when ... ".

"Silence!" ordered Torbald. "You'll have your chance to speak. If you disrupt the course of justice again then it will only serve in proving your guilt. Innocent people have no need to fear the system that's served and kept safe civilisation for millennia."

"But ... ," pleaded Aminatra, before thinking better of it.

Torbald smiled towards the clerk. "Please continue!"

"Thank you, Eltar," said the clerk, bowing towards the judges' bench. "We'll also hear the testimony of the guard who arrested the accused. Despite the risk to his own life, he bravely tackled this now pitiful creature who stands in judgement today.

"Should your eminences find in favour of a guilty verdict, then this court seeks the full sentence of life in the Prison." The clerk held her head high as she finished, content at serving a noble cause.

"Very good," said Torbald, sparing a glance towards his fellow judges. "We shall therefore begin. Please bring in the first witness: Salfort-gula, baker for District Three."

Salfort shuffled in from a side door, wide-eyed and clasping a straw hat. He looked around the room, uncertain what to do next. A guard pointed towards an empty space not a yard from Aminatra.

"Wardyn Utrep," said Torbald, "could I ask you to lead the questions for this witness?"

"I would be honoured," replied Utrep, before disdainfully eyeing up the baker in his dirty work clothes. "Salfort-gula, how long have you baked for District Three?"

"Thirteen years, madam judge. And my father was baker before me for eighteen years."

"You and your family are a credit to Athenia, and we thank you for your dedicated service."

"Why, thank you, ma'am!" Salfort couldn't believe how well it was going.

"And in that time," continued the Wardyn, "how many thefts have occurred?"

"None, ma'am! That is why this is all so shocking for me and my family."

Aminatra shook her head. She remembered trials from her youth relating to thefts at this bakery.

"Please elaborate, Salfort-gula," urged Utrep.

"Well, to know that among my customers there's a criminal willing to stop at nothing to get what they want... and... and...", Salfort stumbled, thinking what to say next. "And poor Alkreg! To know I will never see his face again! He lived for his bread."

Rubbish! screamed Aminatra in her mind. When has Salfort ever spoken to any of his customers beyond a curt word?

"I sympathise, Salfort-gula," said Utrep. "The whole community has lost a dear friend in Alkreg-gula. Now, I appreciate this may be hard, but could you tell us what you saw on the day of this heinous crime?"

"I can," said Salfort. "As always, I was busy. I'd been up before daybreak to ensure the bread and cakes were ready ... ".

"Very noble, of course," interrupted Utrep, "but let us move to the crime!"

"Sorry, ma'am," grovelled Salfort. "I'd just served the accused her allocated ration of bread and was about to move on to the next customer when that little brat of a son of hers starts making a scene and bawling his head off."

Aminatra turned to look ferociously at her accuser, outraged at his description of Karlmon and the fabrication of the truth. The baker stared forward towards Utrep. A sudden painful blow winded Aminatra as a guard stepped in, indicating she resume her forward-facing position.

"Please do not try and intimidate the witness!" instructed Wardyn Utrep. "It's behaviour most unbecoming." She waved for Salfort to continue.

"Well, it was all part of a planned distraction, you see," said the baker. "While my attention was on his theatrics, the mother was pilfering my bread and cakes!"

"So, you did not see the accuser directly take the products, but you're in no doubt that's when they were taken?"

"Absolutely!" agreed Salfort. "It was a short while later I first noticed – what with being so busy and all – but there's no other possible explanation for it!"

"No other possible explanation," repeated Utrep slowly, emphasising it to the jury box. "Thank you, Salfort-gula. That will be all!"

The baker bowed towards the three Wardyns, put his hat on and shuffled out of the room.

"Let's move swiftly on," demanded Torbald to the clerk. "The women? I forget their names."

"Pettrina-gula and Wynoda-gula, Eltar," answered the Moralista.

"Of course," said Torbald. "Well, let's have them! Hradbar, do you think you can manage this one?"

Hradbar gave his brother a withering look, fully aware it was not a simple request, but a criticism.

The two women entered together, their hair immaculate, clothes freshly cleaned. They both sniffed the air as though polluted by Aminatra's presence, then stood proudly upright before the judges.

"Right," said Hradbar. "We'll cut out the Ferral-dung and get this case done. You were both in the same queue as the accused and witnessed the theft?"

The women started to answer in unison.

"Shut up!" demanded Hradbar. "I only need one answer. You, the fat one!" He pointed vaguely at Wynoda. "You talk!"

Wynoda, not in any way fat, simply larger than Pettrina, recoiled at the comment, unaware the barb's ultimate target was the overweight Torbald. Still flustered at the criticism, Wynoda ruffled her hair in distraction. "We both saw her," she said. "While the poor boy was made to create a scene, she brazenly took poor Alkreg-gula's bread and cake."

"Right. That sounds pretty conclusive. You can go."

The women looked at each other, disappointed their day in court was over.

"Go!" urged Hradbar.

"Well, thank you for that in-depth examination, brother," sighed Torbald, exhaling with a dramatic flurry. "You've done Athenia a great service by speeding justice on its course."

"What else do we need to know from those ugly bags?" retorted Hradbar.

Torbald shrugged his shoulders, then leaned closer to his brother and whispered: "It's so due process is seen to be followed and we don't insult the plebeians, you fool!"

Hradbar snarled, but the location was too public to take it further.

Torbald laughed aloud. "My brother, of course, jokes," he said, addressing the jury box. "We all value the insight Pettrina-gula and Wynoda-gula, as exceptional members of our community, brought to these proceedings. Madam Clerk, please bring in Finbarl-apcula for his testimony."

Finbarl had given evidence at trials on a few occasions, but never as arresting officer. He fidgeted, fretting over his script. Catching sight of Aminatra from the corner of his eye, he avoided looking her way.

"Finbarl-apcula," began Torbald, "I will undertake your questions. We don't want to finish too early!"

Finbarl, oblivious to the dig directed towards Hradbar, nodded in the affirmative.

Torbald cleared his throat and continued. "You were tasked with the arrest of the accused, Aminatra-gula?"

"Yes, sir," replied Finbarl, while Hradbar tutted loudly at Torbald's protracted style.

"Where did you locate her and in what state did you find her?"

"We found her in the orange grove at the far end of Eden Valley, Eltar," answered Finbarl. He paused, his eyes moved up and right, constructing the next part of his answer. "It was clear from a distance she was agitated. She paced back and forth and was not picking fruit, as was her duty." Finbarl, aware of Aminatra's head whipping round to stare at him, felt his heart race, his stomach knot and his mouth go dry. His distaste at lying played heavy upon him. However, he firmed his jaw, recalling he did this for justice.

"Really," said Torbald, his face a façade of surprise. "And what did you surmise by such behaviour?"

"That the accused was racked with guilt."

"Yes, of course," said Torbald, now apparently putting the pieces together for the first time. "That would be the most obvious conclusion. And what happened when you confronted the accused and made your arrest?"

Finbarl shuffled, aware his divergence from the truth became more extreme with each sentence. "She went crazy, Eltar. It was Ferral in its ferocity. I've never seen anything like it!"

"That's not true!" protested Aminatra.

"Guard!" shouted Torbald, and the man behind Aminatra stepped forward, hitting her heavily with his club behind the knee. She collapsed to the floor, yelling in pain. The guard bent down, grabbed her hair and yanked her up to her knees.

Finbarl cringed, and for the first time turned to look directly at Aminatra.

"You've been told once before," said Torbald, "about the consequences of speaking out of turn. I'm more than happy to bring in a guilty verdict right now, but I strongly believe in letting the accused have the right to present their defence. So, you've a choice: interrupt proceedings one more time and find yourself instantaneously guilty, or wait patiently to receive the rights of an Athenian. What'll it be?"

Aminatra stumbled to her feet, hanging her head in defeated silence.

"A wise decision," Torbald concurred. "My apologies, Finbarl-apcula. I believe you were about to tell us about what the accused said on her arrest?"

"Yes, sir," confirmed Finbarl. "She denied it at first but, when confronted with the evidence, she tried to blame her son." A collective gasp emanated from the jury box, and a gentle sob from Aminatra.

"Cronax!" exclaimed Torbald, throwing himself back in shock at the revelation. "How could a mother do that to her own son?"

Finbarl stood silent, uncertain if the question was for him.

"I had no idea this case was as dark as this," continued Torbald. "Just shocking!" He looked to his fellow judges for agreement. Utrep shook her head in disgust. Hradbar, unwilling to play along, rolled his eyes at the melodramatics.

"Knowing the type of individual you were tasked with arresting," asked Torbald, addressing Finbarl again, "were you in fear of your own safety?"

Finbarl hesitated, trying to recall his lines. "No, after all, I'm a highly trained Prison guard and think nothing of risking my life to keep the people of Athenia safe." Torbald nodded his encouragement, almost urging the words out of Finbarl's mouth. "But I did fear for the safety of the boy."

"Quite right! Quite right!" endorsed Torbald. "She was trying to condemn him to death by suggesting he was the thief. He wouldn't last a day in the Prison; the poor innocent! What was to stop her murdering him on the spot there and then under the Ferral psychosis gripping her?"

A murmur of agreement came from Utrep and the jury box.

"I know my brother doesn't like to draw these things out, Finbarl-apcula," continued Torbald, "so we'll thank you for your time and for your continued protection from the ever-present evil within our midst. You're relieved from the stand."

Finbarl gave a curt bow and strode from the room. Once outside, his shoulders dropped – he felt rotten.

"So, Aminatra-gula," announced Torbald, looking to the accused, "your time to speak has come at last!" He turned to his brother. "Would you like to ask her the questions, brother?"

Hradbar coloured to a bright red, his muscles tightening. "No, Torbald," he hissed through gritted teeth. "I think you're best-placed."

"Oh, all right then," responded Torbald gleefully. "Aminatra-gula, why did you steal bread and cake?"

"I did not steal anything … Eltar." Flattery seemed a small price to try to win some favour.

"Then why have a number of witnesses come forward to say you did? Are they lying and risking their own liberty by committing perjury?"

"I don't know!" conceded Aminatra, her wide-open hands expressing her frustration. "But I swear before this court, I've never stolen a thing in my life."

"Well, remarkable," rejoined Torbald. "I think I speak for everyone in this court in believing someone who could steal valuable food and then accuse their own child would have no problem lying here in their testimony."

"How … ," Aminatra shook her head in angry frustration. "How can I respond to such warped logic? This is entrapment. All those witnesses lied because instructed to do so!"

"Instructed to do so?" Utrep flinched at the accusation.

"Yes," pressed Torbald. "Why would anybody conspire to find you guilty of a crime you didn't commit? You forget Athenia is the last beacon of civilisation in this world. Our laws are there to protect the liberties of our citizens, not to fabricate evidence against them. Forgive my bluntness, but why would they, against an inconsequential member of our society, such as yourself?"

"To silence me! That's why," blurted out Aminatra.

"Silence you? Why?" queried Torbald, humouring her.

"Your brother is the father of my child," replied Aminatra more calmly. "He got me pregnant and then disowned me and his child."

As Utrep looked uncomfortable, Torbald laughed wildly, enjoying every moment. He turned to Hradbar; whose fists screwed up in fury. "Brother," challenged Torbald, "this is surely nonsense, but still a serious accusation which deserves a response."

Hradbar straightened himself in his chair and gave a fake smile to the court. "This is a desperate act of a desperate woman! In my position of responsibility, I have many women who'd like me to be the father of their child and many who fantasise that that is indeed the case. They're weak-minded and no doubt unsatisfied by their husbands. I'm a happy, contented married man, and those who know me can give assurances I'm also a loyal husband. Now, let's sentence this lying Ferral to the Prison and have some food!"

"Beautifully said, Hradbar," effused Torbald. "The only sin you've committed is leaving so many women frustrated in their lust.

"I must insist you keep your torrid fantasies to yourself. You've embarrassed my brother and besmirched his ... ," Torbald paused for thought and effect before completing his sentence with an incredulous lilt, " ... good character!"

"But it's true!" despaired Aminatra. "The resemblance in Karlmon is clear. Their hair ... ".

"Tut, tut," cautioned Torbald, wagging his finger. "I thought I was clear, to use your son to try to clear your own name is morally indefensible. Those curls of my brother are hardly a family preserve. Though maybe we should invite Karlmon to the court to give his side of the story. Eh, Hradbar?"

"No, no!" pleaded Aminatra. "He's nothing to do with this! Please leave him out of it!"

"Good," agreed Torbald. "So, we concur on that point and won't hear anything more of this ridiculous story. My brother is keen to get drunk, so we'll deliberate and then give our verdict. If the court could please remain as it is. We'll return as soon as possible."

*

It was a full two hours before the judges returned. Torbald and Utrep enjoyed a leisurely lunch, while Hradbar vanished in a huff. On their return they found a frustrated, impatient group, but one who immediately fell silent as they entered.

"We're so sorry for having kept you," said Torbald, as his tongue fought to remove a fibre of peach from a molar. "You'll appreciate the need for every detail to be discussed in full to ensure justice is done. To send an innocent person to the Prison would be as great a crime as allowing a criminal to walk free."

Aminatra, her legs and body weary from standing for so long, slowly lifted her head to acknowledge the words spoken by Torbald. She had accepted her fate. Nothing she said or did would change a sentence decided upon before the start of the trial. She felt guilty. After all, she allowed Karlmon to take and eat the cake. But not of the crime they accused her of. An opportunity presented itself to the Wardyns and they took it. A chance to get rid of an embarrassing episode from Hradbar's past; a chance to wipe out an inconvenient piece of history.

Torbald climbed to his feet, holding his thawb at his chest between finger and thumb. "Citizens! We are civilisation!" he asserted. "We are the legacy of a thousand years of freedom; the bastion of liberty and the beacon of hope in a barbaric world! Blessed are we to have been born into safety, and we thank the Lord for the walls protecting us and food sustaining us.

"Around us are dangers and threats we must fight every day. Together we've found the strength to survive and thrive, but we must never lower our guard! We're alone in this world. Where once civilisation stretched to every corner of the globe, now it burns as a precious ember only in our oasis. And while we may think the biggest threat to our freedom lies beyond the walls, nowhere is the battle for freedom greater than amongst our own. Was it not the criminals who, allowed to flourish in the past, became the cancer of civilisation? These felons exploited the naivety of our ancestors. They brought the vengeance of the Lord; they caused the fire of the sun to burn this Earth, to bring forth tempests and hunger and strip the land of its life. They made the land beyond too dangerous for God-fearing folk; they gave birth to God's fury, the Ferrals. We must not make these mistakes again.

"The desert lies west to remind us of these sins, while the mountains to the east bring us God's blessing in his flowing rivers of tears. The Ferrals, our test and continual reminder of what we will become if we give up our freedoms and succumb to the weakness within us all. All human life is precious, but nothing is more precious than civilisation. The Prison is the price one must pay if you threaten civilisation. You must lose the right to sleep at peace each night; no longer will the walls of this town be your protection. To steal from one of us, is to steal from all. No exceptions! A mother, more than anyone, must be able to uphold the law if we're to raise each future generation as custodians of that civilisation. If she cannot, then she's no mother! She's a felon and a traitor.

"We, therefore, find Aminatra-gula guilty of theft and convict her to life in the Prison. Her son, Karlmon-gula, an innocent victim, will find love and protection under the guardianship of the Wardyns and is thus accorded the name of Karlmon-apcula. At dawn tomorrow, you, Aminatra," – the dropping of the 'gula' suffix a symbolic moment denoting the loss of citizen status – "will be taken to Bruuk's Point and there you'll be left to spend the rest of your life imprisoned."

"You Ferral-whacks!" screamed Aminatra, with nothing to lose. "First you shame me and then you murder me! You're the criminals!"

Torbald smiled. "How right Finbarl-apcula was," he shared with the jury box. "She does have Ferral blood within her. Guards! Restrain her! Take her to the cells!"

A series of blows fell upon Aminatra as the guards interpreted Torbald's command with a degree of flexibility. Aminatra collapsed to the floor screaming while the courtroom calmly emptied, people eager to get on with their daily lives.

Over the general hubbub, Torbald turned to his brother. "Perhaps if you could learn to keep your dick in your pants, we could avoid such distasteful scenes in the future!"

"And if you could learn to keep that mouth of yours shut, you may live longer!" growled Hradbar.

"Oh, another deeply intellectual response, dear brother!" teased Torbald. "Have you been reading Socrates in the library again?"

Hradbar responded with a snarl and barged past his brother, vanishing out the door, leaving Torbald to smile triumphantly at Utrep.

CHAPTER 9

Finbarl sat upon his camel making the familiar trek to Bruuk's Point. It seemed so unfair to him: having first to arrest Aminatra, then the excruciating experience of giving false testimony at her trial, and now tasked to take her to the Prison. Could all this be a punishment for having inappropriate thoughts towards a wayward woman? Maybe a reprimand for challenging Audlech in the square? That would explain why the rascal accompanied them as part of the escort. If so, Finbarl acknowledged the lesson learnt

His mind continued to dwell upon Aminatra. A part of him liked her. She was attractive, strong-willed and interesting, but the Moralistas warned of the ways of women. Their beguiling beauty compelled men to do extraordinary and unexpected things. What was the story Finbarl once read in classes as a cadet? An ancient fable where women lured sailors onto the rocks with their hypnotic songs. He loved the adventure and heroic struggles of the crew, dreamt of a sea of unimaginable size. But as a cadet, he had been too young to appreciate the lesson. Finbarl's mind pushed the complex thoughts to one side and focused on what he understood: he had saved the little boy. Just like his own, the boy's future rested in the hands of the Wardyns as part of the guard cadet school: a hard life, but worthy and honest.

Though lost in thought, Finbarl remembered every now and again to glance behind to check upon the prisoner. Each time, Aminatra gave him a look of pure loathing. It made Finbarl uneasy, but he wasn't about to show it in front of the other men, particularly Audlech. The scoundrel had already enjoyed point-scoring off Finbarl.

"You do have a strange taste in friends," Audlech commented snidely after Aminatra, discovering Finbarl as part of her escort, began hurling insults at him.

Finbarl ignored Audlech, but when striking the prisoner to stop her rants, his clenched fist morphed into an open hand, pushing her to the ground. A subconscious action; a sort of compromise. To strike an Athenian woman was a social taboo, even if it did occur regularly behind closed doors, but prisoners lost their Athenian citizenship and were outside the laws. For Finbarl, however, this woman retained her full humanity. He had looked into her eyes, spoken to her, connected with her child. He had gone to strike her through instinct, to prove to those around he possessed no weaknesses or sympathies. Had they noticed his leniency, his act of rebellious suppression? The glare of pure hatred Aminatra gave, climbing to her feet, made it clear she hadn't.

Finbarl was glad to have Strathbol and Hougat along for the ride. The latter wasn't necessarily a friend, but Finbarl knew he had no love of Audlech and would support him in any confrontation. In fact, he wasn't sure anyone liked Audlech. Even the priest who silently accompanied them had probably formed a negative opinion of the reprobate. Though, considered Finbarl, he had no doubt formed a negative view of all of them.

"Time we stopped for refreshments?" enquired Strathbol from behind.

Finbarl turned and nodded his agreement. "Audlech, Hougat! On perimeter watch." He slid down the camel's flank, not waiting for the beast to descend, and stumbled forward, preventing a fall with a short run and jump. Wiping his brow, he pulled his water bottle from his pack and took a long swig. He was conscious the prisoner stood to his side; her eyes directed on him. For a moment, he refused to return the look, but something compelled him and he found himself offering her a drink from his vessel. Somewhat to his surprise, she took it without a word and drank heavily, gulping down two mouthfuls before pausing and handing the bladder back to Finbarl.

"It's important you drink whenever you get the opportunity," he advised.

Aminatra looked at him, then squirted a stream of water from her mouth at his face.

Finbarl reeled in shock, raising his hand to strike her but restraining himself. "I'm not the enemy, you know," he protested, spreading the cooling water across his face. "I'm sorry you lost your kid, but it's for the best."

"The best!" hissed Aminatra. "In what way is losing his mother best for Karlmon? You Ferral-whack!"

"Cronax!" cursed Finbarl. "He gets to live safely inside Athenia. You were condemning him to the Prison. Whether next year or five years down the line, no child can survive in this hellhole."

Aminatra frowned, unsure what Finbarl knew. Did he know Karlmon took the cake? Did they all know, using the knowledge to get her into an impossible position? "What's that supposed to mean?"

Finbarl shook his head in disbelief. "Your involvement with the black market gang. You were already getting...

Karlmon…," he said the name aloud for the first time and pictured the boy's face, "… to cause distractions for your thefts!"

"You dumb Ferral-whack! You're either stupid or incredibly naïve!" Aminatra sank to her knees, before sitting down, resting her aching feet.

"I'm not the one going to Prison!" retorted Finbarl.

Aminatra gave a condescending smile. "There wasn't a word of truth spoken in that courtroom! You should know, the amount of goat crap you spewed."

Finbarl blushed.

"And what Ferral-arse gang am I supposed to be in? They didn't even let me join the young mothers' club! Nobody wants anything to do with an unmarried mother."

"All the more reason you'd turn to a criminal gang. What with being ostracised for your promiscuity." Finbarl could tell his words struck a nerve as Aminatra's nostrils flared.

"It takes two to become parents! But what would you know about that? You're all the same!" Aminatra swung to face away from the guard.

Finbarl looked at the back of her head, uttering no more words. What more could he say to an inherent criminal? Seeing Strathbol feeding the camels, he wandered over to talk with someone unlikely to call him names. Even conversation with the priest seemed preferable.

Strathbol acknowledged Finbarl with a smile, rubbing the snout of the beast extracting a mouthful of hay from the palm of his other hand.

"She's a fiery one! You can see how the Ferrals evolved from criminals now."

"She's lost her son. She's entitled to be angry," said Finbarl, surprised sympathy still remained within him for the prisoner. "Let's not talk about her."

"Sure," responded Strathbol. "Any more news on your promotion?"

*

Arriving at Bruuk's Point, they found a handful of prisoners already present, peacefully sitting under the shade of the tree atop the tor. The convicts waved at the troop of guards and looked with interest at the new prisoner.

"'Allo, Finbarl-apcula," cried Johansson, climbing to his feet, speaking as formally and respectfully as possible. "Ah, Strathbol-apcula! How lovely-ed to see you both!" He cast an eye at Audlech, refraining from greeting a guard notorious for his brutality.

Finbarl, concerned at seeing the tor occupied, relaxed when he knew its occupant was the harmless Johansson. He acknowledged the wiry figure with a nod of his head.

"Get down from there!" snarled Audlech at the prisoners. "What do you think you're up to?"

"Just getting some-some much-needed shade-ly, Audlech-apcula," replied Johansson, with a deferential bow.

"I'll hang you from the Ferralax tree if you don't move!" threatened Audlech. "Then you'll be in shade." He laughed loudly.

Finbarl ignored Audlech but motioned for the prisoners to descend the tor. Audlech was right. The highest vantage point was no place for a prisoner until the area was secured. "Hougat, hoist the flag up!"

"What news, Johansson?" Strathbol asked, as the prisoner stepped off the final rock.

"Hewton and Alkharg are dead-ed," he answered. The lack of emotion in his voice conveying a familiarity with death. "A Ferral pack raided-ly at dusk by Gudmorg Crescent. Alkharg died-ed instantly-ing. We fought-ed them off but found-ed Hewton the next morning. It wasn't a pretty sight-ly! Partly eaten-ed – cannibalised-ing!"

"Yeah, don't need the details," rebuked Finbarl, trying to keep the image out of his mind.

"Sorry, Finbarl-apcula," said Johansson with due humility, before continuing with his news. "Miltus gave birth-y to a boy but 'e didn't last-ed the night-some. She's all right-y though; didn't want the thing-ing anyway!"

Strathbol shuddered at the sheer disgust of the 'thing', while Finbarl turned to check Aminatra was out of earshot. For some reason, he felt it important she did not hear a discussion on children. However, she was nowhere in sight. Finbarl circled to look wider afield: still no sign of her. No matter, he dismissed, she was already in the Prison. The only escape now was death.

"What brings you and your friends here so early?" asked Finbarl, returning to other matters.

"Just a little shaken-ly by the Ferral attacky," replied Johansson. "Those creatures don't seem-ly to come-ed here too often."

Finbarl nodded in understanding. "Okay. Don't get in the way and you can stay while we get the Jumblar and stuff ready. There's a new prisoner. I'll introduce you to when I find her. She could probably do with a friend."

Johansson bowed and backed away, re-uniting with his fellow prisoners, sitting upon a large boulder thirty yards away. Finbarl smiled in amusement, wondering what made Johansson speak so strangely.

With plenty still to do, Finbarl made out the faint outline of other prisoners approaching in the distance. He glanced up at the tree, seeing the flag fluttering in the breeze. Hougat scurried around, preparing the Jumblar for the priest, who lazed in the shade.

"Where's the new prisoner?" Finbarl called up.

Hougat stopped and straightened, spinning around to check the full 360 degrees. "Don't know," he shouted back. "I saw her about ten minutes ago when Audlech released her bindings."

"Where's Audlech?"

Hougat shrugged his shoulders.

"Don't worry about it. Get on with what you're doing!" But Finbarl was worried. There weren't many places to be out of sight at Bruuk's Point, and for two individuals to be missing concerned him. Ferrals surfaced as his first thought. They silently picked off individuals straying from the group. He walked to his camel, unsheathing his gun.

"Everything all right, Finbarl?" enquired Strathbol, his own hands reaching for his rifle.

"Yes, fine," he replied. "Keep an eye on the arriving prisoners. I need to find the new girl. You've not seen her?"

Strathbol shook his head, glancing around anxiously.

Finbarl climbed to the top of the tor, scanning the local area. Hougat watched him uneasily, at the same time rummaging in his bag for the Jumblar bundles. The smell of the Jumblar tickled Finbarl's senses and he paused to collect his thoughts. He focused his attention to the north-west, the only area not within his or Strathbol's previous range of sight. Dismissing thought of a Ferral attack, he wondered if the prisoners planned something. Should he instruct Strathbol and Hougat to go to alert. But why would prisoners attack them? Killing four guards achieved nothing, only bringing vicious retribution and no more Jumblar. Finbarl decided to investigate further before making a fool of himself. He noticed a line of scrub ahead of a shallow indent about fifty yards away.

"Aminatra! Aminatra!" His shout drew the attention of everyone around Bruuk's Point, but no response from

Aminatra. He climbed down the trickier north side of the tor, making his way towards the patch of scrub. "Aminatra!"

Finbarl stopped. Had he heard something? "Aminatra!" There it was again. A muffled sound from his direction of travel. He started to run, not thinking of the danger ahead. When ten yards from the dip, he saw over the scrub bushes, into the bowl. Audlech lay on top of Aminatra, one hand firmly pressing down on her mouth, the other struggling to pin down her flailing left arm. His robes lifted over his stomach.

"Audlech!" roared Finbarl. "Get off her! You'll pay for this!" He dashed forward, whirling his rifle over his head.

Audlech scrambled up, struggling to fold down his thawb, while Aminatra rained blows upon him. "Don't do anything foolish," he cried towards the ever nearing Finbarl. "She's only a prisoner!"

Consumed by rage, Finbarl charged forward with murderous intent but, as he brought the rifle back one last time to crash upon Audlech's skull, instinct stopped him. Instead he swung at a lower trajectory, smashing the gun against the back of Audlech's legs. The guard howled in pain, collapsing to the floor. He dug desperately in the sand with his fingers, trying to escape further blows, but Finbarl planted his boot firmly on his upper back and pressed down.

"You'll pay for this, Finbarl!" gasped Audlech. "They'll frow you in the Prison for attacking a fellow guard!"

Raising the butt of his rifle, Finbarl brought it down upon the base of Audlech's skull, hard enough to knock him out but not too hard to kill. Audlech's head slumped into the dirt.

"You all right?" Finbarl bent down to aid Aminatra.

"I'm fine! I don't need saving," she snapped, pushing Finbarl away and straightening her clothes. "Nothing happened! The Ferral-whack was too stupid to know what to do. Probably never been with a woman before. Another pathetic guard!"

Finbarl stood and looked down at Aminatra, who sat up and pressed her head between her knees. "Don't cry!" pleaded Finbarl. "He won't hurt you again. I promise!"

"I'm not crying, you goat-lover!" Aminatra glared up at Finbarl, loathing still in her eyes. She then said more calmly, "I'm gathering my composure."

Finbarl offered his hand to help Aminatra to her feet, but she ignored it and eased herself up. Flicking some dirt off her garment, she turned to the prostrate figure of Audlech and swung her boot at his ribcage.

"Finbarl! Finbarl! What happened?"

Finbarl turned to find Strathbol panting at the edge of the bowl. "Audlech tried to rape the prisoner," he answered.

"How he's never become a prisoner himself I'll never know," observed Strathbol, as he walked down to the motionless body of Audlech. "What did you do to him?"

"Not what I wanted to do! He'll live."

"What do we say to Vassel?" fretted Strathbol. "Cronax! Finbarl, you could get into big trouble for attacking a guard, no matter what he was doing."

Aminatra snorted in contempt.

"He fell off his camel," said Finbarl. "At least, that's what I saw."

"Yeah, no, absolutely," concurred Strathbol. "That's what I saw too."

"Well, there's a shock!" Aminatra laughed hysterically, much to the bemusement of Finbarl and Strathbol. "Another lying guard."

"Shut up!" ordered Finbarl. "You've not even bothered to thank me yet for rescuing you."

"Rescuing me!" sputtered Aminatra. "You didn't rescue me. You imprisoned me. You're all as bad as each other. You've taken my son away from me, lied at my trial and dumped me in this Ferral-pit! Thank you! Oh, yes! Thank you!" Tears flowed down her face. "You're afraid of me, of what I represent: an independent woman who doesn't fit your template of obedience."

Finbarl frowned, confused by the outburst. "I'm not afraid of you," he said, side-stepping the truth lying deep within. He was afraid. Afraid at his attraction to this wild, rebellious woman. He, an inexperienced young man playing at the alpha male; she an experienced woman, languishing beyond even the lowest reaches of society. An insecurity festered at Finbarl's core: abandoned as a child and cocooned as a guard. No one prepared him for such feelings.

Aminatra sniffed contemptibly, wiping away the tears. "Then why are you trying to destroy me? Why frame me for a crime I didn't do? Why sentence me to the Prison? Why try to rape me?"

"That wasn't me … ," began Finbarl, before realising her point. He was the symbolic figurehead of her hatred. He wanted to dismiss her words as he would any prisoner's, but he couldn't. "I won't let anything bad happen to you," he promised. "I'll put you under the protection of some of the decent prisoners. They'll look after you."

"Ha! Too late, something bad already happened. You're not my saviour. The sooner you realise what you are, the better: a monster! Why don't you just kill us and be done with all this hassle?"

Finbarl became annoyed. "Because civilised societies don't do that!"

"Civilised?" laughed Aminatra.

Strathbol, keeping out of the argument, interrupted. "Hougat hates Audlech. He'll support our story."

"Yes," said Finbarl, his mind back to matters at hand. "Let's get back to the tor. It doesn't do to be separated for too long."

"What about it?" asked Aminatra, looking down and aiming a further light kick at Audlech.

"He's not going anywhere," said Finbarl. "Strathbol, check he doesn't have any weapons on him! Otherwise we just leave him until he comes around. I don't want the other prisoners seeing us dragging an unconscious guard."

*

Back at Bruuk's Point tor, they found an anxious Hougat attempting to control a growing number of prisoners, while the priest continued to give no assistance. "Where the hell have you been?" Hougat growled. "I was starting to fear for my safety!"

"Big brave guard like you, Hougat?" mocked Finbarl, before catching a warning look from Strathbol. "No, sorry, we had a little issue with Audlech. He's sleeping it off, but we're going to need your assistance in relating the story back to Vassel."

"What?" exclaimed Hougat, stepping away from the hearing range of the curious priest.

"He was trying to rape the new prisoner," whispered Strathbol. "Finbarl had to knock him out!"

Hougat eyed Aminatra slyly. "Yeah, I can see why. But as it's Audlech, I'll say whatever needs to be said."

Finbarl smiled awkwardly, the barrack-room banter so familiar to him. It was only when Strathbol stepped in, saying, "Good man," and steered Hougat away, Finbarl realised he had screwed his fists, poised to land a punch.

"Right," Finbarl said to Aminatra. "Come with me. I'll introduce you to Johansson, who'll help you." He attempted to grab her arm, but she pulled it away. "He's survived over six years in the Prison – don't ask me how - but he has. He talks funny but seems to get on with most."

"Fine," snapped Aminatra. "But don't touch me!"

They found Johansson sitting in a larger group. Finbarl eyed them suspiciously, getting the same look back with interest.

"Johansson, this is Aminatra," said Finbarl. "She's the one I told you about. You happy to watch out for her for a while?"

"What's special about her?" the haggard man to Johansson's left cut in.

"Nothing," replied Finbarl, surprised at the challenge.

"Guards don't ever ask us to look out for a new 'un," added the man. "She your girl?"

"Hardly!" retorted Finbarl, noticing Aminatra enjoying his discomfort. "Will you look after her or not?"

Another voice broke in. "I'll look after you, my dear." It was the old lady who occasionally brought in medicinal plants. "No one will touch you in my company," she assured.

Finbarl looked to Johansson, who nodded. "No one better-er than Maddy," the prisoner said, winking at the old lady. "Been here longer than me. Hell, she's been here longer-er than anyone, 'cept that tree!" He wafted his hand towards the tree on top of Bruuk's Point tor.

"Thanks," said Finbarl, setting off an unexpected ripple of light laughter from the prisoners. "What now?"

"Just not used to hearing gratitude from a guard, that's all," replied the haggard man, smiling a toothless grin at Finbarl.

Finbarl released a frustrated breath and waved for Aminatra to join her new 'family.' "Your Jumblar will be ready soon," he said to the group. "Just collect it and go." He turned and walked back to the tor to help Hougat and Strathbol, just catching the old lady address Aminatra before out of earshot.

"Come here, dear! Your new life and education begin today."

*

"Numbers appear low today," observed Finbarl to Strathbol, as the priest exchanged the last of the Jumblar to the prisoners for their measly scavenged finds.

Strathbol glanced at the remaining handouts and cast around his mind. "Yeah, I don't recall seeing Butt or Claznor. A few more missing too." Finbarl opened his mouth to add a few more names when Audlech emerged cursing and rubbing his neck.

"You should have killed me while you had the Ferralax chance, Orpho!" he snarled.

"You're lucky I didn't!" shot back Finbarl. "No one would have missed you and we could've blamed it on a Ferral!"

"You'll have wished you had! When I get back to Athenia, they're going to roast you alive!"

"Why?" asked Finbarl, aping confusion. "Because you fell off your camel?"

"I what?"

"That's right isn't it, Strathbol?" encouraged Finbarl, and the younger guard nodded tentatively. "Eh, Hougat?"

"Sure," said Hougat, enjoying the charade. "Stupid idiot let the camel get spooked and fell right off! Pretty embarrassing."

"Then give me back my gun!" demanded Audlech.

"You must be joking," exclaimed Finbarl. "You'll get it back when we're within sight of Athenia's walls. Those things have a nasty habit of going off by accident when in the hands of an incompetent."

Audlech spat provocatively in front of Finbarl's feet. "There'll be other times. As you say, who's going to question a story of a Ferral attack and the sad death of a Ferral-whack guard out in the wild protecting the good people of Athenia? Perhaps we'll all be together again, and I can do all three of you in one go!"

"If our story of you falling off a camel is going to ring true," proposed Finbarl, "there's one more detail." He stepped towards Audlech and landed a swift punch to his nose. Audlech staggered back, blood pouring down his chin.

"You … !" protested Audlech, only for Hougat to land another blow to his stomach.

"Strathbol, you want a go?" asked Hougat with glee, as Audlech doubled over.

The young guard grimaced, shaking his head and stepping backwards.

"Suit yourself," said Hougat, and readied to land another punch.

"Enough!" demanded Finbarl, conscious of the priest lingering in view. "We want it to look like he fell off a camel, not got stampeded by a herd!"

"Bah!" Hougat eased his fist down, blowing Audlech a kiss in lieu.

"It's time we headed back," declared the priest, addressing the guards for the first time since leaving Athenia, unperturbed by the state of Audlech. "I understand we have to detour via Alphege Scar to investigate the potential metal find. It'll be getting dark by the time we get home."

Finbarl noticed the fear in his eyes, imagining the complaints when the priest found out about this additional duty. Apart from the further discomfort of the ride, the journey took them deeper into Ferral territory. Even Strathbol showed nerves, pacing back and forth by his camel, desperate to get moving and away from the gaze of Audlech.

"Are we packed?" Finbarl aimed the question at Hougat.

"Nearly," he answered. "Taking a bit longer today as someone's been sleeping on the job!"

Audlech, still clutching his nose, tried to sneer back, but realised the pain of such an expression wasn't worth it.

"Well, get on with it!" urged Finbarl. "You going to be able to ride back, Audlech?"

"I ain't walking!" he hissed.

"We don't want you falling off again!" Hougat chuckled aloud, as he walked away toward the tor to collect his bag.

CHAPTER 10

On the flat, open route north, the guards and priest weaved their way around Sage Bush and Rabbitbrush, occasionally dropping into gentle undulating dips or through wind-carved channels. Looking back, they made out the tree on Bruuk's Point, fading in the heat haze. No one spoke in the poisoned atmosphere.

Occasionally, prisoners reported large metal finds, where the wind-scoured land exposed a tantalising glimpse of an ancient artefact. Its recovery beyond the power of the half-starved wanderers, they traded their information for Jumblar. Such intelligence now led Finbarl and his troop towards Alphege Scar, a well-known landmark about ten miles directly north of Bruuk's Point. The landscape wore the pitiful wounds of the past: faint outlines of destroyed buildings and unnatural shapes claimed by the sand. Alphege Scar hinted at a human creator: a strange, hundred-yard long, twenty-yard wide groove, abruptly dropping twenty feet into the ground. While nature and time reclaimed it, the straight edges and purposeful lines spoke of a superior civilisation of old.

"Rattlesnake!" cried Finbarl, bringing their convoy to a sudden halt. He led, with Strathbol behind and Hougat at the rear, keeping a careful eye on Audlech, who rode uncomfortably in front of him. The priest, with no inclination to wallow at the back, placed himself safely in the middle of the train. The snake, ridiculously small in comparison to the giant beasts before it, raised itself up to threaten the interlopers, blocking their path. A lame or dead camel would be a disaster. Finbarl held position to see if the snake conceded right of way. With a yank of the reins, he pulled his camel sideways. "The Ferral-whack ain't moving!" Finbarl declared. "We'll make our way around. Need to go back a little to get through these thorn bushes."

Each rider, familiar with such a manoeuvre, found themselves riding in reverse order down a shallow slope where the sandstone formed a shelf. A crow sat upon the peak of a cactus, watching them suspiciously as they trotted past. Audlech raised his fingers in the shape of a pistol and let loose an imaginary bullet at the bird. It cawed its disapproval and flew away. Blowing the 'smoke' from his fingertips, Audlech pointed his weapon at Hougat's back, repeating the mime. Strathbol nervously looked at Finbarl.

"Don't worry about it!" Finbarl called out, loud enough for everyone to hear. "Those are the same fingers he sticks up his arse. Hopefully next time he tries, it'll go off!"

Strathbol laughed, while Hougat turned to find out the source of the mirth.

"You won't be laughing with a bullet in your back, Strafbol!" Audlech knew where to aim his barbed comment to target the weakest.

"If someone fell off a camel," opined Hougat, "wouldn't it be usual to have some cactus thorns in them?"

Even though he tried to restrain himself, Strathbol found himself giggling again, his laughter spreading to Finbarl. Audlech sneered in disgust.

✳

The pace of the convoy slowed after a further hour riding in the heat. A light wind brought some relief but blew grains of sand into eyes and mouths, and each man adjusted his Ghutra to cover the lower part of his face. A rabbit or vole occasionally shot across their path, breaking the monotony, while the sun-bleached bones of a beast and even a human, reminded them of the dangers of the wilderness.

The trudge in the heat stirred Finbarl to thought. He reflected on Aminatra and her allegations about the trial. Her guilt proven, she still called everyone else a liar. Why? His own evidence, though not his own, was still truthful. It came from the mouth of a Wardyn, the paragons of justice. The other witnesses had no reason to falsify their testimony. Aminatra confused and intrigued him in equal measure. He hardly knew her, she hurled abuse at him for most of the time, yet he struggled to match the character portrayed in court with the woman standing in the Jumblar queue: the loving mother, willing to stand up for her boy. And what of her boy? Finbarl tried to recollect the day he learnt of his parents' death, but the memories failed to surface. His earliest clear memories were of schooling amongst the cadets; the Orphos and Familos, immediately gravitating to their own kind, competing, befriending, fighting and eventually graduating. All loyal, willing to die and kill for a cause, epitomised through the embodiment of the Governor and the Wardyns.

Finbarl missed those times, particularly the reading and writing classes. With paper a rare commodity, few Athenians were literate and, even if they were, access to books or any reading material was limited. But each guard learnt basic reading and writing, to record details of crimes and deaths and master the codified laws of Athenia. The Moralistas read to them from the old books, saved from past civilisations.

Finbarl loved to listen to and dream about those past times, with a world open to all to explore and marvel at.

A whistle sounded and Finbarl looked up from his daydream to see Hougat's raised arm, signalling a stop. He surveyed the surrounding terrain, checking for threats, and edged his camel to Hougat's side. The guard directed Finbarl with his gun, pointing to a group of five trees in the distance, where large birds circled. "A kill site?" suggested Hougat.

Finbarl nodded sombrely. "Too many scavengers for a single carcass."

"Give me my gun!" demanded Audlech, his voice restrained out of fear. "If there are Ferrals about, I want my gun!"

"Give him his gun!" Finbarl reluctantly ordered Hougat. It posed a risk, but both knew the Ferrals were more of a threat, their personal fight postponed to another time. "You shoot us now, Audlech, and all you'll be doing is saving us from the terrible fate the Ferrals will serve up for the last man standing."

Audlech smiled through his crooked teeth as he snatched the rifle from Hougat.

"We stay together," instructed Finbarl, scratching his head. "If we trail off to the left, we can approach the trees with the sun behind us, along that open section." He waved his finger towards a piece of ground coloured a darker shade of yellow-brown. "If Ferrals are about, they won't have cover and will be blinded by the sun."

"Do we dump our bags?" asked Strathbol, conscious that, when riding a camel and attacked by Ferrals, the smartest thing to do was gallop away.

"Not yet," replied Finbarl. "Once we're on that stretch over there we'll be clear on the situation and if we need to plan for escape."

"What about me?" The priest nervously stroked his camel. "What do I do?"

"You can pray," answered Finbarl facetiously, grateful the priest rode a camel, not a donkey.

"To lose my soul to a Ferral!" whined the priest to the heavens.

"We can feed you to the Ferrals to allow us to escape," quipped Audlech, leaving the other guards wondering if he was wholly joking and the priest even more nervous.

"Come on then!" urged Hougat, easing his camel into a trot. "Let's get this over with!"

"After you." Audlech smiled sweetly at Finbarl, beckoning him with a wave of his hand to lead off.

Finbarl returned the faux smile, giving a nod of his head to indicate he would not be riding in front of an armed Audlech.

"I don't know why I bother with manners when no one else has 'em," moaned Audlech aloud.

"Quiet!" hissed Finbarl. "Absolute silence from now on." He gave another purposeful nod to the priest to go next.

It tested their nerves to go in one direction with every thought focused elsewhere. A knot of dreaded expectation constricted Finbarl's stomach. He knew enough of the signs to know nothing good awaited them. While the horror inevitably lay off to their right under the trees, Finbarl knew, if the Ferrals remained, they could be anywhere. Each large rock, tree or dip in the landscape offered a potential hiding place for those predatory beasts. They even covered themselves in sand or dirt, waiting in silence until their prey stepped upon them before pouncing. Whatever they were, they had humanity's cunning, working in packs, setting elaborate traps. An unwelcome memory of the past surfaced in Finbarl's mind. A year ago, as a small troop ventured south towards Gudmorg Crescent, collecting limestone for glass making, a group of ten Ferrals surprised them, driving Finbarl's troop for cover down a ravine. Atop the cliffs, other Ferrals patiently awaited their unsuspecting prey. Stones and boulders rained down upon them. An expensive discharge of guns drove the Ferrals away, allowing for escape. Luck served them well in the end, with the price of escape no more than the odd bruise and one dislocated shoulder.

They reached the open ground of flattened sandstone, watching the vultures and crows descending to the ground, before taking off again in a squabbling furore. The birds targeted numerous points on the surface, which was evidence enough for Finbarl to confirm his initial fears of a Ferral attack. The birds' presence and courage to land indicated the attackers were probably long gone, but Finbarl took no chances.

"Dump the bags!" ordered Finbarl. "Just keep a water bottle and anything you can use as a weapon." He passed his knife to the priest. "Here, take this. You're staying with the bags."

"What if I get attacked?" exclaimed the priest.

"That's what the knife is for," answered Finbarl. "You can ride away or fight them off until we can get to you."

"But ... ". The priest stopped abruptly, registering Finbarl's blunt stare, terminating the discussion. "I'll wait here."

As they cut the bags from their bindings, an unavoidable noise startled the camels, adding to the tension. Each guard reassured their beast until it was calm again. Then, on Finbarl's signal, they eased them into a trot, heading towards the trees. Following Finbarl's lead, they picked up the pace, ready to steer off in any direction in the event of an attack. At twenty yards, Finbarl brought them back down to a steady trot. His surveying eyes told him no Ferrals remained in the immediate vicinity, only the corpses of their victims.

Four bodies lay blooded and motionless within the copse. The scavenging birds took to flight with a loud chorus of complaining shrieks and caws as the men and camels approached. Two coyotes, standing over the bodies, looked up with annoyance, snarled at the interlopers and trotted away, their meal lost to a larger competitor.

"G'way!" cried Strathbol to hurry them off.

Death was a common companion, desensitising the softest heart, yet the fatal aftermath of a Ferral attack still stirred a shock and revulsion amongst the most hardened guard, even when the victims were common criminals such as these. Two bodies lay slumped at the base of a tree stump; their arms bound to the tree by the shreds of their own clothes. Both lifeless heads drooped to the side. The other two lay on their backs in the sand, their hands and feet splayed out, their faces turned away as though embarrassed by their fate, their skulls smashed: the favoured stunning and killing method of the Ferral. Finbarl hoped death came quickly. No one looked too closely, trying to avoid sight of the exposed intestines, but all came to the same conclusion: the Ferrals had feasted upon human flesh.

"Ferralax!" cursed Hougat.

"At least they won't be hungry," commented Audlech.

Finbarl opened his mouth to admonish, but realised his own thoughts carried similar sentiments. Sated after a meal, like all beasts, the Ferral slept it off. Looking at the mess around, they would be having a long, contented sleep somewhere.

"Audlech," began Finbarl, "cut these two down! Strathbol! Hougat! Stay mounted and out of the trees. I'll see if I can recognise them." He coaxed his camel into the sitting position, climbing off hesitantly, rifle clutched between his sweating grip. Strathbol rode past, nodding assurance he had Finbarl's back. Finbarl waited until both Strathbol and Hougat arrived in position, able to defend those on the ground, or escape to take news back to Athenia.

"That's Craznor," said Finbarl, instantly pointing at the first body leaning against the stump. "Explains why he wasn't at Bruuk's Point today. So, one of these others must be Butt."

"Who cares who they are!" exclaimed Audlech, as he sawed through the rags. "They're just criminals who deserve no better. My only problem is they're keeping those Ferrals alive by providing them with a hearty meal."

"Are you sure your parents weren't Ferrals?" said Finbarl, examining the face of the next bound victim.

"Oh, no, Orpho," said Audlech with glee. "I know exactly who my parents are and where they still are. Good Athenian citizens!"

Finbarl realised he walked right into that slur and decided to ignore it. "I think this is Boule," he said, as much to himself as Audlech. "Though it's hard to be sure."

"Now him I do remember." Audlech stood considering the individual, waving a bloodied rag in one hand, his knife in the other. "I recall having the pleasure of dumping his sad excuse for a boy in the Prison. Cried like a baby!"

"Being in your company can do that to the best of men!" Not the greatest put-down, but Finbarl found it cathartic.

"Yes, that's Boule," continued Audlech, as Finbarl pulled the body of Craznor away from the tree. "Recognise the broken finger on his left hand. I gave him that!"

"You must be proud."

Audlech paused, knife in hand, and looked Finbarl in the eye. Finbarl braced himself, ready to parry an attack by Audlech. But instead the thug nodded and smiled. "Yes, you're right. I am."

Audlech was in his element, and Finbarl realised this passed for a happy moment in the guard's sick mind. "Well, carry on cutting him free and I'll look at the others!"

Finbarl stood in front of one of the pitiful, prostrate bodies. Flies landed on the corpse, and he waved them away knowing full well they would be back in a second. Gently placing his hand upon the body's chin, he tilted the head round and recoiled in shock. The eyes were missing! He controlled an urge to retch.

"This is Butt," he said, recovering his composure. Blood caked his clothes and hands, but he didn't care. He rubbed his own chin, spreading more blood, then turned to the final body.

Audlech already stood over the body, waiting for Finbarl to identify it. He stepped back as Finbarl approached and twisted the head back, this time prepared for what he might find. The face was a mess of cuts and bruises, the nose squashed, the eyes once again removed.

"Erm, not sure we're going to be able to identify this one without working out who's missing. Any ideas, Audlech?"

Audlech raised his eyebrows and pulled his 'why are you asking me?' face.

"We'll bury them! I'll go and get the spades."

Finbarl strolled back to his camel. Behind, he heard a soft grunt and turned to see Audlech pushing the bodies over with his boot, so he didn't have to look at their faces. There was no hope for that man, he thought. He gave a thumbs-up to Strathbol, indicating everything was okay, receiving a similar reassurance back. Hougat, watching from afar, saw the exchange and gave an affirmative sign.

*

Digging in the rocky soil would not be easy, particularly for a pit big and deep enough for four bodies. Finbarl considered trying to burn the bodies, but knew the dangers a smoky fire posed, attracting other curious Ferrals. They might be frightened by fire, but retained a fascination with it, and a plume of smoke would act as a magnet.

The spades were back with the bags and Finbarl found the priest nervously humming to himself as he approached.

"What did you find?" the priest asked reluctantly.

"What we expected. No survivors."

"Then we're done here and can get moving?" proposed the priest.

Finbarl dismounted and hunted for the spades amidst the bags. He paused and looked angrily at the priest. "No, we're burying them first and you're helping." Finbarl thrust a spade towards the man.

"But ... but, why? They're prisoners, I take it. Unloved, unmissed, deserving of their fate. Their souls lost. Surely you're not going to risk all our lives and souls for them?"

"They're human," retorted Finbarl, still holding the spade out. "They deserve a burial. We also don't want to encourage other Ferrals in their taste for human flesh. With your help, we get the job done quicker and can get out of here quicker; without your help, we get pissed off and feel less inclined to come to your rescue."

Looking to the heavens for guidance, the priest whispered a short prayer and grasped the spade.

The trees provided some shade from the unrelenting sun, but the uncooperative, rocky soil made it hot, arduous work. The priest, with his soft hands, contributed little but complaints. With a shallow grave dug, they pushed the bodies in, covering them with a light layer of sand. It was the best they could do.

"We're not going to get back before dark now!" said Strathbol, as the others remounted their camels.

"We can if we skip Alphege Scar," suggested Hougat.

"The Wardyns won't be happy with that!" whined Strathbol.

"We just say we didn't find anything!" Everyone looked at Audlech, owner of the comment.

"I'm good with that," said Finbarl, seeking agreement from the priest.

"Better a lie than getting lost in the dark!" answered the priest without hesitation.

Finbarl smirked at the ease with which the holy man broke his vows of honesty. Hougat and Strathbol nodded their agreement.

"Right," declared Finbarl, "let's collect our bags and get out of this abattoir."

CHAPTER 11

Aminatra provided the main point of interest for the other prisoners for the first hour: a new face, with stories to tell of Athenia. Some sought news of loved ones. Others watched from a distance, assessing, speculating and discussing her with their friends. A few men watched with darker motives, their stares making Aminatra uncomfortable. She hoped Maddy said or did something, but by the time they were ready to head off from Bruuk's Point, it seemed no one spared her a moment's thought. Survival was their main concern now. Just as they arrived in their easily identifiable groups, so they split again into the same factions, drifting away in different directions.

"Why don't we all stick together?" asked Aminatra. "Surely it's safer!"

Maddy smiled gently, feeling the benefits of the Jumblar taken a moment before. "Undoubtedly safer, my dear, but not human nature. Bonds form and break in the Prison, just like in Athenia. Some people you can trust and live with, others you hate and need breathing space from. There's no one and no purpose to unite us. Time changes things too. Sometimes you just need a break from someone. It's a freedom we have that perhaps you don't get in Athenia."

"Freedom!" blurted Aminatra. "How is this freedom?"

Maddy didn't answer but climbed to her feet, lifted her bag to her shoulder and placed a battered hat upon her head. "Come on, we've a long walk ahead of us!"

Aminatra jumped up, eager they didn't leave her behind. She examined the bag holding her few possessions and assessed her travelling companions. Several other prisoners stood and turned south. "Where are we going?" she asked. "Why don't we stay at Bruuk's Point? The Ferrals don't come here much."

"Food and water," the simple response from Maddy, who already strolled on ahead. A hundred other prisoners had asked these questions on their incarceration over the years. She had developed a patient, economical way of dealing with them.

Aminatra slung her bag over her shoulder and ran to catch up. For most of her life she relied on nobody but herself; now she felt lost and needy. Yet following Maddy and her group somehow felt right.

"Who decides where we go?" Aminatra had a hundred questions.

"Nature, memory or need," answered Maddy. "If the Wardyns demand something for their Jumblar, we must go there, but mainly we go where the food is. Just like in the farm, our food is seasonal. They prize the knowledge of us oldies: what to eat, where and when to find it. The landscape's littered with old ruins: places we can find a bit of safety or an artefact. A little knowledge goes a long way here." She tapped the side of her head. "Why do you think they keep me around? It isn't for my fighting ability."

"But I can't fight either," said Aminatra, suddenly conscious of her lack of survival skills.

"My dear, you'll be amazed at what you can do when you have to. To survive, it's just as important to make yourself an asset to the other prisoners. When they need you for their own survival, they'll protect you and this creates the first bonds to make a community. If you offer them nothing, you'll be used and abused like poor little Miltus."

"Who?"

"Never mind," said Maddy. "Just watch and learn from me. I won't be here forever, and you seem like a woman I can pass my secrets on to.

"That guard seemed to like you."

Aminatra shot Maddy a surprised look. "Well the feeling's not mutual. He's the reason I'm here!"

"In what way?" Maddy scrutinised her companion.

"Well, part of the reason." Aminatra told Maddy the whole story: of desertion by Hradbar when pregnant, of how Karlmon stole the cake and of lie after lie at her trial and how she was unable to challenge without exposing the true perpetrator.

Maddy listened politely, putting a sympathetic hand upon Aminatra's shoulder. "You must believe you'll see Karlmon again," she said. "And you've already shown me what skills you have to survive in the Prison."

"I have?"

"Of course, my dear," said Maddy. "You are a survivor and an enabler. Society dismissed you long ago and yet you raised a boy all on your own, without their help – a fine boy, it sounds. One who will now be able to survive the next stage of his life."

"But not with me!"

"No, not with you, but he'll be all right. And you may see him again, one day. Hope is our most important strength in the Prison. It may seem impossible at this moment, but this world is too precarious not to offer the hope of change. Now, tell me why this guard likes you! What's his name?"

Aminatra laughed at Maddy's persistence. She already recognised great wisdom lay within this woman, and this was her way of normalising a traumatic moment. "Finbarl-apcula," she replied. "And to think I did once like him."

"Really, Ami? May I call you Ami?" asked Maddy, feeding her arm through Aminatra's. "Do tell me more!"

Aminatra related how Finbarl intervened when Audlech took Karlmon's toy. It was the first time she witnessed a guard intervene to protect a citizen against their own kind. She thought Finbarl different – until he arrested her without a second thought.

"Ah, you're too hard on him," said Maddy. "He's only trying to do right in a world gone wrong. When your moral guardians are the Wardyns, then it's hard to seem good, but from what you tell me, he does have a good soul."

Aminatra stopped, giving Maddy a quizzical look. Hearing someone criticise the Wardyns so openly was new. It sounded good. But why would any prisoner defend a guard?

Maddy sensed Aminatra's doubts and said: "Another survival tip for the Prison is you have to learn to step back from the avalanche of life and live in the moment. Your anger seeps from you like an open wound. Bitterness is no help to clarity of thought, and you need clarity to survive, my dear. You'll have plenty of time to think and debate openly here; you must be prepared to listen and learn and change. Release your anger!"

Aminatra nodded slowly. Somehow the woman's words connected. Maddy had identified her inner strength, her weakness, had given her confidence and belief. Already Aminatra felt determination returning. "Okay," she said. "I will."

*

Having stopped to collect a hidden stash of primitive weapons buried beneath a pile of stones, the group continued north. They walked at the pace of the slowest member, regularly pausing to examine plants, occasionally digging something up, breaking off the leaves and placing the root in their bag. Maddy explained everything to Aminatra: the names of the plants, which ones to eat, those with medicinal applications and those to make you smell disgusting, dissuading a Ferral from eating you. Aminatra felt particularly grateful for the creamy juice from a short cactus, which Maddy spread over her arms and face, taking the heat out of the sun's rays.

"Whatever you do, dear," Maddy advised, after rubbing the juice into Aminatra's neck, "don't drink it. Well, not unless you've had enough of the Prison!"

"When do we stop to eat and take our Jumblar?" Aminatra started to notice the absence of Jumblar in her system and, combined with her hunger, felt woozy.

"You eat and take Jumblar when you want to. You're free to make your own choices," replied Maddy, before adding, "but you must make good choices and you must take responsibility for yourself! What food have you collected today? None! Dried food is good: it lasts longer. Store that for when you really need it! As for Jumblar, it'll be some days before you get your next supply. You can have some now and feel better. Hell, my dear, you can take it all now and feel wonderful in a helpless, Ferral-welcome coma. Or you can develop the discipline to cope with some discomfort and pace yourself, so you can keep an emergency stash. Then if you miss a dish-out session, you've a chance of surviving until the next one without going mad." She gave Aminatra a haunting look. "Remember, while you must get others to rely on you, you can never rely on anyone but yourself in this world; when you see us foraging for roots or berries, do what we do. You won't be getting handouts from anyone – me included!"

Aminatra understood how the old lady managed to survive so long in the Prison. A combination of brains, determination and rational ruthlessness. "What gives you the hope to keep going?" Aminatra asked.

"Sorry?"

"You said earlier how important clinging to hope is to survive here. Well, I can hope to see Karlmon again one day. What do you have making you hang on?"

Maddy cleared her throat, as though the words proved difficult for her. "My son," she replied. "I'm just like you, Ami. I've been separated from my boy a long, long time."

Aminatra gaped in amazement. "How long have you lived in the Prison? How old was your boy when taken from you? Is he with his father? Why were you sent to the Prison? Oh, I'm sorry. So many questions. Please tell me about your son."

Maddy smiled. "He was about three years of age when I last saw him. A beautiful boy! Very smart, with a nice smile."

Aminatra closed her eyes and saw the image of Karlmon smiling too.

"My husband and I were quite the couple in our day," Maddy continued, grateful to wallow in some fond memories. "I was a doctor and Alfbarl, my husband, oversaw some revolutionary farming techniques, removing the salt that builds up from regular irrigation. We were well respected, and we were busy. We also understood which way the wind was blowing. We made a decision to do what was best for our son."

"What do you mean?" asked Aminatra.

"We enrolled him into the cadets," answered Maddy.

Aminatra gasped. "But ... So he wasn't taken from you when you were imprisoned? You gave him up!"

"My dear, it was the best life available to a child. What parent wouldn't choose that?" Maddy spoke with the same confidence and certainty she might use to describe the medicinal benefits of a plant. Her logic overrode any emotion.

Here was a woman given the opportunities in life denied Aminatra because of a twist of fate: born into a different class. Yet she disposed of the one thing Aminatra valued most: her child. But Aminatra's anger was all spent. Maddy was more attuned to the general attitudes of Athenia and Aminatra knew she was the odd one out. It didn't mean Maddy loved her boy any less, just a form of love Aminatra didn't understand. "So why were you imprisoned?"

"We had power. Too much power, my dear! Alfbarl wanted to see social and political reforms in Athenia. He knew what those Wardyns were up to!

"As his reputation grew, he believed he had the support to challenge them. Oh, it wasn't just him. I drove him too; filling his head with ideas. Would you believe I even proposed prisoners have the chance at redemption? A set term in the Prison and an opportunity to start over, back in Athenia. I would be out of here by now if they had listened to me!" She laughed at the irony. "We had a vision for the future. More accountability for the Wardyns, more transparency in our justice system, a more equal society. We even wanted to see the walls of Athenia come down one day!"

"But how?" asked Aminatra. She never even considered things could change if people wanted it.

"Overcome our fear," answered Maddy.

"But, what about the Ferrals?"

"The Ferrals have become what we made them," responded Maddy, much to Aminatra's confusion. "We wouldn't be hiding behind walls if there were just bears out there."

"What's a bear?"

"Sorry, you probably weren't read The Last of the Mohicans as a child, were you, my dear?" said Maddy, adding further to Aminatra's confusion. "They're large mammals twice the size of humans. Probably hasn't been one in this part of the world for a thousand years.

"My point is, if we consider Ferrals to be beasts, why don't we respond to them like we do to other beasts? If man had always been this scared of wild animals, we wouldn't have bothered leaving the trees. We're the masters of this planet, or at least we were, and can be again. Fear of the Ferrals is the metaphorical wall holding Athenia back. Why not try taming them?"

So much of what Maddy said lay beyond Aminatra's understanding. But despite a limited education, one thing she knew was the danger Ferrals posed. "You can't tame Ferrals," she stated. "They aren't rational. They just know one thing: hunting and killing."

"That's two things, dear," corrected Maddy. "How is that different from a dog's ancestor? They were wolves once."

"Really!" exclaimed Aminatra.

"Yes, all tamed animals were wild once and humans domesticated them. If you control their food source and understand their instincts, you control them."

"And you think we can do so with the Ferrals?"

"Possibly, Ami. You really don't mind me calling you Ami?"

Aminatra shook her head, unwilling to express her true feelings and upset someone in whom she was placing her life. Losing her social appellation of 'gula' hurt, so losing more was delicate. Maddy sometimes addressed her as though a child. But perhaps these were the idiosyncrasies of the old. In truth, Aminatra didn't know many old people.

Maddy returned to her original line of thought, oblivious to Aminatra's own contemplative diversion. "It would take a long time, my dear, and a lot of effort, but I'm not convinced we would need the same approach."

"Why?" asked Aminatra, beginning to understand more, appreciating the possibilities.

"We consider them beasts, but are they?" Maddy enjoyed the opportunity to teach a new pupil. "You see, decisions were made a long time ago, during a difficult period of human history, when we decided the best option was to hide from a problem rather than tackle it. As the environment changed, sea levels rose, some places got wetter, others drier, but everywhere hotter, we ... ".

"How do you know all this?" interrupted Aminatra.

"Athenia's library was obviously far more accessible when I was growing up."

"What's a library?"

Maddy blinked in surprise. "A depository for books, my poor dear. But, as I was saying, due to the environmental hardships, crime escalated out of control and society broke down. Rather than try to solve the social problems causing crime, individuals put bars across their windows; then you had gated communities; finally, society had its solution: civilisation could hide behind the walls, leaving those outside to suffer.

"Now, I'm not saying, Ami, I'd have done anything differently had I lived then. It must have been its own kind of hell. But we're still living inside those walls, while the world has changed. They were a response to a problem but only caused other problems. Civilisation isn't surviving behind those walls; it's choking to death!"

"What does this have to do with the Ferrals?"

"Yes, sorry, I'm taking the long-winded route. It's clear they're humanoid, and we know they don't appear in the classic texts Athenia holds, so can we not assume they've evolved from humans like us during the last thousand years?"

Aminatra laughed. "You mean we're related?"

"Yes, Aminatra!" replied Maddy, annoyed for her ridiculed theory. "Not in the true sense of evolving backwards. I mean digressing from normality in a way I can't explain or understand. But don't you see? If that's the case, they're also human at heart and we can steer them back to normality."

"Have you ever seen a Ferral attack? They don't behave human to me! And what about them stealing souls?" Aminatra remained sceptical.

"I live in the Prison, my dear!" said Maddy by way of an answer, and lifted her shirt to show a crescent-shaped scar. "And don't believe rubbish about stealing souls. Just another brick in the wall of fear."

"Cronax! You're lucky to be alive!"

"Luck is qualitative," remarked Maddy. "I could fight like the best of them in those days and I learnt how to treat wounds with what I had available."

"And you still think they're worth … ," Aminatra searched for the word, " … saving?"

"Clarity of thought, Ami. Remember, clarity of thought. You need to work on it." The old lady smiled at her emerging protégé. "And yet I'm the one meandering with my story!"

Aminatra chuckled, realising with laughter there was hope for her in the Prison.

"So, you see," Maddy said, returning to her theory, "my husband and I became a threat to the establishment. The Wardyns don't want change. Why would they? Each society needs its enemies and every society has it walls – metaphorically speaking, of course – to keep its people in check. Ours are just a little more literal than most. Anyway, there I go again. The point is, we soon found ourselves framed for stealing from the farm and suddenly we'd lost all our friends; some even testified against us. I don't blame them now. They were just protecting their own families. But it was all lies; just like with you. And so here I am!"

"What about your husband, Alfbarl?" asked Aminatra.

"He died after a year in the Prison," commented Maddy without emotion. "Kept me alive for a year and then buggered off to a better place!"

Aminatra clasped Maddy's hand in sympathy. "And what about your boy? Have you heard news of him since you've been in the Prison?"

"I hear a little here and a little there," said Maddy. "I occasionally see him. What I have heard recently is he's a good soul." She looked to Aminatra.

"If he's a guard now … ," began Aminatra, before tailing off to calculate the facts. "I … You … Finbarl's your son! Does he know?"

"No," said Maddy. "I don't want to put Fin in danger. What could he do anyway? He's better off not knowing. As I've said, my dear, his life is better where he is."

CHAPTER 12

Twilight descended as Finbarl and the others entered Athenia's gates. Despite the camels' tiredness, with the shadows lengthening and the heat dissipating from the day, the guards urged the beasts to a fast trot for the last twenty minutes. When the flaming torches from the walls of Athenia finally came in sight, they cheered, but their anxiety only lifted once within the walls. Darkness gave the Ferrals an advantage.

"What the hell happened to you?" cried Gauret at Audlech, as he met them at the stables. "Have you done something to your hair?"

Hougat laughed aloud, while Strathbol cringed at the prospect of having to tackle the issue so soon.

Audlech looked around at his companions, drawing on the tension while he could. "Fell off my camel!"

Strathbol released his breath.

"Cronax! Looks like you fell off a few times!" remarked Gauret.

"His ankle got stuck in the stirrup," explained Finbarl. "Got dragged a few yards." He looked to see Audlech's reaction but got an impassive stare back.

"Well it's done wonders for your looks," joked Gauret, before turning to Finbarl. "And come to think of it, you don't look much better. Cut yourself shaving?"

"Had to tidy up after a Ferral supper!" responded Finbarl.

"Damn!" cursed Gauret. "How many?"

"Four," answered Strathbol. "Butt, Craznor, Boule and an unknown."

Gauret indicated the names meant nothing to him with a shake of his head. "Anyway, Vassel wants to see you all for a debrief on Alphege Scar."

Cronax, cursed Finbarl to himself, do our problems never end?

*

They found Officer Vassel addressing a small group of cadets in a corridor. Each junior guard stood to attention, listening attentively to every word the senior guard spoke. Finbarl remembered being their age. When the real work of a guard started, the youthful passion wore away.

As the cadets, intrigued by their arrival, started to glance towards them, Vassel halted his lecture, inspecting the motley crew with a discerning eye. "Dismissed!" he snapped at the cadets, who scampered away, looking over their shoulders at Finbarl and company. "I'm guessing you've some story to tell?"

"You could say that … some story, sir!" responded Hougat, trying not to laugh, making Strathbol more nervous.

"We'll go into the canteen," instructed Vassel. "No one's around and you look like you could do with a seat and a drink!"

"Thank you, sir," they all muttered, passing Vassel through the doors.

"So," began Vassel after they seated themselves around a table, he one side and they the other, "any problems at Bruuk's Point?"

Finbarl broke the uneasy silence. "No, sir! We safely deposited the prisoner. Only when travelling on to Alphege Scar did we have problems."

Vassel examined Audlech's bruised face intensely. "Go on."

"We'd been informed of Butt and Craznor's absence while at Bruuk's Point," began Finbarl. "We found their bodies and two others just south of Alphege Scar. The Ferrals had got them." Finbarl filled the Division leader in on all the gruesome detail.

"Makes you appreciate those walls," commented Vassel. "And what about Alphege Scar? What did you find?"

Finbarl felt his mouth go dry. "Nothing, sir."

"Really?" said Vassel. "That's strange. The prisoners who reported it were quite excited. We hoped for a substantial find based on what reward they asked for. Seemed to imply a storm unearthed it."

"Ah, yes, that would explain it!" Finbarl scrambled for a plausible explanation. "I suspect the wind has reburied it. May be worth another look, some time. You know how the land can shift when the wind brings the sand in from the desert."

"I suppose that's the case," mused Vassel. "Don't like to risk you boys more than I have to though."

"You don't have to worry about us!" said Hougat, bursting to life now their lie had worked its magic. "Always willing to take a risk for the good of Athenia."

Finbarl groaned inside as Vassel gave Hougat a questioning glance. "Then you'll probably die young!" proffered the officer. "Okay, Finbarl-apcula," he continued, "write up a report on the Ferral attack! Audlech-apcula, you stay behind? I've questions for you."

The others looked at each other anxiously. What would the Ferral-whack say to Vassel? Perhaps they should have killed him, thought Finbarl.

"That will be all, gentlemen!" said Vassel, reinforcing an instruction he thought already conveyed.

Outside, the three guards walked to a secluded spot behind the stables. "Do you think he'll grass us up?" blurted Strathbol, the colour draining from his face.

"Of course he will!" replied Hougat. "We always knew he would. The trick is us sticking to our own story. Three against one! They'll have to 'believe' us officially over that lump of camel dung!"

"Hougie's right," said Finbarl. "We have to remain cool and ensure our stories match!" He looked up to draw some inspiration. "It was as we left Bruuk's Point. A snake blocked our path, Audlech's camel got nervous and he fell off trying to control it. There's enough truth to give it credence."

The other two nodded.

"Right, I'm going down to the stream to wash this blood off," said Finbarl. "Remember, stay calm and keep to the story!"

*

Finbarl walked up Eden Valley, through the farmland and to the valley separating Bymore Tor and Bymore Hill. The river entered the farm there, with a gentle pool sitting parallel to faster flowing water, a spot popular with the guards for bathing. Finbarl undressed, easing himself into the sparkling, glacial water. As the cold hit him, he overcame an instinct to climb straight back out, and released a sigh of satisfaction as his weary body submerged up to his chin. He held his blood and dirt-stained clothes in a screwed-up ball and dunked them in the pool, while a foot searched the floor of the stream for a large, loose pebble. A suitable rock located, he pushed his clothes to the bottom, allowing all the air bubbles to escape, then weighed them down with the stone, leaving them to soak. He closed his eyes and leaned back against the boulder. His body ached after a day in the saddle, fighting with Audlech and digging the burial pit. Pushing himself up with his arms, he swung his legs round into the faster flow, feeling the surge push against his limbs. It felt good. When his feet found the bottom of the river, he edged himself forward so his whole body sat in the torrent, his back acting as another boulder, breaking the flow. He struggled to sit still, with the pressure pushing him forward, only feeling secure when he found a firm foothold.

A small pile of pumice stones lay to the side of the stream, left by numerous other bathers, and Finbarl stretched across to grab one. His footing gave way. He snatched a stone, fighting to find his hold again, pushing himself back up the stream. How he enjoyed these moments! It reminded him of his youth, when the cadets found a rare moment to play in the water.

The blood from the dead prisoners, dried hard on his skin in the heat of the scrubland, broke away at the edges. Finbarl scrubbed the pumice stone hard down his arm: a half-painful, half-pleasurable experience. With his body half numb, it felt more pleasurable today. Tossing the stone back to the bank, he rubbed his skin with a weed plucked from the current. It wasn't perfect, but it would do. He threw himself back to the pool and sank down to a contented recline, opening his mouth to drink in some water. The stars began to show above, and he watched the rich, blue sky ebb to black.

"Finbarl-apcula."

"Cronax!" Finbarl, panicked on hearing his name, struggled to upright himself, splashing wildly.

"Ha! Ha! Did I catch you unaware, guard?"

Squirting a stream of water from his mouth, Finbarl looked round to see a naked Torbald standing on the bank. "Cronax!" he repeated to himself. "Just a little, sir," he replied, wiping the hair from his eyes. He had never seen an overweight individual naked before, but then again, why would he have seen a bare Wardyn before?

"Mind if I join you?" said Torbald, climbing in, and Finbarl realised he wasn't asking for permission.

"A pleasure, Torbald-eltar," he replied, with equal lack of sincerity.

"Well, it's not that common I get to have a cosy chat with a hero in such secluded surroundings."

"Not sure 'hero' is the right word, and you never know who is going to turn up," said Finbarl.

Torbald scrutinised him and then, much to Finbarl's relief, broke out into laughter. "Don't give yourself so little credit, Finbarl-apcula! The only thing keeping the Ferrals from the gates is the brains and leadership of the Wardyns and the bravery of the guards. Those people sheltering in their homes don't know how lucky they are."

"Yes, Torbald-eltar!" he replied.

"Drop the 'eltar' and formalities, Finbarl. What do they say? 'Clothes maketh the man' and two naked men should have no barriers!" Torbald laughed at his own joke.

"That's what the Ferrals would say if they could talk," japed Finbarl.

"Oh, yes! Ha! Very good!" Torbald's laughter grew louder and he slapped Finbarl upon the shoulder. "I like you, Finbarl! You've what it takes to be a successful guard. You understand the complexities and pressures: what one sacrifices to make Athenia a success. Am I right?"

"Of course, you're the one with the brains!" This time Torbald neither smiled nor laughed. Finbarl realising the barrack-room banter inappropriate.

"And I expect you to use your brain to give me a sensible answer!" snapped Torbald

"Yes, sorry."

An expectant look remained on Torbald's face.

"Sorry, Torbald-eltar," said Finbarl to Torbald's satisfaction.

"I trust that wicked woman was successfully placed in the Prison?"

"Yes, T … ". Torbald waved his hand to dismiss the need for formalities. "Yes," continued Finbarl, "I had to hand out some discipline to stop her ranting but, like most of them, once they know it's inevitable, they clam up."

"You did well in court," said Torbald. "That's what I mean by sacrifice. Doing the unpleasant, to ensure Athenia is a safer place. And there's no doubt that woman was a threat to us all."

Finbarl thought about what Aminatra said. Was everything at her trial a lie? Was she a threat? "Absolutely," remarked Finbarl, despite his doubts. "The boy is better off in the orphanage."

"Well, it did you no harm!" laughed Torbald.

Finbarl now took offence, but showed nothing but a weak smile.

The Wardyn leaned across to the bank, dragging his discarded clothes towards himself. His hand rummaged blindly among the pile, clasped hold of something and withdrew a bottle of Kywaczek. "This will warm us up!"

Finbarl's eyes lit up at sight of the maize-based spirit. Kywaczek was a favourite with the guards but a rare commodity, usually only drunk at festivals. He gratefully accepted the bottle after Torbald took a few gulps. It burnt as it splashed down his throat, feeling more ferocious than normal with the icy water chilling his skin. As it hit his stomach, he felt its warming properties trickle through his body. Sitting in the cold, glacial water no longer felt so challenging.

"This is the reward for our loyalty and dedication to Athenia," commented Torbald, as he took back the bottle, taking another swig. "We can't afford for the common citizen to have plentiful access to it. Can you imagine the risks if those uneducated townsfolk got drunk when they wanted? Or if the guards had ready access! They would be starting fires, falling asleep at their posts, shooting each other! It wouldn't be long before the Ferrals ruled Athenia and became bloated from an almighty feast. You need to be of a certain standing and intelligence to have the responsibility to manage your Kywaczek. I reckon you could make it to such a place soon, Finbarl!" He handed the bottle back to Finbarl.

"I would like that," remarked Finbarl, the strength of the alcohol already making him tired and woozy. They continued to exchange and drink from the bottle until it was empty. Torbald tossed it away, smashing it against a rock. In his drunken state, Finbarl felt vaguely aware of the outrageous behaviour, but didn't seem to care.

Torbald, his eyes dreamy from the Kywaczek, tried to stand but, realising the stars were beginning to spin, lowered himself back into the water, instead crawling over Finbarl's legs and out into the flowing water. As he did so he belched loudly, turning in amusement to Finbarl, who giggled back. Once within the channel, he reclined on to his back and stuck out both arms to hold himself in place. His stomach rose like a boulder, water rushing around it, creating a little burst of white water. "What do you make of Hradbar?" asked Torbald.

"He's a fine man to have in a fight," declared Finbarl, fidgeting uncomfortably in response to the direction of conversation.

"Oh, that he is," concurred Torbald. "A fight he's probably started! But is he a man who can lead Athenia? After all, a Ferral is good in a fight but you wouldn't want one of them looking after the city!" For all the Kywaczek consumed, Torbald still possessed his wits.

Finbarl, conscious of things he shouldn't say, still felt compelled to say them. "I don't trust him!"

"Really! Why not?" Torbald seemed more intrigued than angry.

"I he … I hear stories," said Finbarl, fighting to string the sentence together. "He … he hunts Ferrals for sport!" Torbald went to speak but, emboldened by the drink, Finbarl raised a finger to stop him. "And I believe he's the father of Aminatra's son!"

"Aminatra? Who is Aminatra?"

Finbarl pulled a confused face. "The girl at the trial. You know … the girl at the trial!"

"Oh, yes," said Torbald. "Aminatra. I think you've a soft spot for her."

Finbarl shook his head with exaggerated, drunken denial, giggling like a teenager.

"It's nothing to be ashamed of. She's a pretty thing. I hope you didn't find it too hard putting her in the Prison."

Finbarl sat still, his face a picture of sadness. He shook his head again. "No … no."

"Excellent!" exclaimed Torbald, heaving himself into an upright position. "Because we can't be having future officers getting attached to prisoners." He stood, the water battering his lower thighs.

Finbarl continued shaking his head in affirmation.

"I'll leave you to your bath now, Finbarl-apcula. You take care of yourself!"

As Torbald climbed out, picked up his clothes and walked away, Finbarl oppressed his own desire to leave the freezing water. Goosebumps lined his arm, while his bladder cried out to be relieved. He hung on, desperate for Torbald to be out of sight. The Kywaczek blurred his thinking, but he knew an interrogation when he saw one.

With Torbald around the corner into Eden Valley, Finbarl plucked his clothes from the bottom of the pool, cursed the blood and other stains still lingering, and dragged himself onto the bank. He lay on the grass, waiting to get the energy and willpower to dress, then, in a moment of reflection, exhaled a loud curse, "Cronax!"

*

A headache welcomed Finbarl in the morning. It was an apt reminder of the downside to alcohol and, added to his craving for Jumblar, he awoke in a foul mood. He had no recollection of how he returned to the barracks. A vague memory of stumbling over the farm tracks, falling into the edge of the wheat field and carefully trying to straighten the broken stems lingered, but how he entered Athenia remained a mystery. He must have spoken to someone to gain entry, meaning someone witnessed him drunk.

All around other guards rose, climbing out of their beds. The noise seemed excessive, and Finbarl sat on the edge of his bed, head buried in his hands, the summons bell still ringing inside.

"Tough night?"

Finbarl slowly lifted his head to see a sprightly looking Gauret. "You could say," he mumbled.

"I thought you would've hit the sack early after being out in the Prison all day."

"Well something came up!" snapped Finbarl.

"I would say so," continued Gauret. "You made a right racket when you got to the barracks last night. You snored like a Ferral on heat! Anyone might have thought you were drunk."

Finbarl gave him a withering glance. "If you must know, a Wardyn shared some Kywaczek with me!"

"Cronax!" exclaimed Gauret, sitting down next to Finbarl. "Which one?"

"Torbald. For some reason he joined me bathing in the stream."

"What? Scrubbed your back for you?"

"Ha, bloody, ha!" Finbarl ruffled his hair and started slapping his own face to bring some life to his body. "He wanted to talk. Overall, he was friendly and relaxed. My big concern, apart from a killer headache, is how relaxed and talkative I was."

"Cronax!" said Gauret. "What did you say?"

"Something about not trusting his brother."

"Oh, that's all right," reassured Gauret. "You'll be in Torbald's good books."

"I don't know," sighed Finbarl. "It's one thing for a brother to slag off his own sibling but they can get a little prickly if someone else does it."

"Where Torbald and Hradbar are concerned, I wouldn't worry about it. They hate each other so much they'd probably be willing to renounce their brotherly bonds for the chance to stab each other in the back."

"I may also have indicated I had feelings for Aminatra," Finbarl said, blushing at the confession. "The prisoner I helped convict and take into the Prison."

"Ah," responded Gauret. "That probably wasn't so sensible!"

Finbarl pulled his fingers down his face. "Well, I can't quite remember exactly what I said, but Torbald seemed to be testing me."

"And do you?

"Do I what?"

"Have feelings for her?"

Finbarl wasn't about to spill his true feelings to anyone. "I feel sorry for her and the boy, that's all."

"That may be enough to put a black mark against your name," suggested Gauret.

"Nonsense!" replied Finbarl. "We departed on good terms and he as drunk as me. Probably can't remember much either."

"Let's hope so," said Gauret, as he stood. "Anyway, you can't sit here all day feeling sorry for yourself. The last thing you need now is to miss your Jumblar fix!"

Finbarl looked up at his colleague and nodded solemnly.

CHAPTER 13

The doors of the barracks slammed shut and Hougat-apcula, his face red from a short sprint, stood catching his breath. Finbarl looked up from darning a short tear in a sleeve of his thawb.

"We've got a mission," called out Hougat to the room. "Vassel-apculex wants the following outside now!" He shouted out the first upon his list, prompting a smart exit from those named. "Hadyn-apcula! Finbarl-apcula! Strathbol-apcula!"

Finbarl lifted his sleeve and darning thread to his mouth and bit through the thread. He threw the needle and loose thread onto his bed and stood. Following a quick, testing tug on his repairs, he marched out as Hougat continued with his list.

Sixteen guards aligned themselves to attention outside the barracks. Officer Vassel stood before them. "It's your lucky day, boys!" he announced. "I'm leading you out to Alphege Scar. We're going to be treasure hunting and, if you're lucky, you may get to kill the odd Ferral!" The guards cheered in unison. "Now," continued Vassel, quietening the men down with his hands, "go get a day's provisions, your gear for a salvage dig and your camels!"

Finbarl looked around, catching Strathbol's eye. They exchanged a secretive, unspoken acknowledgement their lie risked exposure. Gauret made up one of the sixteen, which helped, but so too did Audlech. Cronax! cursed Finbarl silently. He could do without that, but at least with Vassel in command, discipline would be in check. Just make sure you don't find yourself alone with Audlech, Finbarl told himself, then made an empty prayer they either found no wreckage or the sand had reclaimed it.

After half an hour, lined up on their camels in a disciplined column, with Vassel at the front and the guards two-by-two behind, they were ready to depart. Audlech sat to the fore, thankfully, while Finbarl found himself next to Strathbol at the rear.

"Do you think we'll find anything?" Strathbol leant across and whispered, as they eased their camels forward.

"We find what we find," Finbarl responded. "But we stick to our story!"

*

The journey across the featureless terrain was uneventful, and, after a few hours, they found themselves at the edge of Alphege Scar. To Finbarl's relief a mess of foliage and rocky outcrops obscured the feature, with nothing obvious protruding.

The scar cut into the flat, open ground dramatically, as though furrowed by a giant plough. While its depths offered some shade, it left anyone within exposed to, and oblivious of, encroaching Ferrals. Vassel dispatched eight guards to fan out around the upper edge, providing protection above, and four more followed the officer into the Scar, while four remained protecting the accessible end. To Finbarl's relief, his orders left him guarding the entrance. He watched as Vassel tentatively led his small group down, mindful of the possibility of ambush. Yet another excellent reason not to have visited the other week, thought Finbarl. Why was it okay for four tired men to do the job of sixteen?

After dismounting, tying his camel reins to a nearby shrub and rubbing his sore backside, Finbarl scanned the horizon, the view mercifully devoid of human activity. He settled down in a discreet spot, where anything approaching crossed his line of sight.

"Finbarl-apcula!"

Finbarl instantly recognised the shout as Vassel's.

"Finbarl-apcula! Get your Ferral-arse down here!"

Finbarl scrambled to his feet and ran down into the Scar, vaulting a wind-polished boulder and brushing through the numerous thorn bushes grabbing at his clothes. Vassel stood about fifty yards along with hands on his hips.

"How in the name of Cronax did you miss this?" demanded Vassel, indicting a large tubular, metal object protruding from the vertical edge of the scar. It was a minor collapse of the gulley's side, exposing part of the artefact.

Finbarl racked his brain for a plausible answer. "The sun was low in the sky by the time we rode through, so the light was poorer down here."

Vassel gave Finbarl a suspicious look. "Well, you've just earned the right to lead the excavation team. Go get your spade!"

*

The sandy, crumbly ground made the digging relatively easy, but the more they cleared away, the more obvious it became the object was larger and more sophisticated than initially thought. With the top layer of earth removed, a curved surfaced became exposed, stretching nearly ten yards in length. Dotted along it were protruding pipes, some broken but others leading back into the ground connecting to who knew what. A team of four dug from each corner, with Vassel, returned to the higher ground, monitoring progress while also keeping watch for Ferrals.

"What do you think it is?" asked one of the diggers to no one in particular.

"No idea," replied Finbarl. His other digging companions shrugged their ignorance.

"Reminds me of a boiler," came a voice from above. The diggers looked up to see Vassel watching them. "But on a scale I've never seen before. If it's all in as good condition as what we've unsurfaced already, it could be one of the most important finds ever!" Finbarl and the others stopped digging, taking in the gravity of Vassel's analysis.

"But it'll be worth nothing if you don't finish digging it out!" barked Vassel. "So, get on with it!" He allowed himself a little smile as he turned back to check their surroundings. Finds like this usually resulted in a special celebration for Athenia.

As Finbarl pushed his spade deep into the ground, he heard a distant commotion. He signalled for the others to stop digging, listening intently. Above, Vassel held his rifle to the ready, crouching on one knee, his eyes scanning the direction of the noise.

"What can you see, sir?" called up Finbarl.

"Not sure from here," responded Vassel, craning his neck for a better view. "But something's up! Grab your guns and make your way up to provide support! Not you, Yates! Give me your hand and I'll pull you up. I want you to pass the message down the line, get everyone else together and gradually bring them round in a sweeping movement from there." Vassel pointed north. "If it turns out to be Ferrals, I want them caught in a pincer movement. This could turn out to be a good day … if we're lucky!"

Yates disappeared over the edge of the scar, as Finbarl and the others threw their spades to the floor and, grabbing their guns, dashed through the obstacle course along the scar's bottom. As they neared the slope leading to the surface, they slowed to walking pace, hunching down and edging themselves out, guns at the ready.

"You all right?" asked Gauret, leaning on his rifle.

"What in … ," began Finbarl. "We … we thought you were under attack!" He stood to full height.

Gauret smiled broadly. "So did we for a moment, but it turns out our visitors don't want to eat us." He indicated over his shoulder with a nod of his head, before adding, "Well I hope not!"

About two hundred yards in the distance, ambling in their direction, were a group of prisoners. Finbarl let out a deep breath, feeling the tension release.

"What the hell do you think you're doing?" Vassel's face boiled with anger. "I want you alert and ready for trouble, not chatting like you're waiting for Jumblar!"

Finbarl and Gauret exchanged amused glances before splitting to find some cover. Vassel stood in the open, facing the approaching figures, his hands on his hips. With the group within thirty yards, the officer sauntered forward. "What are you doing here?" he demanded.

After a moment's hesitation, a voice said, "We were on our way to the watering hole at Limbole. Someone saw a camel, so we came to investigate."

Vassel scratched his chin. "Is this all of you?" He looked along the line of eight shabby prisoners, who all nodded in response. "Gauret-apcula!"

The guard came running forward. "Yes, sir?"

"Take the six men to dig out the object," ordered Vassel. "The two women can earn their keep by cooking us some stew. No reason why we should have to do hard labour when we've prisoners to hand."

The group of prisoners looked between each other in disbelief.

"Come on!" demanded Vassel. "There'll be food in it for you too!" This stimulated the male prisoners to an excited chatter as they threw their bags to the ground and followed Gauret, leaving the two women alone with Vassel. "Finbarl-apcula!" yelled Vassel. "Your digging days are over. You can show these women where the cooking utensils and food are and supervise them!"

Finbarl reluctantly stepped forward. He recognised the women from his vantage point: Aminatra and the old woman. Of all the prisoners to meet, why Aminatra?

"Follow me," snapped Finbarl, eager to prove with his manner the details teased out by Torbald the night before meant nothing. "Move it!" He led them to where the camels rested, pointing to a pile of bags. "Pans in the green bag; food in the brown one. Water is hanging on the tree. You're cooking for seventeen plus yourselves. Guards eat first: you get what's left over. So, don't get your hopes too high!" He spoke loudly to emphasise his position as a conscientious and loyal guard, but no one else heard. "And make sure you only use dry wood and scrub for the fire! We don't want smoke inviting the Ferrals to dinner, because there'll only be one thing on the menu, and it won't be those with guns!"

"Ferral-whack!" mumbled Aminatra, as she bent to pick up the utensil bag.

"What did you say?" demanded Finbarl.

"Nothing," Aminatra replied.

"You called me a Ferral-whack!" Finbarl grabbed Aminatra's arm, yanking her up.

"Ouch!" she cried. "You're hurting me."

"If you want to eat, you had better apologise!"

"Go screw a camel!" retorted Aminatra.

Finbarl released her arm, swinging the back of his hand violently across her face. Aminatra fell backwards in pain, as Finbarl stepped forward to land another blow.

"Stop it!" Maddy, watching nervously, stepped forward to put herself between them, her hand resting upon Finbarl's chest.

Finbarl's rage ran free. He lifted his rifle and planted the butt into the old woman's midriff. "How dare you!" he shouted. "You piece of filth! Coming between a guard and his duty. You'll pay for that!" Finbarl lifted his rifle again, ready to bring it down upon Maddy's head.

"Please stop! You don't know what you're doing," cried Aminatra, as she scrambled to her feet.

Finbarl froze, his gun in mid-motion, a foot from striking the old woman. Something in the tone of Aminatra's desperate plea made him stop. Maddy, still bent double, looked up at Finbarl awaiting a response. "What does that mean?" Finbarl challenged, the rifle now relaxed in his grip.

"She's … ," Aminatra looked to Maddy, uncertain whether to continue. The old lady only stared back silently; her face braced for her punishment. "You would regret it," added Aminatra. "You would!"

"You don't tell me what to do!" growled Finbarl, amazed at the temerity of the prisoner. He raised the gun again, ready to strike.

"Cronax! She's your mother!" cried Aminatra, dashing over to stand before Maddy.

Finbarl reeled back, his gun somehow suddenly heavy. "You're lying!" he hissed. "Why would you say such a thing? My mo … ". The anger, still to dissipate, fought to release itself. Yet he couldn't bring himself to strike her. His arm and rifle dropped limply to his side.

"Your mother," confirmed Aminatra softly. "It's the truth! Look at her face. Those hazel eyes are yours. The resemblance! Finbarl, ask her! Maddy, say something!"

"It's true," said Maddy softly.

Finbarl shook his head in bewilderment. It was all lies – he was sure – and yet the words paralysed him. This pitiful woman cowering in front of him in no way mirrored the image forged of his mother: the perfect memory formed in her absence from fantasy and longing. He opened his mouth to admonish and curse, but nothing came out. The old lady watched him intently, her eyes full of wishful hope. Finbarl's own eyes darted around frantically, as his mind searched for clarity. They locked on those of the old woman for an instant. He turned away, as though blinded by a flash of recognition. Aminatra remained silent, conscious further words would make no difference, but exhaled a gasp as Finbarl marched away.

"Let him go!" urged Maddy, as she slowly climbed to her feet. "He's just seen a ghost, and not everyone can cope with that."

"But what if we can't convince him?" asked Aminatra, providing her arm for Maddy to pull herself up on. "What will he do to us?"

"Just give him time."

*

Finbarl realised he didn't know where to head. He was simply getting away; far away from those manipulative prisoners. Only the sound of Vassel barking orders made him reconsider his direction of travel. The next worst place to be right now was under the scrutiny of his commanding officer. He wanted to be somewhere nobody disturbed or questioned him. The stench of the camels caught his attention. They would provide suitable companionship.

There was something cathartic about sharing his woes with a beast of burden. The camel seemed to be enjoying it too, as Finbarl rubbed its neck. "It's ridiculous," he confided to his humped friend. "Why wouldn't they have told me? Someone would've let me know. Guards don't come from corrupted genes." The camel chewed contentedly, while Finbarl continued his outpouring. "And where's my father? You can't trust some people. Not like you, old girl." The doughy eye of the beast seemed to appreciate the compliment as it spared Finbarl a glance. "So, we share the same eye colour – your eyes don't look so different either and we're not related."

"Finbarl-apcula!"

"Cronax!" swore Finbarl.

It was Vassel. "Where are you? Why aren't you doing what you were ordered?"

"I'm here," answered Finbarl. He patted the camel and whispered towards its ear, "I may need you to lie for me."

"So?" demanded Vassel, as Finbarl walked over.

"There was something upsetting the camels. I went to see what it was."

Vassel looked across to the serene herd and back at Finbarl. "Hmm, they seem fine now, so get back to what you were tasked with doing!"

"Yes, sir," snapped Finbarl, reluctantly making his way back towards Maddy and Aminatra. To his horror, Vassel followed. He hoped to get away from his watchful gaze and loiter at a good distance from the women.

"Why isn't the fire going?" Vassel shouted at the women. "You should have it alight by now! You see what happens when you neglect your duties, Finbarl-apcula?"

Words failed Finbarl.

"It's my fault, sir," said Maddy. "I had an attack of something in the stomach and the guard here was helping me recover."

"Nurse and vet? You have been busy!" said Vassel, admonishing Finbarl with another accusatory look. "Go and supervise the digging team! I'll keep an eye on these two. I'm old enough not to have my head turned by a pretty face."

Finbarl stood motionless looking at Maddy.

"Something the matter, guard?" Vassel pressed.

A strange sense of familiarity flitted in Finbarl's mind, causing a wave of unexplainable emotions to wash through his body. "I ... I ... no, sir."

"Good, so bugger off and let these prisoners get on with their cooking. I, for one, am hungry!"

"Yes, sir." Finbarl walked away with a sense of relief, but found himself turning for another look at the old woman. Now dismissed, he felt an urge to ask more questions, to expose her as a charlatan.

The next hour passed painfully slowly for Finbarl. He sat on the lip of the scar watching the prisoners scrape around the edges of the object. While other guards bullied and cajoled the convicts to work harder, Finbarl sat quietly, thinking to himself.

The structure of his existence no longer felt stable. Life should not be complicated. The good and honourable battled to save civilisation; the depraved and dishonest fought to undermine it. Within the walls of Athenia resided the former; beyond, the latter. If what the old woman said was true, then he'd built his entire life on a lie: those within the walls lacked honour. That is why it can't be true, Finbarl reasoned to himself. A wave of anger flushed his cheeks. How could people sink so low, attacking his greatest vulnerability? He tried to think of his mother, to conjure up the face created as a guiding companion throughout his youth. But every time Finbarl closed his eyes, all he saw was the cringing prisoner, claiming to be his mother. He tried to do the same for his father, but now only Vassel's or the Governor's faces formed on his mind's canvas. Each time Finbarl pushed the possibility of it being true from his mind, another combative thought surfaced.

What if she hadn't died? What moments had he lost from his childhood? Dancing at festivals, birthday parties, just holding hands in the street. It stung at his core. An anger built. He felt cheated and robbed. All irrelevant because she died! Yes, concluded Finbarl, at the end of another internal battle, she died.

A cry went out that the food was ready, followed by the clanging of dropped spades and a rush of famished guards to the feeding station. Vassel looked to the sky in despair, but queued eagerly for his own serving.

*

Maddy handed Finbarl a bowl of stew, her hand brushing his. It was agonising. Part of him disgusted, the other the small, lost child who wanted his mother. The food held no interest, even though his stomach gurgled in anticipation. He sat down, staring lost into the rich, brown sludge steaming in his bowl. Vassel, slurping his food on the other side of the circle, watched everything. Finbarl casually turned to see Maddy distributing the final few helpings of the stew, her eyes looking straight at him. He turned away and blushed.

"Not hungry?" Gauret eagerly eyed Finbarl's full bowl, his own scraped clean.

"No," answered Finbarl vacantly. Before Gauret made an offer to assist in eating his portion, Finbarl rose to his feet and slouched away, bowl in hand, whispered mumbles slipping from his mouth.

The nausea in Finbarl's stomach added to the spinning thoughts in his mind. It felt like Jumblar's vengeance, but with little hope of relief. The feelings were hard to identify. anger, shock, fear, confusion or even realisation? Sight of the sorry-looking prisoners, all sitting patiently, hoping for a meagre share of the food, broke Finbarl's maudlin thoughts. He loathed them for what they represented, but couldn't help feeling some sympathy. They worked on the boiler under the oppressive sun as hard as any guard. More unfamiliar thoughts surfaced. He noticed their faces, the scars, the hungry eyes, the hopeless smiles pleading for compassion: he saw them as someone's daughter, son, brother, sister, father or mother. He saw their humanity.

"Johansson!" Finbarl beckoned to the prisoner. The request came out instinctively. "There's a problem with one of the camels. I want your help with it."

Johansson nervously climbed to his feet, eyed by his fellow prisoners. "I don't know-ing about camels."

"I don't want your opinion," responded Finbarl. "Just your help."

Johansson obediently followed Finbarl in the direction of the tied-up camels, his eyes watching the bowl of stew the guard casually carried. The camels sniffed at the food as Finbarl passed in front, as though conscious it was one of their own in the bowl. Their torsos blocked the other guards and prisoners from sight and Finbarl handed the bowl to the surprised Johansson. "Enjoy it!" Finbarl instructed, as the prisoner wolfed down his unexpected meal. "You'll make yourself sick."

Johansson looked up and just smiled. It seemed a small price to pay to enjoy such a feast.

"I want you to do something for me," said Finbarl, his tone still guard to prisoner. Johansson's eyes watched him carefully. "I want you to get a message to the prisoner called Maddy."

Johansson's curiosity and confusion manifested itself through raised eyebrows but his determination to fill his mouth with as much food as possible remained unabated.

"You know Maddy?" asked Finbarl.

The prisoner nodded.

"I can trust you to give her, and no one else, a message?"

This time Johansson paused before nodding.

Finbarl weighed up the reaction, wondering whether he had asked the right prisoner. "Good," he eventually said. "Tell her I want to speak to her alone." The words out, Finbarl felt his face flush. He spoke with fuelled emotion, not clear thought. Each decision committed him deeper and deeper into he knew not what. "I can't be seen talking directly to her now," he explained, as much for himself as Johansson. "But I want you to ask her if she'll meet me at a certain time and place."

Johansson swallowed a mouthful of stew and controlled a gentle burp, thumping his chest at the inevitable indigestion his bolting technique caused. Only an inane smile remained, awaiting Finbarl's next utterance.

"Do you understand what I'm asking you to do?" pressed Finbarl. The absurd face continued looking back at him without answer. "I ... ," began Finbarl, before an almighty belch erupted from Johansson. "Cronax! I told you not to eat too fast."

"Like-ed food," said Johansson.

"Good," sighed Finbarl. "Now you have to do something for me."

"I give-ed Maddy message."

"Yes!" exclaimed Finbarl, relieved he hadn't wasted his time. "Right, you tell Maddy I'll come to the dry river channel at the first major bend outside of Athenia an hour after sunset in two days' time. I'll be on my own."

"Why, sir?"

"Sorry, what do you mean 'why'?"

"Why do-ing you need-ly meet-ed with Maddy?" asked Johansson, his tongue searching for trapped morsels of meat between his teeth. "No one leaving-ly Athenia at night. Well, not unless-ing they're mad or a prisoner."

"What?" queried Finbarl, trying to fathom out his confidant's question. "Why doing ... Oh, why do I need to meet with Maddy?" It was the question; one without an answer. Like a grain of sand on the wind, he moved forward without knowing where he might end. Speaking with the old woman again, he reasoned, would stop his torment. "None of your business," he answered but without ferocity. "Repeat the message to me ... please."

Johansson looked uncomfortable at the prospect but intrigued by the courtesy. No guard ever said 'please'! "Of course-ed I will, sir. First bend-ing on the river, an hour after sunset."

"First major bend beyond Athenia. In two days' time," reiterated Finbarl, keen to ensure Johansson remembered correctly.

"That's what I said-ed," stated Johansson.

"Yes, good," said Finbarl, unconvinced the message would get through in the form intended. He sighed and took back the cleaned-out bowl. "Now I'll shout at you to make it look like I'm telling you off."

Johansson looked hurt.

"So no one works out what we're up to!" hissed Finbarl, trying to explain the intricacies of his plan.

The prisoner nodded slowly, signalling acknowledgement but indicating confusion.

"Now get back to work!" yelled Finbarl, gesticulating with a finger at Johansson's face.

Johansson stood still, not sure if the anger was real or not.

"Move!" Finbarl grabbed him by the shoulders, twisted him in the opposite direction and shoved him away. "Thanks," he whispered.

*

They finally excavated the boiler after another two hours, the protruding pipes detached and collected. With ropes fed beneath and secured, it became clear the prisoners alone did not possess the strength to pull it up and over the lip of the scar. Vassel conscripted several further guards to the work gang. Finbarl found himself at the front of one of the ropes, straining with every sinew to make the object move; the activity providing some distraction from his frenzied thoughts.

"You two!" yelled Vassel towards a couple of guards still pacing the perimeter, keeping watch for Ferrals. "Get down here and push the boiler to get it moving!"

They hesitated, scanning the horizon. But an order was an order.

"Right," continued Vassel, when everyone was in position and he at the end of one rope, "on my command we all push and pull as one! One, two, three, now!"

A mass of groaning and cursing erupted from the group as they laboured in the sun. The boiler rocked forward and then back to its original position.

"Again!" shouted Vassel. "One, two, three, pull!" This time the boiler rocked forward and then slid upward on the sand. "Keep going! It's moving! Heave!"

It edged further up as the men beneath scrambled to get a firm foothold to push. Climbing into the hole where the boiler once rested, they crouched in its shadow, hands shoving upwards on its curved surface, their safety in the hands of those holding the rope.

"Come on! Again!" cried Vassel. Another mighty effort got the boiler balanced delicately on the rim. Any relaxing in rope tension risked bringing the mass crashing back down to the depth of the scar; one more pull would bring it clear on the surface. "On three! One, two, three, pull!" The huge cylinder rested safely on top. "Left rope – keep pulling!" demanded Vassel. "When we've the long side parallel to the edge, we can roll it away." A few frustrated expletives rumbled down the line of those holding the left rope, but they kept up the strain and, once a few of the men from the other rope ran to the back of the cylinder and started pushing, it moved easily over the loose surface.

"Stop!" ordered Vassel, everyone dropping to the floor exhausted. "Well done! Well done all!" The triumphant officer collapsed on to his back.

It wasn't long, however, before everybody realised lying flat on the baking ground provided little relief. Strathbol collected water bottles and passed them around to grateful recipients, even offering to the prisoners without a thought, their efforts considered worthy of reward.

Finbarl noticed Johansson and Maddy sitting together and wondered if his message had been conveyed. Maddy's face gave no sign, just a look of exhaustion. Finbarl looked for Aminatra. She sat alone, examining her blistered hands. For all the grief she directed his way, he still felt drawn to her: a fascination he didn't quite understand.

"That's enough lazing!" Vassel climbed to his feet, rousing others to follow his example. "I want to get this cylinder onto our wagon as soon as possible. Gauret-apcula! Bring the wagon as close as we can get it but unhitch the camels before. I don't want them freaked. They're going to be grumpy enough pulling the darn thing back to Athenia!"

The guards chuckled in appreciation, knowing their camels' temperaments.

The wagon, a simple contraption with four large wooden wheels reinforced by lead strips and a simplistic suspension of underpinned metal springs, sat awaiting its load. Its previous cargo of food and supplies had been removed and distributed amongst the guards' camels for the return journey. Whether the wagon took a load this size remained questionable. Vassel appeared confident as he walked around, contemplating the best way to get the thing on it. "We'll take the rear wheels off," he declared. "Make it into a natural ramp and roll the cylinder on. We then raise the wagon with the jacks and reattach the wheels."

The wheels slipped off easily and two men either side slowly lowered the rear to the ground. Tired muscles provided the challenge, as they again tried to move the cylinder. Finbarl found himself behind the mass, ready to push, on Vassel's command. A few camels stood to the side curiously watching the shenanigans.

"Last piece of hard work today and then we're homeward bound!" declared Vassel. "It has to be central in the wagon or it's going to cause problems. Now, are we all ready?"

It took a mere ten minutes to position the cylinder on the ramp and edge it into the centre. Bound securely with rope, they raised the creaking frame with jacks before refitting the wheels. Vassel held his breath as it rested, motionless, whispering a prayer it didn't collapse under the weight. Finally, they attached the three camels to the front of the wagon and, despite their protestations, the load inched forward.

"Mount up, boys!" cried Vassel. "We're going home!"

A chorus of whoops rang out from the guards as they dashed for their own beasts. The prisoners, ignored and forgotten, stood watching. Only Finbarl spared a thought, glancing back as the train pulled away to the east and home towards Athenia.

CHAPTER 14

"Excellent!" Governor Elbar circled the cylinder, rubbing his hands as it glinted in the morning light at the stables. All the Wardyns were present, wallowing in their moment of glory at the discovery. "This will mean lots more bullets, gentlemen!" The Governor addressed the large group of guards.

"Could it not still be used as a boiler?" opined Torbald, rapping the surface with a knuckle, producing a deep, resonating clang. "Pity the pipes were hacked off, but I for one would like some regular hot water."

"As would we all," replied the Governor, hiding his irritation at this somewhat public challenge. "But hot water is not much use if we can't defend ourselves against the Ferrals! Our prime objective must always be to defend civilisation. You find me ten other boilers like this and then we can spoil ourselves. With this metal we can make guns as well as bullets."

"If there's one thing the Ferrals are good at," said Hradbar, sensing an opportunity to side with his father against Torbald, "it's breeding. For every one of them we shoot, they seem to produce two more. The only way we're going to wipe them out is to ensure we can kill them faster than they can reproduce, and, for that, we need more guns and bullets."

"What a pity!" declared Torbald. "I was looking forward to a hot bath." He winked at the mass of guards, receiving a light ripple of laughter in response.

Governor Elbar, smiling for the benefit of appearances, held his hands up for silence. "This is a big day for Athenia. I commend you all for what you've done in retrieving this treasure and securing civilisation's future. I will be making a public announcement tomorrow to bring the momentous news to the citizens and will, of course, be reminding them of how you've all risked your lives to protect their liberty."

A loud cheer went up for the Governor, Finbarl as loud as anyone. However, he had changed. He listened as before, but the words now sounded hollow.

The Governor's public announcement, scheduled for tomorrow, proved a stroke of luck. With celebrations planned to follow, the opportunity to sneak away unnoticed fell into Finbarl's lap. All the noise and alcohol would keep the minds of the sentries elsewhere. He knew from experience, while the town partied, guards succumbed to the temptation of Kywaczek.

"How many new guns do you think that will make?" asked Strathbol, his usual enthusiasm contrasting sharply with Finbarl's mood.

Finbarl shrugged. "Don't know. I suspect bullets will be the priority. After all, a gun's no good without bullets."

Gauret joined them. "I'm not helping them move it to Saul. I can hardly move myself after yesterday's fun."

"You're getting old," joked Strathbol.

"It's because I worked harder than you!" parried Gauret. "I had to pull twice as hard because you weren't pulling at all."

"Didn't want to chafe my hands!"

Gauret laughed, slapping Strathbol on the back. Finbarl remained sombrely unaffected. "What's the matter with you?" asked Gauret. "Missing your woman?"

Finbarl looked at Gauret in alarm, before realising he referred to Aminatra rather than the woman claiming to be his mother. "Oh, yes. Missing my Prison trash." He smiled weakly. A part of him wanted to tell Gauret and Strathbol what had happened, but he knew guards weren't the people to share problems with. "No, like you, tired and sore after yesterday. Relieved nothing further was said about not finding it first time round."

"Amazing what a bit of metal can do to refocus minds," said Gauret. "But I'm with Torbald. I could do with a regular hot bath!"

"You don't really think the Wardyns would let us benefit from it even if they agreed to use it as a boiler?" The words were out before Finbarl could stop himself.

"What do you mean?" Strathbol turned to him.

"Nothing!" said Finbarl, shocked at himself for uttering such unworthy words. "Ignore me. It's a moot point anyway. No one is getting any hot water."

"You'll be getting in some if you keep speaking your mind like that!" Gauret's accompanying grin put Finbarl at ease, but he appreciated the serious point the smile covered.

"You need your Jumblar," suggested Strathbol to Finbarl.

"I think you're right," replied Finbarl, eager to move on from the discussion. "It's been burning a hole in my pocket since I picked it up this morning!"

"You've survived this long? I always take mine straighta-way," said Strathbol. "I like to get charged as early as possible. Sets me up for the entire day."

The young, sanctimonious guard was beginning to annoy Finbarl, but he meant no harm. Maybe a dose of Jumblar would help straighten things out.

*

The Moralistas hurried across town, passing on news of Governor Elbar's upcoming speech, with promises of a special announcement. Finbarl took his Jumblar but still found himself unsettled and tetchy. For his part in bringing the artefact back, he enjoyed a rare afternoon off. Others from the troop tried to catch up on sleep but, for the restless Finbarl, the barracks felt unsuited to his mood. He wanted the secret rendezvous with the old lady over, his life back to normal, but time refused to humour him, progressing at a torturously slow pace.

Wandering to the northern reaches of Athenia, up the slopes of Cragor Hill, Finbarl stood outside a typical ramshackle house. "Is Mistress Komov-morex in?" he enquired.

A woman, perhaps a few years older than he, stood nervously in the doorway, assessing the surprise visitor. "She is but she's not well." The woman's eyes scanned down Finbarl's green guard's thawb.

"Are you her daughter? I'm a former pupil of hers," explained Finbarl. "I just want to ask her some questions about the old days."

The woman still didn't appear entirely comfortable, but nodded her head slowly, opening the door wider. "She likes talking about the old days."

Finbarl stooped through the low doorframe. "Thank you. I have fond memories of your mother reading books to me and teaching me to read and write."

"She misses her books. Even if we'd some to read, her eyesight is too poor now." The woman led Finbarl into a second room, stinking of stale air. A woman, in her early fifties, lay asleep upon a lumpy straw mattress. "Mother! You've a visitor."

"It's Finbarl, Mistress Komov-morex." Finbarl bent down to his knees, as the old lady slowly opened her eyes. "Do you remember me?"

She smiled. "I remember all the children I taught. How's my little Finbarl?"

"I'm well. I thrive in the guard. I'm Finbarl-apcula now."

"Good," said the old woman, reaching out a shaking hand.

Finbarl held it in his, feeling the bone protrude through a wasting body.

"I sleep well knowing people like you are keeping the Ferrals at bay: keeping my soul safe."

Finbarl nodded, recalling the many stories Mistress Komov told a receptive class all those years ago, of the Ferral danger and the fate of those who betrayed Athenia. "How are you?" he asked, conscious it sounded a cruel question, given what was plain for all to see but aware of the respectful thing to do.

"I'm as an old woman should be; content with what I have given, demanding no more from life."

"You're as I remember you," said Finbarl, fulfilling his part of the pre-ambling etiquette. "Wise and kind. A good Moralista."

"I'll leave you to it," said the forgotten daughter. "I have work to do."

"She's a good daughter," commented the old woman once alone. "I had ten good children, though only three survive to this day. Sushen's had her own hardships to suffer. Her husband is dead a full year now. She's in need of a good new husband to start a family." A suggestive glint brought her tired eyes to life.

On many occasion, Finbarl thought his time was due to be married, but not to his old teacher's daughter. He quickly changed the subject. "I wanted to ask you about my parents."

The old lady closed her eyes, as though to access buried memories. "I remember your father, Alfbarl. A great man. And your mother, Madeleine. They were a wonderful husband and wife. A good marriage is so important. That's what I'm always telling Sushen."

Finbarl smiled awkwardly. "What do you know of their deaths?"

"You talk to a dying woman about death!" Her eyes opened again, conveying the stern discipline Finbarl remembered from her classes.

"I'm sorry, Komov-morex. I wouldn't ask if it wasn't important."

"I may remember all those I taught, but to remember how everyone died is too much to ask in this world."

"But they did die?" pressed Finbarl.

"You were always an impertinent little one, Finbarl-apcula." The effort to chide her former pupil caused the old lady to pause for breath. Finbarl waited patiently, still as fearful of the teacher's wrath all these years later. "You've been told what happened to your parents," continued Mistress Komov. "Each Orpho has a terrible loss to bear but each is so fortunate to find love and nurture under the care of the Wardyns."

It was a line told to Finbarl a hundred times before, and he nodded gratefully at his old teacher. He climbed to his feet. "I must be going," he said, much to the obvious disappointment of his host.

"Stay and read to me!" she implored.

"I have nothing to read. Do you?"

She shook her head, disappointed once more. "Then stay and talk some more. Not of death, but of life."

"I can't," said Finbarl, shifting awkwardly. "I have to get back to work." He felt frustrated at her reluctance to talk about his parents, but maybe that very reluctance said something.

"Pass me my cup before you leave!" The old lady stretched out her arms, conveying both helplessness and disappointment in the gesture.

Finbarl looked behind to where she motioned. A shiny metal cup rested on the sideboard. "It's beautiful," he said, picking it up.

"My husband found it in the wasteland," said Mistress Komov proudly, omitting to explain why he hadn't handed it in.

Finbarl raised it in the dim light, examining the delicate engraving and polished surface. A convex image stared back. The warped reflection lost his nose and mouth but, fixed at the knee of the curve, were his hazel eyes, the light brown iris ringed with a thin, dark edge. He closed his eyes in contemplation only for his memory to summon those same eyes to stare back again: though now they belonged to Maddy. "I'll come to visit you again," said Finbarl, quickly passing the cup to his old teacher. "Goodbye and tomorrow's fortune to you, Komovmorex." As Finbarl ducked out of the house, he knew he would never return.

CHAPTER 15

Thousands gathered to hear the Governor's public announcement, packed into the town square. People mingled in good spirits; expectations were high at what might be coming. Finbarl hovered on the outer edges, on guard duty, watching the throngs sweltering in the heat. He had volunteered, ensuring escape from duties later in the day.

"Citizens!" began Governor Elbar, standing proudly in a vibrant red thawb, adorned with gold lapels, under a shade-giving gazebo. "I wish you well on this special day. It pleases me to see so many faces; so many people coming together to celebrate our continued achievement in maintaining civilisation in a barbaric world." A light ripple of applause met this acknowledgement, the Governor encouraging with melodramatic nods. "When I wake each morning and think of the challenges I face, I gain strength from knowing I'm not alone. None of us are alone! We all depend on each other. I may steer the camel train through the desert, but I need bread and the baker needs his flour for that bread and the farmer needs the guards' protection to grow the grain to produce flour and the guards need the blacksmith to make their bullets and the blacksmith needs his wife to keep him strong. Does a Ferral have this support, this family?" Elbar shook his head, the crowd reciprocating with their own answer. "No! You're right! The only thing a Ferral has is an instinct to kill. It's what separates us from those monsters. We function as a community, supporting each other and making sacrifices for the good of the community. The only thing they need each other for is to pick lice from places they can't reach themselves!" This earned a healthy laugh.

"It's days like this when civilisation rewards its loyal followers. I recently made a difficult decision to send several of our brave guards out into the Prison with one objective: to find and bring back a hoard of metal." The crowd murmured its excitement. "Despite the risk from Ferrals and prisoners, these men laboured through the heat of the day to locate and retrieve the largest single metal find I have ever seen!" Uncontrolled cheering erupted. The Governor stood preening with the adoration, uncaring in his demonisation of the prisoners, despite their assistance in the metal's recovery. Silencing the crowd with his hands, he continued. "This will enable key repairs to essential machinery around the town and in the farms. It will enable us to make ten more rifles and two years' worth of ammunition. The Ferral does not fear much, but it knows what a guard with a gun can do! You can tell your children to sleep at peace because we've secured the fragile walls of civilisation!"

Another round of cheering erupted, the crowd surging forward. Finbarl watched with concern, aware of the dangers with too many people in too small a space. The unthinking, uncontrollable mass movement threatened a crush. Guards at the front held a firm line, shouting for the crowd to stand still. Their voices were unheard as pressure built and the single entity continued to press forward.

Bang! A gunshot cracked across the dry air, bringing everybody to a silent paralysis. All eyes returned to the stage, where a beaming Torbald stood holding a smoking pistol.

"Don't worry, father," said Torbald, just loud enough to carry to the Governor, "we've plenty more bullets now and we don't want anyone to hurt themselves!"

Finbarl let out a relieved breath. Disaster averted, but the gunshot could have easily compounded the crush, leading to a stampede.

The Governor shifted uneasily, shocked by the noise and at nearly losing control. He spared his son a discerning glance before presenting a broad smile for his audience. With silence returned, he had his cue to continue. "I hereby declare the rest of today a festival of thanks. Bring your instruments and voices to your district public space, enjoy some dancing and singing. By way of thanks to all of you, the Wardyns will donate the drinks!"

"Three cheers for the Wardyns!" cried out someone suspiciously close to the honoured few. The crowd dutifully obliged, much to the supposed embarrassment of the Governor.

Silencing the crowd once more, the Governor stood still, his face changing to a harsher, determined set. "You deserve your festivities," he continued, "but there are some among us who strive not for the stability and longevity of our society but purely for their own gratification." The crowd hushed to absolute silence, recognising what was to come. "We know the Ferrals try to destroy our beautiful town from beyond the walls, but we must always be on guard against those seeking to destroy us from within. Were it that today was only for good news, but alas, due to the selfish criminality of a small minority, we must report the rationing of maize for the next year." A more threatening rumble emanated from the massed citizens of Athenia. "You've every right to be angry. I'm angry! And I can assure you, we will hand out swift justice to those responsible. They know who they are, and we know who they are! They're those self-seeking felons who have been stealing food for themselves.

"Now we can make more bullets, a swifter form of retribution can be implemented. But justice is the bedrock of civilisation. We hold dear the ancient principle of good government, that life is sacrosanct. Therefore, today we'll live to celebrate; tomorrow we'll arrest the guilty and, when justice is served, you've my assurance they'll spend the rest of their lives in the Prison!" With raised fist, the Governor walked off the stage to a tumultuous roar from the crowd.

Yet amid the celebrative mood, some citizens responded with less enthusiasm: the managers, the local leaders, those who dabbled with power. Not one of them was guilty of stealing food, but some were guilty of treading where only the Wardyn's walked: a dalliance with power, an independent spirit, a word misspoken. They feared tomorrow's knock to their door; a precursor to arrest and a charge of treason. Each searched their memory, trying to recall a word out of place or a wayward ambition. Most felt reassured; their stagnant endeavours and blind obedience no threat to anyone. Others struggled with doubt, conscious tonight could be their last of freedom.

Finbarl stood at the edge of the crowd, his arms folded, watching the Governor as he walked off stage with a mix of disappointment and disapproval. All those times before, when the Governor's words and promises stirred hope, gratitude and understanding in Finbarl, now provoked an embarrassed regret. The superficial rhetoric and lies screamed out to him today. No repairs, just bullets and guns. No thefts, just a crop failure and scapegoats to punish. How many times in his life had they lied to him, manipulated him? Could he trust anyone any more? Finbarl felt alone and lost. The excuses conjured up during the day to avoid meeting up with Maddy in the Prison seemed pathetic. He longed for dusk, to slip away to make the rendezvous. Another liar, but at least one he could challenge, putting an end to the tormenting she had caused.

CHAPTER 16

As the light faded from the day, the sound of revelry drifted across Athenia. Against the backdrop of music and boisterous merriment, Finbarl made his way through the narrow streets, avoiding, where possible, the pockets of drunk citizens hunting their next drink. He headed towards the farm exit at the east end of Athenia. His destination was a poorly guarded spot on Cragor Hill, where an outcrop of rock gave the impression of inaccessibility, but where he had once climbed for a dare as a youngster. He remembered the natural 'staircase', cut sharply from left to right up the shallow precipice. They were memories from years ago, and captured in daylight.

"Got any Kywaczek?"

Finbarl swung round to see a man and woman he had walked past without seeing. They stood in a doorway embracing, looking at him expectantly. "No," he replied, without breaking his stride.

"You must know where we can get some!" They started following Finbarl.

"I'm on duty. Now, piss off!"

"Miserable Ferral-whack!" cursed the man.

"He must be one of those maize thieves!" called out the woman, emboldened by the Kywaczek already consumed. "Wants everything for himself!"

"Yeah," echoed the man. "Thinks he's too good for the likes of us!"

Finbarl turned to see them still in pursuit, catching the attention of others with their brazen indignation and accusations.

"What you done with our maize, you bloody thief?"

Enough was enough. Finbarl slowed, abruptly changed direction and sent a fist flying at the man's face. A sickening crack sounded as Finbarl's knuckles hit his nose. The man crashed to the ground, blood flooding down his face. Finbarl rubbed his knuckles to confirm the crack belonged to the man's snout. Standing over the prostrate figure as he groaned, Finbarl growled, "No one calls me a thief!" He stomped away, leaving the stunned woman kneeling over her wounded boyfriend. It felt good releasing his anger, even if on some stupid drunk.

At the exit gate, he found Adekobe-apcula on duty. One last human hurdle to get past. Adekobe, one of the oldest guards, chewed on a piece of straw and sat with his feet resting on a table.

"Evening, Finbarl," he said. "What brings you out here tonight of all nights? Don't you have a girl you should be dancing with?"

"I wish," replied Finbarl. "Got roped into taking a message to Liberty Wall. They promised me a bottle on my return."

"Well, if you're looking for someone to share it with, you know where I'll be!"

Finbarl laughed, making for the door.

"Hang on!"

Finbarl froze.

"Can you tell Joseptinius I'll help with his roof on Friday?"

Finbarl released a held breath. "Sure, no problem."

Once out of the town walls, Finbarl scanned the valley for signs of life. In the poor light, he saw no one and, more importantly, no one saw him. He made his way left towards the base of Cragor Hill. An olive grove ran up the slope and Finbarl followed the well-worn footpath weaving its way through the trees. The flaming torches lining the ridge stood out in the twilight, allowing Finbarl to see the sentry posts and silhouetted figures within. The nearest lay roughly fifty yards to his right, beyond the range of sight of even the most able guard in this light.

At the summit Finbarl stopped, attempting to get his bearings. He crouched to the ground, straining his eyes, trying to make out familiar landmarks. Perhaps he should have risked trying an hour earlier, to use the extra light, but there was no point considering the 'what ifs' now. He looked to his left, recognising the dominant shape of the windmill and the jagged line of rooftops of Athenia clinging to the lower slopes at the far end of Cragor Hill. By his calculations, twenty yards remained to the outcrop. He scrambled a little way forward on his hands and knees, then, still stooped, ran down the ridge of the hill in the direction of Athenia. A protruding root almost sent him flying but, keeping his balance, he came to the intended spot. He crouched again, trying to catch his breath. In the darkness and silence, his breathing seemed too loud. He struggled to slow it down, thinking of the dangers lying ahead.

Down the outward facing slope, man-made obstacles, stakes, pits and barbed wire, designed to maim or kill, ensured only a fool would try to scale into Athenia here. What word described him for trying to get out?

Finbarl relied on a distant memory as he edged down the gradient. Judging distance in the fading light proved difficult.

One foot wrong and he could find himself tumbling down and over the edge. He sat on his backside, walking with his hands and a foot, testing every inch with his other limb. The rock beneath his hands, sharp and painful, forced him to pause frequently. His right foot dangled in the air, feeling down for terra firma but finding nothing. He had found the edge. He shuffled forward to sit upon the precipice, both legs hanging over.

"Cronax!" Finbarl whispered. The elusive first foothold evaded him. An urge for calming Jumblar popped into his thoughts. Beneath him lay a ten-yard drop and possibly a few stakes to make his end more excruciating. His brain encouraged him to call the whole thing off. "Why am I risking everything to confront this woman?" he asked himself aloud. The rest of the conversation continued silently. Why not wait until another prisoner drop-off at Bruuk Point? Just forget about tonight and ignore her; let nature or the Ferrals remove the problem. She probably wouldn't even be there tonight anyway.

Then, a few seconds later, with the negative thoughts and arguments reverberating through his brain, Finbarl found himself hanging by his fingertips, his feet desperately trying to locate something to cling to. Something deep inside committed him, deciding his fate.

Immediately below lay nothing beyond an inch-wide lip. Finbarl rested upon it, easing the strain on his fingers. He stretched a leg to the side, feeling for something more substantial. Eventually his toe hit the rock, but, at maximum stretch, he got no sense of anything substantial. He tried to edge along the lip with his fingers, but a sharp ridge forced him back. His fingers ached badly. Taking a deep breath, Finbarl reset his grip and pushed off with what little leverage his feet could manage. His right foot sniffed for ground like a pig scavenging for food. A surface! He felt the strain in his groin and fingers as he adjusted his body, transferring his weight to the right foot. Success depended on edging his fingers to the sharper rock. He grimaced with the pain but felt the secure base beneath his feet. With one final, nerve-racking push from his palms, he found himself hugging the face of the outcrop, with the only thing keeping him from falling being the thin ledge. There was no going back now. Going up would be just as hard as going down.

The detail of his descent and ascent as a cocky young cadet failed him. His feet stuck outwards in opposite directions and he carefully lifted his left foot, turning it the other way. Feeling the cold stone pressing against his face, Finbarl pushed in harder, somehow believing the closer the contact the more secure he would be. He slid his cheek and body slowly down the face of the rock, his arms sticking out wide, acting as counter-levers. His hands felt blindly for the ledge before he tentatively moved one foot off. A leg stretched down while the other, still clinging to the narrow shelf of rock, bent painfully. Everything rested on there being another convenient ledge to find! Locking his arms, he dragged his remaining foot off the sill and slowly eased his weight down. One final tricky manoeuvre required; he would have to let his whole body go and cling to the ledge with his fingertips. No time for thought. He relaxed his shoulder and wrist muscles, letting gravity take him down. His fingers hit the lip and he tensed up, fighting to keep a grip. A jutting rock hit his midriff, knocking the wind out of him. Struggling to recover his breath, he flapped his feet, attempting to gain some hold. Finding nothing of substance, he lifted his right knee to the protruding rock and hauled himself onto the ledge. Then he started the process again.

Finbarl's luck changed as his feet found the perfect base to support himself. He calculated the lower end of the outcrop must be close. If memory served him right, a few large boulders rested at the bottom, then normal ground for the rest of the way. Peering down, he felt sure the smooth, curved surface of a boulder lay below, and he reached out with a leg to make contact. "Gotcha!" he exclaimed, a little too loudly, as his foot touched the surface. He felt the curvature, recognising the familiar shape of a boulder, and let his full weight rest on its surface. Glancing up at the rock face, he pondered the challenges required for his ascent later. It looked impossible in the darkness. A problem for later, he concluded, with time pressing.

The row of stakes he expected to find littered the ground, but to Finbarl's relief, and disgust, they provided inadequate protection. Far too much space remained between, allowing any attacking Ferral or AWOL guard to easily weave through them. Mindful other hazards lay in wait on the hill, Finbarl continued down at a steady walking pace, snaking around the bushes and foliage. At the bottom he broke into a run, veering away from Athenia's walls, out of sight of any conscientious guard not distracted from his duty. With the town lit by a hundred torches, he easily maintained his bearing and, once past the north side, cut south knowing the river channel lay in his path. Every now and again an eruption of cheering and frivolity floated through the night air, making Finbarl wonder what any Ferral in the vicinity would make of it. Although his real concern lay with what they would make, or do, with him if discovered.

A faint reflection of moonlight bounced off the channel water. At the water's edge, Finbarl paused to catch his breath, scooping up some liquid to quench his thirst. He looked back, the flickering flames atop Athenia's walls still visible, then continued along the channel path. A coyote howled in the distance as Finbarl stuck to the soft ground next to the stream. Regularly glancing over his shoulder, he checked the view of Athenia, until eventually it vanished out of sight. He had arrived at the rendezvous site. No one awaited him. He was alone, the old woman absent. Finbarl cursed to himself. Had all his efforts and risks been in vain? Had he underestimated how difficult it would be for Maddy to get to this point? Or maybe she had no intention of meeting him. Exposed and alone in the Prison, the negative thoughts dominated, but an optimistic spark within urged Finbarl to give her more time. He rested against the old riverbank, his ears monitoring for signs of movement. Despite his attempts to stay alert, within a few minutes Finbarl fell fast asleep.

*

A hand gripped Finbarl's shoulder, rocking him. He woke startled, leaping to his feet, instinctively grabbing for his absent gun. A line of faces confronted him and his mind, still foggy from the sleep, struggled to take it in. Only when a voice sounded did he recall where he was and why he was there.

"Finbarl, it's all right! It's me, your mother."

He tilted his head back in relief, looking to the stars, and exhaled a long breath, "Maddy? I didn't think you were coming." Finbarl looked suspiciously at the other faces. "You were supposed to come alone."

She smiled. "I haven't survived this long by being a fool. No one travels in the Prison alone. It wasn't the most thoughtful plan, and we don't like to be this exposed at night, but everyone was happy to come with me, including Aminatra."

Finbarl looked around the faces, spotting the stern expression of Aminatra at the end. "It was more like no one was happy for Maddy to come alone," said one of the men, who inspected Finbarl disdainfully.

"Thank you," said Finbarl, unsure what purpose the gratitude served other than inviting them to refrain from killing him. "Here, I've brought you some food." He reached behind his back and into his trousers, pulling out a small pouch. "It's not much. I didn't realise there would be multiple mouths." It was another token gesture he thought might spare his life.

The eyes of the other prisoners glowed at the mention of food. As they crowded round to examine the treat, Finbarl stepped back, partly out of instinct and partly due to a stink he couldn't quite place emanating from them.

"What news of Karlmon?" asked Aminatra. Her face was dirty and aged by the persistent exposure to the sun; her eyes lost and tired.

Finbarl shook his head. "Sorry, he's in the cadet school. I haven't seen him."

Whack! Aminatra's hand lashed out, slapping Finbarl around the face. She abruptly turned and walked away.

"What was that for?" whined Finbarl, holding his hand to his throbbing cheek.

Aminatra stopped and looked back. "For pushing me over when you escorted me here and slapping me at Alphege Scar," she answered coldly, before sitting down with the other prisoners to rummage through the pouch of food, leaving Finbarl alone with Maddy.

"You deserved that, dear," whispered Maddy. "Word of Karlmon may have softened her mood."

Finbarl looked to the sky in disbelief, rubbing the sting out of his cheek. "I didn't know I was going to see her."

Maddy's hand gently touched his and, despite an initial urge to pull it away, Finbarl did nothing.

"We've got lots to discuss. It's good we can talk without fear," said Maddy.

"Well, as long as no Ferrals are about!"

"We would've heard them if they were," Maddy said, reaching into her own pouch to pull out a gourd. "Here, apply this to your exposed skin just in case."

Finbarl recoiled at the odour, the same he'd noticed a moment ago on the prisoners. "What is that?" he asked, his face screwed-up in disgust.

"Just herbs and a few other ingredients," replied his mother. "The Ferrals don't appear to like the smell. It makes them less inclined to attack. And they definitely won't eat you if you wear it."

"I don't blame them," joked Finbarl, strangely more relaxed in her company than intended. "It's put me off my own dinner. How can you bear to wear it?"

Maddy gave him a disappointed look. "We do what we have to, to survive. Smelling nice is not high up the list of priorities."

"I guess not," said Finbarl, still not entirely convinced, as he gingerly applied a little bit of the mixture to his arms.

"What have you done to your hands?" asked Maddy, spotting the blood.

Finbarl examined his palms, feeling the pain for the first time. "Oh, nothing," he replied. "Just floundering in the dark on the way here."

"Finish applying the salve and then wash your hands in the water. I'll give you something for your wounds."

Ignoring the urge to wash all the pungent lotion from his body, Finbarl complied, offering his hands to the old woman.

"Doesn't it hurt?" she enquired.

He shrugged.

"Well this might!"

Finbarl grimaced as she applied a pure white balm.

"Tree sap," she said before he could ask. "Helps prevent infection, though I would prefer bandages if I had any. Moss is also good, but impossible to come by on the flats. You can find it halfway up the mountains, but you also tend to find Ferrals there too."

A jolt shot up his arm and Finbarl pulled away. "Stop! I didn't come here to be mothered." He regretted the choice of word instantly. Composing himself, under the scrutiny of the other prisoners, Finbarl continued calmly, "I mean, you need to explain yourself."

"Explain myself? Explain what?"

"Why you claim to be my mother!"

"Because I am your mother."

Finbarl felt anger building inside, his emotions fluctuating. Why persevere with these lies? He turned away, annoyed at letting her kindness disarm him. Feeling her hand rest upon his shoulder, he turned back to her, ready to release his thoughts in a barrage of vitriol. "I ... I ... ". The words failed to come. In the darkness, the moonlight caught Maddy's face, highlighting her eyes and mouth. It was like looking at his reflection, thought Finbarl, as the anger dissolved.

"You were trying to say something, Fin," encouraged Maddy.

"I ... can you prove you're my mother?" Finbarl straddled the realms of acceptance and denial. He wasn't about to give up a lifetime of understanding on the word of an old woman, but those eyes were his eyes.

Maddy smiled. "It's good you've a sceptical, challenging mind. We should never take what is before us for granted."

Finbarl breathed heavily, anxious for proof rather than compliments.

"I can tell you about your birth, your early birthdays, your father, your home," offered Maddy. "But none of that will convince you. How about a scar? You have a short scar on the inside of your foot arch, beneath the medial cuneiform." Maddy paused for thought. "The right foot, I recall."

Finbarl nodded slowly. "I don't know what a medial cuni-thing is, but I've such a scar on my foot."

"It's a bone," explained Maddy, almost oblivious to the impact of her words on Finbarl. "You cut yourself on a jagged rock while playing. There was a lot of blood. Your father wasn't particularly good with that sort of thing."

"Father," repeated Finbarl, as though the word possessed special powers.

"Yes, you remind me of him. You've his nose and cheeks, similar zygomatic bone structure."

Finbarl smiled awkwardly, the long words washing over him. "Where is he?" The challenge gone from his voice. With the truth out, he felt as though he should be in shock but, somehow, he had known for some time. Why else take the incredible risk of meeting up? He just hadn't admitted the truth to himself.

"He's dead, Fin," answered Maddy, with no emotion. "He died a long time ago in the Prison. He kept me alive for the first year. I never appreciated until too late what a sacrifice he had made for me. What little food he found ... well, let's just say he was a selfless man. I thought I would be the first to go, but through his death he gave me strength to survive."

Finbarl listened. He felt no sadness for a man he already thought dead. "Why do you call me Fin?"

"It's what we called you when you were a baby."

Finbarl nodded. He had no memory, but it felt right. "How do you know so much: about bones and things?"

"I was a doctor in Athenia – a good one too," answered Maddy. "I had access to some wonderful books and even a rudimentary laboratory. Of course, I've had to learn so much more out in the wilderness, but a good education prepares the mind for learning throughout life. Fighting for survival is wonderful for sharpening the mind."

"A doctor?" repeated Finbarl. "That's a responsible position. You must have been important."

"I was from a good family," said Maddy, before adding, "you're from a good family with status – Alci. We served Athenia well for many generations."

"And my father? What did he do?" For the first time Finbarl owned the truth through his questions.

"He did remarkable things. I mentioned how much you remind me of him?" Maddy reached out and stroked Finbarl's cheek, causing him to blush unnoticed in the dim light. "He was an agricultural scientist. Not sure you have them any more! I'll tell you all about him another time, but I need to know about Athenia's rotten heart. If for no other reason than one day they may try to bring you down, just as they did your father and I."

"I'm beginning to see it myself now," said Finbarl, a frown forming on his brow.

"So, you do believe I'm your mother now?" asked Maddy, already knowing the answer.

"I do," answered Finbarl.

The two words pleasurably wafted through Maddy's soul.

"The scar, the stories. I can't believe I was so blind before. Not just about you, but about the Wardyns."

"Why shouldn't you be? Mankind, for such a clever creature, is also one prone to accepting the familiar. We crave what we know and what makes us feel comfortable. 'Home' is a powerful word because it represents everything we relate to on several levels. We are then particularly susceptible to fear as a tool for manipulating and controlling us."

"But I'm not afraid of anything!" bragged Finbarl.

"Rubbish!" retorted Maddy. "You live behind walls, you've never loved, and you carry a gun most of the time."

"Yes, but that's just common sense with the Ferrals around!" Finbarl avoided the reference to love.

"The Ferrals," repeated Maddy. "Don't kid yourself that's all you're afraid of! You're afraid to live. You're afraid of freedom. You're afraid of losing 'civilisation' when it was lost many years ago."

"How can you say that when you're the prisoner and I'm the free citizen of Athenia?" challenged Finbarl.

"Are you free to say what you like, to go where you like? No place with walls is ever free and that applies to psychological and physical walls. You're as much a prisoner as I am."

"But what choice do we have?"

"Ah, is choice not a key element of liberty?" answered Maddy. "What prevents you from having a choice?"

"I don't know," grumbled Finbarl. "What stops you from having a choice?"

"Jumblar!" answered his mother without hesitation. "Why does any prisoner rely on the benevolence of Athenia once outside its walls? That is my chain. Without my dependence on it, I could go anywhere I wanted."

"But there's nowhere to go. Desert to the west and endless mountains to the east. You would be dead within days."

"Perhaps," reflected Maddy. "But I would die free. For someone who is afraid of nothing – apart from Ferrals, deserts and mountains – you appear to fear an awful lot. I would have thought someone from Athenia, a place claiming to be the last bastion of civilisation, would want to know what lies beyond."

Finbarl thought hard. Maddy's words all made sense, but were still hard to accept. "I thought Jumblar bound us together. It helps us cope with an unforgiving world; provides energy and clarity. It's a gift from God." Finbarl found himself echoing the distant doctrine of Komov-morex.

Aminatra wandered over, sitting down quietly on the other side of Maddy.

"I think you confuse clarity for relief, dear; faith with control," said Maddy to Finbarl, welcoming Aminatra with a gentle pat on her thigh. "The people of Athenia gave up on the God, who forgot about them, long ago. It's just an empty ritual now, continued because no one knows any different." She turned and looked Finbarl in the eye. "And if you don't get Jumblar, what then?"

"I've never thought about it," Finbarl confessed. "It is, and has been, the constant in my life and is always available. I couldn't imagine going without it."

"I've had to go for a number of days without in the Prison. It drives you mad. Look at Johansson! He went five days without and has never fully recovered."

Finbarl looked across to see Johansson sitting alone, talking to himself.

"There was a time before Jumblar," continued his mother. "I don't know when or how it became part of our lives, but it was an accursed day when it happened."

"So, what are you suggesting we do about it?" asked Finbarl.

"I'm not suggesting we do anything," Maddy replied. "I'm simply stating what is stopping me being free. You on the other hand have a bigger problem. The Wardyns and Governor Elbar for starters."

Finbarl laughed. "Are you suggesting I get myself thrown in the Prison to liberate myself?"

"No, of course not!" responded Maddy. "I'm an old lady who's easily pleased. You're a young man who can shape not only your own future but the destiny of civilisation itself."

"Cronax!" expelled Finbarl. "You've grand expectations for someone who was willing to hit you with a rifle butt not so long ago. What are you suggesting I do? Stage a coup and overthrow the Wardyns? Make myself the new Governor?"

It was Maddy's turn to laugh. "Of course not! I've no doubt you could do it, but you would just turn into a new Governor Elbar." She paused and grimaced. "And I couldn't have my son becoming him."

"But I would give power to the citizens!" declared Finbarl, as he grew into his new revolutionary role. "They would no longer be oppressed; trials would be fair."

"No!" snapped Maddy, her stern tone surprising Finbarl. "Don't you get it, Fin? Power to the people is not the answer. Do you trust they'll make better decisions? Just because someone is poor or rich, on their own or speaking as a crowd, it doesn't mean they'll make the right decision. Come the next famine and, just like now, they'll find scapegoats to punish. First it'll be the Ferrals, then the prisoners and finally, with no one else to blame for their children starving, they'll blame the Governor and, if the Governor is no fool, he'll have a force of loyal armed guards who will stop the citizens from ripping his throat out and he'll never trust the people again. You have your next Elbar!"

Finbarl nodded in painful understanding.

"Liberty is no easy mistress. A wise man once said, 'Truth can be stated in a thousand different ways, yet each one can be true.' I say, 'Liberty can be defined in a thousand different ways and yet someone will always feel imprisoned.' Are the Ferrals free? They've no rules, don't rely on Jumblar or live behind walls. But they're bound by their ignorance of the world, their inability to farm or to read. Civilisation defeats some of those things but liberty must be curtailed in the world of laws and powers. There's no pure form and it exists in the same orbit as anarchy. To keep them apart you need a framework of authority based on good morals and an understanding that the journey and fight for liberty never ends."

"Cronax!" exclaimed Finbarl, scratching his head. "That's too deep for me."

"No, the way you can save civilisation," continued Maddy, ignoring Finbarl, "is to destroy the pitiful skeleton claiming to be the final embodiment of civilisation!"

Finbarl gasped in shock.

"Until those walls come down; until we break free from our reliance on Jumblar; until mankind decides to come down from the metaphorical tree for a second time, then civilisation has no chance to flourish again. Liberty remains bound. It's a new, better civilisation you have to build, with the lessons and skills from the past!"

Finbarl looked across to Aminatra, trying to find companionship in his disbelief, but her eyes only confirmed agreement with Maddy. Everything was happening so fast. A moment ago, he accepted Maddy as his mother, now she proposed revolution. "But how do we achieve that? No one will agree to it. The first person I suggest it to will hand me over to the Wardyns for treason."

"At least the charge would be fair for once!" said Aminatra, breaking her silence to snipe at Finbarl.

"Seeing what's wrong is so much easier than making something right," opined Maddy." The place you start is to bring down the Wardyns and the Governor."

"But ... " began Finbarl, before his mother cut him off.

"Not with guns and bullets, but with information: discredit them. Destroying a political power base is dangerous because it creates a vacuum, and you can't always control what fills it. Therefore, it's better to unite everyone with knowledge than just remove the core with violence. Bureaucracy appears to be unavoidable for civilisation, and with paper and books so precious, it's unlikely they'll throw anything away. Every tyrannical state enjoys its place in history recorded for posterity; gives them a sense of ancestral connection and belonging to heroes and heroines, even if they share no blood whatsoever! If you can find where they keep the records, you'll find the dirt to bring them down. I suspect you'll be able to find evidence to move every sector of society against them. You must ensure it's shared anonymously around the town. If you can get the guards revolting with the citizens, you'll create the will that's needed."

"And then what?" Finbarl cried, feeling caught in a fantastical dream.

"To be honest, I don't know," confessed Maddy. "I know what I'd like to do, but I'm not sure it's the right solution."

"What?" asked Aminatra.

"Why, burn the Jumblar crop, my dear Ami!" declared Maddy.

"You're crazy!" derided Finbarl. "I think you've been off your Jumblar a little longer than a few days. Eh, Ami?"

"Don't speak to your mother like that!" snapped Aminatra, glaring at Finbarl. "And my name's Aminatra. Only Maddy calls me Ami!"

"It's all right," laughed Maddy. "It is crazy at this moment. I need to think on it some more." She reached out both hands, gripping Aminatra's and Finbarl's shoulders. "Don't worry, there'll be a solution! You don't need to believe or commit to everything I've suggested, Fin, but will you find the Wardyns' records?"

Finbarl looked to the ground in thought. Breaking out of Athenia for a chat was one thing, but stealing from the Wardyns and bringing about the collapse of civilisation was a risk and challenge on an entirely different scale.

"You can't go back to your old life. You know that, don't you Finbarl?" Aminatra now offered the words of wisdom. "You've three choices: start beating prisoners and your mother again or, in the not-too-distant future, get caught being kind to your mother and her friends and get thrown in Prison yourself or, three, expose the Governor and Wardyns for the corrupt pigs they are."

"Nicely put," said Maddy. "I see you're learning fast."

"Yes, nicely put," said Finbarl, less enthused.

"Are you sure the future of civilisation's safe in his hands?" asked Aminatra, her tone unclear as to whether she was teasing or serious.

"Why, of course not, dear," replied Maddy with a smile. "I expect you to help him. You're Eve to his Adam." Finbarl and Aminatra turned away in obvious embarrassment, while Maddy laughed aloud.

*

Maddy hugged Finbarl, bringing a lump to his throat. No farewell ever felt like this before. As his head nestled against her hair, Finbarl's heart conceded the affection dormant since childhood. It brought pain and joy at the same time.

Aminatra curtly nodded, which Finbarl interpreted as carrying some token of acceptance, even if his sore cheek told him otherwise. She seemed a different woman to the one abandoned in the Prison; still angry, but there was something. Finbarl couldn't quite find the right word. 'Liberated' kept coming to mind, but that couldn't be it, not for a prisoner.

Walking back alone to Athenia, a restless excitement filled Finbarl. Having arrived with such anger and confusion, it felt strange to be departing with such clarity and purpose. Despite the bewilderment, anxiety and conflict raised within, he found it cathartic.

Under the town walls, Finbarl noticed the silence. Curfew had brought an end to the festivities, returning peace to the valley. All but the guards sheltered behind closed doors, and Finbarl hoped drink and fatigue undermined their effectiveness on watch.

The flames again provided a point of reference, guiding Finbarl around the northern edge of the walls. He looked upon Athenia with a conflicted eye. The walls and watchtowers, seared into his mind as emblems of protection and safety, now appeared as symbols of a trapped existence: he as much a prisoner as his mother or Aminatra. The darkness lent its weight to the oppressive atmosphere and, within himself, Finbarl felt a similar conflict. The thought of breaking into the Wardyns' sanctuary and stealing documents, ran contrary to everything he believed in, and yet he knew it was the right thing to do. Aminatra was correct: he had no choice.

Finding himself at the foot of Cragor Hill, Finbarl worked his way along the side until he recognised a distinct bush, one registered on the descent. A gentle breeze brought a faint odour of Kywaczek to Finbarl's nose and a shiver ran through him: this was the life he would be destroying.

At the outcrop's base, Finbarl pawed with his hands at the rock face. With no idea where to start, he wondered whether to wait until the sun rose. A screech in the distance brought the threat of Ferrals to mind. His mother's lotion still smelt like a rotting hog's stomach, but, without a gun, he had no desire to test its effectiveness. He looked along Cragor Hill to the watchtowers. Could he sneak past them? In the darkness, the tripwires, with their alarm bells, posed the biggest threat. Discovery would be instant; his fate a bullet.

As he edged along the bottom of the rockface, he slipped, his left foot landing at the base of a stake. Whistling in relief, a thought came to him. Along the end of the outcrop, a steep sandy-soiled slope soon took on a gentler gradient. Finbarl bent over, waggling the stake free from the soil. It took some effort, but eventually he withdrew it, immediately extracting another. Standing with two stakes in his hands at the foot of the slope, he held one above his head, thrusting it into the surface. It hit a rock, bouncing back. Finbarl cursed, as the shock reverberated down his arm. Picking a replacement stake, he tried again. This time it sunk in and he pushed hard to embed it as deep as possible. Gripping tight to the stake, he jumped, pulling up on it and, at the same time, thrust in, with all his strength, the second stake a little higher. It held. He found himself lying strangely flat on a seventy-five-degree gradient, his feet dangling a quarter of a yard from the foot of the slope. His hands stung like crazy, but he overcame the discomfort through necessity. The challenge involved repeating the action, stabbing in the stakes at short intervals and pulling himself up until he reached a gradient where his feet found traction of their own. Somehow it worked, and Finbarl lay at the top, sprawled flat, gasping for breath. He inspected himself: his dirt-covered clothes, his blood-stained hands and shins, together with his shredded thawb. This would take some explaining, but it felt good to be safely back within the boundaries of Athenia.

Having washed the worst of the muck and blood off in the river, Finbarl made it past an amused Adekobe at the town gate with a simple "don't ask!" He found the barracks quiet on his return, most off-duty guards sleeping their way to a powerful hangover in the morning. Stripping off his torn and thread-bare thawb, Finbarl climbed straight into bed. With roll call due in a few hours, he needed sleep. He also needed Jumblar. Its demanding call cried through ever sinew. Perhaps his mother was right about the Jumblar too, he thought. Could he live without it if he chose? Exhaustion, however, won the fight, and soon Finbarl feel deep asleep.

CHAPTER 17

"All guards stand to!" The order cut through the barrack room, piercing the sleep of the guards, bringing their attention to the headache set to plague most for the next few hours. Equally startled, Finbarl possessed wits enough to ease out of his bed as though burdened by a hangover.

"You look as bad as I feel!" said Gauret from two bunks along.

"You look pretty crap yourself!" replied Finbarl.

"Enough chatter," reprimanded Officer Vassel. "We've a lot of work to do. There are traitors to be punished."

Damn! thought Finbarl, finding himself caught up in undertaking the Governor's purge. He planned to betray the Governor, but today was not the day to forgo the pretence of loyalty.

"Get yourselves smartened up," continued Vassel, aware his shouting helped no one and enjoying it. "I want to see you all outside in ten minutes!"

As soon as Vassel left the room, Finbarl slumped back on his bed, his body urging him back to sleep.

"You can't fight it," called across Gauret. "The best thing to do is get up, drink some water and have your Jumblar. It can't get any worse, can it?" He massaged the sides of his temple.

"Good idea," replied Finbarl, thankful for the good advice, even if given for the wrong reason. As he stood, an idea occurred to Finbarl to confide his own plan to those innocents due for arrest, but he dismissed it. The first chance, they would try negotiating their release by grassing him up. He could trust no one.

Outside, the air was chilly, the sky overcast, but already the sun had begun burning away the cloud in preparation for another hot and stifling day. Finbarl dressed in his only other thawb, and wondered how to explain the damage to the other one. Perhaps swapping it with one of Audlech's would work?

As they lined up outside the barracks, Vassel persisted in his shouting. "You're a bloody disgrace! I can still smell the alcohol on your breath. A parade of Ferrals would look more presentable than you lot!" Only Finbarl appreciated the quality of the joke, laughing out loud, catching Vassel's attention. "What the hell happened to you, Finbarl-apcula? You look like you went a few rounds with a Ferral last night."

"It feels like I did, sir," responded Finbarl in character.

Vassel came and stood before Finbarl, looking him over closely. "So, what happened? And what is that smell?"

"I don't remember, sir. I think someone must have played a joke on me when I passed out: came to in some manure." This did elicit a laugh from the other guards, their heads soon regretting the gesture.

"Well remind me not to eat whatever they grow with that shit," said Vassel, before lowering his voice slightly and speaking in Finbarl's ear. "Why is it, guard, that ever since you've been earmarked for promotion you've been getting into trouble? Am I going to have to review my recommendation?"

You can stick your recommendation up Governor Elbar's arse, responded Finbarl in his mind. "No, sir. Sorry, sir," he replied aloud.

Vassel gave him another appraising, disdainful look, twitched his nose and returned to address the men. "Upon the noticeboard is the Governor's proscription announcement. Each name recorded accused of treason for either stealing food, destroying food or plotting to overthrow the state. Needless to say, each is dangerous and desperate. You're allowed to use whatever force you consider appropriate and, if any of them threaten your own safety, you've the authority to shoot to kill. However, the Governor has promised justice, so let's try to send them to Prison if we can. Designated teams are also on the noticeboard, so don't let me keep you."

Finbarl joined the shuffling mob of guards as they crowded around the noticeboard.

"You've got to be joking!" came a familiar voice at the front of the group. "Working with Finbarl is like working with a stale fart." It was Audlech.

"And where there's a fart there's an arse!" retorted Finbarl. "Oh, it's you, Audlech."

His nemesis sneered back.

"So, which lucky soul have we been assigned?"

"Kaspirlu," answered Audlech, stressing the name's ending. "You'll be right at home with a loo."

Finbarl knew Kaspirlu. A Commissioner for District Two with a wife and four kids. What had the poor sap done to deserve this fate? What would his family do when he was gone?

"Are you coming?" huffed Audlech, before adding, "I'm not walking next to you while you smell like that."

"Fine by me," answered Finbarl. "In fact, I may sleep in manure every night if this is the dividend." Cronax, this stuff really does keep the Ferrals away, he thought.

*

At the early hour, the majority of Athenia still slept, leaving the streets relatively empty. Finbarl strolled about two yards behind Audlech, the former snarling at any poor citizen up and out for their work. District Two lay at the north end of the town at the base of Cragor Hill. The tight, claustrophobic streets remained in darkness, despite the sun already creeping above the horizon. Each house was a shambolic mishmash of necessity and availability, constructed from whatever variety of materials people found. Wood provided the main structural framework, collected from the forest at the foothills of the mountains, complemented with odd pieces of constituents collected from the wilderness and past, providing a patchwork character.

"Where's Kaspirlu's house?" Audlech demanded from a terrified street sweeper, who pointed to a shack at the end of the street. "I'll shoot him when he causes trouble," explained Audlech to Finbarl as they approached the door.

"There won't be any shooting," Finbarl replied. "Kaspirlu's about half our size and you heard Vassel's instructions."

"I did. Any trouble and we're allowed to shoot to kill."

"You give me any trouble and you'll find my fist saying 'hello' to your nose again!" threatened Finbarl.

Audlech smiled. "You're just making my revenge all the sweeter when it comes ... and it will come soon."

Finbarl rolled his eyes. "Come on, let's get this over with."

At the door, Audlech lifted his rifle and brought the butt down with a loud thud. "Kaspirlu-gula, open up! You're under arrest for treason."

Finbarl noted the insulting use of an incorrect social nomenclature by Audlech. Soon the poor sod would have no suffix at all.

No immediate response came, but Finbarl saw movement in the upstairs window. A moment later, a scream pierced the air.

"Break the door down!" cried Finbarl. The fragile structure gave in easily. Audlech and Finbarl rushed through, finding a hysterical woman in her night clothes halfway down the stairs. In the middle of the room, a body hung from a rope tied to a ceiling beam. It was Kaspirlu. Finbarl leapt forward to support the body's weight but, as soon as he felt Kaspirlu's legs, he knew he had died some time ago. With the writing on the wall, Kaspirlu chose his own way out. Finbarl couldn't blame him.

"Well, that's saved me a bullet," commented Audlech.

"Have a heart!" growled Finbarl, before addressing the woman. "We're so sorry."

"Speak for yourself," said Audlech. "He was a thief and a traitor! Cronax, why would you commit suicide if you weren't racked with guilt?"

A group of children appeared at the top of the stairs, the wife attempting to shoo them back. Finbarl realised it probably wasn't the best time to punch Audlech, but he too could wait for revenge.

"Cut him down, Audlech!" ordered Finbarl. They needed to bring the body back as proof. One further indignity for Kaspirlu.

The children cried wildly, the widow trying to comfort them as best she could. Finbarl climbed the stairs, saying softly, "Go into your bedroom. It's best the children don't see this. I'll try to make sure his body is well looked after."

"Go to hell!" came the response. "You did this to my husband! You killed him!"

"I'm sorry," whispered Finbarl, realising from the look in her eyes nothing he said would help. He slowly backed down the stairs and went to assist Audlech to get the body away as soon as possible.

Despite his small stature, Kaspirlu was still surprisingly heavy and difficult to carry. Finbarl held his wrists, Audlech the ankles. They waddled along under the frightened eyes of the neighbours, woken by the disturbance.

"It would probably be easier if just one of us carries him," suggested Finbarl, at which his carrying partner promptly dropped his end.

"Be my guest!" said Audlech, always eager to avoid responsibility. "Rotting corpse should add to your aroma!"

"He's not rotti ... Oh, what's the point. Shut up, Audlech!" Finbarl pulled Kaspirlu's body up under his armpits, bent down and rested the limp torso over his own back, throwing him up so the arms went around one side of his neck, the legs the other. He then straightened his own legs and shifted Kaspirlu's body into the most comfortable position. "Maybe this isn't going to be easier!" But Audlech had already started walking away, beyond hearing, halfway down the street.

*

"What happened?" asked Officer Vassel, as Finbarl staggered into the barracks with his load.

"Suicide!"

"A sure sign of guilt," observed Vassel, much to Finbarl's annoyance and Audlech's delight. "Put him in the corner! I'm sure there will be others to keep him company."

Finbarl examined Vassel. A good, honest man, with integrity, but trapped by a corrupt regime. He would die fighting to defend it, with no normal argument able to convince him things could be different. He was who Finbarl had been destined to become. Only by pulling the world from under Vassel's feet would his eyes finally open. That meant Finbarl fulfilling the plan to expose the Wardyns and bring down the walls.

Laying Kaspirlu's body down as respectfully as possible, Finbarl rubbed his sore back and went to the water trough to try to wash away the lingering odour and touch of death, as other guards returned with their prisoners. With water trickling down his face, Finbarl looked up to see Strathbol and Hougat manhandling a despondent individual towards the holding cells. Hougat was enjoying the drama, but Strathbol looked disgusted at mixing with someone from the criminal class. The prisoner, a pitiful, nervous wreck, still dressed in his night attire, saw Kaspirlu's body and wailed. Finbarl didn't recognise him but felt an instant empathy as an image of Kaspirlu's family flashed through his memory. As the door to the cell opened, the prisoner struggled, digging his heels in the ground. A sharp blow to the kidneys by Hougat encouraged movement, and the guard shoved him into the small, claustrophobic room. Soon he would have plenty of company.

"Where's your prisoner?" asked Strathbol, as he walked across to the trough to wash the stain of criminality from his hands.

Finbarl nodded over to the dead body in the corner.

"Cronax!" exclaimed Strathbol. "What did he do to make you shoot him?"

"We didn't shoot him," grunted Finbarl. "He hanged himself. Probably last night."

"Cronax! Talk about a sign of guil ... ".

"It wasn't a sign of bloody guilt!" seethed Finbarl, before Strathbol finished his sentence. "It was fear." Finbarl stormed off without further explanation, leaving a shocked and confused Strathbol behind.

CHAPTER 18

Aminatra spent the morning with Maddy, her mentor demonstrating the art of finding buried crickets. It seemed impossible: identifying their location through discreetly disturbed sand, digging quickly to prevent escape and finally reaching blind into their burrowed tunnel to catch them. Maddy made it look easy, but each bit of ground looked the same to Aminatra. With patience and perseverance, the pupil achieved success, even if her first triumph felt pitiful when added to a bowl already containing fifteen collected by the tutor. They now sat by a small fire frying their bounty, Maddy occasionally adding a pinch of herb.

"Do you think Finbarl will do as he promised?" asked Aminatra, pushing the crickets around the cooking stone with a short stick.

"Of course," replied Maddy. "Why? Don't you?"

Aminatra squirmed, reluctant to answer.

"Come on, don't be shy, dear," pressed Maddy. "You asked the question."

"Well, he's a man," said Aminatra, poking at the crickets more than necessary. "They can't be trusted."

Maddy laughed. "I see. That's interesting."

A pregnant silence hung in the air before Aminatra responded. "What's interesting?"

"Your distrust of men."

Aminatra turned from the fire to look at her companion. "I don't trust anyone."

"But you said you didn't trust Finbarl because he was a man."

"So?" answered Aminatra.

"You were abandoned and betrayed by the father of Karlmon, weren't you, my dear?" asked Maddy.

Aminatra didn't answer.

"What about your father?" asked Maddy. "Did he leave you?"

Aminatra frowned. "What's he got to do with it?"

"Did he, or didn't he?" The question lacked vehemence, despite its bluntness.

"He died when I was eight. I don't have many memories of him, but he didn't walk out on me."

Maddy nodded. "As an eight-year-old girl, your psyche may not have accepted it like that. Have you had any relations since that ... what's-his-name deserted you?"

Aminatra shifted uncomfortably. "No. Why?"

"You've built a wall around your heart as a coping mechanism. Anyone you've ever loved has left you and so, to shield yourself from pain, you don't let anyone in."

"I love Karlmon!"

"And he loves you, my dear," reassured Maddy, "but a mother's and child's love are unconditional. Once again, though, you've been torn apart from the person you love. No wonder you're full of anger. Losing Karlmon has reinforced your wall."

"So, what are you saying?" asked Aminatra, a little frightened at how Maddy delved inside her mind.

"Oh, nothing," said Maddy, with a whimsical flourish. "Don't forget to keep the crickets moving! We won't be forgiven by the others if they're ruined."

"Sorry," said Aminatra, caught up in the discussion.

"However," began Maddy, as Aminatra prodded at the crisping insects, "just because you're stuck in the Prison, it doesn't mean your heart should be imprisoned. I found a man I could trust and fall in love with. Alfbarl was a wonderful man."

"I could fall in love if the right man came along," protested Aminatra.

"And what are the qualities of this special man who could make it through to your heart? Yep, I think those crickets are done now. Flick them onto the bark!"

"I don't know," pondered Aminatra, as she held a flat, peeled strip of bark by the frying stone and pushed their feast onto it. "He would need to be brave, honest ... loyal ... ".

"Oh, yes, my dear," agreed Maddy, "You definitely want loyal."

"Err ... humble ... ".

"Harder to find in the male species I'm afraid, Ami," joked Maddy. "Anything else?"

"Someone who ... , I don't know!" exclaimed Aminatra in a fluster, before adding facetiously, "someone with a nice singing voice."

Maddy tilted her head, assessing the response.

"Well, it doesn't matter anyway," responded Aminatra. "Not in this graveyard."

"And yet ... " said Maddy, whipping a cricket from the bark and popping it in her mouth. "And yet you began to answer my question." She bit down upon the insect. Crunch. "Oh, yes, very tasty. So that tells me you hold out some hope."

"Do I?" questioned Aminatra, edging a cricket towards her mouth.

"You do!" confirmed Maddy. "You just need to open your heart a little. You'll be surprised at who can find a way in."

"And how do I do that?"

"I don't know!" exclaimed Maddy with a shriek of laughter. "I'm an old woman for whom love … ". She let the sentence fade as though distracted by fond memories. "You could start by letting your heart make some decisions for you.

"Now," continued Maddy, quickly taking another cricket and sharing a childlike grin with Aminatra, "we'd better tell the others their food is ready before I eat them all."

As Maddy turned and called to their fellow prisoners, Aminatra observed her. The old woman analysed every topic. Sometimes it felt cruel, impersonal and intrusive. That, however, considered Aminatra, biting into a cricket, was one of the stranger conversions. After all, she'd only asked Maddy if Finbarl would do as he promised.

CHAPTER 19

A warm, midday breeze curled through the deserted streets of Athenia, whipping up eddies of sand and dust, while most residents locked themselves indoors, favouring a hollow sense of safety. A total of sixteen citizens awaited their fate in the crowded holding cell. A public announcement, stating legal proceedings would begin in the afternoon, failed to stem the fear of more arrests. The process moved with indecent haste. The fate of those accused was already determined and prepared for. Finbarl seethed at the injustice, but recognised it provided his opportunity to break into the Wardyns' sanctuary and hunt for incriminating evidence.

The sanctuary lay on a gentle elevation behind the guards' barracks, enjoying a view over much of the town. Like the rest of Athenia, the building was constructed from a makeshift cornucopia of materials, but exuded a sense of superiority. Bright, shiny marble provided a base, with cedar wood neatly fitted above. Coloured glass, embedded into the wood, sparkled in the light, declaring itself the centre of power: those residing inside, separate and privileged. Its structure provided a statement of control.

Accessing the sanctuary required going past the barracks. Few citizens of Athenia ever entered its sanctified corridors.

Even Finbarl, who spent many a day guarding the entrance, had only entered a handful of times. The last time was his unexpected summons to the council meeting. He knew what to expect beyond the doors: the Moralistas milling around, writing and filing, and finery like nowhere else within Athenia. Getting past the guards at the entrance posed the main challenge. Once inside, no one would think anything of a guard supposedly going about his business.

"Finbarl! What are you doing here?" challenged Walberg-apcula, as Finbarl approached the pine doors.

"Been sent by the court clerk for some papers needed for one of the trials," replied Finbarl with a practised ease.

"What are they like?" rebuked Walberg. "It's a wonder they ever manage to secure any convictions with their level of competence!"

Finbarl didn't quite know how to respond to such wayward logic, given he couldn't recall a trial ending any way but with a guilty verdict. If you told people lies often enough, they started to believe them, repeating the pomposity as though their own. *Was I really like that?* he thought before refocusing. "Do you know where the records are kept?"

Walberg shrugged. "No idea. Ask one of the Moralistas to help you find what you need."

"Good idea," said Finbarl, already intent on ignoring the advice.

A long corridor greeted him on the other side of the doors. Every now and again, a body emerged from a room in the distance, quickly vanishing into another on the opposite side. Finbarl took a deep breath and walked down the passage. He needed a brazen approach. Catching the eye of a Moralista bureaucrat sitting at her desk in the first room, Finbarl acknowledged her with a nod. As expected, the clerk ignored him, continuing to scribble at her desk.

Finbarl recognised some of the rooms from his previous visits, but had no notion of where he should be heading. Before entering, he reasoned anything with the potential to embarrass or destroy the Wardyns was hardly likely to be accessible to a lowly administrator. Rather, it would be somewhere secure and under the protection of the Wardyns themselves. Only one place met the description: their personal quarters at the far end of the sanctuary, a place unseen by Finbarl.

"Everything okay, sir?"

Finbarl swung around to find a timorous-looking clerk standing behind him. "Yes, of course!" he replied. "Governor Elbar-ensi has sent me to collect something he needs." If he was going to lie, then Finbarl decided to go big.

"Is there anything I can help you with?" The Moralista sniffed and scratched her ear nervously.

Ideas flashed through Finbarl's mind but, before he argued against himself, he dug the hole deeper. "What's your name?"

"Lowe-mora, sir."

"Excellent, Lowe!" exclaimed Finbarl, omitting the formal suffix to appear friendlier. "The Governor told me to ask for you."

"Really?" responded Lowe, half confused, half delighted.

"He did indeed. He needs some personal papers for a confidential meeting and said you'd be able to take me to the room."

"Meeting? What meeting is this?"

Finbarl feared overplaying his bluff. "Something's arisen at one of the trials."

"Well, do they need me to attend?" asked the clerk, becoming more emboldened in familiar territory.

"It has nothing to do with you!" replied Finbarl. "As I said, it's a confidential matter and the Governor was clear in his instructions. So, if we could get on with it! The Governor does not like to be kept waiting!"

Lowe, still a trifle perplexed, understood the importance of not upsetting the Governor and nodded her head. "Of course, please follow me!"

They took a right turn down a further corridor, bringing them to a courtyard, verdant and colourful. Finbarl's eyes marvelled at the splendour. It possessed a tranquillity impossible to find elsewhere within Athenia, nor, indeed, beyond the walls. So many flowers, so much fragrance, so at odds with the harsh world outside. At the centre, a circle of empty, reclining couches stood under the shade of fluttering sheets. Finbarl visualised the Wardyns relaxing on an evening in this idyll, feeling another surge of bitterness and loathing.

"It's beautiful!" gasped Finbarl, his nefarious task forgotten for a second.

"Is it?" questioned Lowe. "I suppose it is. I understand gardens were common in the past. This here is a chilli tree. Have you ever tasted a dish with chilli?" She brushed her hand through the compact green foliage, a small red chilli coming to rest between two fingers.

Finbarl thought she might pick it, but the clerk withdrew her hands.

"No, me neither: exceedingly rare. Now, this is the Governor's office." She indicated towards the room with the best view into the courtyard. "If you want to tell me what it is you need, I should be able to locate it for you."

"That's good of you," said Finbarl, trying a more sensitive tone, "but I know what I need to find and, as it's of such a sensitive nature, I can't allow you to see."

Lowe frowned. "This is most irregular! I don't understand why the Governor would not entrust a Moralista with this task. We're trusted with sensitive material all the time!"

"Ah, but that is precisely why it can't be a Moralista," explained Finbarl. "I can't say too much, but you'll know all about the treason trials and how the traitors have been able to infiltrate into all corners of Athenia?"

The clerk nodded with intense comprehension.

"Well," continued Finbarl, "and I shouldn't be telling you this, but a trial exposed a mole in the sanctuary. They're investigating all Moralistas and while the Governor, of course, trusts you – after all he did ask for you specifically to bring me here – they'd be foolish not to check out everyone."

"But ... but I'm entirely loyal to the Wardyns!" spluttered Lowe.

"I can see that," remarked Finbarl, gripping the clerk's shoulder reassuringly. "But it's important you show them by following the Governor's instructions."

"Of course, of course! I'll leave you to it. But if you do need help, let me know! I'm as eager as anyone to capture the enemies of the state."

"A true Moralista!" boomed Finbarl, conscious of the enormous hole dug with his lie. He hoped his plan played itself out before his exposure. "Remember, I didn't say anything to you, so not a word to anyone!"

"You can trust me!"

Finbarl watched Lowe disappear through the courtyard, relieved he hadn't needed to hoodwink a less naïve invalided guard in the Moralistas. He entered the Governor's office. It reminded Finbarl of his youth in the classroom: a majestic wooden desk occupying the far end, surrounded by shelves stacked with books. His heart yearned to spend a day looking through them all; his head thought only of the mission and limited time. Where to look? The desk. Papers lay strewn across it. His eyes flickered between the sheets, fingers lifting and sorting them as he absorbed key words. But it was all routine stuff. The only thing of interest was a dirty plate from an eaten meal: a stripped corn cob lying in congealed gravy.

Sitting down in a sumptuous leather chair, Finbarl pulled open a drawer. More papers, but nothing of interest. He shut it, opening another, finding a similar stash. Rifling through this pile proved equally fruitless. Finbarl realised, without knowing what he needed to find, it would prove hard finding it. It seemed so straightforward when planning the intrusion: incriminating documents, exuding guilt, leaping out at him. But he realised the Governor spent most of his days on trivial governance. Finbarl lacked the skill or knowledge to analyse or recognise the wheat from the chaff. He slammed the drawer shut in frustration, leaning back in the chair. What to do? A small box on the top of the desk caught his attention. It contained a strange collection of small, miscellaneous oddments, leaving Finbarl wondering on their purpose. His eye spotted a ring of three keys. Few things in Athenia required locks, piquing Finbarl's interest. He quickly matched the smallest to the already unlocked desk drawer. Two left to find. One fitted the office door. The cupboard under a shelf was nothing more than it seemed, containing cups and a few bottles of Kywaczek. Finbarl considered reinforcing his courage with a quick swig, but abstained. Perhaps the key unlocked another room? Perhaps the documents he needed resided in another room? "Cronax!" he cursed softly, aware of the risk of venturing further into the sanctuary.

Finbarl tentatively turned the handle on the inner door, easing it open a crack, and peered through to an empty hallway. Several closed doors adjoining the hallway compounded his nerves, with potential for danger lurking beyond each. With a fateful determination, Finbarl opened the first door, his body primed to fight whomever resided within. A wave of relief washed through him on finding an empty bedroom. The bed looked so inviting, so soft and clean. Finbarl controlled an urge to reach out and stroke the smooth, cream sheets, so in contrast to the coarse, itchy blanket he struggled to keep warm under, but the key, gripped in his clammy hand, reminded him of his purpose. Was this a room for secrets? It no doubt held its fair share, but not the sort he hunted. A gut feeling led him on. The key, he thought with a smile, was key. Whatever it opened would give him the answers he sought. The bedroom – neat, tidy and lacking any locked cupboards – held nothing of interest.

Finbarl backed into the hallway and went to open the next door. As his hand gripped the handle, he stopped. A vague, subconscious recollection of something out of place in the hallway surfaced. He turned to examine the scene again. What had stirred his interest in this nondescript place? The bare walls, the plain stone floor, the doors … the doors! The door at the end stood out, made from a subtly darker wood but … Yes, it alone possessed a keyhole! Finbarl inspected the key in his hand, his hopes rising. What needed locking away in one of the most secure buildings in Athenia?

Finbarl confidently pushed the key into the hole and nodded with satisfaction as the lock clicked open. A cool, musty smell wafted through as he pushed the creaking door open. The odour stirred a distant memory from youth. He stepped into the dim light of the room, gaping in awe. Books! Books everywhere! He was in a library. Row upon row of shelves, each crammed with ancient books and manuscripts, squeezed together, gasping in the limited room. In some places they flooded down upon the floor in a mess. Finbarl's impulse to touch and feel got the better of him this time, and he ran a finger down the dusty spine of the tome before him. So many books in one place. Why had he never heard of this place before? Here before him lay the wisdom, imagination and memory of a golden time; a treasure greater than any Finbarl had seen or found in the sandy waste of the wilderness.

"Hello," said a voice from nowhere. "What's your name?"

Finbarl jumped out of his skin, his eyes searching the darkness for the source. "Show yourself!" he demanded, with a bravado at odds with the alarm of his racing heart.

"They don't usually leave the door open," said the voice, as three books disappeared from the shelf, leaving a hole through which Finbarl looked upon the gnarled face of an old man.

"Who are you?" asked Finbarl, feeling less fearful, but still alarmed at this unexpected encounter.

"Dul-biblex," came the reply from the old man, as he shoved the books back onto the shelf, vanishing from view.

"Dul-biblex?" repeated Finbarl with a little confusion. "I've not heard that name before."

The old man appeared at the end of the shelf and tottered towards Finbarl. "And I've not heard your name at all … ".

Finbarl watched the man closely as he approached. He had never seen anyone of such great age before; so old he couldn't put an age to him. His stooped frame was so strangely out of proportion against the large head upon it, hosting a big nose and huge ears, the skin a sickly, yellow hue. The eyes still possessed vigour and life but seemed more interested in the ajar door behind Finbarl. "It's Finbarl-apcula."

"Ah, a guard," said Dul-biblex, his eyes adjusting to look at Finbarl's green thawb. "What do you want?" He shuffled past a bewildered Finbarl, standing with an appetising eagerness in the light of the open door.

Finbarl watched as the intruding light highlighted the wrinkled face of the old man. "What do you do?" was all he could think to say back.

"Oh, you've curiosity and questions," said a delighted Dul-biblex, flashing a mouth half-empty of teeth at Finbarl. "I like that. This, after all, is the place for answers. Come, follow me! The light is hurting my eyes." He shuffled away, vanishing behind the shelves. After a moment of indecision, Finbarl followed.

The library went back twenty yards, a depth not appreciated from the vantage point at the door. Thin rays of light trickled in from blind-covered windows in the ceiling, catching the dust dancing through the air. Dul-biblex made his way between the maze of books with a familiar ease. Finbarl followed, tripping in the dark upon the clutter on the floor.

"You like books?" asked Dul-biblex. "Who doesn't," he added, before Finbarl could answer. "Look around. This is but a tiny fraction of the thinking and thoughts of mankind. Can you imagine what we've lost? It's a tragedy, but we must be grateful for what we retain. Socrates, Aristotle, Virgil, Ibn Khurdadhbih, Dante, Shakespeare, Montesquieu, Bronte, Dickens, Steinbeck, Beckett, Ibsen, Chopra, Emecheta.

"Biblio is the original word for 'book' from an ancient language called Greek," mumbled Dul-biblex aloud, as he shuffled along. Finbarl assumed he still addressed him. "It forms the basis of many words in our language such as Bible and bibliophile. Have you seen our copy of the Bible?" There was no way to tell if the question sought an answer, as Dul-biblex pressed on. "An interesting read and once, I believe, held precious by many." The old man stopped. "What was I saying?"

"You were telling me what you do,' replied Finbarl.

"Of course," said Dul-biblex, annoyed at his own forgetfulness, ambling forward again. "Books! I look after books. My name, it represents books: learning. When society became stratified in its current form, those looking after education adopted 'bibl' as a suffix in our name. We were wont to do pretentious things like that! But it is a proud label we all wore to identify those custodians of learning: the teachers, librarians and archivists."

"I've not heard that before," commented Finbarl. "My teacher was a Moralista."

"Really?" said Dul-biblex, his face showing disdain. "A teacher should only teach so their pupils can think for themselves. But it explains a lot. After all, they made me biblex. Would I have reached the top of my social strata had they not made us all but extinct! So, what is a guard doing visiting a librarian?"

"The Governor sent me," answered Finbarl, sticking to his lie.

The old man whipped around with surprising speed. "Don't lie to me, young man! I did not earn my position through stupidity. I'm the custodian of this reservoir of knowledge. Do you think I don't know a fib when I hear one?" His tone suddenly softened. "I've seen only Wardyns for too many years to remember. Where once I shared this hallowed space and this learning with my colleagues and eager pupils, now it and I are prisoners to the Wardyns' greed and paranoia. Loneliness is my companion and when I do hear a voice, it's that of a Wardyn. I listen carefully: I hear what they say and what they mean." Dul-biblex nodded his head thoughtfully. "Yes, they lie a lot, so I know what lying sounds like."

Finbarl stood stunned and confused. "Sorry."

"Tush." Dul-biblex waved his large hand through the air, dispensing forgiveness. "I've said my piece. Now tell me the truth. I'm intrigued by your treachery."

Finbarl gulped at the use of the word, but somehow felt safer in the old man's company. "Why have they locked you and the books away?" he asked, keen to discover more, rather than expose his own purpose.

"Ah, we both want the truth. Excellent! Excellent! Here, sit!" He motioned to a clear space on the floor. "An exchange of information. It feels like the old days." Dul-biblex rummaged through a pile of personal belongings, pushing a tin towards Finbarl. "They do keep me well-fed. Here, I can offer you a biscuit."

"Thanks," said Finbarl, taking a tough oatmeal biscuit and crunching it between his teeth.

"I'll tell you my truth first as the host," offered Dul-biblex. "All around you in this room is the most powerful weapon you'll ever see."

Finbarl glanced around at the chaotic shelves, unsure what to make of it all.

"The ancients had a saying: the pen is mightier than the sword. You build civilisation upon knowledge and learning, one generation passing on to the next, then the following generation building upon that. Maybe our ancestors built too high – like Icarus, they flew too close to the sun – but as I see it, they left us with another valuable lesson to learn from. Just because they ruined the world by their excesses and short-sightedness, it doesn't mean we disregard all the other wonders they discovered and invented. Through these books and documents, we have access to some of those wonders and inventions; to the lessons of the past that can light the path to the future. The knowledge only exists in this room and in the heads of those who've read the books. That is power!" Finbarl made to ask a question, but Dul-biblex pushed on. "So, when all this power was available to many citizens, it made the Wardyns uneasy. People could learn about the past: how others had governed themselves or thrown off tyrannical government."

"And because you know everything, they locked you up too," Finbarl blurted out.

Dul-biblex laughed. "I'm not all-knowing. My strength is I understand how much I don't know; how much I've still to learn. It keeps me going. Every answer you achieve in life should open the door to a new question. When you stop asking the questions, that is when you're doomed. When mankind started building walls, he chose to avoid asking the tough questions and facing up to the difficult answers: the Wardyns made an equally fatal mistake by locking the door to this library.

"When I die, there is no one to replace me. Quite what the Wardyns will do then, I don't know. I think they're too afraid to confront that moment and so have chosen to ignore it. Mankind is good at doing that." The old man stopped in thought and peered closely at Finbarl. "Tell me, your face reminds me of someone. An old student of mine."

Finbarl understood instantly. "Maddy? My mother." The way Dul-biblex spoke, the way he thought, it reminded him of his mother.

"Madeleine," confirmed Dul-biblex. "She was my favourite. How is she?"

"She's been in the Prison for nearly twenty years," answered Finbarl, bitterness saturating his words. "For most of that time I thought she was dead. That's what I was told."

Dul-biblex placed his palms together before his mouth, tutting with each revelation. "Then truly Athenia is doomed. For she was its future."

Any reluctance Finbarl bore to tell the truth suddenly vanished. This connection to Maddy, the parallels in his punishment and suffering, it made Dul-biblex a kindred spirit in Finbarl's eyes. He was someone he trusted and somebody who could help. "The real reason I'm here," he began, "is to destroy the Wardyns and the walls."

The old man took the confession with casual acceptance. "Of course, I already surmised that. But what is it you're seeking to achieve this?"

Finbarl detailed to Dul-biblex the full extent of the plan to expose the Wardyns' corruption and crimes and ultimately destroy the walls and civilisation itself; to start again and build a better world. He explained how it was his role to find the evidence to undermine the Wardyns' power. Dul-biblex responded thoughtfully, stroking his chin and humming. "Well," said Finbarl at the end, "can you help us?"

"Ambitious. Extremely ambitious," responded Dul-biblex. "Perhaps foolhardy. Certainly dangerous. I trust this plan is the brainchild of Madeleine?"

Finbarl nodded.

"I thought so. She always thought big, as did your father Alfbarl. I guess that's one of the reasons they upset the Wardyns. An idealist is a dangerous thing to the status quo..." The old man paused before adding, "... they can be dangerous for everyone. Seeing and saying what is wrong is the easiest of things; making things right is the hardest of things. You need to be careful. To progress, you can't destroy everything. You must understand what is good and important within the bad. A pesticide is no good if it kills the fruit as well as the pest, and even the pest may have an important wider role in the ecology."

"I don't understand," confessed Finbarl.

"I mean," answered Dul-biblex, "society is a complex thing. There's never one solution, just as there's never one problem. Everything becomes intertwined and interdependent. To unpick it to make it right is no easy task. What you're proposing will destroy society in its entirety. To think you can rebuild and make it better is ... ". Dub-biblex threw his hands up dramatically, "... reckless, arrogant and stupid."

"So, you won't help us?" said Finbarl.

The old man smiled. "Of course, I'll help you! Those are the very qualities driving history." A sudden coughing fit engulfed Dul-biblex, set off by an attempt to laugh. His face turned red, but he waved Finbarl away and gradually calmed. "I'm being frivolous. My apologies. They've held me against my will for longer than I can remember. How can I not wish for change, revenge and perhaps an end? Now, let me show you how I can help." He eased himself to his feet. "One advantage of me locked away as a secret is I'm among all the other secrets. I'm the keeper of all knowledge. They've no compunction in dumping their dirty laundry in this room, and I've no compunction in sharing them with whomever asks."

"We need something big," said Finbarl, following Dul-biblex to his feet. "Do you have proof they're taking the best crops while the rest live off scraps?"

"My dear boy, that won't do! It isn't a secret. Who doesn't suspect such a practice takes place? Man has the capacity to accept a certain level of corruption from its leaders, so long as they deliver on the basics: security and stability. No, what you need is a secret to undermine people's faith in them." Dul-biblex's fingers started to dance along a shelf. "Now let's start with this." He pulled out a narrow book, opened it and withdrew a parchment.

"What is it?" asked Finbarl.

"Proof we're not alone," answered Dul-biblex.

"You mean … ," began Finbarl.

"I mean civilisation has not shrunk down to just this pathetic husk. They found the parchment upon a dead body in the foothills several years ago – one of a small party of unfortunate souls. The Wardyns claim our Ferral friends found these strangers first, making easy pickings of them, but we must keep an open mind."

"What does it say?" Finbarl couldn't hide the amazement in his voice.

"It's a letter of introduction from a place called Mandelaton, somewhere far over the mountains. Can you imagine, a civilisation still with the spirit of adventure, sending out its envoys to seek friendship and trade?"

"Can I see?" requested Finbarl, his hand held out eagerly.

Dul-biblex passed the letter to Finbarl. "You can have it. Some of the language is different from ours, but it's easily decipherable. It has the power to destroy a crucial facet of the Wardyns' control. They've told the people we're alone in this world. It's a lie reinforcing the walls: why leave the security of Athenia if there's nothing beyond. You build the walls higher to protect all that's left."

"This is wonderful," said Finbarl. "I mean, to think we're not alone! Why would they keep this from us?"

"And I don't think it's the only contact over the years," added Dul-biblex, leaving Finbarl's question unanswered. "But I don't think it will be enough on its own to start your revolution. You'll need something to make the citizens question everything they believe."

"You've something that powerful?" exclaimed Finbarl.

"Mightier than the sword!" declared the old man.

A distant noise from the far end of the library interrupted their discussion.

"What was that?" whispered Finbarl.

"Hello." A new voice cut the silence.

Dul-biblex put a finger to his lips.

"Dul-biblex, are you with someone? Why is the door open? Grandfather, is that you?"

Finbarl mouthed a silent curse. Why hadn't he thought to close the door behind him?

Dul-biblex motioned for him to remain stationary and moved towards the approaching voice.

"Grandfather?"

"Hradkarl-eltar," acknowledged Dul-biblex, converging on the Governor's grandson. "Your grandfather's not here. I'm alone."

"I heard voices," declared Hradkarl.

"What is a lonely old man to do but talk to himself?"

"Don't take me for a fool, you decrepit prune! I heard two voices. Who's with you?" Hradkarl pushed Dul-biblex aside, stepping past, causing the old man to stumble back over a pile of books onto the floor.

Hearing the commotion, Finbarl strode forward. "It's Finbarl-apcula, Eltar," he announced, much to the surprise of the teenager.

"What are you doing in here?" He gave Finbarl a distasteful, suspicious inspection.

"I'm collecting some papers for your grandfather," replied Finbarl.

"What papers?" Hradkarl barked back.

Finbarl strained for an answer. "Err, well, I don't know. He just told me where to find them."

Despite their contrasting sizes, the short teenager stepped up to face Finbarl with an intimidating manner. He held himself like his grandfather, with the arrogant air of someone born to power. "No one is allowed in the library apart from the Wardyns! My grandfather would never send a guard."

"These are exceptional times," answered Finbarl, conscious his bluff felt weaker and weaker. "All the Wardyns are tied up in important business. The Governor wanted someone he could trust to ensure the papers didn't get into the wrong hands."

"Someone he could trust?" repeated Hradkarl. He almost touched Finbarl now, peering down at the parchment in his hands. "Show me the document you have for my grandfather!"

Finbarl looked down at the letter and then at Hradkarl, desperately thinking of his next line. "This document?"

"Of course, that document!" shouted Hradkarl. "Show it to me now, you insolent Ferral-whack!"

"The … the Governor did ask me to pass on a message to you, if I saw you," said Finbarl, tentatively offering the letter.

"Really? You had better tell me then, hadn't you?" Hradkarl snatched the parchment. "Well?"

Instinct took over. Finbarl's fist shot out, smacking against the doughy face of Hradkarl. He stared into the boy's bulging eyes, before watching him collapse with a vacant look, falling backwards unconscious. Finbarl whipped the letter out of Hradkarl's flailing hand and stepped back, shocked by his own action. Even though he plotted to bring down the Wardyns, to strike one felt so wrong.

"Does that count as reckless or stupid?" asked Dul-biblex, painfully pulling himself up with the support of a shelf.

Finbarl rubbed his knuckles. "Both, I guess. But what choice did I have?"

"And now what?"

"I don't know," replied Finbarl. "He knows I've been here. He'll ruin everything if he tells anyone. I'll have to kill him."

"You'll do no such thing!" insisted Dul-biblex. "Do not compound your stupidity with inane brutality. It won't take them long to work out you're the perpetrator. I presume you were seen entering the sanctuary?"

Finbarl shrugged, ashamed at his murderous intention.

"Of course, you were!" said Dul-biblex, answering his own question again. "No, your choices have narrowed. You leave the boy to me: I'll keep him here as long as I can. What you need now is time. Your fate's sealed, but the future isn't. You will be caught and thrown in the Prison – that's inevitable – but knowledge can still be your weapon."

Finbarl looked down at the boy, lying senseless between the bookshelves. A congealed stream of blood painted a scarlet line from his nose to the floor, but his chest slowly heaved up and down, confirming he lived. "What should I do?"

"I have something for you to read," announced Dul-biblex, ambling to another row of books. "It's something I've been working on. A history of the world. I've been trying to plug the shameful gap between the end of the Golden Age to our times. It's a brief read, for paper, as you know, is not easy to come by, but there's much in there you'll find of interest and help." The old man returned to Finbarl, handing him a sheaf of papers loosely bound together by string, and then added somewhat proudly. "It's my life's work, so I do hope you like it.

"Now, I suspect you'll only have a few hours before you're found, so you need to find a good hiding place: somewhere you won't be disturbed." The old man shook his head, looking to the ceiling. "To think my life's work can be read in but a few hours!" Lowering his eyes to look directly into Finbarl's, he solemnly added, "You read my history and carry the 'weapon' with you to the Prison!" Dul-biblex tapped the side of his head. "They can't take the knowledge we possess up here away from us."

"Thank you," said Finbarl.

"You'd better go! Time's not on your side." The old man turned, mumbling about books again.

Finbarl nodded and, stepping over Hradkarl, made his way towards the door.

"Give my best to your mother," Dul-biblex called after him. "I hope to see her soon."

Finbarl hurried along the corridor, his path crossing the same Moralistas passed on his way in. He knew the eyes nonchalantly watching him would soon be glaring with hatred, his name cursed and vilified.

"Got what you were looking for?" asked Walberg amiably, as Finbarl finally reached the exit doors.

"Yes, thanks," answered Finbarl.

"Looks like the Governor will be kept busy," continued Walberg, indicating the bundle of papers in Finbarl's hands.

"Oh, very busy!" replied Finbarl, as he slipped through the doors, his pulse racing.

*

Fortunately, the everyday occurrence of a guard going about their business brought no attention to Finbarl as he marched at pace towards the eastern end of the town. Getting through the east gate, past the guard and into the valley, presented a major risk, but was his best chance at finding a place to hide. As he approached the gatehouse, he slowed, ducking into a narrow alley, hiding in the shadow with a line of sight to the guard. Adekobe was on duty again. He sat stationary in a chair; his face turned away. There was no way past for Finbarl without crossing Adekobe's gaze. He needed a distraction, something to take Adekobe away from his post for a few moments, giving Finbarl time to scurry through the door. As he considered his options, the door to the farm opened and Finbarl jerked his head back into the shadow. Edging forward to look, he saw two young guards returning from their shift, deep in conversation. They stopped suddenly and smiled towards Adekobe. Finbarl frowned. Their chatter became secretive and mischievous as they tip-toed towards the seated guard. What was going on? It then dawned on Finbarl: Adekobe was asleep at his post! Finbarl cursed his misfortune at missing the opportunity. If only he had realised earlier. The guard would swear no soul had left Athenia under his watch to cover his dereliction of duty, putting the hunting pack off his scent for much longer. Finbarl sensed what the two youngsters planned to do. One snuck behind the snoozing sentry, while the other stood poised in front.

"Stand to, guard!" shouted the one facing Adekobe. "The Governor wants to pass!"

Finbarl watched as Adekobe jumped to his feet, even from afar his confusion clear. The young guard before him laughed strenuously as Adekobe slowly realised he was the victim of a joke. "Very funny!" he grumbled. "Now piss off!"

The fun, however, continued. While Adekobe rebuked one guard, the other, still unnoticed, stealthily pulled his chair away. As the older sentry attempted to sit back down, he fell on his arse, his arms swinging wildly up as he tried to steady himself. This time, both youngsters exploded with laughter, congratulating each other for their slapstick jape. Adekobe climbed to his feet, rubbing his backside, while the jokers edged away, conscious, through their hysterics, of the retribution his expression promised.

"You'll pay for that!" yelled Adekobe, as the two scallywags ran away, whooping with delight. He chased them, cursing with promises of revenge.

Finbarl managed to smile, recognising a good joke and seeing his opportunity, as all three ran past him. He dashed for the door, glancing behind to ensure Adekobe wasn't returning, and vanished into the valley unseen.

CHAPTER 20

Aminatra held her bare foot up to her face, examining the sole. She ran an index finger between her big and index toe, removing a line of dirt, and pressed her thumb into the sore inner arch, then lowered her tired foot into a small pool of water and sighed. Her boots lay to the side, their soles thin and loose, the cause of her blisters and discomfort. Most of the other prisoners wore primitive sandals fashioned from animal hide, their original footwear long disposed of. Aminatra longed to hang on to this simple vestige of civilisation but knew the day fast approached when she would need to follow suit.

They had ventured as far north from Athenia as they dared, into the foothills, where the line of trees reaching up into the mountains ended. A natural spring encouraged rich and plentiful vegetation. Hoof and paw prints from others seeking water and shade littered the exposed mud.

"It's good to rest upon grass for a change." Maddy lay under the shade of a cedar tree.

Aminatra glanced back at her friend. "It's so nice. Why don't we spend more time here?"

Maddy pointed at a hoof print. "Where the deer comes, so does the mountain cat." She indicated a large paw print in the same vicinity. "This is Ferral territory, my dear! They prefer the cooler habitat of the foothills and, just like us, they need to drink."

Aminatra sat upright, fearful of eyes upon her. "Are we safe?"

"Of course not, dear!" chuckled Maddy. "There's nowhere we're safe. They don't usually visit the watering hole this early in the day, but never lower your guard. We come here because it does us good to experience what the world could offer us and, if we're lucky, we may find some tasty mushrooms."

"Why hasn't Athenia established a farming community here?" asked Aminatra, hastily putting her boots back on.

Maddy shrugged. "Don't know, dear. Maybe they did a long time ago and it failed."

"Because of the Ferrals?"

"Possibly. Or the crops didn't like the soil. There's only a thin layer."

A howl broke the serenity, its source a mystery as it echoed all around.

"What was that?" Aminatra jumped to her feet, looking around in panic.

"I don't know," answered Maddy nervously. "It might be time we were on our way!" The other prisoners grabbed their belongings. "Get your stuff! Quickly!"

The group formed into a loose column, their makeshift weapons gripped tightly, their eyes searching for movement in the surrounding trees and hills. A sudden shadow from a passing cloud caused further agitation, their pace increasing to a jog.

"Could it be a wolf or dog?" asked Aminatra of no one in particular.

"Could be," answered Obidon, a hardened prisoner with a disfiguring scar across his forehead and as tall as anyone

Aminatra had ever met. His appearance, however, did a disservice to his personality, which Aminatra found kind and considerate, if sometimes a little blunt. "But it's also how Ferrals communicate when they're hunting."

"They wouldn't attack a group this large. Would they?"

Obidon gave Aminatra a disbelieving look. "They attack a walled town of nine thousand people regularly. Of course, they'd attack us!"

Aminatra tightened the grip upon her improvised weapon, a crude piece of knapped flint bound to a short stick. It was yet to be used in anger, and she examined the deer tendon binding holding the stone in place. It looked so pathetic compared with the weapons others in the group brandished. Only Maddy possessed a weapon of equal questionability. She carried a good, solid staff, used while walking and for digging roots, but it would not, Aminatra imagined, be much good in a fight. "What do we do if they attack?"

"Fight, my dear!" came the terse response from Maddy.

"You can try running," added Obidon, "but they can run faster and longer than we can. They'll just wait until you're separated from the rest and pick you off; like a wolf pack hunting a deer herd."

"I wish-ed I were a deer," said Johansson.

He said the strangest things at the strangest times, thought Aminatra. "Do they have a weakness?"

"Can't say I've ever considered it when I'm fighting for my life!" replied Obidon.

"They seem to behave entirely instinctively," answered Maddy more sympathetically. "While some always appear willing to sacrifice their lives to make the initial breakthrough, the others will give up if we hold our shape as a group and inflict enough injuries or mortal blows on them."

"You sound like you've survived a few attacks."

"My dear," said Maddy, "you don't survive the number of years I've lived in the Prison without getting attacked by the Ferrals more than a few times!"

"Of course not," agreed Aminatra. "When will we know when we're safe?"

"When the last breath of life leaves our bodies," remarked Obidon. "If the Ferrals are on our trail, then a clash is inevitable. What we need to do is get to a place we can defend more easily, without getting trapped ourselves."

"I think I know of such a place," offered Maddy. "Not too far from here. Come on!"

The grass vanished as they returned to the arid sand and stone on the edge of the plain. Aminatra glanced over her shoulder every few seconds for signs of their pursuers. Occasionally she thought she saw movement but couldn't be sure. The brain played cruel tricks under the influence of fear.

The party soon became stretched out. Jogging in the dry heat tested the healthiest individual and, for malnourished prisoners, it quickly separated the weak from the fit.

"Slow down!" came a shout from behind.

"Hurry up!" someone countered.

Aminatra suddenly realised she had become separated from Maddy. She looked behind to see the older woman lagging about twenty yards back. "Come on, Maddy!"

"Go! Go!" Maddy waved Aminatra on through rasping breath, but the younger woman slowed to a walking pace, allowing her friend to catch up. "Don't let sentiment be your downfall, dear," Maddy gasped as she came level. "Darwinism is God in this place!"

"Eh?" Aminatra had no idea what Maddy meant. "You're my friend. I'm always going to be there to help you, as you've helped me."

Maddy considered trying to explain her words further, but instead just replied, "Thank you!"

"How much further?"

"Not far, Ami," reassured Maddy. "It's a ruined settlement on that hill over there." She indicated some 300 yards to the south-west. "It'll give us some defence, but more importantly, give us time to start a fire."

"And that'll keep any Ferrals away?" asked Aminatra.

"They certainly don't like flames but … ".

A spine-shivering shriek shattered the silence to their left. Before Aminatra or Maddy knew what to do, a naked figure, its face painted vividly with raw umber mud, was upon them. Aminatra screamed, swinging her axe wildly through the air. Elsewhere, more figures sprang from nowhere, their piercing cries creating a fearful cacophony. They ran and leapt in all directions, hurling stones at their prey with unerring accuracy.

"We've let ourselves spread out too far!" cried Maddy, flinging her satchel to the ground and rotating her staff round her head. "Group up! Group up!" But it was too late. The Ferrals surrounded them, targeting each small unit of prisoners. Blurred movement and echoing shrieks created a sense their numbers were overwhelming.

In front of Aminatra and Maddy, a single Ferral stood, its eyes impassively locked upon them. "Stand with me!" instructed Maddy. "If it goes for one of us, the other can fend it off!"

A stone caught Aminatra on her forehead, causing her to reel back stunned. She felt the warm flow of blood trickle down her face, but adrenaline allowed her to stay focused and she stepped back to Maddy's side. The Ferral snarled, exposing its stained teeth, emitting a peculiar hiss. Aminatra had never been this close to a Ferral, and though a human body stood before her, she saw the monster portrayed throughout her life. A grotesque beast, hunched down, neck protruding, creeping around them.

"I think the smell of the salve is confusing it," whispered Maddy. Shouts and screams around indicated other Ferrals suffered no such qualms, throwing themselves at the desperate prisoners. Aminatra caught sight of Obidon from the corner of her eye, swinging a large club pitted with flint and glass shards at the head of a charging Ferral. The beast yelped pitifully and slumped to the floor dead. Perhaps hope remained.

"Get away!" screamed Aminatra, lashing her axe forward at the Ferral. Its eyes now fixated upon her, the blood dripping from her chin exciting its bestial senses.

"I'm going to get something from my satchel," declared Maddy abruptly. "Have you got me covered?"

"You're what?" exclaimed Aminatra.

"I'm going to try to reason with it. Offer it some dried meat."

"Cronax! Maddy! This isn't the time to try out one of your theories."

Maddy slowly lowered herself, blindly feeling for the bag, her eyes remaining fixed on the Ferral. Aminatra reluctantly positioned herself in front, slashing her axe through the air as menacingly as possible.

"Got it!" announced Maddy triumphantly, standing with a couple of pieces of dried meat upon her palm. She tentatively offered out her hand, smiling meekly at the Ferral. For the first time the creature's eyes lost their intensity and looked with interest at the gift. "It's for you, dear," said Maddy. "Very tasty. Yum, yum." She extended her arm a little further. "I think it's working." The Ferral stepped a little closer, a perplexed look upon its face, while its nose twitched in exploration.

"I can clobber it as it takes the meat," suggested Aminatra, through the side of her mouth.

"No, no," implored Maddy. "This is going to wo ... "

From nowhere another Ferral sprang, landing upon Maddy's back, its teeth digging into her neck. She screamed, swinging around, trying to dislodge the attacker. The distraction triggered an attack by the other Ferral, his interest in the dried meat forgotten. It leapt forward upon Maddy, knocking both victim and attacker to the floor. Aminatra staggered back in shock. With no idea what to do, her survival instinct kicked in. She brought her axe down as hard as possible upon the neck of one of the Ferrals. Her binding held firm. The block of flint crashed down with a sickening sound. Aminatra followed up with a swing of her boot into the beast's midriff, but as the kick landed, she knew the Ferral was dead. It lay unmoving upon the writhing mass beneath as Maddy and the other Ferral continued their own struggle. An odd sensation swept through Aminatra. Light-headed and disorientated, she raised the axe again, then dropped it as she fell backwards in a faint.

CHAPTER 21

Finbarl found a hiding place within a small shack used to store tools. A strong, musty smell accompanied the stifling heat inside, the odd rat keeping him company. He cleared some spades from the corner and squeezed in out of sight of anyone entering. On his way through the valley he had picked up a fallen orange and peach. He placed the orange in his lap and took a satisfying bite out of the peach. It tasted so good fresh. Licking his fingers clean, he picked up Dul-biblex's manuscript, opening it at the first page. Although taught to read as a child, with so little practice, his standard of literacy remained poor.

Tracing his finger over Dul-biblex's text, Finbarl absorbed the content, occasionally stopping to say an unfamiliar word aloud, hoping it made phonetic sense. When this failed, he read on, filling in the blanks with logic and common sense. With time against him, Finbarl was grateful for the brevity of Dul-biblex's manuscript.

The narrative fascinated Finbarl. The introduction he knew already: the end of the Golden Age, global warming, the rise in crime and anarchy, the collapse of the old order. But Dul-biblex, with his vast knowledge and access to the library, managed to illuminate the great void of time stretching back from the present. The more Finbarl read, the more confident he became and the faster he progressed, but time moved forward and he realised Hradkarl would have raised the alarm by now. He needed to read even faster.

Some four hours later, a noise from outside the shack broke Finbarl's absorption in the book. As the chatter got closer, he quietly closed the manuscript, laying it by his side. Voices spoke firmly, the tone indicating they may be guards. Finbarl breathed out slowly, preparing himself for this final act in his life as an Athenian citizen. They came closer and closer, until he heard their every utterance.

"Fan out and ensure you keep the man next to you in sight!" Finbarl couldn't quite recognise the voice, but knew they hunted for him. He made himself smaller, squeezing his knees to his chest. Silly thoughts entered his mind. Could they hear his breathing? It sounded incredibly loud to him. The more he thought about it, the harder it got to take a breath. What would they do to him? Would they summarily execute him for attacking a Wardyn? Should he tell those about to apprehend him all he had discovered from the manuscript? Would it be enough to convince them straight away and start the uprising? Or perhaps he should try to fight his way out? That damn breathing!

Footsteps crunched outside, the door to the shack creaking open. Finbarl held his breath. He refused to look towards the door, irrationally convinced if he couldn't see them, they couldn't see him.

The voice of authority boomed again from outside. "Anything?"

"No!" came the reply from within the shack.

To Finbarl's relief the man turned to leave. Something familiar in the voice intrigued him, but he hadn't said enough for Finbarl to place it.

"You were in there for a second! Look properly!"

Cronax! Finbarl silently cursed the diligence of the commanding officer. The door to the shack rattled shut. The guard's breathing now sounded incredibly loud. A sudden crash of tools pushed to one side startled Finbarl and he blew out a slow, measured breathe. He dared to angle his eyes towards his pursuer. Through the shelves and aligned row of tools, he made out some movement, recognising the green of a guard's uniform. The face, however, remained hidden.

"You wait 'til I find you, Finbarl! I'm gonna so enjoy watching you suffer!" It was Audlech.

Finbarl's heart plummeted. Why did it have to be him? Perhaps he should surprise him, steal his gun and make his escape. By the time he climbed to his feet, shook the cramp from his legs and climbed over the barrel, Audlech would have shot him at least twice, and perhaps a few more times for fun.

His foe continued to treat his surroundings without respect, shoving the farming implements to one side and kicking boxes. The tools stacked to the side of Finbarl tumbled and collapsed, a small container dropping from the shelf onto Finbarl's head. An instinctive yelp may have escaped his lips. He couldn't say – he recalled hearing it, but not releasing it. Silence followed. Audlech stopped his destructive search and stood motionless. Finbarl solemnly closed his eyes.

"Well, well, well! Finbarl! You fieving, cheating, Ferralwhack traitor!"

Finbarl opened his eyes to see a smug Audlech looking down at him from behind a barrel. "Audlech! You've got to hear me out!" he implored. "I've got something so important you and everyone in Athenia need to know about."

"Is that so, Orpho?" replied Audlech, bringing his rifle butt crashing down on Finbarl's head, knocking him out cold.

*

A burning pain in his arms stirred Finbarl back to consciousness. He opened his eyes to a foggy world, immediately aware his arms were bound behind him. A face appeared in his blurred vision.

"You've been a bad boy!" said a stern voice. "I never did like you much! I don't know what my brother saw in you."

Finbarl's vision sharpened, his brain adding voice recognition to its computations. It was Hradbar. Their location was still in the valley, with Finbarl propped up against the outside of the shack. He tried to say something, but his stifled mumble confirmed the strange sensation he felt across his face: a gag.

"That was my boy you attacked!" growled Hradbar. "You broke his nose!"

Finbarl tried to speak again, but a muffled nonsense came out.

"You don't get the right to defend yourself! You lost your rights the moment you broke into the sanctuary and stole. The Governor wants a word with you about that. But before he does, the facts must fit the story. You know, the one where you put up a tremendous fight as you tried to escape, and we only managed to apprehend you after the most vicious of struggles."

Realising what awaited him, Finbarl emitted a high-pitched yelp.

"Okay boys, he's all yours! Just remember, and it pains me to say it, the Governor wants him alive."

Finbarl observed several bodies closing in. He recognised Audlech's grinning face leading the pack. The guard held a spade in his hands, lifting it and bringing the flat head down upon Finbarl's knee. Finbarl tried to scream, but only a diluted whimper passed through the gag. Another blow came from the right. Finbarl turned his torso in a vain attempt to protect himself. Green guard uniforms surrounded him, leading to blow upon blow and a chorus of laughter. The initial excruciating pain lasted a few minutes before he drifted into unconsciousness. As the light faded from his vision, one last image seared upon his mind: Strathbol's angry face behind a determined strike to his gut.

*

"Ah, you're back with us at last," said Governor Elbar, towering over the bed. "You shouldn't have resisted arrest. You of all people should know that."

Finbarl hardly had the strength to open his eyes.

"Now, don't try to move," instructed the Governor. "Apart from the pain it'll cause, you'll soon find you're not going anywhere. Our special prisoner has had quite special treatment! You'll remain bound until you're disposed of in the Prison. You've caused quite enough excitement in Athenia as it is."

Half expecting to find himself still gagged, Finbarl was surprised when words came out. "What do you want?" he croaked through his painfully dry mouth.

"Me? I want justice."

"Justice!" exclaimed Finbarl, as loudly as his voice allowed. "I've read our real history. I know your dirty secret!"

"It's not my secret," corrected the Governor, picking up Dul-biblex's manuscript from a side table. "It's Athenia's, and a secret it's going to stay."

"Your Ferral of a son should have killed me while he had the chance!" spat out Finbarl. "I'll ensure the story is eventually heard. Even when I'm in the Prison I'll be able to somehow make sure it filters back to Athenia. And once they know, you Wardyns won't last a day!"

The Governor laughed. "Oh, you're going to the Prison all right. After all, justice has got to be seen to be done. But from my experience, it's the ex-guards who don't last a day when they find themselves in the company of those prisoners they used to torment."

Finbarl managed to open his eyes wider. "What ex-guards? I don't remember any guard sentenced to the Prison before!"

"You wouldn't," answered the Governor. "We never burden the town with a trial of a guard. What would that do for law and order if the citizens learnt about an enforcer's disregard for the law they're supposed to uphold? A select few smuggle them out of the town and we let the prisoner scum mete out their own justice. We could always leave you to the Ferrals if you preferred."

Finbarl closed his eyes, wishing the nightmare away, hoping, when he opened them again, his old life would be reset. The Governor's voice broke the fantasy.

"I don't know what went wrong with you, boy. I honestly thought you could make something of your life and serve Athenia honourably for a long time. The Orphos make the most loyal guards ... usually. They don't have the family loyalties and self-serving attitude of the Familos. I suppose you found out who your parents were and got delusions of grandeur. Is that what happened?"

"Yeah, right," retorted Finbarl, his eyes still closed. He thought about retaliating by challenging the Governor on his parents' fate, but stopped. Any mention of Maddy risked exposing the fact she lived, putting her in danger. "You forget, I can see right through your lies and manipulating words now. Nothing you say means anything to me."

"You're a stupid fool!" chastised Elbar, his tone suddenly full of anger. "We're all servants to this fragile civilisation, and we all have to make sacrifices to keep it going!"

Finbarl snorted in contempt before the Governor continued.

"You're right when you say what's in the book will destroy us if it gets out, but it won't just be the Wardyns. It'll be all of us!

How long do you think we'll survive without direction, without firm leadership, without justice? The history in that book is a chronical of a civilisation that's continued for thousands of years, and I'm not willing to be the last chapter."

Finbarl opened his eyes again, looking directly into the Governor's. "What about the others? Those who've made contact. I've seen the letter! We're not all that remains of civilisation. What did you do to them to keep this façade up? Have them killed!"

"Bah!" dismissed the Governor. "What did that fool Dul-biblex tell you? They found it on a Ferral-devoured corpse. One of five bodies. They may come from a place beyond the mountains, but there was no evidence they were civilised. They didn't even have guns."

"Perhaps that was an indication of how civilised they were," rasped Finbarl.

"Nonsense! More like an indication of how stupid! Civilisation's just as much at risk of corruption or dilution from those deluded degenerates, as by criminals or Ferrals."

"I'm beginning to like them already!" Finbarl smiled, as the Governor's face brightened to a rich rouge.

"And yet they all fail," the Governor hissed.

"All?" queried Finbarl. "There have been more than one!"

"You'll be given a week to recover from your injuries," asserted the Governor, changing the subject, "and then you'll be ceremonially marched through the town to the Prison. You've made a little too much noise for us to discreetly pack you off to the Prison, so we're going to make an example of you. Then we'll see how well you're liked! At this moment, the guards hate you, the citizens want to tear you apart and, well, the prisoners will tear you apart. The Ferrals can have the scraps. You deserve everything that's coming to you."

Finbarl opened his mouth to continue the sparring, but the pain stopped him. Instead he closed his mouth, turned his head away, ignoring the Governor until he left.

CHAPTER 22

The Governor had been right. The hatred directed towards Finbarl, as they dragged him through the streets was like nothing witnessed before. Thousands turned out to jeer and throw camel dung his way. The guards took great delight in humiliating him, tripping and spitting at him. Deprived of Jumblar for nearly thirty-six hours made the experience still worse, every sensation exaggerated. Finbarl now understood why a quiet death was not to be his fate. Nothing unified the mob like an easily identified and defeated enemy. Finbarl wanted to shout, tell them all about the truth and the lies, but the gag covered his mouth again, completing his humiliation.

It was a relief to finally leave the walls of Athenia and enter the silence of the Prison. Finbarl walked alone with his guard of dubious honour, including Vassel, Audlech, Gauret and the obligatory taciturn priest. Gauret, one of his few friends, had not spoken to Finbarl or looked him in the eye since his arrest. The image of Strathbol striking a blow during his arrest haunted him, but Finbarl understood. Only recently he was that naïve youngster, captivated by the lies. But Gauret always possessed a healthy scepticism, and Finbarl hoped he might understand or at least, in the absence of any facts, want to understand.

"Let's kill him ourselves!" proposed Audlech, as he triumphantly looked down from his camel upon the bound Finbarl. "Why should the prisoners have all the fun?"

"Because that's not what we've been tasked with doing! Now shut up!" shouted Officer Vassel, in a foul mood, at the front of the column. One of his prodigies had been found to be a traitor, and this duty was his punishment.

After a long, torturous walk, they arrived at a deserted Bruuk's Point. Finbarl hoped to be free of his gag and bindings as soon as they got there, but instead, they dumped him against the tor, telling him to wait in the stifling heat. His mouth felt so dry, the gag absorbing any moisture. He watched the guards go about their usual business, setting up a perimeter and preparing the Jumblar for distribution. Despite his precarious situation, Jumblar dominated his thoughts. Would they let him have his allocation, or was it part of their cruel game to make him go mad by depriving him? His imminent death at the hands of the prisoners probably made it a moot point. But, Cronax, a bit of Jumblar would be welcome now!

It was hard to tell how much time passed before the first prisoners arrived. An exhausted Finbarl drifted in and out of sleep, Audlech ensuring he stayed awake with the occasional sharp kick of his boot. Each arriving prisoner inspected Finbarl, combining hatred with satisfaction. Nothing made a person at the bottom of the pile feel better than seeing someone from a position of authority fall below them.

Audlech, who never spoke to prisoners unless threatening them, appeared in deep conversation with a couple. His head turned regularly to look at Finbarl, his gruesome grin exposing his sentiment. Finbarl suspected the topic of the discussion was his own fate.

With the prisoners milling about, Finbarl's eyes hunted for his mother. She was his only hope. With the guards ignorant of their relationship, after their departure, his survival depended on her influence with the other prisoners. But he saw no sign of her nor anyone he recognised from her group.

Only when his despondency fell to its lowest ebb did Finbarl notice a further troop of prisoners emerge from the haze. His vision was foggy from roasting in the sun for over an hour, but he still easily recognised the figure of Aminatra amongst the others, his hopes soaring. Readjusting to an upright position, he craned his neck to look for Maddy. She always hung back a little. Where was she? He needed to see her face, feel the love recently discovered.

"Right, come and trade for your Jumblar!" cried Vassel. The prisoners converged on the tor, forming a disorderly queue, as the guards rotated around them with disdainful and suspicious eyes.

"Finbarl!" A barely audible whisper came from above Finbarl. "Don't turn your head! Just listen. It's Gauret."

Finbarl fought off the urge to turn, wanting badly to look his friend in the eye and implore his help.

"Everyone else is distracted but we don't have long," continued Gauret. "What have you gone and done, you Ferral-whack?" Any criticism was lost under the affectionate tone. "I've dropped a small knife behind the stone you're leaning on. Don't ask me how I got it but you're going to need it to survive. There's also a small amount of Jumblar as you'll probably be needing that yesterday!"

Finbarl mumbled his gratitude.

"Yeah, well it came from my own supply, so I'll be cursing you later when the heebie-jeebies start to bite! Take care of yourself. I'll try to get you some extra rations if you're still alive next time I'm here."

Further words failed to get through the gag as Finbarl tried to engage Gauret, but it soon became clear his friend had gone.

*

With the guards mounted on their camels ready for departure, Vassel came over to Finbarl. The officer signalled for him to stand, yanking upon his elbow as he struggled to his feet. Their eyes met but there was no friendship in Vassel's, only disappointment. He pulled out a knife, crudely rotated Finbarl round, and cut the bindings holding his hands. Finbarl rubbed at his sore wrists and pulled the gag from his mouth.

"I was told to leave the gag on until the last minute," said Vassel. "Your mind's been poisoned, and you want to spread it. Well, I've also got instructions to shoot you in each kneecap if you say a word before me and the boys are over the horizon. Do you understand me?"

Finbarl nodded his head, grateful to be able to breathe through his mouth again.

"You can have this." Vassel threw him a gourd of water. "But we aren't wasting anything else on you. You'll be dead by nightfall and forgotten by tomorrow."

Finbarl opened his mouth to say something, but a finger lifted to his own lips by Vassel stopped him.

"You're a great disappointment to me, Finbarl, but I don't want to have to cause you any more pain than you've had. I sincerely hope your death is quick and painless."

As soon as Vassel left, Finbarl tipped the gourd up to his mouth, letting the sweet water flow into his mouth, quenching his thirst. His body ached, his skin felt raw in the burning sun, but he didn't move, preferring to stand as proudly as possible while his former colleagues rode away. With the guards far enough away, Finbarl turned, reaching into the darkened gap between two boulders. He hoped a snake or lizard hadn't made it their sanctuary from the midday sun. The coolness on his hand felt welcome, in sharp contrast to the almost unbearable heat his other hand endured resting atop the boulder. His fingers touched the smooth metal blade of the knife and, with a little manoeuvring, he pinched it between two fingers, pulling it out. The Jumblar had fallen deeper into the crack, just beyond his reach. He made it out in the shadow, tantalisingly close, but beyond his touch. In the guards' absence, the noise amongst the prisoners rose and Finbarl decided to leave the Jumblar for the time being to find his mother. While dying at the hands of another prisoner would ease some of the torment of Jumblar's vengeance, he wasn't about to give up on life just yet.

The other prisoners kept their distance, suspiciously looking over to inspect their former oppressor, nervous with a 'guard' in their company. Finbarl took another swig of water. He tucked the knife in an inner pocket, safe and hidden until needed: for how long he didn't know, but not long. Killing a former guard was probably the only pleasure available to a prisoner. The sooner Finbarl found his mother, the better. Walking over to where he last saw Aminatra, he discovered her reorganising a bag amidst her companions.

Finbarl spoke her name tentatively. "Aminatra."

She turned, displaying a prominent wound upon her forehead, beneath which her tired features acknowledged Finbarl with a resigned smirk. "I see you're one of us now. I'm guessing you failed."

He shrugged. "I guess I did. Where's Maddy? I need to speak with her."

"Your mother's been badly injured," explained Aminatra. "She's too weak to travel, so we left her in Bluebecker Woods."

"You left her alone!"

"We'd no choice!" snapped back Aminatra. "We got attacked by Ferrals. Your mother's lucky to be alive but her wounds are bad. She can't walk, and we can't carry her. I did all I could for her and if we leave soon, we should get back to her today."

"But if the Ferrals find her alone … ?"

"I know," said Aminatra more sympathetically, "but she'd have been just as vulnerable if we could somehow have carried her. She can't run or fight. She's well-hidden where she is. It was the best option."

Finbarl nodded. "Sorry, I'm grateful for all you've done. This has all gone so wrong. I didn't even get a chance to check up on Karlmon. Are you all right?" He pointed a finger at her wounded head.

The mention of Karlmon sent a wave of pain through Aminatra, but she possessed more resilience under Maddy's stoic tutorship "Welcome to our world. I'm fine. But don't worry, your mother's a fighter. You can talk to her tonight."

Finbarl, conscious of some of the male prisoners watching him closely, their intention clear, moved his hand to the hilt of his dagger. "Perhaps we could leave sooner rather than later. I'm not sure I have much of a future hanging around in the company of some of these goons."

Aminatra inspected the scene. "You certainly won't if you keep referring to them as goons. We'll be heading off in a few minutes."

"Can I trust your group?"

"They know what you mean to Maddy," answered Aminatra. "But we lost a few of our number in the Ferral attack and others are carrying injuries. I'm told this is when new alliances and partnerships are formed, so we may have some fresh faces."

"I see," said Finbarl uneasily. "Well, you've got me now too. I can help protect you."

"You need to think about protecting yourself first. I think it's time we were off." Aminatra noticed a quartet of men approaching, trouble written across their faces.

"Hey, guard!" The tallest of the group and obvious leader stood behind Finbarl. "Your Ferral-whack friends have left without you on their camels. You should get after them!"

Finbarl slowly turned. "They aren't my friends," he said as placidly as possible. "I'm a prisoner, like you."

"What you are is a dead man," snarled the man.

Finbarl recognised him as the one conversing with Audlech earlier. He gripped the knife hilt tightly. "Well I feel remarkably alive and that's the way I intend to stay. Now, go on your way! I've no beef with anyone here."

"You've no beef?" mimicked the man. "Is that right? You ain't in charge no more. You don't tell us to go on our way!"

Aminatra, watching nervously to the side, intervened. "He's Maddy's son! He's been trying to bring the Wardyns down."

The man gave Aminatra a look of hatred. "Well the old hag can try her herbs on a dead body, see if they do any good."

No amount of talking was going to resolve this situation. They intended just one outcome. Finbarl drew his knife. "If you don't want that dead body to be yours, I suggest you piss off!"

The man stepped back in alarm. "Once a guard always a guard."

"I don't know what that means," said Finbarl, waving the knife in front, "but if I were still a guard, you'd be dead by now. So, save your energy for finding food and leave us alone!"

"This ain't over, guard!" The man drew a finger across his throat and indicated to his colleagues to back off. They trudged away in conspiratorial discussion.

"Have you ever noticed," commented Finbarl to Aminatra, as he let out a relieved breath, "there are fewer people willing to fight for what's right than those willing to start a fight for what's wrong?"

"Some people in the Prison deserve to be here," commented Aminatra. Does Finbarl know how much he sometimes sounds like his mother? she pondered to herself. "Come on, let's get out of here!"

"Who was that?" asked Finbarl, replacing the knife back in the pocket.

"I only know him as Dove," replied Aminatra, as she sealed her satchel and hoisted it over her shoulder. "A touch of irony there."

As Aminatra led Finbarl into the safety of her own group, they passed a solitary, wretched figure Finbarl recognised. The man, securing his Jumblar in his satchel, looked up slowly. It was Gorwell, whom Finbarl escorted into the Prison not so long ago. His hair was wild, his face drawn beneath a bushy beard.

Finbarl felt a jolt of guilt and looked away quickly.

"Welcome to hell," croaked Gorwell.

Finbarl stopped. "I'm sorry for what I did to you. I didn't understand things then." Gorwell just nodded slowly, leaving Finbarl uncertain whether he accepted the apology or not. "Where is … ," Finbarl paused to trawl his memory for the other prisoner deposited that day, " … Pryfol?"

"Dead," answered Gorwell impassively. "His type doesn't stand a chance out here."

Finbarl wanted to know what he meant, but Aminatra tugged at his sleeve. "Come on! We must go."

"I'm sorry," repeated Finbarl, leaving Gorwell to himself.

*

The route to Bluebecker Woods was a well-trodden one for the group, consisting of fourteen prisoners, four of whom were joining anew, like Finbarl. Indeed, Finbarl recognised one woman as a victim of the recent purge. The poor soul still owned the bewildered appearance of someone who couldn't believe their life had fallen apart. Perhaps, considered Finbarl, the same look adorned his own face.

A man called Crixus, with an obvious air of authority, appeared to be leading the party, his red hair marking him out, his manner firm and organised as the column set off. Finbarl didn't recall seeing him when digging out the boiler, further proof of the ever-changing dynamics of the wandering groups within the Prison. When Aminatra introduced Finbarl, he received a grudging grunt of acknowledgement, the lingering resentment towards a past guard obvious.

The piercing blue sky possessed a beauty hard to appreciate as it continued to expose them to the unrelenting heat of the sun. A light dust cloud stirred under their feet, leaving a hint to others of their route. Finbarl's suspicious and watchful mind noticed this breadcrumb trail and he mentioned the risk to Aminatra.

"Others will know where we're heading anyway," Aminatra observed. "They'll have heard about Maddy and told others. Soon it'll get back to Dove and his goons."

Finbarl smiled at her adoption of his term. "Who can we rely on in your group?" he asked, out of earshot of the others.

"Just yourself," answered Aminatra tersely. Maddy would have been proud of that answer.

"Let me ask a different question. If those guys come looking for me, will your friends help?"

Aminatra appeared a little tired of the subject. "I really don't know, Finbarl. They've no reason to help you; you're a former guard and you've a lovely knife they wouldn't mind themselves."

"But you indicated at Bruuk's Point we could trust them." Finbarl reassessed the line of people.

"They won't kill you themselves but they're not going to risk their lives for you either. Listen Finbarl," sighed Aminatra, "there aren't any rules out here, except the strongest and smartest survive and then only if they're lucky. Your mother has survived because she's smart and everyone else knows it, but the rest of us have to go with the current and hope it doesn't drag us under."

"You sound pretty smart yourself," complimented Finbarl.

"I'm learning from your mother."

"Well, if it means anything, you can rely on me."

Aminatra smiled amicably but looked sceptical.

"What?" pressed Finbarl.

"You've got to do an awful lot to earn people's trust here, including my own. Do you fully understand the part you've played in ruining so many lives?"

"I was doing what I thought was right," countered Finbarl. "It's proper to fight for what you believe in." Aminatra remained silent, letting Finbarl's thoughts meander, searching for justification. "I was lied to just like everyone else and only following orders. Sometimes you have to do some bad for the greater good."

"Listen to yourself," chided Aminatra. "You sound like a Wardyn."

"What does that mean?" Finbarl asked, unaccustomed to losing an argument with a prisoner.

"Nothing," said Aminatra. "As you say, you were lied to like everyone else."

"Why are you helping me at all? I'm responsible for taking your boy away from you, remember?"

"I'm glad you're taking responsibility!" scolded Aminatra, before stopping to draw upon some inner strength. She closed her eyes, took a deep breath and started again. "I'm learning from Maddy to let go of the past and focus on the now. It isn't easy, but I'm trying. That's why I'm helping you now." She took another deep breath, before adding, "I'm doing this for Maddy."

Finbarl recognised the opportunity to change subject. "Is she going to make it?"

A meek smile formed upon Aminatra's face. "Maddy? I don't know. It was a bad injury; infection may set in. Only your mother could have lasted this long. I think the thought of you and what you were trying to do is keeping her alive."

"What happened?"

Aminatra relayed the story of the attack and how, overwhelmed by Ferrals, they seemed doomed. "I fainted from blood loss and didn't expect to wake up again," she recounted. "The last I saw of your mother, she had one dead Ferral on top of her – my first kill! – and a live one under her trying to rip her throat out. When I came to, the Ferrals were gone, we were safe in a small enclosure with a raging fire and your mother helping the wounded, despite her own injuries." She paused for dramatic effect.

"But what happened?" pressed Finbarl, impatiently but in good spirits.

"I said your mother was clever. When she offered the meat to the Ferral, she also retrieved some powder from her pocket in case things didn't work out. When all seemed lost, she had the wherewithal to throw it in the Ferral's eyes. Seems it burns like hell! Anyway, this Ferral throws her off and is making the most frightful noise, unsettling the rest of them. I'm told he must have been a pack leader or something. This allows the other prisoners to get the upper hand and soon the Ferrals are fleeing, leaving five dead, including the one I killed!"

"Yes, you mentioned that bit before." Finbarl smiled. "So, what was this mysterious powder?"

"Chilli powder!" A faint, sly grin emerged on Aminatra's face. "Your mother found some chillis growing wild years ago, dried them out and ground it into powder. She's occasionally been adding a pinch to the broth for flavour. It's supposed to be a luxury, but no one noticed."

Finbarl laughed out loud, venting a mixture of pent-up nerves from the day and relief the conversation had found a more amiable subject. Aminatra allowed her grin to widen.

A voice came from behind. "You shouldn't be 'appily 'ere. No, this isn't the place to be 'appily."

Finbarl and Aminatra turned to find Johansson following in their wake. "You need to be 'appily whenever you can," said Finbarl and started laughing again. He looked to Aminatra for approval but found her straight-faced, their moment of frivolity over.

*

The shadows stretched to their limit as the sun hung above the horizon. This was the best time of day, as the once overpowering heat cooled to a pleasant temperature ahead of the cold nights. A positive mood swept through the group of prisoners as Bluebecker Woods came into sight. It wasn't 'home,' but it was familiar. Finbarl felt relief too, as his injuries ached, slowing him down. He didn't like to show it, but Aminatra sensed his discomfort, slowing her own pace.

"Will there be food?" asked Finbarl, his stomach gurgled, demanding a more forceful enquiry. "I've nothing."

"On my first night they shared food with me," answered Aminatra, "but after that you must contribute, or you get nothing. It's not easy, but I can teach you what your mother has taught me."

"Thanks, I don't think I've ever felt hungrier. Though that may be to do with … ," Finbarl stopped dead in his tracks, a look of consternation upon his face.

"What?" asked Aminatra.

"I forgot to pick up the Jumblar Gauret left for me! Cronax! I got so caught up in getting out of there and pumped up on adrenaline that … Oh, Ferral-whack! What am I going to do?"

"I don't know. Some of the prisoners have collected emergency supplies but I doubt they'll share with you."

"I'll go mad! I'll have to go back to Bruuk's Point tomorrow."

"Don't be stupid," chided Aminatra. "No one will go with you and you can't go alone. Sleep on it and we'll see what solutions tomorrow brings."

"I guess you're right, but I'm not sure how much sleep I'm going to get without Jumblar."

CHAPTER 23

They found Maddy shivering under a deer hide in the thorn bush enclosure, her brow wet from a feverish sweat. The woodland cut out the last of the daylight, leaving her in darkness. Aminatra ran to Maddy's side, hugging her. Finbarl hung back, unsure how to greet his mother.

"How you feeling?" asked Aminatra, aware Maddy's eyes lacked their usual lustre, her skin its colour.

Maddy smiled weakly. "I'll be better when you start a fire to warm me up, my dear." She noticed Finbarl standing awkwardly in the faded light and her face fought to light up amid the pain. "Fin! Am I to take it my plan has got you into a little trouble?"

Finbarl grinned uneasily. "Just a little."

She waved him towards herself. "Come, tell me all about it, my dear! I may not have much time."

"Don't talk like that!" he said, sitting by her side. "Now Aminatra and I are here, we'll look after you and you'll be better in no time."

"That's nice," she whispered, leaning her head upon his shoulder as though a regular occurrence. "What did you find that got our friends so annoyed with you?"

Aminatra got the fire going, the light from the flames exposing a green, mossy slime covering Maddy's neck wound.

240

The surrounding red skin gave away the signs of infection. "Is that some of your medicine?" he asked, pointing at the slime.

"Yes, but I want to hear what you discovered. You did find some dirt on them?"

He nodded. "I did, and I also found an old friend of yours."

"You did? Who?"

"Dul-biblex."

"Dul? Cronax!" gasped Maddy. "He must be over seventy by now. He's done well to survive so long. Is he well?"

Finbarl shook his head sombrely, explaining Dul-biblex's and his library's fate, behind a locked door, off bounds and a secret from the rest of Athenia.

A tear welled in Maddy's eyes. "But he helped you find what we need?" she asked.

"He did, and it's explosive." Finbarl grimaced. "But they got the evidence back when they caught me. Now it's only my word against theirs."

"Sod that!" exclaimed Maddy. "I want to hear it. Ami, get everyone to join us! Fin's going to tell us a story."

With everyone arranged around the fire, Maddy nudged Finbarl. "Your audience awaits."

He shuddered, unaccustomed to addressing groups or strangers. The audience and subject was a little different from the more familiar barrack-room banter. Jumblar's vengeance also toyed upon his nerves. What he wouldn't do for a leaf right now. A bowl of dates was passed round the circle, Finbarl gratefully taking a couple, easing his hunger. A further nudge from Maddy encouraged Finbarl to begin.

Jumping straight to how he found Governor Elbar's keys, Finbarl described his discovery of the library and Dul-biblex. For all in the audience, except Maddy, the news of such a room and man proved a revelation. They listened in awe as Finbarl tried to describe the vast collection; they laughed when he tried repeating the authors' names. He held news of the letter back, moving on to how Hradkarl discovered him and how he knocked out the Governor's grandson. Much to his surprise, the attentive group cheered and laughed and, realising he had them hooked, Finbarl relaxed, growing into his storyteller role.

"Knowing there was no way of covering up, I ... Dul-biblex decided all I could do was escape to the farm with the material he gave me, buying myself some time, allowing me to find out what the Governor doesn't want the rest of Athenia to know. I managed to slip through the town unnoticed, finding shelter in a small toolshed in the farm. It took them over four hours to find me. From my time with Dul-biblex and reading in the shed, this is what I found out.

"Firstly, we're not alone. Other remnants of civilisation do still exist!" A loud gasp escaped from those listening. "They've sent emissaries to make contact with us. I don't know how many, but I've seen evidence of at least one. According to the Governor, who gave me the pleasure of his company on my capture, the Ferral killed this group. I think I believe him, but what they retrieved was a letter from the government of a place called Mandelaton." Someone in the audience repeated the name in awe. "They're from beyond the mountains," continued Finbarl. "The letter only gave a vague location, somewhere westward. Some of the words they used I didn't recognise. I don't know what level of civilisation they've retained or achieved, but I believe the fact they're reaching out to other people can only mean they're more civilised than Athenia!"

"I agree, my dear," interjected Maddy, her weak voice only just carrying. "Exploration and diplomacy are two facets the Wardyns have never known or attempted. The fact they try to hide this from the citizens suggests they're fearful their tyranny becomes exposed by comparison with a more just society."

"That's an awful lot of conclusions from a simple letter and one we haven't seen!" Obidon shifted uncomfortably as everyone looked his way.

"True, Don" responded Maddy. "I can think of more frightening interpretations if you want a sleepless night, but what is a fact is the Wardyns hid the knowledge from everyone else. Any civilised government, discovering it isn't alone in this world, would at the least give its people some hope and attempt to find out more. Think how much life would improve if we could start trading again. If we could mix up the gene pool again."

"The what?" asked Aminatra.

"Never mind, dear," responded Maddy. "I'll explain later. We're stopping Fin from telling his story. There's more, I take it?"

"I haven't got to the good part yet," announced Finbarl. "Dul-biblex has spent his time studying and writing a book. It's the chronicle of Athenia's history. He gave me it to read. Momentous dates are recorded, capturing the collapse of the Golden Age and Athenia's isolation from the rest of the world." A buzz of conversation erupted, neighbour turning to neighbour expressing interest and excitement.

"But we were taught our history in school." One of the new women found confidence to speak.

"I was taught exactly the same as you," responded Finbarl, "but it turns out what the Moralistas teach isn't the true history. Yes, the world imploded as temperatures soared and resources became sparse. Wars broke out, walls were built, et cetera, et cetera. All that is true. But the cream of civilisation didn't come together from around the world to one location, founding a new city called Athenia in the hope they might save humanity. What our history lessons didn't tell us is other walled communities existed in the first few centuries after the collapse. A healthy trade in goods and ideas existed between them all for a while, as they battled the common foe of the bandits beyond the walls. But as the desert encroached further and food and water became scarcer, they started fighting each other for precious resources. Athenia was the victor, laying waste to any rivals." Finbarl noticed the shocked faces surrounding him and paused.

Maddy broke the silence. "If Athenia was able to defeat other towns, why couldn't it defeat the criminals and bandits, reclaiming the land?"

"A good question," noted Finbarl. "Partly because by defeating the other towns, they got rid of valuable allies in fighting the bandits. Also, it was one of the ways they managed to defeat the other towns. Through guile and deception, they managed to destroy just a small part of a town's walls and then left the bandits to raid and bring the town to its knees. They then surrendered to Athenia for protection and, when their arms were handed over, they found themselves betrayed."

A rumble of disgust passed round the fire. "It's in those Wardyns' blood to be cheating, stealing Ferral-whacks!" said Crixus, his red hair visible from the light of the fire.

Finbarl held a hand up to quieten his audience. "Let me continue! This did allow Athenia to try to reclaim the land and farm on an area more extensive than we could ever imagine. But by using the bandits in their duplicity, they emboldened them, giving them access to weapons from captured towns. The criminals didn't just stop raiding at the defeat of the other towns. But now it was Athenian property they stole from! They were a more formidable foe and all this extra cultivated land Athenia secured stretched their resources, making it difficult to defend. The bandits escaped into the safety of the mountains, emerging when they wanted something, while Athenia became more and more compact."

"And the criminals evolved into the Ferrals?" enquired Obidon.

Finbarl found himself laughing. "No. That would be too easy and is perhaps the biggest lie of all. As time passed and the status quo became more settled, those outside the walls became more envious of those inside, with their houses, families and remnants of civilisation. The bandits started to attack the town itself. They had the numbers to undertake an effective siege and, cut off from their food supplies and with no allies, the rulers of Athenia agreed to surrender." Perplexed frowns formed on many of those enthralled. "Large numbers of the citizens were killed or evicted, and the bandits replaced them, taking some females of Athenia as their wives, whether they wanted that union or not! We, my dear friends, are descendants of those bandits! The criminals those walls were built to keep out."

As Finbarl expected, this disclosure caused an eruption of excited chatter, and he sat back down to let it burn itself out. He imagined they felt much as he had on learning the truth: slightly dirty, undeserving and hypocritical. All his life he viewed criminality as the biggest threat to civilisation, and yet it had already taken over. What right did he or anyone else from Athenia have to spout off about righteousness now?

"So, the original inhabitants of Athenia are the ancestors of the Ferral then?" queried Aminatra, looking to others in the group to see if they agreed.

"This is where the book only provides conjecture," answered Finbarl, climbing to his feet again. "It suggests the majority of those sent into exile perished, completely unsuited to surviving in the wild. But the bandits held captive the previous government and administrators, trying to extract secrets from them: where they hid things and how to run Athenia. Now, it seems the bandits already used Jumblar at this stage, but not those in Athenia. They used it on their captives to soften them up, withdrawing it and promising more if they told them what they wanted. By the end of this process it sounds like most lost their minds. Of no help any more and no longer a threat to the bandits, they found themselves dumped outside the walls. The Ferrals gradually emerged in the decades following. There's no proof linking them to those poor souls, but the chronicle speculates, despite their madness, instinct allowed them to survive and mate. Their offspring, with no sane guidance, grew up as uneducated, unspeaking beasts. There were, of course, still other bandits living in the wilderness, but over the centuries they died out in direct competition with the Ferrals and the new custodians of Athenia."

"What I don't understand," said Obidon, "is why the criminals perpetuated the myth they're the descendants of the original inhabitants, why they became so obsessed with civilisation. Surely, people of such evil disposition wouldn't care about law and justice?"

"I don't know," replied Finbarl honestly.

"Every usurper needs to build a myth to justify their rule," opined Maddy. "The first bandits wouldn't have given a hoot, but for future generations, they had to establish order and control and to do that they would also have needed to establish legitimacy. Remember, they allowed many original inhabitants to stay. For them to accept a new ruling class, they needed some pretence at continuity with the past, no matter how false. After only a few generations, and the passing of the original bandits, the truth would have been lost amidst the lies."

"But what does this all mean for us?" asked Obidon. "It's shocking and kind of makes sense, but it doesn't change anything. We're still stuck out here rotting and the Wardyns are behind those walls getting fatter."

"Maybe this is our punishment for our ancestors' crimes," suggested another prisoner.

"Ferralax!" retorted Maddy. "It means the future's a blank slate. The Wardyns' legitimacy to rule is a sham. A new world awaits if we want to create it, and it has no walls."

"That fever is affecting your mind!" said Obidon, sounding crueller than intended.

"Maybe, dear," replied Maddy. "Our punishment is knowing what mankind can achieve without being able to achieve it ourselves. Now, all this talk has made me tired."

"I'll sing a song to help you sleep," offered Obidon, surprising Finbarl as he sang in a beautiful baritone voice.

Many a man has died in her arms
And laid down his life for her favour
Crossed mountain and desert to be by her side
Fought demon and foe as her saviour

Many a man has cried out her name
Found courage and strength in danger
Lost family and loved ones on the way
Sacrificed all just to save her

Oh, Liberty, my femme fatale,
I'd give my life for my precious belle
Oh, Liberty, your price is high,
But I'll pay the cost 'til the day that I die

"I recognise the tune," whispered Finbarl to Maddy, who lay beside him, her eyes closed. "But not the words."

A smile formed on her face, while her eyes remained shut. "It's 'Brave Are We'," she explained. "You would have sung it with the cadets. More fitting now, don't you think?"

Finbarl nodded in recollection and smiled.

"Stay by me, Fin," requested Maddy, as Obidon finished singing and the party broke up. "I would like to talk some more before sleep takes me. Tell me about Dul."

Finbarl helped adjust the deer skin to cover his mother's entire body. "Of course, I'll stay by you all night and keep watch. I fear sleep will be hard to come by for me. I've not had any Jumblar for two days now!"

Maddy eased herself back up, grimacing with pain. "And how do you feel, my dear?"

"Absolutely terrible! The only good thing is it's keeping my mind from all the other horrible things happening in my life! But I fear for my sanity."

"Here, have some of mine." Maddy reached into the satchel and pulled out a small bundle of Jumblar.

"But what about you?"

"I've got plenty, Fin," she answered. "I've been squirrelling it away for years for emergencies. I believe this counts as one."

"I wish I'd known you sooner," said Finbarl, as he kissed his mother's forehead softly.

"I'm glad you're with me now, my precious dear," Maddy responded, lying down again and closing her eyes.

Finbarl chewed on some Jumblar, feeling the stress lift from his body. He spoke softly to his mother about Dul-biblex, but quickly noticed her drifting off to sleep. Closing his eyes, he soon followed her.

CHAPTER 24

The fire, reduced to white embers, released its remaining heat to the chilly night. The only sound was the heavy breathing of sleeping prisoners. The call of an owl cut through the darkness, but no one stirred. Even the cracking of a dried stick, under the misplaced step of an approaching intruder, failed to disturb those at slumber. The owner of the wayward step winced at the noise, pausing to see if anyone reacted, then continued stealthily forward. He was not alone. Behind came three others, all creeping towards the thornbush enclosure. The leader held his hand up, signalling a halt, then indicated to two of his companions to remain stationary, the other to follow him. A simple gate of bound sticks, wound with thorny vines, provided the entrance to the enclosure. Despite the darkness, the gate, designed to keep scavenging beasts out, opened easily. The leader, reiterating the need for absolute quiet with a finger to his lips, tip-toed into the inner area. They examined the face of each sleeping body passed, silently continuing until they found their goal: Finbarl.

Finbarl rolled away from his mother as he drifted off and lay with a contented look upon his face. Although only his first night in the Prison, the session around the fire, combined with the effects of Jumblar, left him feeling good, a bond already forming with his fellow prisoners. How could they not appreciate his sacrifice to gain the truth? He slept exposed, with no blanket, his head resting on nothing but a pile of sandy dirt. An occasional grunt or snort came from his mouth as he fidgeted against the cold, the knife, removed from his pocket, and stabbed into the ground above his head for easy access.

One of the interlopers bent down, plucking the knife up, examining it as best he could in the darkness. They exchanged a series of visual instructions. The man holding the knife knelt over Maddy, the other placed one hand firmly over Finbarl's mouth, one round his throat. Finbarl's eyes flashed opened in shock, a faint murmur of distress escaping. He glared up, seeing Dove's face staring down at him. Dove smiled as Finbarl struggled. Removing his hand from Finbarl's throat, Dove put his finger to his lips, nodding in the direction of Maddy. Finbarl lifted his head and saw the other man holding the knife to the oblivious Maddy's exposed throat. The threat and message clear, Finbarl nodded he understood. Grabbing Finbarl by the back of his collar, Dove yanked him up, keeping his hand firmly over Finbarl's mouth. The other man nervously looked around the enclosure to check no one stirred. With Finbarl on his feet, the man left Maddy, handing the knife to Dove, who prodded it in Finbarl's back, prompting him to start walking.

They rendezvoused with the other two, who grabbed an arm each, dragging Finbarl deeper into the wood. When sufficiently distant from the sleeping prisoners, they threw Finbarl to the ground.

"What did Audlech promise you?" snarled Finbarl, getting to his knees.

"We don't need any payment to kill a former guard," said one of the men. "We're doing this for fun!"

"I wasn't speaking to you! I was speaking to your boss, Dove. He's the one who made the deal with Audlech." Finbarl fished for the truth, hoping to drive a division between the men.

"We don't have bosses in the Prison," said the man.

"Shut up!" commanded Dove. "He's trying to distract and divide us. It ain't gonna stop us killing you, guard."

"Heaven forbid," responded Finbarl, his face a picture of cool over his nerve-racked interior. "By the way, I want my knife back when you've finished."

"Humour to hide your fear. I like it!" commented Dove, running a finger lightly over the blade of the knife. "I'll tell you what, I'll lend it to you for a while – through your heart – then I want it back as a reward for doing all the work."

"I don't want it if you're going to get it dirty," ribbed Finbarl.

"Perhaps I'll give you a choice," said Dove, enjoying the joust. "My colleagues here could bludgeon you to death with their clubs, or I can make it nice and swift with my lovely new knife. What's it going to be?"

"There's not a third choice of you bludgeoning each other to death, I suppose?"

"The third choice is a slow and painful death with my lovely new knife," declared Dove. "Yes, I like that one best."

"I can live with that," said Finbarl, delighted to see his flippant answer causing the gang to laugh amongst themselves, delaying his fate a few more seconds: vital seconds. For in the background, among the trees, Finbarl thought he saw shadows moving. Perhaps tricks of his sleep-addled mind, but he hoped something else.

"I'll tell you what, lads," announced Dove. "So I'm not the only one having the fun, you can soften him up with your clubs first."

The three club-wielding men closed in on Finbarl, giggling like excitable adolescents. Time had run out. The first man raised his club. A twang followed by a whoosh. The man dropped his club and, with a strange gurgling sound, slumped to the floor. Twang! Whoosh! Twang! Whoosh! Before the other two could react, they too collapsed to the ground in agony. Finbarl looked around in bewilderment, only the equally bemused Dove visible, seeking a place to run, but not knowing which way to go.

Finbarl slowly climbed to his feet, nervously watching Dove to ensure he didn't try anything stupid.

A voice emerged from the darkness. "Didn't I tell you Obidon is a crack shot with a bow?" It was Aminatra. She emerged with the large figure of Obidon behind her, his bow drawn and aimed at Dove.

"Cronax!" cursed Finbarl. "Am I glad to see you!" His head collapsed in relief. "How have you kept your bow secret? The guards wouldn't be happy to know a prisoner is in possession of such a lethal weapon."

"The guards can screw themselves," replied Obidon with gratifying clarity.

"He keeps it in the woods for hunting deer," explained Aminatra. "He's promised to teach me to use it."

"I presume these goons woke you when they dragged me away?" asked Finbarl, as he put a boot into one of the injured men.

"Oh, no," responded Aminatra. "We were never asleep. Maddy said the goons wouldn't have the patience to wait and do the job properly and would try tonight. So as soon as you were asleep, Obidon, Crixus and I snuck out and hid up a tree overlooking the enclosure. If things didn't work out, others are awaiting our call, but I think we can judge that a success."

"Cronax and Ferralax!" exclaimed Finbarl. "You could've told me! I've been crapping myself."

"You wouldn't have behaved naturally had you known, and you deserve to suffer a little."

"Fair enough," said Finbarl, willing to give Aminatra her quota of barbed comments. "Where's Crixus?"

Aminatra shrugged: "What do you want to do with him?" she nodded towards Dove, who knelt nervously under the watch of Obidon, ignoring the groans of his incapacitated colleagues.

"I don't know," pondered Finbarl. "I'd like to question him, find out what Audlech offered for my death."

A figure stepped out from behind a tree, a club held aloft in his hands. It was Crixus. He made for the kneeling prisoner and, before Dove could react, brought the club crashing down upon his skull. A sickening crack followed and Finbarl's former tormentor crumpled down dead.

"Whoa!" shouted Finbarl. "What did you do that for?"

"You were beginning to think about his future, meaning you weren't planning on killing him. He had to die. If you let him go, he would have eventually killed you, and us. This isn't the place for sentiment and idealism."

"I ... I ... ," Finbarl stuttered, lost for words at the immediate, uncompromising, and unfamiliar form of justice.

"Crixus is right," said Aminatra, sounding only half convinced, "he wasn't someone you could reason with."

"I know, but ... I guess you're right. I'm just not used to the ways of the Prison yet, but I'd have liked to have known what was offered for my life."

Obidon bent down and picked up the knife lying beside Dove's dead body, offering it to Finbarl.

"You keep it," said Finbarl. "Think of it as a thank you for saving me."

The big man beamed, admiring his new weapon.

"May I borrow it for a moment?" asked Crixus, his hand held out in expectation. Obidon passed it to him and then, to everyone's horror, Crixus bent down and cut the throats of the unsuspecting injured men. "Didn't want them screaming when you retrieved your arrows," Crixus explained pragmatically, handing back the knife to Obidon.

"That was very generous or very stupid," said Aminatra, after Obidon and Crixus vanished back into the darkness. "You might need that knife."

Finbarl shrugged. "So far it's only brought me trouble. To be honest, I'm glad to be rid of it. I rather fancy having a bow like Obidon's, and now he's a knife, he should be able to make us one each."

"How clever," commented Aminatra, "let's hope that brain of yours doesn't get you killed."

"Thank you for saving my life," said Finbarl, oblivious to Aminatra's sarcasm. "I don't deserve your help." It was gratitude left lost in the night, as Aminatra started to walk away, leaving Finbarl alone in the darkness wondering what to make of her.

CHAPTER 25

D espite the excitement of the night, the prisoners still rose at dawn. They revived the fire and put the water on to boil. Finbarl woke feeling good, the imminent threat to his life removed. He began to envisage a future in the Prison. Amid the morning bustle, he watched his rescuer of last night as she scurried about chatting to other prisoners, undertaking the first tasks of the day. Aminatra turned and caught his eye. She nodded a curt acknowledgement. She was beautiful, considered Finbarl; the Prison hadn't stolen that yet. He liked her company, her alluring spirit for life, the way she smiled, the way she moved. How she felt about him remained a mystery. A lot of the feelings she stirred in him were a mystery.

As Finbarl ruffled his hair and rubbed his arms to generate some warmth in the chilly morning air, he glanced across at Maddy. She lay awake, wrapped under her deer hide.

"Morning Maddy," said Finbarl. "How you feeling today?"

She smiled but expressed no joy. "Not good, Fin. I'm burning up."

Finbarl shuffled across and felt her brow with the back of his hand. "Is there anything I can do?"

A faint shake of her head answered him. "I've taken all the herbal medicine that might help; now my body must fight, but there's something I need to tell you. Get yourself some rabbit broth and sit with me."

"Rabbit!" exclaimed Finbarl. "My, we're living like Wardyns out here."

"That bow of Obidon's has its uses," said Maddy, squeezing Finbarl's arm affectionately. "Imagine what we might achieve if truly free. Not tied to Athenia by dependence on Jumblar, able to forge our own tools, go wherever we want. We could eat like kings every day. Now hurry before Johansson asks for seconds. Here, use my bowl!"

Finbarl returned, his hands enjoying the warmth from the bowl and the rich aroma of the thick broth. "When did father and you know you had a connection?" he asked, giving Maddy no time to get off her chest what she wanted to say.

"What a strange question," answered Maddy. "What's the real question you want to ask?"

Finbarl blushed slightly. "Just interested. It can be quite difficult to tell the signs, particularly if the person has no reason to like you."

"It can be." Maddy looked her son in the eye, trying to extract further information. "And?"

"Nothing," answered Finbarl, raising his bowl and sniffing. "Smells good! You should have some to keep up your strength."

"Maybe later," replied Maddy. "There's something you should know, Fin. I've stopped taking Jumblar."

"What! Are you crazy?" Finbarl attempted to keep his surprise to a minimum, but the outburst caused some heads to turn. "Why would you do that?" he whispered.

"It's an experiment," confided Maddy. "I've been weaning myself off it for a while now, using a mix of medicinal plant roots to combat the withdrawal effects."

Finbarl recoiled in further surprise. "And you haven't gone mad?"

"That's a matter of opinion," quipped Maddy. "But thank you for noticing, my dear! You see, since we last met, I've been thinking. Jumblar is the problem. It's what keeps us reliant on Athenia; it's what gives the Wardyns their power over everyone. To destroy the crop would destroy their power. But it would also likely send everyone crazy and cause a bloodbath with everyone turning on each other in panic. If we can offer an alternative, a life with no Jumblar, think of the freedom it would give everybody."

"And you've succeeded?"

"Unfortunately, I hadn't planned on getting attacked and wounded by the Ferrals," explained Maddy. "For the experiment to be a success, I'd have liked to have a whole month. After the attack they gave me some Jumblar to ease the pain, which has somewhat skewed the test. I'm not sure if I'm going to be around to see it through."

"Maybe you need more Jumblar to help you recover," implored Finbarl.

"No, it has no healing properties," said Maddy. "Maybe coming off it dulled my reaction times when the Ferrals attacked, but beyond that it can't help me now. It was hard when I started, but I've had none for the last four days and my mind remains fine."

"And what do you want me to do now?" asked Finbarl, a little afraid of the answer.

"I want you to destroy Athenia's Jumblar crop. I want you to prove to everyone here it's possible to come off Jumblar and survive; to do so you need to stop taking it yourself."

Finbarl puffed out his cheeks and exhaled. "You remember I said I wished I'd known you for longer? I may need to revise my words." Maddy stretched out her hand and clasped Finbarl's. He noticed how clammy it was from the fever.

"Will you do it, my Fin?" she asked.

"Only if you tell me your secret. I'll need help."

"You can have that secret," said Maddy. "As for the secrets of the heart, you'll have to find your own way."

*

The morning chill quickly lifted as the sun rose in the sky. A flurry of activity took place within the enclosure, each person readying themselves for a day of foraging and hunting. The prisoners collected the light dew clinging to the leaves, topping up their precious water supplies before it evaporated. Aminatra ran a simple comb made from antler through her hair, before making a minor repair to her boots, replacing the inner sole with a piece taken from one of the dead attackers of last night.

"You have to come with us, Finbarl," she asserted. "Otherwise you won't learn what to look for and won't be contributing anything to the pot. They won't let you stay if you do your own thing all the time."

"But what about Maddy? I can't leave her alone. She's in a bad way."

Moments before, Maddy appeared to drop off to sleep again, but she still listened. "Ami's right." Her voice was weak but coherent. "It's important you go; prove you're of value to the group. I'll be all right."

"But you need looking after," protested Finbarl.

"We're not in Athenia any more, Finbarl," said Maddy. "You have to adapt to new ways. And anyway, why would I want a grumpy, Jumblar-deprived son hanging around me all day?"

"Jumblar-deprived? You still haven't had any?" questioned Aminatra, looking at Finbarl.

"I have. I'll tell you about it as we walk," answered Finbarl, conceding defeat.

"Take my bag, Fin!" instructed Maddy. "You'll need something to gather all those berries, roots and grubs you're going to bring me. Also find yourself a sturdy stick whilst in the woods. You'll need something to dig and maybe to fight with as well."

"I've got one of the clubs the goons were going to tenderise me with last night. Looks like a fine weapon."

"Can you dig with it?" challenged Maddy.

Finbarl reluctantly confessed not.

"Well it won't be much good to you then, will it?"

"I'll find a bloody stick to dig with!" Finbarl held his hands up in mock surrender, then smiled at his mother. "Look after yourself, and I'll bring you something tasty for later."

"Don't worry, all mothers are like that," whispered Aminatra as they left the enclosure. "We do like to make our point heard. Particularly with wayward sons!"

*

Crixus took charge of the party, instructing everyone on their objectives for the day. About ten years older than Finbarl, he possessed a gaunt, hollow frame, a legacy of his time in the Prison. Finbarl had still to determine whether a natural hierarchy existing within the group or whether they shared responsibility. All he knew, for now, was that it made sense to follow those with the experience.

Obidon found Finbarl a sturdy digging stick, proudly carving a sharp tip with his new knife. Everyone told Finbarl you looked after yourself, not anyone else, to survive in the Prison, but already he saw the bonds of community formed from small acts of kindness. It kept his mother alive. Each night the prisoners shared their food and fire with her. It was payment for the years she had given them with her knowledge and experience. What these prisoners had built was, in some ways, stronger than that existing within Athenia. Could the town claim to have a community when the leaders stole from and cheated those they ruled over, or when people so easily turned on their neighbour with false accusations? The bond holding them together was fear, and the walls were the greatest symbol of that fear. It took some time, but Finbarl at last understood what his mother meant. Civilisation didn't survive behind those walls; it had long ago suffocated to death. The future lay in starting over; building on the spirit found in the Prison.

"She'll be fine," said Aminatra, catching up with Finbarl.

"Ah, you're not ignoring me," said Finbarl, conspicuous in his lack of company on the walk. "I was beginning to think no one likes former guards."

Aminatra gave him a withering look.

"I hope she will," he said, eager to reignite the conversation.

"So, what's the story with the Jumblar?"

Finbarl grimaced. "Maddy believes she can successfully wean people off it, isn't taking it herself and has convinced me to try."

"Are you both crazy?" exclaimed Aminatra.

"Hmm, that's what I said when she told me," said Finbarl, "it's a little more complex though." Finbarl explained Maddy's theory on Jumblar as the Wardyns' Achilles heel and, by destroying it, setting people free.

"So, how do you come off it without going Ferral?" asked Aminatra.

"I cut back usage gradually," explained Finbarl, "and supplement it with a dose of two other substances, one called Valerian, the other Ginseng. God knows how she worked out they might help, but she still seems of sound mind."

Aminatra nodded thoughtfully. "I've seen her collect their roots. They grow in the cooler places such as in the foothills."

"Basically, where the Ferral are most populous."

"You didn't think Maddy would make it easy, did you?" Aminatra gritted her teeth, lost in an internal debate, then added, "I'll join you. It'll make a more convincing case to the others if we can both come off Jumblar."

Finbarl couldn't hide his surprise. "A moment ago, you called me crazy."

"Who said crazy is a bad thing in this world?"

*

They walked nearly four miles before Crixus called a halt at the first foraging site. In the open, arid terrain, Finbarl saw no evidence of food. Yet a bountiful harvest lay before him.

"They're called pitaya or dragon fruit," explained Aminatra, demonstrating how to use a stick to remove the fruit, brushing off the ferocious-looking spines. "I've learnt so much since I became a prisoner – mainly from your mother. You'll enjoy them."

Finbarl cursed, struggling to avoid the spines or damage the fruit, but soon grasped the technique, grateful for his sharp stick which removed the fruits so easily. Others searched the floor, looking for the signs of edible roots called cassava, which Aminatra explained they boiled and roasted to eat or made flour from, even fermented it as a drink or syrup. After half an hour in the oppressive heat, they stopped for a break. Finbarl reached for his water gourd but Aminatra stopped him before he took a sip.

"Save that water and watch Obidon," she advised.

The prisoner towered over a barrel cactus. Using his knife, he made a deep cut, then slid in a piece of wood with a narrow channel carved along it. A trickle of gloopy water flowed along the wood into a bowl beneath.

"It's a little bitter but quite refreshing, once you get used to it," explained Aminatra. "There's another one called the hoody gordon you can chew on to suppress hunger."

"I had no idea," said an impressed Finbarl. He never appreciated cacti offered such bounty.

"You can't do this with all cacti," elaborated Aminatra. "In some the water is toxic, so make sure you can recognise this type. It's just as important you know what's poisonous as what's edible."

"Absolutely! I wouldn't want to accidentally kill myself."

"I meant so you can deliberately kill yourself if you want." Aminatra recognised the uneasy look on Finbarl's face as the same one she pulled when informed by Maddy. She gave Finbarl the same answer she received. "It's what prisoners do when they've had enough: better a death of one's choosing."

"Perhaps we could poison the Wardyns. Slip something in the food we trade for Jumblar."

Aminatra raised a discerning eyebrow. "How would you guarantee the Wardyns would eat it and not a cadet?"

Recognising the reference to Aminatra's son, Karlmon, Finbarl nodded his understanding. "Stupid idea."

"Doesn't stop most of the prisoners spitting on or rubbing the food in dung before they trade it though," remarked Aminatra casually, making Finbarl wince in memory of past meals. "I'll show you how to locate underground water sources later," continued Aminatra. "It's something Maddy taught me and she, believe it or not, claims she learnt it by observing the Ferrals."

As Crixus signalled the end of a successful gathering and pointed north-west for their next direction of travel, the prisoners gathered their harvest and belongings together. Finbarl's contribution seemed poor in comparison with his colleagues, but he felt pleased with his first efforts. Behind him, Johansson struggled to tie his bag to the end of a staff. As he lifted and swung it upon his shoulder, the bag came loose, flying at Finbarl, hitting him on the back of his thigh.

"Hey, prisoner!" yelled Finbarl, turning in anger. It hadn't hurt, just startled him. He marched up to Johansson, grabbing him by the scruff of the neck. "You show some respect to your betters, you Ferral-whack!" Finbarl looked into the terrified eyes of Johansson, suddenly conscious of the silence. He looked around to see every face staring at him, hands firmly gripping weapons. Anger collapsed into regret. He let go of Johansson and stepped back. "I ... I ... ".

"It was an accident, Finbarl," chided Aminatra.

"I know. I know."

"You can't go treating people like that any more! You're one of us now."

"I know." Finbarl re-examined the jury of prisoners surrounding him. There was a mix of anxiety and hatred on their faces. "I'm sorry," he said, conscious a former self had taken control. Only when his past life fell apart had Finbarl recognised the hypocrisy of his behaviour; how he'd upheld values and ethics but at the same time justified breaking them by dehumanising his victims. It made him sick to think himself a fraud, and now he feared he couldn't help himself. "It was just instinctive. It won't happen again."

"If it was instinctive, how you gonna stop it happening again?" challenged Crixus.

"What he means," said Aminatra, "is he's going to let us make him a better person. Eh, Finbarl?"

"Absolutely," answered Finbarl, uncertain of its truth but grateful Aminatra's anger had dissipated.

"You're no better than anyone here now," said Obidon. "You never were."

"You're right," conceded Finbarl, eager to move on.

"So, apologise to Johansson!"

"Of course." Finbarl offered his hand to the shaken prisoner. "I'm sorry. Here, let me help you repack your bag."

Johansson accepted the handshake and watched perplexed as Finbarl scrambled about the ground collecting his scattered belongings.

"Good," said Obidon. "We can get going now. It's forgotten."

"A little humility goes a long way," muttered Aminatra in Finbarl's ear as they headed off.

"I know," replied Finbarl, "I've a lot to learn."

✷

"We're not too far from Athenia," observed Finbarl, catching up with Aminatra. He'd been walking and talking with Johansson for the last hour, trying to make things right.

"Far enough away so they won't bother us," remarked Aminatra. "You'll know better than me how rare an encounter with the guards is, other than at Bruuk's Point. That time at Alphege Scar was an exception."

"So, this land does belong to us?" suggested Finbarl, pleased Aminatra was talking to him.

"And the Ferrals," added Aminatra.

"Yes, the Ferrals," echoed Finbarl, his mind consumed with further thoughts. He spent a lot of time thinking about them since learning the truth of their origins. His past prejudices no longer held sway. He recognised them as victims, just like the prisoners. He still feared them, or perhaps respected was the word now, but they deserved better than the unquestioned hatred inculcated in every Athenian.

"You good with Johansson now?" asked Aminatra.

"Yes," answered Finbarl, a little reluctant to revisit his meltdown. "He's fine. It's like nothing happened with him."

"He's like that. I don't know if it's his memory or something else. He can be quite childlike: easily upset but quick to recover. You did the right thing though; spending time with him, I mean. It's important others see some humanity in you."

"I'm not a bad person," protested Finbarl, "I've been trained to react to provocations by prisoners. I just need to be trained to ... "

"Stop thinking of us as prisoners, for a start," cautioned Aminatra irritably. "Look, don't worry about it. You're not the first person to lose it as they adapt."

"I'm probably the first former guard though," added Finbarl.

"You're missing Athenia, you're disorientated and you're feeling vulnerable; that's no different from the rest of us when we were imprisoned. Get over it!"

Finbarl nodded thoughtfully, allowing Aminatra's outburst to go unchallenged. He looked in the direction of Athenia. The town remained over the horizon, the heights of Cragor Hill and Bymore Hill, sheltering Eden Valley on either side, just visible. Finbarl thought of the people going about their business, tending the crops and the livestock, building furniture, making fabrics and paper, baking bread or brewing Kywaczek; all sorts of skills handed down from generation to generation. Aminatra was right, he missed it: the familiarity and security. Since his assault of Johansson, his future felt in doubt. The prisoners would cast him out if he didn't control his temper or prejudices, leaving him alone and dead within days.

"What will you miss most from Athenia?" asked Aminatra, stirring Finbarl from his drifting thoughts.

"You mean other than regular food, water, shelter and guns?"

"Don't be flippant," chided Aminatra. "Think about it."

Finbarl looked up to the sky, considering his fondest memories. "The view of the valley from Bymore Hill."

"Yes, I like that," said Aminatra, smiling as she summoned the image in her own mind. "Keep that memory to hand for the tough times. One day we may see it again."

Finbarl smiled and wondered again at his contrary companion. He knew he annoyed her, yet they shared these moments.

Ahead, Crixus stopped, signalling for everyone to halt. Finbarl looked at Aminatra for advice, following her lead as she crouched, a finger to her lips. After about a minute, Crixus waved everyone forward.

"What's the problem?" whispered Obidon.

"Ferrals!" replied Crixus, setting off a wave of nervous glances. "A couple of them, but they've gone now. Something attracted their attention in the copse over there." He pointed towards a small group of trees.

"Perhaps there's a dead animal down there," suggested one of the prisoners.

"Shouldn't we find out?" pressed Finbarl.

"What if there are more Ferrals about or they come back?" asked another anxiously.

"I presume we were heading in that direction for a reason," stated Finbarl. "Our need for food is no less, so we might as well have a look on our way through!"

Crixus nodded his assent. "Let's be smart about this. If two go on ahead while the rest remain here, then they can signal if the route is clear."

"Sounds like a good plan to me!" declared Finbarl, taking a step forward. "Who's coming with me?" It felt the right thing to do, compensating for the earlier incident with Johansson. No one volunteered, but Finbarl noticed a glint in Aminatra's eyes hinting at her intent. "Hey, Obidon! Could be a good chance to try that knife out."

The big man thought about it and nodded. "Yeah, good idea. I'll go."

Aminatra looked disappointed. Finbarl felt strange about her: over-protective and needy of her company. They had spent so little time together, yet their lives had become intrinsically intertwined over the last year. Finbarl gently touched her shoulder as he walked past, feeling a desire he couldn't explain. It was hard to know what she felt for him.

"How did you get your scar?" asked Finbarl of Obidon, as they crept down a gradual slope towards the copse.

"My wife."

"Really? Is she in the Prison?"

Obidon shook his head. "No, I killed her before they could convict her."

"Oh! So, you're not here because you pissed off the Wardyns?" Finbarl considered whether it sensible to continue the conversation, but curiosity got the better of him.

"She was a sister to one of them, so I probably did piss them off a little."

"I'd say so!" exclaimed Finbarl, before another question popped out of his mouth. "Do you think Aminatra likes me?"

Obidon stopped and looked at Finbarl. "I usually find when checking for Ferrals, it pays to be silent."

Finbarl grimaced. "Of course, sorry. It's just one minute she's friendly and helpful, the next hostile and distant."

"There's something down there," whispered Obidon, holding his hand out abruptly to halt Finbarl. "It's a man!"

Finbarl pushed past Obidon's arm and started running towards the figure. "There's movement. He's alive!" Memories of Alphege Scar flashed through Finbarl's mind as he approached the bound, slumped body. Despite the blood smeared everywhere, Finbarl only made out one grisly wound to the abdomen. He suddenly remembered Obidon owned the knife and turned to check he followed. The big man ambled down the slope, his eyes darting back and forth scanning for threats. Finbarl waved furiously for him to speed up.

"It's Torbald! Cronax! Quick, cut him down. He's still alive!"

Obidon whipped his knife across the bindings as Finbarl supported Torbald, lowering him to the floor. "Those are sophisticated knots. Not Ferral," remarked Obidon.

"Screw the knots!" exclaimed Finbarl. "Pass me my water bottle!" He splashed a little water on Torbald's blood-smeared face, allowing a trickle to pass over his lips. Torbald's tongue flicked to catch the moisture and he slowly opened his eyes.

"Finbarl!" he croaked "I thought you were dead."

"I think you're mistaking me for you!" answered Finbarl. "You don't look so ... alive! What happened?"

"Hradbar! He betrayed me. Too stupid to succeed father on his own merits and so ... ," Torbald violently spluttered before trying to finish his sentence, " ... so he gets rid of his smarter rival. Should have seen it coming!"

"Yeah, that modesty of yours may have blinded you to the bleeding obvious." Finbarl no longer felt deference for Torbald. "So, it wasn't the Ferrals?"

Torbald slowly shook his head, gasping for breath. "No, my soul is safe. A couple came sniffing around. I thought they were going to finish me off, but they seemed spooked by something and left."

"As they didn't tie you up, they probably thought it was some tribal rival and ran away to alert their own kind," suggested Finbarl.

"I always ... liked you, Finbarl." Torbald wheezed, "we could have made a fine team had I succeeded."

"Where were you when they arrested me then?"

"You did rather burn your bridges by stealing from my father. Though I commend you for punching Hradkarl." Torbald paused, trying to bolster his fading strength. The other prisoners arrived, crowding round. Torbald's eyes weakly acknowledged them. "Ah, your woman!" he gasped, recognising Aminatra's face. "I'm glad we could bring you together." He tried to smile at his joke, but the pain overwhelmed him. "Listen, fulfil a dying man's wish for him, won't you?"

"Depends what it is," replied Finbarl.

"There ... there are two things. Bury me ... when I'm dead. Make sure the Ferrals don't get my ... soul." A harsh, rasping breath punctuated Torbald's plea. "Most importantly though ... there's a secret tunnel ... a tunnel leading from the Wardyns' sanctuary to outside Athenia's walls. Built centuries ago as an escape route. Find the three boulders shaped like a clover at the base of Cragor Hill. There's a camouflaged door above them. Kill Hradbar for me!" Another outburst of coughing erupted, then nothing but a slow, hissing, solitary breath.

"He's dead," confirmed Finbarl, as the group gathered round to verify with their own eyes. Finbarl felt torn. He hated what Torbald stood for and his overwhelming arrogance, but also admired his character, charm and intelligence, and maybe Athenia would have improved under his stewardship.

"Stand back," asked Finbarl. "I have an idea!" He brushed the sandy surface with his hand, removing the footprints around Torbald's body. With his finger he scratched out a message. It read: 'Hradbar a traitor!'

"That should cause some trouble!" commented Aminatra, as those around her chuckled in appreciation of Finbarl's emerging plan.

"If we clear our footprints as we leave, they'll never know we were here," explained Finbarl, brushing the sand from his hands.

"We not-ing bury-ling him?" asked Johansson.

"No," answered Finbarl firmly. "We need his body found. His soul's long gone anyway."

Finbarl put little faith in his message causing anything more than a moment's concern. He knew the process now: a constructed story, someone else found to blame and Hradbar painted as a hero. But it planted a seed of doubt in Hradbar's mind – someone knew his secret, fermenting his paranoia – and that was enough for Finbarl.

*

Despite a successful day of foraging food, the discovery of Torbald and his subsequent death cast a cloud over the group as they journeyed back to Bluebecker Woods. The oppressive heat added to the malaise and they walked in near silence. Each man and woman had been rejected and punished by Athenia, yet ingrained within their being was a subconscious respect for the Wardyns and their symbolic status as custodians of civilisation. While each prisoner dreamt of killing one, the murder of a Wardyn disturbed them. It felt like a portent of a coming storm.

Finbarl's thoughts grew heavy with speculation of what Torbald's death meant for Athenia. If Hradbar made a play for power, would it stop at Torbald? With a man so brutal as Hradbar in charge, what fate would befall the prisoners? Those rumours he once dismissed, of prisoner pitted to fight against Ferral, now seemed frighteningly plausible. Perhaps if they brought Maddy's plan to overthrow Athenia forward, while the Wardyns fought among themselves, it might work. Finbarl dismissed such frivolous hopes. They didn't know if the lotion to come off Jumblar worked yet; they needed more time and more numbers, and they needed to think of a way to break through … Finbarl stopped. Of course, the secret tunnel Torbald informed them about. That offered the way into Athenia! Finbarl felt a wave of excitement, imagining how Maddy would feel when he told her. It almost felt like fate throwing them the final piece of the puzzle. He caught up with Aminatra and smiled. He would tell her the great news when he told Maddy.

*

Bluebecker Woods was a welcome sight after a long day of walking in the heat. The slight drop in temperature, as they came under the shade of the trees, proved a spur for an energetic final few hundred yards, and chatter broke out among the prisoners. Johansson appeared particularly gleeful, running ahead to the enclosure, singing a repetitive little ditty. As the rest of the group approached journey's end, they removed their bags, ready to share or trade their day's bounty. Johansson stood at the enclosure entrance, his face ashen.

"What is it?" asked Obidon.

"Dead-ed," replied Johansson.

Realising what Johansson meant, Finbarl dashed forward into the enclosure and to his mother's side. Maddy lay still, her eyes open, her mouth formed into a subtle but contented smile.

"Mother!" cried Finbarl, using the term for the first time, bending down to touch her skin. Stone cold. A hand gently touched Finbarl's shoulder and he looked up to see Aminatra.

"I'm sorry," she said. "I think she knew it was coming."

Finbarl shed no tears; his hard life had stolen those. He nodded. "I just wish I'd known her longer."

"I'm glad to have known her for the brief time I did," said Aminatra. "She was a remarkable lady. She taught me so much." A murmur of agreement followed from behind, as the whole group crowded round, their heads hung in deference and sympathy.

"Yes, remarkable," repeated Finbarl.

"She'll be honoured on her journey to the next world," announced Obidon, his face showing emotion for the first time.

CHAPTER 26

"**M**ove!" cried Obidon, cradling a nest of smoking tinder within his hands. Those adding to the bed of dried sticks, scrub and dung stepped back, allowing Obidon to gently place his volatile nest amid the prepared kindling. Brushing his hands free of the flecks of dried fungi and moss, Obidon prostrated himself before the smoking stack, blowing heavily until the first flame leapt upwards, taking hold of its surrendering host. Easing his heavy frame up, Obidon stood back, watching with the surrounding crowd of prisoners, as the fire quickly consumed the bed of wood. Within ten minutes, a mass of competing flames engulfed the whole structure, the tremendous heat forcing everyone to retreat further. Amid the inferno, the silhouetted outline of Maddy's body lingered in sight before it too became lost amid the shimmering heat.

Finbarl stood next to Aminatra, staring soberly into the flames. The tune of the song sung in Maddy's memory bounced around his head, stirring his emotions. Death, a regular companion for Athenians, felt different to Finbarl this time. Finding his mother, after all those years, unearthed the deepest of latent feelings. Losing her again left him feeling empty and lost. All the plans they discussed, all his hopes, now seemed futile and cruel.

In the wake of the funeral, a pragmatism soon returned for the rest of the group. Death never got in the way of living, of finding food, water and safe shelter. Maddy's passing marked a mere comma in their struggle for life. For Finbarl, however, it felt like a full stop. Only Aminatra seemed to suffer with him.

"I need to start taking Jumblar again," he confessed to Aminatra a few days after the funeral.

"Yes, now's not the time to implement Maddy's plan," agreed Aminatra. "It hurts too much at the moment." She hugged Finbarl. "We'll give it a month and then we'll have collected more of the necessary ingredients. We must stay committed – honour her memory – but only when she's properly mourned."

The Jumblar immediately made Finbarl feel better. His grief lifted with indecent haste. The thoughts remained but merely floated with a harmless banality. Soon Finbarl joined the others, getting on with life. Aminatra too found relief through the drug, spending the days talking of Maddy with Finbarl, trying to explain all his mother had taught her, showing him where to find food and other tradable goods from the wasteland. Having lost Maddy, they discovered some comfort in each other.

CHAPTER 27

Three weeks after Maddy's death, they arrived back at their temporary camp in the valley at Limbole after a foraging expedition. Seated against a rock, alone and unmistakeably dead, rested a female prisoner; not one of their group but a familiar face, recognised from Bruuk Point.

"How did she get here?" asked Obidon. No one answered because no one knew.

Johansson edged to the front of the gaping prisoners to look. "Dead-ed," he stated in his unique manner.

"Her ankle's swollen," observed Aminatra. "Abandoned by her group because she couldn't keep up?"

Finbarl held back. The scene felt so familiar. His memory flashed back to the discovery of Maddy's body. The chamber of emotions, dormant since her death, erupted. A wave of nausea consumed his stomach, his head swam in a pool of anxiety, and then nothing. Something changed inside the Jumblar couldn't fix. The numb feeling felt at Maddy's funeral returned. Life lost its colour. He couldn't explain it; he didn't have the inclination to explain it.

*

Every place the group scavenged and half the foods they discovered over the next week were new to Finbarl, yet it all felt mundane and pointless to him. The stick Maddy had urged him to take for foraging now half-heartedly pushed the sandy soil around, the joy of unearthing a prized tuber gone.

"The month's up," declared Aminatra, conscious Finbarl wasn't himself but confused about what to do. "I've made enough of the remedy for both of us. If we start the first week cutting back Jumblar by a quarter, taking our daily dose of Maddy's medicine, then cut back another quarter the following week. Okay?"

Finbarl smiled weakly and took his quota without a word.

His poor contribution from foraging trips was beginning to grate with the others. While Aminatra started to cut back on her Jumblar, Finbarl remained taking the full dose. The idea of feeling more pain terrified him. Did it matter anyway, honouring Maddy's plan without Maddy?

"Finbarl, you've got to start pulling your weight," stressed Aminatra. "The others are starting to talk. You could be cut off from the group."

Finbarl shrugged. "I'll go out on my own then."

"Don't be stupid!" Aminatra tried to remain calm and understanding, but Finbarl's self-pity was becoming tiresome. She had persevered with Maddy's experiment, reducing her own Jumblar intake, but withdrawal made her irritable. "You wouldn't survive a week and what would you do for Jumblar? You can't collect it from Bruuk's Point yourself."

Finbarl said nothing. He sat looking into space.

"Argh!" exclaimed Aminatra. "I thought we had something. I thought you cared about me. It seems you only care about yourself!"

Aminatra's confession of a connection caused Finbarl to stir and look at her. "I'm sorry," he said passively. "I do care about you and I don't mean to hurt you. I'm just … I'm just … In truth I don't know. I wake up and I can't see a future."

"Well, I can and Maddy could too," said Aminatra, in a cooler tone. "Do you think she'd have wanted you to give up? She told you exactly what we needed to do, and she trusted you to do it. I'm doing well with giving up Jumblar. It's tough, but I haven't lost the will to see it through and I haven't gone mad. I'm starting to believe Maddy was right. It is possible and, if she was right about that, then ... ".

"I'm not sure I can cope without Jumblar at the moment," said Finbarl.

"Ferral-crap, Finbarl!" snapped Aminatra, the anger returning. "Can't you see? That's exactly why you must come off it. You're a prisoner to it: your reliance makes you a prisoner of Athenia. You'll never be free. I thought you were smarter, but you're just like the rest – a brainless sheep following the flock."

"Ouch! Say what you think," said Finbarl, a little more impassioned in his response to Aminatra's vitriol.

"One of the things your mother taught me was, 'If liberty means anything at all, it means the right to tell people what they don't want to hear.' It's from some writer in the Golden Age. Well, you need to hear some home truths right now, and I want a future where liberty means just that." She paused. "And I want that future with you!"

"I know, I know," acknowledged Finbarl, as he closed his eyes, taking a deep breath. "It's what I want too."

"Then stop wallowing in self-pity and let's make that future happen!"

Finbarl opened his eyes and stared into Aminatra's. "I love you!" He had wanted to say those words a hundred times before, but courage failed him. Even as he lent forward to kiss Aminatra, he felt trepidation. Her lips remained passive as his pressed against them. He could withdraw, pretend nothing happened. As the negative thought entered his head, Aminatra threw her arms around him in a passionate embrace, her lips consuming his. Where Jumblar failed, a kiss worked wonders.

*

Finbarl sat quietly, lost in his own thoughts, rhythmically tenderising a strip of leather with a stone. Three days without Jumblar. Yesterday, he felt things progressing well, this the longest he had ever been without. The medicine, made as instructed by Maddy, tasted terrible, making his stomach growl uncomfortably but, with the additional ingredient of love, it made a difference. Today, however, his muscles felt like lead: the tormenting tickle of a thousand imaginary ants marched through his veins. Every thought led to Jumblar. Every smell reminded him of it. Every taste experienced brought a yearning for its calming intervention. Even his ecstasy at discovering Aminatra shared his feelings had become muted, and she bore Jumblar's vengeance too. Starting a week ahead of Finbarl, he noticed her becoming more irritable, irrational and short-tempered. He smiled in recollection of his neurotic doubts of the past. As he had grown more certain of his own feelings toward her, so he had become more convinced she disliked him. But with that neurosis vanquished, Jumblar deprivation eagerly took its place. Finbarl needed work to keep his mind occupied. He whipped the leather strip in front of him, testing whether his scraping made a difference.

Raised voices in the distance caught his attention. He looked up, his hand patting the ground to his side searching for his staff. Two women stood facing each other, arguing. His hand gave up its search and relaxed. Craning his neck forward, Finbarl tried to make out the exchange. He recognised one as Aminatra, the other Helenta, a skinny thing with one foot missing a toe, making her walk with a slight limp. Fingers pointed and arms waved. Then Aminatra appeared to throw a small object at Helenta before storming off in Finbarl's direction. He slowly and painfully climbed to his feet, awaiting her approach.

"What was that all about?" he asked.

Aminatra's face glowed a bright red. "Stupid Ferral-whack accused me of stealing her comb!"

"She what?" Finbarl felt his own blood boiling.

"Don't worry about it!" she said, her tone abrupt.

"We can't have people accusing each other of stealing," continued Finbarl. "Those are the lies the Wardyns use to destroy us."

"I said forget it!" Aminatra kept her voice level but her annoyance obvious.

"I'll go and have it out with her. Was that the comb you threw at her? I'll get it back." Finbarl reached out to touch Aminatra, but she jerked her shoulder away.

"Forget it!" The words left Aminatra's mouth as a scream; her eyes adding to the outburst with a ferocious stare. "I did steal the bloody comb! Are you happy now? That's what you do to survive in this shithole. That's what you do in Athenia to survive. You steal! Are you so naïve to think people could live on the pittance we got through the rations? I've had nothing my whole life: you've had it easy. Why shouldn't I be able to have something nice every now and again?" The eruption of anger out, Aminatra collapsed to the ground, tears flowing.

Finbarl stepped back in shock. "But … ," he began, uncertain and confused. It wasn't Aminatra's anger confusing him but the content of the confession. "But you said you were innocent."

She looked up through tear-soaked eyes, a little anger remained in them mixed with exhaustion. "I didn't steal the things I was convicted for. I am innocent!"

"But you're a thief," Finbarl gasped, a sense of betrayal burning inside. His personality, forged at the cadet school, recoiled at such behaviour.

"And you're a fraud!" yelled back Aminatra. "You've spent your entire life playing at being some macho hero but you're not. You're acting the part, compensating for losing your parents. In truth you're as scared as the rest of us. The only thing I'm guilty of is surviving!" Aminatra jumped to her feet and stormed off, leaving Finbarl alone, craving Jumblar as never before.

*

"Don't worry," Obidon said to Aminatra a week later, finding her sitting alone while the rest of the group circled the fire. "On the next trip to Bruuk's Point, we'll ask him to join another group. It's probably what he wants too. He can take his new friend with him." They looked across to the fire where the silhouetted figures of Finbarl and Helenta sat shoulder to shoulder, an alliance from the wrath of Aminatra.

"Perhaps I should be the one moving on?" suggested Aminatra.

"No!" said Obidon, the speed and unequivocal nature of his reply surprising Aminatra.

"Don't tell me you'll miss my hunter instincts or cooking. Or is it my friendship?"

Obidon shuffled awkwardly, hoping not to answer.

"It's all right," reassured Aminatra, enjoying the big man's discomfort. "I know I'm the best you've got to replace Maddy."

"I do consider you a friend," insisted Obidon, "but having a friend is no substitute for having someone with survival skills in this place. It's brutal but true. Maddy tried to teach us some of her medical stuff, but you're the only one smart enough to grasp it. They only keep me around for my strength."

"Don't underestimate the quality of your grub and cactus gruel," teased Aminatra. "But we need both Finbarl and Helenta too. It's important we stick together." Perhaps she felt a tinge of jealously, seeing Helenta moving in on Finbarl, but one fact convinced her everything between Finbarl and herself would eventually be all right: they both persisted with their abstinence from Jumblar. She knew the worst was over for herself, otherwise she would have snapped Obidon's head off. If Finbarl continued for one more week, then he would be okay: they would both be okay

*

"We need to follow the crest of the hill," instructed Crixus, leading the group on a gathering expedition.

"No," said Finbarl without further explanation.

Crixus paused, looking back at the dissenter. "Yes," he replied sternly. "It gives us the best vantage point."

"It makes us sitting ducks," yelled Finbarl. "Every Ferral within a mile will be able to see us." A firm hand gently rested on his shoulder. It was Obidon.

"Crixus is right," he said gently. "In this landscape it's best to have the high land."

Aminatra watched from the rear of the group. Something felt wrong; she sensed it. A strange look emanated from Finbarl's eyes. She feared he could hit someone. As a guard, he usually got his way. Could his Jumblar-deprived mind be about to revolt? What happened next surprised her. Finbarl collapsed to the floor, crying like a baby.

Obidon looked down at him perplexed.

"It's sun fever," said Crixus, with little concern. "I've seen it turn the sanest of men into quivering wrecks. There's nothing we can do for him. Come on, we have to keep moving or we will be sitting ducks!"

Obidon stood awkwardly, unsure what to do. "Come on Obidon!" cried Crixus. A column of other prisoners, including Helenta, passed by, ignoring the prostrate and tearful Finbarl. Obidon shrugged and walked on. Only Johansson stopped.

"You 'ave-ed to get-ing into the shade," he urged, trying to lift Finbarl to his feet. The ex-guard proved a dead-weight, too much for the diminutive prisoner. "Need-ing to get-ing out of the sun."

"Go on. Leave him to me!" said Aminatra. "It's all right, Johansson. I'll look after him." The prisoner smiled sheepishly, as though possessor of an intimate secret, giggling as he walked on.

"Finbarl!" She laid a hand gently on his shoulder, kneeling to his side. "It's the withdrawal. You're almost there. Just a few more days and it'll all be over."

Finbarl looked into her eyes. "I can't protect you any more!" he sobbed. "We have to keep in the valley. If they see us, I can't protect you."

"It's okay," cooed Aminatra, noticing a childlike innocence in his eyes. "There are others who can protect us while you're not well, but you can't stay here. You've got to stick with the group. Just a few more days and you'll be feeling right again."

His face collapsed in pained confusion, oblivious to Aminatra's words. "I'm all alone. Everyone leaves me. Who's going to protect me? I've only ever known how to be a guard. Protecting other people: it's what I do. Now I'm nothing! If the Wardyns hadn't stolen me away from my parents I might have learnt to be something better, but all I know is how to be a guard."

Aminatra winced. Now wasn't the time to disclose the truth to him: no time would be right to tell him that. "These dark thoughts you're having, they're not real. Or at least they'll be gone soon. You've got to focus on something else. What would Maddy tell you to do now?"

The last sentence caused a reaction. "Maddy? I miss my mother. She was the most intelligent person I've ever met, apart from Dul-biblex."

"But what would she do now?" pressed Aminatra, shocked at the insecurity she saw in the man who showed no doubts. Abandoned as a child, exiled and vilified by his society, reunited with then ripped from his mother and now ... ? Had their argument tipped Finbarl over the edge – spurned by the woman he loved? The vulnerability made him more normal, but the thought she might be causing this pain made Aminatra feel terrible.

Finbarl frowned. "The Jumblar! We have to come off the Jumblar."

"That's right. You're nearly there. A few more days. That's all."

Finbarl's face, with no discernible movement, lost the little boy look. He sniffed, rubbing his nose on his sleeve. "Right!" he declared, climbing to his feet, wiping away the tears dampening his cheeks. "We've got some catching up to do. Excellent, they're following the crest. It provides the best vantage point in this country." With that he set off, leaving Aminatra standing shaking her head in bemusement. A smile crept onto her face as she followed in his wake.

*

Finbarl and Aminatra exchanged no further words until two days later, when Finbarl appeared before her at breakfast. "Can we talk?" he asked.

She smiled nervously and nodded.

"I ... I wanted you to know I understand."

"Understand what?" asked Aminatra, the conversation not going as expected.

"Why you steal," explained Finbarl, as Aminatra's eyebrows rose, warning him to tread carefully. "I mean, you were right. I've always had everything on a plate as a guard. Never had to look after anyone but me. What I'm trying to say is 'sorry'."

"Are you still suffering the effects of Jumblar withdrawal?" teased Aminatra.

"No," said Finbarl, oblivious to the joke. "I think I'm over the worst. I can't explain it, but everything suddenly feels … ". He hunted for the word.

"Clear?" suggested Aminatra.

"Clear," repeated Finbarl. "That's it."

"I'm sorry too," said Aminatra.

"What for?"

"For anything and everything I said when I wasn't myself."

"I think we should marry," blurted Finbarl.

"Marry!" Aminatra laughed nervously, before wrinkling her petite nose and adding mischievously, "but what about your friend, Helenta?"

Finbarl blushed. "I wasn't myself."

"There are no formal means to undertake a marriage in the Prison."

"Then we'll start something new," responded Finbarl. "And at the ceremony, we announce to the group what we've achieved. We'll ask them to join us in our quest! We'll encourage them to give up Jumblar, spelling out our plan for bringing down the Wardyns and the walls of Athenia."

Aminatra clapped her hands in excitement. "Do you have a nice singing voice?"

Finbarl froze in perplexed anxiety. "Not really."

"Oh, never mind. I do!"

"You 'do' what?" queried Finbarl.

"I accept your marriage proposal, and the 'bringing down civilisation' thing."

Finbarl gathered her in his arms. "I've been wanting to ask you for so long but I ... well, I've not been brave enough."

Aminatra tilted her head back to look Finbarl in the eyes. "What were you afraid of?"

"Being rejected," answered Finbarl sheepishly. "I've only ever been a guard; never a ... ".

"A lover?" answered Aminatra for him. "And what's changed to make you overcome this fear?"

"I have," said Finbarl. "The Prison, it's ... I don't know. It's freed me. Does that sound strange?"

Aminatra affectionally placed her hands either side of Finbarl's head. "Not at all. Had you asked me earlier, I would have rejected you. I honestly thought I could never trust anyone ever again, but the Prison's taught be to have faith in others, in you."

"And I'll never leave you or stop loving you," said Finbarl, stroking her hair. "The only thing that could make me look beyond the Jumblar was my love for you. I can now see everything so ... clearly. We can bring the prisoners together, destroy the Wardyns, rescue Karlmon, start a new life, a new civilisation and a new family."

"When shall we get married?" asked Aminatra.

"Any time we want! After all, there are no formal rules to follow in the Prison."

"Tomorrow!" said Aminatra.

"Tomorrow," repeated Finbarl, leaning forward and kissing his fiancée.

*

A rare, torrential rainstorm arrived in the night, waking everyone, provoking a scramble to collect the water. The flashes of lightning and rumbling of thunder added a dramatic backdrop, with the prisoners revelling in their drenching.

A joyous mood swept the camp and, as the first rays of the morning sun started to warm the ground, a miraculous transformation took place. Colour exploded as plants everywhere answered the call of the rain and flowered. The once harsh landscape became a green and pleasant land, promising a rich harvest of food in the coming weeks.

"It's a good omen," suggested Obidon. "You've picked the perfect day to get married."

Aminatra decorated her hair with yellow and blue flowers. "I never thought I would be happy again," she said, "but now, well, I think I've rediscovered hope."

"Cronax!" exclaimed Obidon. "You're only getting married. Not sure that's a reason to be hopeful. Not from my experience, anyway."

Aminatra laughed. "No, I mean things are falling into place, as opposed to falling apart. I'm in love, getting married and, well, Finbarl will tell you all about it at the celebrations later."

Obidon looked serious. "I hope you're not pregnant! This is no place to have or raise a child."

While Aminatra agreed, it still hurt to hear Obidon say it so bluntly. "No, I'm not pregnant. But it would be none of your business if I were!"

"Sorry," said Obidon, looking flustered for the first time Aminatra could recall. "I didn't mean it to sound so callous. It's just … you know."

Aminatra touched his shoulder. "I'm sorry. Shouldn't have snapped your head off. I just can't think about children until I've got my Karlmon back. Let's forget about it and enjoy today."

*

The prisoners formed a circle around Finbarl and Aminatra, as the couple held hands facing one another. "You look beautiful," whispered Finbarl.

"The flowers look beautiful," responded Aminatra, adjusting a bright yellow bloom behind her ear. "I look like I've lived in the Prison too long."

"You look beautiful," repeated Finbarl. "You always have and always will."

Aminatra ran her hand affectionately down Finbarl's cheek. "To think I once slapped that handsome face of yours."

"I treasured your touch," joked Finbarl.

The rare day of celebration, in a world usually devoid of hope, brought genuine pleasure to the faces of everyone. As the first marriage to take place in the Prison, they followed no traditional format: no priest undertook the ceremony. The other prisoners chattered, excited to be involved, but oblivious to what to expect.

"Can we have your attention!" called out Aminatra, taking hold of Finbarl's hand again. A respectful silence fell. "Thank you for your support today. It means everything to Finbarl and me.

"As you know, we are very much in love and we want to spend the rest of our lives together. We want those lives to be long and worthwhile. That's not going to happen in the world we live in. So, we want to change the world." This caused a murmur among the prisoners and one or two wry smiles. "We wanted to start through our vows. Athenia has passed judgement on and dismissed us and so we reject their ways. We reject their society, their rules, their beliefs. We believe in making a better world: a world of liberty, equality and justice for all." Aminatra, conscious a few of the prisoners rolled their eyes, mocking the high aspirations and sentiments of her address, pressed on. "Finbarl will tell you some incredible news later," she added, hoping to keep the majority with her. "But there's no better symbol of how society behaves than in how two people brought together through love treat each other in the bonds of marriage. We have, therefore, composed new vows – if Finbarl can remember his lines."

Finbarl smiled at his lover's prompt, conscious she pinpointed the very thought terrifying him. "I, Finbarl, give my heart, my love, my life to Aminatra." He blushed, hiding his head against his chest, as he exposed his feelings in front of others. Focusing his eyes upon Aminatra's, he found the strength to continue. "I will respect, cherish and care for you ... her ... you." Aminatra mouthed the correct word and Finbarl continued, "her, through good and bad times. We will be as one. What is mine is hers; what is hers is mine."

"Doesn't sound like liberty to me!" came an anonymous quip from the congregation.

Finbarl ignored it, desperate to get the most stressful few minutes of his life over with. "I will support her in what she aspires to do, in what she aspires to be. I offer myself as a loyal and loving husband." He let out a relieved breath as Aminatra squeezed his hands.

"I, Aminatra, give my heart, my love, my life to Finbarl." She possessed none of the nerves of her lover and spoke with pride to all around. The words mirrored those uttered by Finbarl, and she breezed through to the end. " ... in what he aspires to be. I offer myself as a loyal and loving wife."

A moment's silence followed, the prisoners unsure if the vows were complete or not, until a curt nod from Aminatra stirred Finbarl to action. He sheepishly turned to one side of the circle and said aloud: "I accept Aminatra's offer and declare myself her husband." Turning to the other half of the circle, he repeated the declaration.

"I accept Finbarl's offer and declare myself his wife," cried out Aminatra, as soon as Finbarl finished. "I do accept

Finbarl's offer and declare myself his wife," she called out again with even more gusto. As cheers erupted from the prisoners, Aminatra threw herself into her husband's arms, sealing their marriage with a kiss.

*

"I have to tell you all something," announced Finbarl around the fire, as the celebrations stretched into the evening. "It's what Aminatra alluded to earlier." The chatter and laughing ceased. "Both Aminatra and I have stopped taking Jumblar and have been free of it for weeks." A collective gasp emanated from the group. "We've suffered no ill-effects ... well, I haven't. As Aminatra has chosen to marry me, her sanity could be questioned!" Aminatra gave him a withering look. "Sorry, what I mean to say is, Maddy showed us it was possible, and we've succeeded. It feels great! The world is a new and wonderful place and no vengeance has been reaped upon us from on high." Finbarl reached for Aminatra's hand, clasping it affectionately. "We want you to experience this world with us. You can achieve a freedom you've never enjoyed before. Jumblar is not a gift from God, it's the chain imprisoning us. Coming off it isn't easy. You may have noticed us behaving ... oddly."

"You've been as miserable as always!" yelled Crixus to much mirth.

Finbarl laughed with them. "Once you're free of Jumblar, then Athenia will no longer control you."

"But they still have guns," shouted someone from the darkness.

"They still have guns," repeated Finbarl, "but we don't just want you to be free; we want everyone in Athenia to be free! Maddy had a vision: a worthy vision of a world without Jumblar, without the Wardyns and without walls. A world where humans break free from fear and oppression. Our bodies and minds can go where we want. We're no longer reliant on a few ancient books to keep us alive – we'll write our own! We'll find out what lies over the mountains – literally and metaphorically."

"What about the Ferrals? They breed like rabbits and have a habit of eating us."

"We know they're not beasts now," asserted Aminatra. "They're like us. They lost their way generations ago due to the trickery of some of our ancestors. Don't we owe them a chance to find their way back onto the path of humanity?"

The plea got a mixed response.

Finbarl cut in. "Listen, freedom isn't about ducking tough decisions! It's about facing up to the truth. We, and our ancestors, hid behind a fortified wall to avoid the truth for millennia. Most of you have lived outside those stone walls for years, yet you've built further walls for yourselves!" Finbarl's voice grew in strength and emotion as he got into his stride. "If you can free yourself from Jumblar's hold, you'll see more clearly and better understand what I'm talking about. We should spread the word amongst all the prisoners; give them the hope they deserve and unite them behind this common cause. I now know a way to get into Athenia undetected. We target the arsenal first and then fight our way to the farm and burn the Jumblar. What do you say? Are you with us?"

"If you can get me a gun, I'm in!" said Crixus. "I've got some scores to settle." This caused several other prisoners to hoot in agreement.

"The intention is not to start a massacre," admonished Aminatra. "We just want to topple the Wardyns and burn the crop."

"What about the Ferral-whacks who betrayed me!" cried another prisoner.

"And those Ferral-whacks who turned their back on me when I was sentenced!" shouted another.

"There will be no murders!" shouted Finbarl. "The reason you're bitter and angry is because you were innocent of any crime. Don't prove them right now by becoming a criminal."

"Finbarl's right," said Obidon, his voice gentle but authoritative. "I'm a true criminal. I murdered my wife and it's haunted me ever since! We've a chance to do good, but we can't achieve that by doing wrong." The big man's intervention swayed the majority, who voiced their consent with a cheer. The rest grudgingly acknowledged his rationale.

"Good," said a relieved Finbarl, leaning over toward Aminatra and whispering, "You'll soon have Karlmon in your arms again."

She smiled warmly and responded with a whispered tease. "And what if we're not so innocent of a crime?"

Finbarl still felt uncomfortable thinking about Aminatra's transgressions, and chose to acknowledge her comment with an edgy laugh before addressing the group again. "It will not be easy, but, well, life as a prisoner is never easy. You'll need to continue your visits to Bruuk's Point and play the part of a dependent prisoner. We can't let on what we've planned to anyone who may let slip to a guard."

"We'll have to venture into the foothills to harvest the ingredients to break Jumblar's grip," added Aminatra.

"Will I be cured-ed?" It was Johansson, standing with a childish grin on his face.

Aminatra faltered, lost for words. She hadn't thought about Johansson's condition. "I honestly don't know," she confessed. "I hope so."

CHAPTER 28

"Guilty!" One after another the circle of prisoners called out a judgement. Their declaration was aimed toward a solitary man standing awkwardly in the middle. Justice, a concept left to nature and fate in the old world of the Prison, now fell under the control of the Jumblar-free community, biding its time as it prepared to bring the walls of Athenia down.

The six months since Finbarl and Aminatra convinced the other prisoners to join them and give up Jumblar had brought enormous changes within the Prison. Their movement slowly grew as word spread and hope rose. The pretence at Bruuk's Point continued, but rather than splitting on their departure into divergent factions, they reunited into a single community, defined by a purpose and common cause. This brought its own problems. There were more mouths to feed and the need to establish a form of organisation and governance. The latter was unavoidable if they were to successfully challenge the Wardyns. While the removal of Jumblar helped transform the place from a collection of self-serving individuals battling to survive into a group pulling together for a common goal, rivalries and flaws remained. It only needed one malcontent to tip off the guards, exposing their intentions. These details never crossed Finbarl's mind when he dreamt of a

Jumblar-free future. Now a reality, there was no escaping the need to impose order and justice.

Amid the circle, Finbarl, last to cast his judgement, looked across to the accused. He offered the final chance for the defendant. Only one from the jury needed to find the accused not guilty to give them their freedom. Finbarl spoke the word with pain, knowing the consequences. "Guilty!" It matched the other twenty returned verdicts. The man collapsed to his knees, crying out in anguish. The sound of sobbing also broke out from beyond the circle, where the accusers sat, having delivered their indisputable evidence of theft and assault against the man. Aminatra sat with her arm around one, a woman not much younger than herself. She sobbed uncontrollably, whether at justice served, revenge gained or at the fate to befall the guilty, Aminatra couldn't tell, but she needed comforting.

Finbarl, as chair of the jury, rose to his feet and, with heavy heart, announced the sentence. "You have been found guilty of theft and assault by your peers and of endangering the security of the community." Finbarl paused for breath, contradicted by a feeling he somehow echoed the words of the Wardyns. This was different, he argued inside, then uttered words he knew to be different. "You'll therefore be executed. Your suffering in this world will be over and the community safer and stronger."

The condemned man yelled an incoherent lament, causing all around to lower their eyes. This was the only sentence available to the court. Anyone who challenged the rules of the community posed a risk of betraying them and the plan. What choice did they have? They had no means of holding them captive. To ostracise them would drive them into the arms of the guards. A physical punishment, such as whipping, meant death anyway, from infection or the inability to scavenge.

Execution, they decided, was the only just and practical solution.

Finbarl hated the extreme and flawed system, hanging on to the flimsy justification that in this brutal world, where a horrible death awaited most, a quick, controlled execution seemed almost a blessing. He watched the man escorted away by Crixus and two others to a secluded spot. Out of sight, a stone swiftly smashed his skull. One quick strike ended it humanely: no one wanted to know if the act was always so clean, the suffering so short.

*

Finbarl proposed an army of 150 for the raid on Athenia. They selected a group of fifteen commanders, each in charge of ten men and women, and each with a specific role in the raid. With his expert knowledge as a former guard, Finbarl made the natural leader. He knew the routines of the sentries, the layout of the barracks and arsenal and how to fight like a guard. All rested on securing the arsenal. Without guns, they stood no chance; with them, the odds still felt slim. The darkness of night would be their other ally: most Athenians, including the Wardyns, would be safely tucked up in bed. If they captured the Wardyns together, no point of opposition would develop.

"Our main advantage is surprise," explained Finbarl to the massed group of prisoners sitting anxiously before him. "If we secure the sanctuary and barracks without a shot fired, we stand an excellent chance of making it to the farm without any on-duty guards reacting in time. If they raise the alarm, we'll be up against better trained marksmen and they'll pin us down and defeat us. We know our objectives. Once the Jumblar is on fire and destroyed, the best thing we can do is withdraw. There'll be so much confusion, we'll be able to exploit it, vanishing back through the tunnel. With the Wardyns our captives, no one else will know about it, and in the cold light of day the citizens will find they've no leaders, no Jumblar and no enemy within those walls."

Aminatra took over. "With all the Jumblar we've stored over the last six months, we hold the winning hand," she explained. "They'll have the choice of going mad or surrendering and taking our offer to wean them off Jumblar. Once people are free of their addiction, they'll start to see us as liberators rather than conquerors."

"No one needs to die tonight!" urged Finbarl. "This is a revolution for freedom! We're building our future on a solid foundation, not upon the bones and blood of our fellow man! Are you ready?" An almighty cheer erupted. "Then we march for freedom!"

The first moonless night provided the darkness required, the only light coming from the flickering torches upon Athenia's walls. The prisoners gathered in the dry river channel, their mood boisterous. Finbarl, fearing detection, urged silence.

They divided into units of ten. There were three units to lead the initial assault – locating the tunnel, accessing the sanctuary and securing the arsenal – with the main contingent following, heading straight for the arsenal to arm themselves, before spreading out across the town to pacify all opposition. Finbarl, as part of the primary incursion, led unit one, its objective to capture the Wardyns; Aminatra's unit, as part of the secondary wave, aimed to burn the Jumblar.

"Units one to three with me!" ordered Finbarl in a hushed tone. "We'll head for the third light from the left and inch around the perimeter to try and find these boulders. If you hear gunfire, retreat and split up! Remember, stealth is everything from now on!"

The train of thirty men and women headed off, shaking hands with their friends and anyone offering a gesture of good luck. Finbarl kissed Aminatra quickly on the lips and dashed into the darkness, neither contemplating failure nor the chance of never seeing his wife again.

Their approach gave little cover to the bottom of Cragor Hill, but with visibility limited to ten yards, the chances of a sentry spotting them was slim. Once within sight of the walls, they progressed in twos, sprinting the last section, working their way around, keeping as close to the defences as possible. They aligned along the base of Cragor. Finbarl gave the signal and they spread out, edging up the slope, trying to identify the three boulders guarding the tunnel entrance.

After what felt like an eternity, a burst of clicks sounded. Three bursts was the agreed signal notifying success in the hunt. Another series of clicks! Finbarl held his breath. A third burst! Someone had found the tunnel to his right. He scampered over stones and undergrowth, directed by regular guiding clicks. A charcoal vision of hunched men above greeted Finbarl. He held out his hand. Someone grasped it, pulling him up. Sure enough, there were three boulders, surrounded by overgrown bushes, marking the entrance to a well-hidden passageway. Finbarl nodded to a man holding a leafy branch collected earlier in the day. He vanished down the slope, placing it as a marker to the main group at the foot of the hills. With all thirty men and women present, Finbarl led them into the tunnel.

The dark night grew darker as they entered the pitch-black hole. Finbarl wondered how Torbald or the Governor managed to fit through the narrow entrance, as he squeezed himself between two sentry rocks. The prisoners felt their way along, stooped and blind in the cool, dank air, their progress slow. A curse escaped every now and again as prisoner stepped upon prisoner. After 100 yards, Finbarl reached the end. A sliver of light appeared above, exposing a rudimentary ladder against a wall. Finbarl reached forward trying to find a rung and took his first step up. With the others standing silently below, he climbed the ten yards to the top. A heavy wooden trapdoor blocked his way. He listened for activity above and then, on detecting nothing, tried to push the trap open with his hands. It refused to budge. Finbarl positioned his shoulders under the end where the light emerged, precariously leaning out from the ladder with one hand gripping, and tried again. A creak indicated some movement, but the door refused to open. "It's bolted on the other side!" Finbarl whispered into the darkness. "Somebody, climb up and help me!" An uneasy shift of the ladder signalled someone else ascending. "Who's that?" asked Finbarl, as a head of hair caught in the light.

"Crixus," came the reply.

"Good," said Finbarl. "Now ease yourself to the right of the ladder. I'll lean out to the left. I'm hoping brute force will break whatever's locking the door, otherwise we're in trouble!"

Crixus huffed and puffed as he awkwardly positioned himself, the ladder creaking under the strain. "I'm in place."

"On my mark. Push!" Again, the door promised more than it gave. "Again! Push! And again!" On the fifth attempt the squeaking morphed into a crack. "It's working."

"I'm cramping!" complained Crixus.

"Hang on!" urged Finbarl, his own shoulders beginning to cramp too. "One more push should do it."

The door jumped opened a few inches before gravity brought it back down, hitting Finbarl's and Crixus' heads. They wobbled at the top of the ladder as the pain shot through their bodies. "Cronax!" cursed Finbarl. "That hurt!"

"Get moving before I fall!" growled Crixus, as he climbed back down a few rungs.

Finbarl pushed the door with his hands, easing it open. The light of a single candle flooded through, shocking Finbarl's eyes. He shielded his face behind his arm, unable to discern if anyone awaited to attack or give the alarm. Silence prevailed. As his eyes adjusted, he made out their point of entry: an unassuming storeroom. He heaved the door to full height and pushed it over. It crashed down, banging loudly. Finbarl cringed, gripping the club tied to his belt. Frozen for a moment in anticipation of discovery, he breathed out with relief as the silence persisted. Pulling himself out of the tunnel, he instantly noticed the pungent smell of Athenia; contrasting with the pure air of the Prison. Walking over to the storeroom door, he eased it open a crack and peeked outside, straining to discover their exact location within the sanctuary, assessing what awaited them. Finbarl recognised nothing.

No one appeared to be about, but the burning candle must surely have been for someone's benefit? Finbarl hesitated by the door, doubts filling his mind. If someone had been in the storeroom but gone for assistance, then he could be leading his raiders into a trap. There was time to abandon the whole thing, disappear back down the tunnel and lead the prisoners away from Athenia for good. If only Maddy were here to provide her wisdom, thought Finbarl.

Crixus' face appeared from the tunnel entrance, breaking Finbarl's thoughts. "What's going on?" demanded Crixus in a hushed tone.

Words came out of Finbarl's mouth out of alignment with his thoughts. "Get everyone up here!" he ordered. "As quietly as possible."

One by one the prisoners emerged from the tunnel; the storeroom quickly became tightly packed with sweating figures eager to get this night's work over with.

Finbarl leaned across to Crixus. "I suspect someone's been working in this room." He indicated the burning candle with a nod of his head. "We may have to assume they know we're coming."

"Better to die trying than continue in that hellhole!" replied Crixus, surprising Finbarl with his purposeful response.

"Okay," said Finbarl. "I'll lead everyone to the arsenal; leave you there with two units to secure the weapons, whilst I go and round up the Wardyns."

Crixus nodded and grinned.

Opening the door of the room, with men and women crammed in thick, became an unexpected challenge; Finbarl was only just able to get it ajar enough to squeeze through. Gradually, as more and more emptied into the corridor, they opened the door fully. Finbarl gripped his club tightly as he made his way down the corridor. He recognised their location as they came to the main aisle leading to the sanctuary entrance. Access to the arsenal meant passing through the entrance and past the sentries. Finbarl signalled a halt, indicating for three others to follow him to the door. Two guards stood on duty, their heads facing the opposite direction, with no expectation of danger from within the sanctuary. The four prisoners tip-toed forward, prepared to rush the guards at the first indication of discovery.

Two yards away, their breathing gave them away, and the guards turned. The look of surprise on their faces hardly formed before the prisoners threw themselves upon them. No sound escaped from the guards' mouths as the clubs landed their blows. The men slumped to the floor senseless, the prisoners stepping back, silently revelling in their first victory.

"Drag them out of sight!" ordered Finbarl, beckoning the main group forward. The contrast in the emaciated bodies of the prisoners, pulling the two well-fed guards into the corner, told a tale, reinforcing Finbarl's concerns that in a close-quarters fight, the odds were against them. "The closer we get to the arsenal, the more guards there'll be," he explained, as others edged forward, eager to land another blow against Athenia. "We manage them exactly like this: a quick and silent strike and move on. We have to make it to the arsenal without the alarm being raised."

Memories resurfaced as the smells and sounds of the town hit the prisoners' senses, nostalgia washing through them. Finbarl estimated the time to be around one in the morning. The second wave would be starting their passage through the tunnel now. They had to push on, ensure they secured the arsenal and readied the guns to be handed out by the time the others arrived.

A camel emitted a low grumble in the silence, indicating the barracks and arsenal were nearby. A door squeaked open and Finbarl stepped back into the shadow, the line of men behind following. Peering into the torchlit area in front of the barracks, Finbarl observed a guard emerge, take a few steps forward, stretch his arms skywards, then press his fists into his lower back to relieve muscle tension. Signalling for the others to remain still, Finbarl strode brazenly towards the guard.

"Excuse me, Apcula," said Finbarl. "I have a delivery for Officer Vassel."

The guard looked round unperturbed, before recognising the approaching face. "Finbarl!" It was Strathbol. Finbarl harboured no ill will against the boy but knew there would be no reasoning with him. The young guard opened his mouth to ask that most pressing of questions – "what are you doing here?" – when Finbarl's club caught his brow. A pained, confused look consumed Strathbol's eyes as he slumped to the floor. Finbarl felt a pang of guilt, hoping only a nasty headache awaited him in the morning. He stripped Strathbol of his knife and waved for the others to join him. The chatting of guards from inside the barracks drifted in the air as the prisoners hurried on.

With its precious content, all guards carried guns at the arsenal. Finbarl knew what to expect: two sentries outside and up to ten stationed within. Theirs was a dull duty, and Finbarl hoped to find them in a state of relaxation, but first there was the small matter of the bolted door, only opened from the inside.

A small group of prisoners vanished in the opposite direction, while Finbarl and Crixus stepped to the edge of the shadows, just within sight of the two external guards. Finbarl pushed his comrade upon the chest, a first act in their staged argument. Crixus pushed back, their mock fight soon drawing the attention of the guards. After a brief discussion, one tramped over to investigate.

"Hey! What are you two up to?" the guard demanded.

Finbarl and Crixus stopped fighting, the former turning his head away.

"Sorry, sir," answered Crixus. "Just a little family disagreement."

The guard came closer, his rifle hanging casually over his shoulder. "Well, if you're heading to work, hurry up and get there! Otherwise you shouldn't be out at this time! Go on, get home!"

"You're right, sir. It's just … ". Crixus left the sentence hanging, enticing the guard still closer.

Within touching distance, Finbarl spun round, placing Strathbol's blade at the shocked guard's throat. "Not a sound!" Finbarl instructed, as the guard flinched in terror.

In the distance, as planned, the remaining guard appeared distracted by his partner's excursion. The darkness was to the attackers' advantage. Finbarl watched the sentry's hesitancy turn to shock as a group of figures emerged from the shadows, charging silently towards their victim. A pathetic yelp carried to Finbarl as the man disappeared under a mass of attacking bodies. Clubs rained down on his prostrate body, and Finbarl cringed, hoping the pain inflicted was fleeting before unconsciousness overcame him.

"We've a little job for you," whispered Finbarl into the ear of the captured guard. "We know where your family live and have men there already. If you want to see them alive again, you'll do exactly as you're told!" Finbarl prayed he hadn't picked an Orpho.

The guard nodded timidly.

"Good," said Finbarl, relaxing the pressure of the knife against the guard's throat. "Now we want you back at your post!"

Crixus removed the guard's gun, proudly examining it, aiming directly at the guard's head.

"Lower that barrel!" snapped Finbarl. "If that goes off accidentally, we're screwed!"

"Just practising!" replied Crixus, resentment colouring his tone. "Need to know the sight lines up with the target."

"I'm hoping we won't have to fire a shot!" said Finbarl sternly. "Once we've the Wardyns and arsenal, it's possible we can force the guards to surrender peacefully." Crixus didn't respond but gave a knowing smile, making Finbarl uneasy.

With the knife still to the guard's throat, Finbarl manoeuvred him back to the arsenal doors. The other guard lay prostrate, stripped of his clothes, as one of the prisoners changed into his thawb. "Right," said Finbarl to his captive. "You're to knock on the door and calmly ask them to open up!"

"For what reason?" asked the guard.

"I don't care," hissed Finbarl. "You want a drink of water! Any attempt to give the game away and you'll be shot, and on the sound of any gunfire, my friends have the order to kill your family!" Finbarl shoved him toward the door and scurried to one side, Crixus aiming the gun back at the guard's head.

With the uniformed prisoner standing as though on duty, the real guard knocked loudly upon the solid oak door. Silence followed, then a mumble.

"I want a glass of water," said the guard, with no great theatrical flair.

A spyhole opened in the door, this time the voice resonated clearly. "You've only been on duty for five minutes, Pantlin!"

"It's actually been two hours," answered Pantlin. "There's dust in the air."

Finbarl allowed himself a wry smile at the guard's creativity. The spyhole slammed shut, accompanied by a sigh. A moment later, the distinct sound of a moving bolt: they'd taken the bait. Finbarl braced himself. The handle rotated, the door crept open, allowing a head to poke out to inspect the scene. Pantlin stood rigidly, unsure what to do next, while the uniformed prisoner maintained his outward facing posture. The head then vanished inside before the door opened fully.

"Now!" yelled Finbarl.

The disguised prisoner acted first, turning and thrusting the butt of his rifle at the head of the emerging guard. Pantlin stood back in alarm, a forgotten man. As the first guard fell back through the door, Finbarl and the others piled in, trampling the dazed man as they went. The noise merely stirred curiosity rather than fear among the other guards. They emerged from side rooms, intrigued by the disturbance, only to find themselves swept up by the surge of prisoners. It was over in a flash. Nine pitiful guards sat on the floor, a posse of prisoners with guns watching over them.

"I'm going to secure the Wardyns," called out Finbarl, his adrenaline pumping at the thrill of this major victory. "My unit, all of you grab a weapon and some bullets and come with me! Secure the bolt after we're gone and get the guns and ammunition ready to hand out when the others arrive."

CHAPTER 29

Finbarl led the ten men of his unit back to the sanctuary. They examined their new weapons excitedly. "Keep it quiet!" ordered Finbarl. "We don't want to stir the hornets' nest yet." They passed not a conscious soul on their return; all unconscious ones lying serenely where left.

As they marched up the main sanctuary corridor, Finbarl reminded his men of their instructions. "The Wardyns all live around the atrium. Pair up and take a room each. Women and children will be present, so keep violence to a minimum. If they make a noise, hit them. I want all brought to the atrium." He already knew which room to take himself. There would be something deeply satisfying in seeing the Governor's face when he awoke.

The Governor's office had changed little since Finbarl last enjoyed its decor. Accompanied by a prisoner named Herzog, Finbarl went through the office's inner door and into the corridor. He spared a look at the library door. Now wasn't the time to rescue or involve Dul-biblex. Once they secured the town, he would return for him. The librarian would be a useful ally in the days ahead. "It's this one here," whispered Finbarl, slowly turning the handle on the first door. A contented snort came from within. Sliding his body through the partial opening,

Finbarl stood looking down at an occupied bed. A solitary figure lay asleep amid the crumpled sheets. The Governor's wife died years ago, and he never remarried. Finbarl spent a moment watching the Governor in his peaceful slumber, then yanked the sheets away. The naked body stirred in a semi-conscious state, feeling around for his missing warmth. Something clicked within and an eye opened to discover an explanation. A second later, the Governor sprung upright in alarm.

"What the hell's going on?" he cried, still confused and uncertain who stood before him. "Who are you?"

"I'm justice!" announced Finbarl. "Come to set the people free."

"What are you t … Finbarl?" The Governor strained his eyes to confirm the ludicrous notion forming. "Is that you, Finbarl? I thought you were dead."

"No, just a little annoyed. Now get out of bed and put some clothes on!"

The Governor eased his considerable bulk off the bed, sitting on the edge. "You won't get away with this, Finbarl! All I have to do is make a noise and the guards will be summoned."

"I'm not alone," said Finbarl with satisfaction. "I've brought quite a few friends and we've already taken over the arsenal." He waved his own rifle towards Governor Elbar, whose head sank at the realisation Finbarl held the upper hand. "Now, get moving!"

After the Governor hurriedly threw on his thawb, they marched him back to the atrium. A group of dishevelled and bewildered men, women and children stood huddled in their family groups. Utrep stood with her husband and three children, Rhyd with his wife and child, Hradkarl, the Governor's grandson and a few Moralista clerks. A commotion sounded to the right and Finbarl looked over to see Hradbar dragged along, nursing a bleeding forehead, his wife following in tears.

"Had a little disagreement," said the prisoner holding Hradbar's left arm, promptly releasing it, letting the groggy Wardyn drop to his knees.

"What do you plan to do with us?" enquired the Governor, still speaking with the voice of authority but with a hesitancy in his eyes.

"What would you do with someone who had condemned you to a slow and painful death?" challenged Finbarl.

"If I made decisions that seemed unfair, it was always with the good of Athenia and civilisation behind them," said the Governor. "Sometimes sacrifice is necessary for the greater good."

"I'm pleased to hear you say that, Elbar," responded Finbarl. "Because we're here to help you make a big sacrifice for the greater good."

"What do you mean?" asked Utrep, recovering from the shock of her rude awakening.

Finbarl went to answer, when one of the prisoners ran up to him, whispering in his ear. "Excellent, thanks," said Finbarl, turning back to his captive audience. "Our other comrades have arrived. They're on their way to the arsenal." Multiple steps sounded faintly in the distance.

"How did you all get past the walls?" asked the Governor.

A gruff, mumbled voice spoke. "Torbald!" It was Hradbar, gradually recovering his senses.

"Spot on," said Finbarl. "His dying words informed us of the tunnel and sought a promise of revenge on the man responsible for his death. I don't suppose you know it was Hradbar who murdered your other son, do you Governor?" The face of the Governor showed no reaction, the truth dawning on Finbarl. "Cronax! You arranged Torbald's death! But why? He was your son!"

Utrep and Rhyd both appeared shocked, suggesting purely a family plot.

"You wouldn't understand," said Governor Elbar. "Power's not something you put in just anyone's hands."

"But he was your son!" repeated Finbarl.

"And he would have done anything to wield power, including killing those in his way." The Governor looked indignant.

Finbarl shook his head in disbelief. "You deserve each other."

"What about this 'sacrifice'?" asked Utrep again.

"You're going to give up power and we're going to destroy the Jumblar," answered Finbarl.

"But that'll condemn the citizens and yourselves to madness!" exclaimed Utrep.

"I've not touched Jumblar for over six months," declared Finbarl. "All the prisoners have been successfully weaned off it. We'll offer the solution to all those that'll follow us in destroying the walls of Athenia and starting a new civilisation."

The Governor burst out laughing. "I'm not sure your solution has saved you from madness. Why would anyone want the walls destroyed?"

Finbarl opened his mouth to respond when a thought stopped him. He turned to Utrep. "Why did you say, 'condemn the citizens' rather than 'condemn us'? It's not like the Wardyns to think of others before themselves."

Utrep shifted uneasily, reluctant to answer.

"Oh, just tell him!" cried Hradbar, now on his feet, recovered of his full faculties. "We don't use Jumblar. Never have."

Finbarl gripped his gun tightly, the urge to use it strong, but he knew it would change nothing to shoot them. Even his promise to Torbald to kill Hradbar was one he had no intention of keeping. It was the last thing Maddy would want. "So, you used it to control everyone else."

"Like I said, you can't possibly understand what is required to keep civilisation alive," said the Governor.

"Maybe not, but I've an idea how to destroy it," retorted Finbarl. "Enough talking! We're taking you on a little journey outside the walls while we do just that." Before Finbarl had time to convey orders to his men, the sound of approaching steps stopped him dead. He lifted his gun, aiming it in the direction of the noise.

"Ah, Finbarl. I see you've successfully rounded up our foes." Crixus stood at the door with his unit.

"What are you doing here?" asked Finbarl, lowering his gun.

"Don't worry," answered Crixus. "The arsenal remains secure and all the guns and ammunition have been allocated to our people."

"Yes, but what are you doing here? This isn't part of the plan."

Crixus walked up to the Governor, looking him directly in the eye, before whipping round to address Finbarl. "Plans change. The boys and I were having a chat while we waited. Some things in the original plan just didn't make sense to us. Like the bit where we don't kill the Wardyns. Or the bit where we make life harder for ourselves by trying to kick-start civilisation again! I mean, come on, we've been languishing out in the wilderness for years. Why would we want to give up the rewards of our victory? Look around you!" Crixus pointed at the lush green atrium. "This is ours now!"

Finbarl turned a bright red as his anger grew. "Don't be a fool, Crixus! We're not doing this for just our benefit, but for everyone's."

"Speak for yourself! I don't owe these people anything! Who do you think betrayed me?" He lifted his rifle and shot the Governor through the head. Finbarl gasped as a thunderous volley erupted from other guns. Screams and whimpers mixed through the smoke as he watched the Wardyns, their families and the Moralistas fall to the ground in a hail of bullets.

"No!" cried Finbarl amid the stench of gunpowder. Then all became silent and black as a rifle butt struck him across the head.

CHAPTER 30

Aminatra realised something was wrong when Crixus and his party crossed her path as she approached the arsenal. He ignored the question she threw his way and vanished into the darkness, leaving her with Obidon and Johansson, and looking perplexed.

"I'm sure everything's fine," commented Obidon. "Plans always have to change a little."

"But why wouldn't he talk to us: tell us where he's going?"

"There are 120 prisoners just arrived," said Obidon. "He can't explain to all of us. Someone at the arsenal will tell us."

"I guess you're right," replied Aminatra, unconvinced. "Come on, let's do what we came for!"

"Burning-ly the Jumblar," said Johansson, clapping his hands together in excitement.

Aminatra hadn't come to collect a gun from the arsenal. She despised guns. Her only focus was setting alight the Jumblar and finding Karlmon.

A disorganised mass built up outside the arsenal. Prisoners, eager to get a weapon, were pushing forward, trying to force their way into the building. An excitable noise rumbled from within, a voice here and there becoming animated and aggressive. Aminatra gripped Obidon and Johansson by the arm and pulled them away from the rabble.

"Something's wrong," she said. "I don't know what, but it feels wrong."

"In what way? asked Obidon.

"Firstly, there's Crixus leaving the arsenal and then there's something about the mood here."

A muffled shot sounded in the distance, quickly followed by a volley. Silence and confusion fell upon those struggling to gain access to the arsenal, before a wild "yeeha" came from within and a voice shouted: "Athenia is ours! It's time to wreak our revenge!"

"Cronax!" cursed Aminatra, as another gunshot went off, this time from within the arsenal. "The fools are going to try and even their personal scores."

Those without guns backed away from the doors as others, brandishing their weapons, emerged from inside.

"What do-ist we do-ist?" implored Johansson, his childlike enthusiasm turning to terror.

"Obidon, secure a gun from the arsenal!" instructed Aminatra. "I've a feeling we may need it."

"Should have brought my bow," grumbled the big man, as he took a step forward. A whooping prisoner confronted him, doing a jig with his newly acquired rifle.

"Gonna have me some fun!" said the man, grinning widely.

Obidon gently smiled in reply, then thrust his fist into the man's face. As he collapsed in a heap, Obidon pulled the rifle from his relaxing grip and turned back to Aminatra. "The arsenal was too crowded."

"Okay," said Aminatra, sternly eyeing her friend. "As you say, plans often have to change."

Prisoners disappeared in all directions, their discipline gone, their shouts waking any soul unstirred by the previous commotion. The first scream sounded in the darkness. All knew something dreadful was occurring.

"This is going to be a bloodbath!" cried Aminatra. "No one will be safe. I've got to find Karlmon now!"

"What about the Jumblar?" asked Obidon, still looking to Aminatra for leadership amid the chaos.

"That plan is shot," declared Aminatra. "I suspect Crixus and his cohort undermined it a long time ago. It's back to the laws of the Prison: we look after ourselves now. Why don't you head back to the tunnel and sit it out? Take Johansson with you."

Obidon shook his head solemnly. "No, I'm sticking with you to find your boy." He looked to Johansson.

"I'm coming-ly too," said the smaller prisoner, his eyes still full of fear.

"Thank you," said Aminatra. "You're good friends. Now Karlmon is likely to be in the barracks, which won't be a good place to be any time soon. It'll likely be where most prisoners want to attack first."

"We're prisoners," interjected Obidon. "Why don't we go with the flow and join the attack? What better way not to get noticed."

"And what if Karlmon's defending the barracks?" Aminatra pressed her face between her hands in despair.

"He'll be defending it whether we're involved or not," replied Obidon. "I don't propose we contribute to the violence, just use it as a smoke screen to get us in as soon as possible."

"I know! I know!" fretted Aminatra. "We don't have many options. Come on, let's go before another plan runs out of our control!"

*

As expected, prisoners, drawn by a desire to sow their revenge on the guards, converged upon the barracks hoping for easy pickings. Three bodies already lay dead or wounded outside but the once brazen prisoners remained fixed in siege positions in the surrounding area.

"Why aren't we advancing?" cried Aminatra, as she arrived with Obidon and Johansson.

"Blondel and Kahan tried that," answered one of the prisoners poised with his rifle. "The fools got ambushed inside. Now the guards have two guns!"

Aminatra looked again at the prostrate bodies on the ground and noticed one was a prisoner. "They can't have much ammunition," she suggested.

"It only takes one bullet to kill," replied the prisoner. "If you want to storm the barracks now, be my guest!"

Aminatra looked to Obidon and Johansson, both crouching behind her. "If you lay down some fire, I'll make a dash for it."

"No!" snapped Obidon. "What'll you do if you make it in there alive? The place is full of guards, all armed with knives and truncheons. They aren't going to care you're someone's mother. You'll be dead within a minute."

Aminatra fidgeted. "We've got to do something! The longer we wait, the more prisoners will arrive. Those inside will be overwhelmed."

"Let the guards escape-ed," said Johansson.

"What?" queried Obidon.

"He's right!" exclaimed Aminatra. "If we can provide the guards with an option to escape the barracks then that'll remove the threat."

"Yes, but if they all escape, we won't know where Karlmon is any more. He'll be in just as much danger on the streets of Athenia."

"Not if their escape route is unobserved, except by us," opined Aminatra. "If Karlmon tries to leave, we follow him."

"But if there were such an escape route," pressed Obidon, "don't you think they'd have used it already?"

"These are guards remember. They aren't much good at taking the initiative, only following orders and fighting."

"And you married one!" commented Obidon.

Aminatra ignored the quip, her mind too focused on Karlmon. "My point is, it won't have occurred to them to do anything other than fight. If we offer them an alternative, they may take it."

A round of gunfire burst forth from the prisoners around, causing them to duck and cover their ears. "Okay," assented Obidon reluctantly. "We'd better do something sooner, rather than later. Lead on!"

Aminatra cut back behind the besieging prisoners, Obidon and Johansson in her wake. The barracks, hemmed in by the sanctuary on one end and the stables on the other, made the side walls inaccessible. But Aminatra moved with purpose, clear where to head. As they passed the stables, she turned to Obidon and instructed, "Get two bales of straw and bring them to the front!" The camels and donkeys housed in the stables, distressed by the ongoing noise and commotion, welcomed the additional intrusion with a fresh chorus of groaning, bellowing and neighing. Obidon emerged carrying the two bales together, the only prisoner Aminatra knew strong enough to do so. "Put them on top of each other down here!" she instructed. "We're going onto the roof."

As they helped Aminatra upon the straw mount, a young Athenian man and woman ran past, terror etched upon their faces. They acknowledged the activity of the three prisoners with a fleeting glance, adding to their fear and indecision. Aminatra thought of warning them of further perils ahead, but realised danger awaited them in every direction and only fate would decide if they took the right path. They were soon gone from sight and mind.

From atop the bales, Aminatra was able, with some agility, to stretch a leg to the roof gable, pulling herself up with hand and foot. While Johansson followed with a modicum of grace, Obidon's size made his ascent a spectacle worthy of future campfire tales. Eventually, his great bulk lay flat, face downwards, on the lower edge of the roof. Aminatra and Johansson rolled him over to his front, away from the edge, allowing him to sit upright. "I don't do heights," he confessed.

"Today you do!" declared Aminatra, as they shuffled along the roof. An acrid smell caught her attention and she looked up with alarm. "Fire!" she exclaimed.

"Where?" asked Obidon, not willing to look himself.

"I don't know, but I suspected it wouldn't be long before fire became another tool of revenge. We'd better hurry before they decide to burn the barracks down!"

Aminatra and Johansson stood on the roof at the back of the barracks, awaiting Obidon to catch up on all fours. Behind them the building cut into a rising bank where invasive shrubs took over. "If we remove a block of tiles and see what's on the other side," suggested Aminatra, as Obidon finally joined them, "we can tempt the guards out the way we came."

"Why do I suspect 'we' means me?" said Obidon, now gingerly standing upright.

"Because speed is everything," urged Aminatra, patting his back.

"Stand aside!" commanded the big man, as he ripped up the tiles, passing them to Johansson and Aminatra. Beneath, a light framework of wood provided the support for the tiles. A firm stamp from Obidon's boot broke one narrow beam and, after a few further hefty kicks, a sizeable hole, big enough for a man to climb through, appeared. Only a thin board lay between them and the barracks. "It won't take my weight," advised Obidon, as his foot assessed the situation. "It'll need someone of a more effeminate build."

Aminatra brushed past her comrades and vanished down the hole.

"What can you see?" called out Obidon.

"Not much in the darkness," answered Aminatra. "It doesn't feel too stable. I hope it holds my weight!" As the words left her mouth, a series of gunshots and shouts erupted beneath. "Cronax! I think the barracks is breached." The gunfire became more intense. Screams followed, littered with the occasional triumphant cry.

"What do we do? What do we do?" cried Aminatra, climbing back onto the roof.

Obidon stood to his full height, held the rifle upright against his stomach and face, and stepped through the hole in the roof. He fell straight down upon the board, his weight and momentum taking him right through with a terrible crack, plummeting to the barrack's floor. Aminatra screamed in shock, looking up to see Johansson's terrified face watching from above. She edged forward to peer through the splintered remains of the hole. Below, the big man hobbled back and forth, his gun swinging round his head, clobbering the guards still stunned by his unorthodox arrival. "Come on!" he yelled. "You're missing all the fun."

CHAPTER 31

Finbarl came to in a scene worthy of a nightmare. Bodies lay around him, blood covering the tiled floor. They had spared no one. He climbed to his feet, rubbing his sore head. No matter how much he hated the Wardyns, this barbaric crime sickened Finbarl. He looked away from the sight of the children lying dead next to the limp bodies of their parents. He would make Crixus pay.

Muffled gunshots sounded with regularity from beyond the sanctuary, the element of surprise gone. Soon those guards on duty at the perimeters, armed and angry, would be making their way back into town, ready to fight.

Finbarl's gun was gone, no doubt in the hands of Crixus' cronies, but other things occupied his mind as he staggered out of the sanctuary. Was Aminatra safe? Her unit's objective was to burn the Jumblar. If she made it to the farm, she would be the first to meet the guards regrouping on their way back to Athenia. Finbarl picked up his pace, unsure where to go in his dazed state. Flames lit up the night sky, coming from the town, not the valley where the Jumblar grew. Against the pain of his throbbing head, Finbarl struggled to understand what had gone wrong or where he should head.

Athenia was wide awake, boiling in a cauldron of violence.

Screams and bangs sounded everywhere and Finbarl soon stumbled upon more dead bodies in the street, both guards and common citizens. What had he done? The foxes ran amok in the chicken run! He cursed his naivety in believing mankind could see beyond its own self-interests. History provided the warning signs, but Finbarl had fallen into the familiar trap of thinking his idealism provided a simple solution. Burning the Jumblar still offered some hope. At least it would scupper Crixus' plans to control Athenia. He just had to find Aminatra.

"Aminatra!" People rushed past Finbarl in panic. "Aminatra!"

"Finbarl!"

Finbarl leapt around to find Gauret staggering towards him, blood leaking through his thawb.

"What the hell's going on, Finbarl?" yelled Gauret. "What have you done?"

"It's not how it was supposed to be," said Finbarl, steadying his old friend by the shoulders. "I'm sorry."

"I knew you were involved as soon as I heard the first gunshot," said Gauret, a weak smile forming on his face. "Never could keep out of trouble."

"Have you been shot?"

Gauret shook his head. "No, stabbed! Guards are fair game for anyone now."

"You mean this wasn't a prisoner?"

"No, news has spread the Wardyns are dead," answered Gauret. "Anarchy's filled the power vacuum. They're looting the food stores, some are drunk, women are fearful for their safety and everyone is paying back old scores! People are free to do what they want."

"Cronax!" cursed Finbarl, looking to the sky in despair. "Have you seen Aminatra? Is she safe?"

"I think so," said Gauret. "It was hard to tell in the light, but I thought I saw her on the roof of the barracks. Looking for her boy, no doubt. I hope she finds him alive! They haven't shown guards any mercy but as he's a child ... ".

A series of loud bangs caused Finbarl to jump. He swung around, catching sight of a shadowy figure down one of the side alleys, a cloud of smoke rising from what was obviously a gun. "Come on!" he urged, turning back to Gauret. "We need to find her!" Finbarl moved away but noticed his friend remained motionless; a strange, surprised look covered his face. "What is it?"

Gauret tried to open his mouth but instead thick, dark blood dribbled from his lips. He slumped to his knees, his eyes staring out in shock. Another ring of blood grew upon his thawb. "You've been shot!" cried Finbarl. A whoop echoed from the side street and Finbarl saw the shadowy figure running away. Gauret collapsed to his knees, falling face down in the dirt, dead. Finbarl cried out in anguish, knowing to go after Gauret's killer would be futile while the whole of Athenia succumbed to retribution and violence. He dragged Gauret's body to a more discreet, deserving resting place at the side of the street and gently closed his friend's eyelids. The only thing making sense to him was his love of Aminatra. He needed to find her!

Danger littered the way back to the barracks. Fighting took place everywhere and between everyone. Occasionally a former prisoner ran past, brandishing a gun, holding a bottle of half-drunk Kywaczek, but most of the time citizen fought citizen, holding makeshift weapons and releasing a lifetime of frustration. Finbarl found a dead guard and removed his truncheon.

"Hey, don't I recognise you?" A man stood in Finbarl's path gripping a spade. "You're a guard!"

"You're mistaken," responded Finbarl. "Do I look well-fed?"

"Your eyes say you're a guard! You've just changed your thawb."

Finbarl feigned subjugation by slumping his head to his chest. "And your eyes say you're an idiot!" he shouted, raising his head and swinging the truncheon at his unprepared opponent. The man took the hit upon his chin, stumbling back stunned. With no time for further discussion, Finbarl placed his boot in the man's groin and hurried on his way.

He passed a priest on his knees, surrounded by three men and a woman. Blood trickled from the priest's mouth. "Someone save me!" he pleaded. Finbarl ignored the cry for help, his mind focused on Aminatra.

The area around the barracks felt strangely devoid of noise and activity, like a tornado had ripped through it, passing on to tear up the rest of the town. Finbarl walked through the familiar doors, accompanied by a feeling of horrible trepidation.

CHAPTER 32

The gunfire subsided to an occasional shot as Aminatra and Johansson safely lowered themselves onto a table, positioned by Obidon under the hole. Bodies lay all around. The majority of guards had been shown no mercy as the prisoners burst in; a few dead prisoners lay among them, overwhelmed by numbers, stabbed to death. Aminatra's ashen face searched the candlelit room for signs of her Karlmon, becoming guiltily happy at the realisation all the dead were adults. Only a couple of other prisoners hung around, the rest either frightened off by the scale of the destruction or on the hunt around Athenia for new game.

"We've got the barracks secured," said Obidon to the other two prisoners. His tone carried a clear threat. "You can go and find somewhere else to play."

They eyed him suspiciously before deciding easier fights lay elsewhere and backed out the front doors.

"Are you all right?" enquired Aminatra, in the relative silence of the room.

"I may have broken my ankle," replied Obidon without fuss, as though talking about the weather.

"That was reckless, what you did," reproached Aminatra, "but thank you."

"Reckless-ing," repeated Johansson, attempting to chide his friend but only prompting a laugh from Obidon.

"Can you walk?" asked Aminatra. "We need to search deeper in the building and can expect some resistance."

"I can if I use the rifle as a stick," replied Obidon. "Best if you both grab a weapon from one of the dead."

They made their way from the sleeping quarters, down a corridor toward the canteen. A single body lay in their way. The blood pattern on the floor suggested he had retreated here injured, only to lose the battle for life in the stark surroundings of the corridor. They carefully stepped over the corpse and crept into the canteen. It appeared empty. Several overturned tables were set out in a distinct defensive formation. Aminatra looked to Obidon, who silently nodded his understanding. He staggered to an upright table, painfully lifting his knee to rest against it, then raised the rifle to aim toward the mass of up-turned tables.

A sudden disturbance behind caused all three to turn in panic. Two guards, hiding somewhere further along the corridor, made a dash for freedom. The draught as they ran past the canteen doors made them swing open a few inches and close. "Let them go," said Aminatra. "They're not after us and we're not after them. From the noise they made they were adults." A more discreet noise, perhaps a sniff, came from behind the tables, refocusing their attention forwards.

"Come out!" demanded Obidon. "We're not here to hurt anyone."

"Come out! Please!" reiterated Aminatra, conscious her words sounded less threatening.

A bloodied, bandaged head appeared, slowly rising from the centre of the tables, followed by a set of wide, frightened eyes.

"I know you," said Aminatra. "You were in the troop that took me to the Prison."

"I will fight if you come any closer," the guard challenged, brandishing his truncheon.

"And I'll shoot you if you threaten us again," retorted Obidon.

"No, no!" implored Aminatra. "We're not here to shoot anybody. You were Finbarl's friend. What's your name?"

After a moment's hesitation he answered. "Strathbol-apcula. I was Finbarl's friend but not any more. He betrayed us all and did this!" He pointed the truncheon at his bandaged head. "You can kill me but let the cadets go."

"The what?" Aminatra's face became animated. "We're not going to kill anyone. Honestly!" She took a step closer. "Have you got the cadets with you? Karlmon! Karlmon! It's your mother!"

A small head peered around the tables. He had grown so much since last seen by Aminatra, but there was no mistaking her boy. "Mum?"

"Karlmon!" She held her arms wide and, before Strathbol could stop him, Karlmon climbed over a table, running to his mother. Tears flowed down Aminatra's cheeks as he flung himself into her embrace. "Oh, my precious baby! I never thought I'd see you again."

Strathbol, realising these prisoners wanted nothing but this reunion, lowered his truncheon. "What's going on outside?" he asked.

Obidon tilted his gun down. "Nothing you want to be involved in," he said. "How many you got behind there? It's all right, we'll protect you the best we can."

A nod from Strathbol encouraged the other cadets to stand. Fourteen of varying ages and sizes climbed to their feet.

"Cronax!" said Obidon. "A right little mother hen, aren't we? You were willing to give your life to protect them?"

"Of course," replied Strathbol, hurt by the insinuation he wouldn't do his duty.

"Good man," said Obidon, to the young guard's surprise. "Someone who's willing to fight for what's right."

The canteen doors burst open and three prisoners strode through, all armed with rifles. Aminatra hugged Karlmon a degree harder. "What do you want?" she snapped. "We have the barracks secured. These are our prisoners!"

The tallest of the new arrivals glanced disdainfully towards Aminatra. "Usually hug your prisoners, do you?"

"He's my son."

"He's a brainwashed guard," countered the man. "As soon as you turn your back, he'll betray or stab you. Best you let him return to his real family over there." He nodded to the group of cadets, now standing nervously behind Strathbol.

"We don't want no trouble, Hermangog," said Obidon, indicating he knew the prisoner. "Go and do your looting somewhere else and leave these cadets to us."

"Obidon, what are you doing with this rabble?" He spared a disparaging look to Johansson. "We could do with a man like you. Why don't you leave this guard's whore and imbecile and join us?"

"Us? Who's 'us'?"

"Why the new government of Athenia!" declared Hermangog.

Obidon looked at Aminatra impassively, then at the cadets. "Oh, why didn't you say." He pushed himself off the table and stood facing Hermangog, showing no pain from standing on his broken ankle. "On one condition."

Hermangog frowned impatiently. "What?"

"You let my friend here cut your throat!" Before Hermangog had time to react, Johansson was upon him, his knife swiftly slicing from ear to ear. Obidon's finger pulled the trigger on his gun, sending one of the other prisoners to the ground. The remaining prisoner swung his rifle up in alarm, aiming towards Obidon but, before he got a shot away, Aminatra was on him, a knife planted into the side of his stomach. The man groaned in agony as Obidon hopped forward, smashing his rifle butt across his head, killing him. "I said you should pick up a weapon before we searched any further, didn't I."

Aminatra looked at him and burst out laughing and crying in hysterical relief, taking Karlmon back in her embrace.

Obidon turned to hobble back to the table and rest his ankle, finding Strathbol in his way, truncheon in hand. In the commotion the guard had leapt the barricades, now within striking distance. The earlier tension resurfaced, but Obidon saw the look in Strathbol's eyes and realised the boy had intervened to tackle those threatening the cadets. With the threat over, the guard again appeared the innocent youth, and Obidon placed a hand upon his shoulder and squeezed. "Stay here with the boys. They're going to need you today and tomorrow."

Strathbol nodded his understanding. "What about you? What will you do now?"

Obidon looked to Aminatra for an answer.

"We need to find Finbarl," she said.

CHAPTER 33

"Aminatra! Thank Cronax you're all right!" exclaimed Finbarl, as the barracks doors closed behind him. Aminatra, with Karlmon, Obidon and Johansson, emerged from the shadows at the back of the room. He ran across and took her in his arms. "You found Karlmon. Thank God!" He glanced nervously down at the boy, who watched the scene with curious eyes. The last time Finbarl saw him, he arrested his mother. He feared the boy possessed only hatred for him. "How is he?"

"He's okay, thanks to Johansson, Obidon and Strathbol."

"Strathbol?"

"Yes," replied Aminatra. "He stayed with the cadets to protect them all. Quite the hero. He's through in the other room but not perhaps ready to forgive you just yet."

Finbarl grimaced in recollection at knocking out the guard earlier. "So, what happened?"

"We were with the group attacking the barracks. We didn't want to be but, well you know, things didn't go as planned!"

Finbarl nodded grimly.

"There was nothing we could do to stop them killing the guards," continued Aminatra. "All the cadets are safe though! They're only children but they were going to kill them! Obidon kept his cool. He saved us all."

Finbarl recognised the irony in Obidon, one of the few people probably deserving to be in the Prison for murder, being among the best of them all. "Thanks," he said.

"This isn't how it was meant to be!" said a downcast Obidon.

"No, it isn't." Finbarl thought. What more could he say?

"Karlmon. This is my friend, Finbarl," said Aminatra, changing the subject.

Finbarl dreaded the boy's response.

"Hello," said Karlmon smiling. "You rescued my toy."

Finbarl laughed in relief. "Have you still got it?"

Karlmon presented a dignified air. "Of course not! Toys aren't for cadets."

"You're not a cadet any more," said Aminatra, holding Karlmon to her. "You're allowed to play and be a child again."

"But I want to be a guard."

Aminatra looked at Finbarl with concern.

"We'll need you to guard us," said Finbarl. "But you'll have to play again as part of your duties." From his own experiences, he knew the child never died inside, but became buried under discipline and fear.

"Okay," concurred Karlmon.

Finbarl rose and walked to peek through the door outside. "Crixus massacred the Wardyns and started all this," lamented Finbarl. "What went wrong? We offered them freedom and they chose ... ". Finbarl threw up his hands in disgust.

"We gave them freedom; freedom to choose," answered Aminatra. "Maddy often stressed nothing is straightforward. Is true freedom the right to be wrong and make mistakes?"

"To be stupid, more like!" fumed Finbarl. "Sod the philosophical arguments! They could've lived without walls, travelled anywhere."

"'Ope is the beacon pulling-ly mankind forwarded, but greed-ing is what fuels 'im." Johansson piped up from the shadows, receiving a nod of admiration from his friend Obidon for the wisdom hidden beneath his mystifying syntax.

"And temptation leads him off the path," concluded Aminatra, as she quizzically examined Johansson.

"But we live for the present, not for the future," added Obidon. "People want food, security and familiarity. You could argue we're no different to the Ferrals. Is freedom anything else than the right to live as we wish?"

"Precisely!" declared Finbarl, less inclined to dismiss their philosophical musing. "That's why we still have to destroy the Jumblar. It takes away the power to choose. We have to achieve something: create the pathway to freedom."

"No, Finbarl!" replied Aminatra, holding Karlmon tighter, making him squirm. "Athenia is not the future. It was always our plan to destroy it but save its people. Well, its people are going to destroy Athenia, and perhaps themselves. To keep your mother's dream alive, we have to save ourselves: start anew."

"I think Maddy was joking when she referred to us as Adam and Eve," quipped Finbarl, as he wandered back from the door.

Aminatra touched his cheek sensitively as he sat beside her. "We have to keep hope alive: stay on the path. Get away from here; find a world we can live in, or create something ourselves."

"You mean beyond the mountains?"

"It's either there or through the desert, and I know which way has more water."

"You're right," agreed Finbarl, his enthusiasm returning. "But we'll need to stock up on as much food, water and supplies as possible. It may have more water, but it's no less challenging. Obidon, can you find some tools?"

The big man slowly shook his head. "I'm not going. My place is here. There are children who need guidance." His eyes looked through the wall, in the direction of the cadets. "I know there may not be much of a future in Athenia but … I made my future in the past and I don't need to find a better life, just peace of mind for what I did to my wife. My prison has always been in here." He tapped his head and heart. "You need to get away. You're future's unwritten."

"Johansson? What about you?" asked Aminatra. "Will you come with us?"

"I stay-ed."

*

Fire ravaged the town, spreading fast between the fragile wooden buildings. No one thought to tackle the flames while the internal fire of revenge consumed them. The years of suspicion and paranoia fostered a culture of blame. A domino effect carried the retribution across town. Revenge sated in one place fermented a release of further vengeance elsewhere.

Finbarl held tightly to Aminatra's hand, and she to Karlmon's, as they weaved through the mess, ducking to avoid the occasional sundry items thrown for destruction's sake. With the doors to the sanctuary in sight, Finbarl came to a halt, yanking back on Aminatra's arm as she raced past.

"What is it?" demanded Aminatra, gasping for breath, conscious time was against them.

"Get plenty of supplies from the sanctuary. Then get Karlmon to the tunnel. Wait for me at the outer end!" ordered Finbarl.

"What is it?" Aminatra left no doubt in Finbarl's mind she was going nowhere without knowing what was going on.

"Crixus!" said Finbarl. "I just saw him. There's unfinished business I need to take care of."

Aminatra inspected Finbarl's determined eyes and understood. She kissed him and sprinted away with Karlmon. "I love you!" she cried without turning, leaving Karlmon to look back, bemused, at the new man in his mother's life.

Finbarl felt the heat of the fire carried on the breeze as he ran off in pursuit of Crixus. He was making for the main square and Finbarl darted through the crowded streets in pursuit. At the edge of the square, Crixus' distinctive ginger hair marked him out as Finbarl closed in. He recognised several prisoners following in Crixus' wake but thought nothing of them, only the man responsible for gunning down the women and children in the sanctuary.

A few yards from his prey, Finbarl cried out his name, causing Crixus to jump in surprise. He held a rifle but had no time to react before Finbarl caught him on the side of his head with a truncheon. Crixus reeled backwards, dropping the gun, fighting to stay on his feet. Some of the other prisoners raised their rifles, aiming at Finbarl.

"Don't shoot!" yelled Crixus. "He's mine!" A cruel smile formed on his lips as he wiped blood from the wound on his head, withdrawing a large knife from his belt. Finbarl remained impassive, ready for whatever Crixus had.

"What do you make of what you've achieved?" asked Finbarl, as they circled each other, awaiting the other to make the first move.

"What I've achieved!" exclaimed Crixus. "It was your plan to destroy the Wardyns and bring down civilisation."

"My plan was to destroy the Jumblar and the walls. Not the people! Not innocent women and children!"

"Innocent! Those innocent children are the ones who'd have replaced the Wardyns in a few years. Those innocent women are the ones who've been enjoying a life of luxury while everyone else suffers." Crixus made an initial feint, testing Finbarl's concentration.

Finbarl skipped to the side. "Those flames burn both innocent and guilty."

"That's God's vengeance on the people of Athenia."

Finbarl snorted in derision. "God had his vengeance on mankind a long time ago. He's forgotten Athenia even exists; just like Athenia has forgotten God exists." Even as he struggled for his life, Finbarl called upon the words of his mother.

A sudden lunge from Crixus caught Finbarl flat-footed. Only a side-arch of his torso enabled him to avoid the thrust. With Crixus committed, Finbarl swung his truncheon at the knife-holding arm, clasping Crixus' neck with his other hand. The knife dropped to the ground, as they struggled for supremacy in a locked embrace. Finbarl released his truncheon to free his right hand and push away Crixus' fingers clawing at his face.

"I knew you were trouble as soon as you joined our group," hissed Crixus, as he tried to wrestle Finbarl to the ground. "Should've killed you then."

"Why have just one murder then, when you can be a mass murderer tonight," retorted Finbarl.

A blow struck Finbarl's brow as Crixus headbutted him. Nausea swept through his body and he found himself flailing backwards as his legs collapsed beneath. The back of his head took a further whack on hitting the floor. Finbarl lay groggy and vulnerable upon the ground, while Crixus retrieved his knife, placing his foot upon Finbarl's upper chest. "Tonight," declared Crixus triumphantly, "all guards, the oppressors of the people, die!" He pushed down, squeezing the breath from Finbarl, who grasped his assailant's leg with his hands but without the strength to move it. In defeat, Finbarl's arms collapsed to his side, as Crixus bent his leg, lowering his knee down to replace his foot, the knife now at Finbarl's throat. "It doesn't end here!" snarled Crixus. "When you're dead, that bitch of yours will need company and protection – until I'm bored of her."

Finbarl stared weakly in protest as Crixus opened his mouth to utter another tormenting threat.

A painfully loud bang erupted from nowhere and Crixus' body slumped on top of Finbarl. He could breathe properly again, but still didn't have the strength to push off the leaden mass of the distinctly dead body of Crixus. Only the stars above were in sight, with the prisoners accompanying Crixus long since gone in search of other game. Finbarl lay still, trying to recover. A face veered into view above him. The familiar sneer of Audlech. Finbarl closed his eyes in resigned despair.

"Look what I've found!" declared Audlech to himself, holding a smoking rifle. "A traitor of Athenia, committing unspeakable crimes."

"Audlech!" croaked Finbarl.

"Now I don't want you to fink I was saving your life just then," lauded Audlech. "It's just that chap pushed in. Everyone knows I have first dibs at killing you! I can't abide poor manners, particularly from a prisoner."

"You don't know what manners are!" wheezed Finbarl.

"Oh, is that the best you can do for your final words? Come on, push that lump of dung off and let me hear you try and insult me again!"

"I can't!" gasped Finbarl, as his efforts to remove Crixus' body failed.

"You always were weak," said Audlech. "Weak of mind and body. They should have snuffed you out when they got rid of your diseased parents." He put a boot to the torso of Crixus and rolled his limp body off Finbarl. "I want to see the hole in your chest when I shoot you."

The crooked teeth of Audlech and the barrel of his rifle was all Finbarl made out as his oxygen-starved body lay prone upon the dirt. "Just like you to kill like a coward!"

Audlech placed his boot on Finbarl's chest and pressed down, mimicking the actions of Crixus. "A Ferral-whack coward is someone who attacks in the dead of night while people are asleep." Finbarl tried to speak, but Audlech's boot squeezed the breath from him again. With a satisfied grin, Audlech released the pressure. "You have something to say? You'd better say it. They'll be your last words. Make them memorable!"

"I … ," Finbarl wheezed and coughed violently, leaving him breathless for a few seconds more. "I think … it important … you know something." He paused for a couple of deep breaths. "We haven't seen eye to eye much. I … I guess you could call us … best of enemies – an Orpho and a Familo. We've each done bad things to … to the other." Again, Finbarl paused to inhale a reviving lung of air. "But despite all that … you should know that … ," another reinvigorating breath. " … you should know that … ," Finbarl sat up, Crixus' knife clasped in his hand, " … you never give up your advantage over your enemy!" He drove the knife into Audlech's groin.

The guard staggered back in horror, a jet of blood shooting from a severed artery. "You … you … !" Audlech tried to react, lifting his gun to aim at Finbarl, but it was either shoot his foe or try to stop the bleeding. His shocked brain failed to decide. He fell heavily upon his backside, eyes glaring out in alarm and bewilderment. Finbarl watched with anxious anticipation, still without the strength to react if Audlech somehow rallied. His nemesis fought with all his strength to stem the flow of blood. A dark pool formed in the sandy dirt, slowly skirting and outlining the victim's supporting hand. Audlech's arm started to shake, his mouth gaped open and then shut. Even in the darkness, Finbarl could see the colour drain from his face. The arm gave way and Audlech fell backwards, releasing a pitiful wheeze. Time ran out: Audlech was dead.

Finbarl let out a relieved breath, before mirroring his foe's action and slumping backwards in exhaustion. The stars above appeared more beautiful as he sucked in the best-tasting air he had ever breathed. "I thought that was pretty memorable," he reflected, turning to look at Audlech's lifeless body.

CHAPTER 34

Finbarl staggered back to the barracks, toward the sanctuary, grateful to avoid further excitement. The first light of morning broke through, catching the smoke in the air, adding an eerie atmosphere to the town. He passed Officer Vassel wandering the streets in tears, a broken man. His eyes followed Finbarl but contained no malice or hatred, indeed no recognition at all. Finbarl felt a pang of pity. He knew Vassel was a good man at heart, just born at the wrong time.

As Finbarl approached the doors of the sanctuary, he became conscious of smoke creeping under the lip. The fire had spread this far, or perhaps someone had started a new one. Finbarl ran towards the danger. Aminatra and Karlmon resided within, hopefully safe in the tunnel, but in danger of separation from him. As Finbarl swung the doors open, a plume of smoke engulfed him, taking his breath away. He turned to cough and gasp at the fresher air wafting in from outside. He raised his arm, covering his nose and mouth with his thawb sleeve, and headed down the corridor. The acrid smoke stung his eyes, but he strained to keep them open to avoid the wreckage covering the floor. Looters had ransacked the building, stripping anything of value or interest, destroying everything else. A discarded blanket caught his eye. He picked it up. Who knew what would prove of use for their journey? Whatever

Aminatra had already accumulated, it was better to have too much than too little.

The smoke thinned the deeper he progressed, allowing him to breathe with a little more ease. Escape via the tunnel in the storage room was within reach, but Finbarl stopped. Dul-biblex needed rescuing. The old man remained trapped within the library. Once the smoke and fire reached his sanctum, he stood no chance. Spinning on his heels, Finbarl took another corridor, making for the atrium. The same sorry scene of death met him there, and he looked away as he crossed to the Governor's office. Inside, he made for the desk, finding the keys.

"Dul-biblex!" he cried, as he fumbled to fit the key into the lock of the library door. "I'm coming!" As the door swung open, only silence greeted him. "Dul-biblex!" No reply came. Finbarl scrambled through the darkness and obstacles. A faint smell of smoke mixed with the musty odour of the books. Eventually, he came to Dul-biblex's personal corner, and found the old man, laid out on his mattress, eyes closed. "Dul-biblex," said Finbarl softly, memories of discovering his dead mother returning. He knelt and placed his hand upon Dul-biblex's shoulder. The old man stirred.

"What is it?" grumbled Dul-biblex, one eye opening to assess the disturbance.

"Dul-biblex!" exclaimed Finbarl. "I thought you were dead."

The other eye opened, giving Finbarl a critical glare. "Dead?" He pulled himself slowly up. "When I die, I'll be working with my books. Can't an old man enjoy his sleep without being disturbed?"

"The sanctuary's on fire. The whole of Athenia's on fire. You've got to get out of here!"

"So, you've succeeded," stated Dul-biblex, rubbing a stiff knee, sniffing at the air.

Finbarl sheepishly looked down. "No. Our plan got hijacked. The prisoners are running riot. They've killed the Wardyns and their families. Everyone's using the chaos to get revenge. It's terrible."

Dul-biblex tilted his head and sighed. "Liberty can only ever be a compromise between those in power and the rest of society: there have to be limits. If you give each individual freedom to do whatever they want, you just get anarchy and monsters. A family doesn't remain strong if the children aren't given the right balance of love and discipline."

"What's done is done," said Finbarl tersely, not there for a lecture. "You've got to come with me! I can get us out of Athenia and to safety."

"Ah, the tunnel," remarked Dul-biblex, surprising Finbarl, before he realised there was probably no secret the old man wasn't aware of. "I suppose that's how you got in."

Finbarl nodded. "Torbald told me just before he died. Get your shoes on!"

"I'm not leaving," said the old man.

"You've got to! The fire will soon be upon us. Once the books catch alight, it'll be over in minutes."

"That's why I can't leave. My books. I told you, I'll die working with my books."

Finbarl expelled an exasperated cry. "We can take some books; as many as we can carry."

The serene smile upon the face of Dul-biblex remained unchanged. "You must take some books, of course," he said. "But I must remain with my library." He staggered to his feet. "Now, I presume you'll need to travel light if you're to cross the mountains."

"How did you know that's where we're heading?"

"Because you're a young man with adventure and discovery in his heart; that's where Mandelaton lies and that's where I'd go if I were you. I'm surprised you think I could make such a journey too."

Finbarl didn't know how to respond. He hadn't thought far ahead, but realised the truth in Dul-biblex's words.

"Ah, this is what you need: an encyclopaedia." Dul-biblex lifted a large book from a shelf and handed it to Finbarl. "Now, what else?"

"If we just got you out of Athenia until the fires subsided," suggested Finbarl. "You could then return. Maybe some of the library will survive."

"A book on medicine," said Dul-biblex, ignoring Finbarl. "Yes, that will come in useful, and your mother will enjoy that."

Finbarl opened his mouth to impart news of Maddy's death but thought better of it: why upset the old man at this time.

"Yes, here it is." Dul-biblex passed a second book to Finbarl. "I haven't read that for a while. Now, there's one more you should have." He vanished down another aisle. "It's a light one but contains great wisdom."

Finbarl stood impatiently holding his small collection of books. "Will you at least come to the tunnel with me?"

"Found it!" cried Dul-biblex from a few rows away. "It's one of my favourites. The children love it too." He re-emerged and handed Finbarl a thin novel. "Now, you must get going. There's nothing keeping you here."

"You … ," Finbarl curtailed his plea, looking deeply at the steely determination rooted within Dul-biblex's eyes. "I'm not going to convince you to leave, am I?"

Dul-biblex smiled. "No. I've lived a long life. I'm tired. Death no longer frightens me, but life without the library does."

Finbarl nodded. "I understand."

"Go! Go!" urged Dul-biblex, unwilling to let emotions surface.

"Thank you," said Finbarl, lifting the books in acknowledgement. "I'll write to you when we get to Mandelaton." It was a white lie both parties recognised and appreciated. Finbarl vanished, leaving the old man to straighten his books.

*

In the storage room, Finbarl lifted the trapdoor to the tunnel, looking down into the depths. At the bottom of the ladder, shielding their eyes from the burst of light, sat Aminatra and Karlmon. They gazed up with a look of concern, unsure as their eyes adjusted if they were in danger or not.

"It's okay," reassured Finbarl. "It's me!"

"Thank Cronax!" exclaimed Aminatra, tears in her eyes. "Are you all right?"

"Better for seeing you both," he replied. "Move back! I'll drop some things down."

"Did you find Crixus?" Aminatra awaited an answer before moving.

"Yes," confirmed Finbarl. "He's dead. So is Audlech."

"Good," stated Aminatra, stepping back.

Finbarl wrapped the three books in the blanket and dropped them down the shaft. A soft thud signalled their impact on the bottom, and Finbarl gingerly moved his aching limbs onto the ladder. He shut the trapdoor, climbing down into the darkness. As his feet found the ground, he felt the arms of Aminatra wrap around his body, hugging him.

"I feared I'd lost you!" she sobbed.

"You may still do so if you don't release your grip a bit!" teased Finbarl. "I think I may have broken a rib."

Aminatra let go apologetically.

"Don't worry," laughed Finbarl. "It's amazing what love can help you endure." He felt a playful punch on his arm. "Come on! Let's get out of here! I've never wanted to be out of Athenia so much in my life."

"Me too," said Aminatra, slipping her hand in Finbarl's. "Karlmon! Hold my other hand! We're going on a journey."

*

The light at the far end of the tunnel beckoned them on. It felt good to finally step out into the fresh air of the morning. Blue skies lay before them but, behind, a dark cloud of smoke hung over Cragor Hill. For the first time, Finbarl saw what Aminatra and Karlmon had collected for their journey. Both carried a couple of bags way too big for them.

"I had hoped you would smuggle a few camels with you," said Aminatra.

"I would have but my hands were full," replied Finbarl, pleased to hear Karlmon laugh in response. "I rescued some books instead." He decided not to mention Dul-biblex. "Here, I got one for you." Finbarl pulled out the short novel Dul-biblex chose. He looked at the cover. "It's called Animal Farm."

"Well, we can't eat those in an emergency," said Aminatra, "but we can always burn them if we can't find wood." This caused Karlmon to squeal in delight, and soon they were all laughing.

When the laughter subsided, Aminatra reached into her pocket. "I rescued this!" She held a pistol between her finger and thumb. "To scare off any Ferrals."

CHAPTER 35

There was no fast route through the foothills. They followed the natural paths, the tracks made by animals in the woods, along the valley bottoms or clambering over exposed rock. The air got cooler the higher they went, and eventually they found themselves slowly ascending the first mountain.

Finbarl carried the heaviest load; a large bag slung across his shoulder. Something hard within stuck into his back. He stopped, removing his load to allow for some reorganising. Aminatra and Karlmon, following behind, welcomed the opportunity for a breather and dumped their bags to the ground. Despite the cold, thin air, the sun brought a pleasing warmth through its touch.

"What's that?" asked Karlmon, pointing down the line of the mountains. A pier of rock protruded, providing a wonderful vantage point across the landscape below. Perched serenely at the far end, they looked upon the naked figure of a Ferral, balancing comfortably in a crouched position, staring out across the vista. At a little over a hundred yards away, it felt too close for comfort. Finbarl's body tensed, his hand feeling for the pistol. With casual grace, the Ferral rotated his head to the side, sparing a moment of contemplation on the three interlopers, before calmly returning his gaze to the vast expanse below.

"I don't think he's interested in us," said Finbarl, more from hope than certainty. "Come on, let's keep moving before he changes his mind!" His hand squeezed Karlmon's shoulder in reassurance. "Hey, what do you have there?" he asked, noticing the boy grasping something in his hand.

Karlmon smiled up at Finbarl. "It's a new toy mother found for me." He held up a simplistic but beautifully carved figure Finbarl recognised as a deer.

"Maddy gave it to me," commented Aminatra. "It's made from antler. They've used the natural shape so well. It's almost alive."

"Who are 'they'?" queried Finbarl.

"Your mother said she found it on a dead Ferral. She thought they'd made it."

Finbarl took the figure from Karlmon, admiring its grace and capture of the spiritual essence of a deer. He turned to re-examine the Ferral on the outcrop – wondering how the monster he had grown up in fear of created this beautiful object. "He's gone!"

Aminatra emitted a light, unexpected laugh.

"What?" asked Finbarl, handing the deer back to Karlmon. "What is it? We should keep moving!"

"It was something Maddy once said to me," remarked Aminatra, climbing the slope, sparing the occasional glance backwards. "Something I thought a bit crazy at the time but now I'm not too sure. Have you ever actually seen a Ferral eating human flesh?"

Finbarl thought for a moment. "Well, no, but I've seen the remains of those they've feasted on."

"Have you ever seen a coyote or vulture eating a Ferral victim?"

"Yes, of course, you often find the carrion beasts defiling the dead." Finbarl frowned. "What's your point?"

"It was Maddy's point," corrected Aminatra. "Are the Ferrals who we thought they were, or have we made them into the monsters we thought we needed?"

Finbarl opened his mouth to contradict his wife but stopped. A lifetime of stories and stereotypes tried to form his words, but his world had changed. Too many lies and secrets lay exposed for him to accept what once he took to be the simple truth. "I hope you're right," he said. "Maybe they're the future."

*

After another hour of climbing, they reached the mountain pass leading them away from their old world and into a new one. It was time to say goodbye to Athenia. They paused and turned, looking back upon the expanse below. The vista went from the white, snow-bound heights, to the green wooded and grass-covered foothills, the sandy, parched scrubland wilderness with a narrow strip of fertile green where the river flowed, and finally the ruddy yellow blanket of the desert stretching to the horizon. Eden Valley nestled as a green oasis in the wilderness, with Athenia a smoking husk at the far end. Finbarl thought of all those tiny figures down there striving to survive in the wake of the raid.

A faint aroma carried in the wind and Finbarl sniffed, trying to place the smell. It was smoke carried high on the rising air currents. Something familiar in the nasal flavours teased his sense. It included the recognisable taste of the burning structures of Athenia but something more: Finbarl struggled to think what.

"Jumblar?" suggested Aminatra, reading his thoughts. "The Jumblar is burning!"

"Possibly," agreed Finbarl, recognising the familiar craving it triggered. "Do you think someone set it alight deliberately? Obidon? Johansson?"

Aminatra shrugged. "Should we go back?"

"No," answered Finbarl without hesitation, turning to look in the opposite direction at the battalion of mountains lined up before them.

"So where are we heading?" asked Aminatra, conscious they had simply left Athenia behind.

"To freedom!" declared Finbarl.

"And what direction is that?" asked Aminatra, as she scanned the distant valleys beyond the mountains, stretching out toward the unknown.

"I don't know," answered Finbarl honestly. "But we get to choose, and that's a start."

The End

ABOUT THE AUTHOR

Nathaniel M Wrey studied history at Reading University before becoming a Civil Servant. He has worked in central government for over twenty years, largely in health and nursing. His literary influences include the social commentary of George Orwell, the adventures of John Buchan and the foresight and imagination of Ray Bradbury. Combined with a continued love of history, Wrey's writing delves into the past to understand the present and speculate on the future. He has also published a short collection of short stories, The Dividends of Love and Other Stories.'

website: www.nathanielmwrey.com
twitter: @nathanielwrey

Lightning Source UK Ltd.
Milton Keynes UK
UKHW040651040520
362749UK00001B/25